I knew the moment I set eyes on Michael, when I walked up on him in the park. He was sitting calmly next to the river on a rock ledge, day dreaming, wearing nothing but a pair of jeans. His image quickened my heart and stopped my breath, and I found it almost impossible to approach him with my duties as a park ranger. Then he turned when I called out and it felt like I melted within his eyes. He spoke, and the sound of his voice crawled over my skin like electricity. He was sad, and I had an overwhelming urge to comfort him, to figure out a way to help him find peace. I tried to play the role of a ranger, but I was most anxious to cast that aside and get to know him. I wanted to stay there with him all day, and when we talked about where he might stay, I knew I had never wanted anything in my life more than I wanted him to come to my house. I was compelled to ask him to do just that, and thrilled when he accepted.

A SONG IN THE PARK

MARTIN BRANT

Genesis Press Inc.

Le Marais Stories

An imprint of Genesis Press Inc.
Publishing Company

Genesis Press, Inc.
P.O. Box 101
Columbus, MS 39703

ISBN: 1-58571-125-X
Manufactured in the United States of America

First Edition

Visit us at www.genesis-press.com
or call at 1-888-Indigo-1

DEDICATION

This novel is dedicated to my wife Cathy,
who has shared with me the important
things in life for seventeen years.

CHAPTER 1

Michael Anderson's horrified gaze shifted from the lifeless little girl to his bloody hands. The doctors and nurses standing about the operating table looked on in disbelief. A gloom fell quietly over the room that felt like foul oil on their skin. Michael had repaired the little girl's heart valve with his well known, some say incredible, skill. This time he had overlooked a small ruptured vein. The little girl's breath stopped only moments after he had closed her small chest.

In the frenzied half-hour they had fought to repair the damage and bring the little girl back, Doctor Michael Anderson suffered anxiety he had not known in his entire ten-year career. As he labored for reason, his mind swirling with blind thought, he stared at the little girl, transfixed, not yet aware that the turmoil in his head was about to set his life on a new path. While the assisting staff milled about, the reality of this tragedy accepted, the head nurse, Shannon Mason, still hadn't taken her eyes off Dr. Anderson.

Shannon watched him with heart wrenching concern. He had pushed back his surgeon's hairnet with the back of his hand, his sandy blonde damp with perspiration. She ached for him, his tanned chiseled face twisted in angst, his blue eyes, always warm and disarming, now distant with fear, his broad shoulders drawn and small.

Stunned, for a long moment she didn't know what to say or

do. She had been a nurse at the hospital for nearly a year, and had worked with Michael much of that time. Though she had not shared her feelings with anyone, least of all Michael, she had fallen in love with him.

A twenty-nine-year-old transplant from the Midwest, Shannon had found her small apartment in San Diego and waited, it seemed forever, to be accepted for her current position. Having worked side by side with Michael for several months, she had finally gathered the courage to ask him to dinner. When he accepted, though he didn't know, it had set her heart sailing. She had taken off early that day, got a sharp new haircut that gave her blonde hair that carefree California look. She also bought a sexy, short black skirt. As radiant as any woman could be when he picked her up, she wondered if her efforts might tempt a suggestive invitation. It never did. He had been charming, and attentive, and how time seemed to fly that night as they sipped coffee and talked until three o'clock that morning.

There had been a few more dinners and a couple of evenings at the theater since then. She knew, had it not been for her friendship with Michael, she would eventually leave San Diego, for she had learned she was not meant to be a city girl. But she had fallen in love with Michael. Having debated the idea for weeks, she still had not found the courage to invite him to her apartment, nor had the suggestion fallen from his lips.

Now this. She had never seen such grief possess a man's face. She stepped forward, quietly, and stood beside him. He glanced at her as if he didn't know her, lost in the anxiety of being responsible for losing the little girl's life. She wanted to take his arm, comfort him in some way, but nothing she might do seemed appropriate. Finally, her voice soft and filled with compassion, she said, "Michael, we can take care of things here. Why don't you go wash up?"

"I killed her. I killed this little girl," he muttered, wanting to take hold of the little body and shake her back to life.

"Michael," she pleaded, "it was a mistake we all made together. Just go and wash up. Let me finish up here and then I'll join you. We can sort it out. We can ..." She averted her eyes when she saw a tear run down his cheek.

He turned like a zombie and walked aimlessly out of the operating room. Shannon then watched an intern wheel the gurney through those bleak stainless steel doors, upon which lay the small lifeless body.

Doctor Jacobs approached. "Anderson is going to have a hard time with this," he said. "It's the first time I've seen him leave an operating room without everyone slapping him on the back with accolades."

Shannon looked at the doctor, her concern etched on her face.

"I'll do the report," he said. "He won't be worth a shit any time soon. I just hope his malpractice insurance premiums are current."

Shannon's expression took on an edge of contempt. "That's an awful thing to say."

"It's a fact of life, my dear. Do you think that little girl's parents are going to sit still for this? And every discriminating detail has to be recorded, because I'll be damned before I get caught trying to cover something up."

"No one said anything about covering it up," she said hotly.

"It was a mistake, an oversight that might happen in any procedure. That doesn't necessarily have to lead to a lawsuit!"

"Maybe not in Kansas, honey, but consider it a foregone conclusion in California," said Jacobs.

She turned her head in exasperation. She hadn't liked Doctor Jacobs from the moment she met him. In fact she didn't care much for most of the hospital staff, for it seemed like a world of back stabbing, long tedious hours, self-possessed complainers and unbridled ambition.

Shannon found Michael in his office, staring out the window, unaware he had already drawn his conclusion as to why the mistake had been made. Instead of a good night's rest the night before, he had recklessly stayed out most of the night, responding again to the call of those never ending escapades found in a bathhouse. The shock of losing the little girl had now turned into a demon of self-loathing.

Shannon took a few tentative steps into the office. He had changed into his street clothes, denim jeans and a pullover shirt. Though Michael had a wonderful sense of style—he wore Armani when they went to dinner—he had acquired a rather eccentric reputation with his affinity for casual dress. She was looking at the back of his head, the fairly long sandy hair, the shoulders of a man who lifted weights. At five foot eleven, he stood an inch or two taller than her. Every time she looked at him, she remembered how it had delighted her to walk into a restaurant with him; his tanned face a display of perpetual optimism and boyish charm, his demeanor a wonderful blend of casual sophistication. Though his sensual lips were thin and straight across, his nose rather narrow, what Shannon loved most was his crystal blue eyes.

He stood trance-like, staring out a window. He had rolled up his sleeve and had tied a rubber tube around his arm. It looked like he had just drawn a sample of his own blood. It seemed odd to her that he would do this just now, adding to her discomfiture. She saw the vile on his desk when she stepped up behind him.

"Michael …"

He seemed on the verge of panic. "I've got to get out of this hospital," he said, interrupting her.

"Michael …"

He turned suddenly, his blue eyes red and puffy from tears.

She swallowed hard, groping for the right words. "I'd like to be with you for awhile. We both need a little fresh air. Let's take a drive to the beach. Maybe you should eat something. We could get a hotdog at Sonny's Grill."

"You could eat?" he said angrily.

"Well, maybe a cup of coffee then. We could talk for a while. I just don't want you to be alone right now."

He looked at the floor in thought. *Why am I snapping at her? I killed a little girl. I don't have to take it out on her. God! Shannon, help me!* He looked back up. "Forgive me, Shannon. I'm sorry." He closed his eyes and nodded. "I'll meet you there."

When Shannon returned to the picnic table with two cups of coffee, Michael was staring out across the beach. A salty breeze came off the Pacific and fluttered his fine sandy brown hair. She detected his anger had melted back into a state of despair. Placing the coffee on the table, she sat down opposite him, her back to the ocean, and his eyes rested on his coffee.

She released a deep breath and said, "We were all there. None of us saw the ruptured vein. You can't take all the responsibility yourself."

His forearms rested on the table, his hands were knotted in tight fists. "Why do you think they call me the *head doctor*? That title doesn't come with the luxury of blaming others for your own mistakes." He looked at her for a long moment before he added, "Shannon, if you wanted to be with me to help invent some kind of excuse, forget it. I'm the one who killed that little girl today and that's all there is to it."

"She was dying before we put her on that operating table," Shannon said in his defense.

"That doesn't matter. She was dying because she needed a routine operation. Any competent surgeon could have saved her."

"Competent surgeon! I've never heard of a more competent surgeon than you. Think of the hundreds of lives you've saved or improved with those beautiful hands of yours. I won't try to deny this was tragic, but you couldn't possibly believe that you'd go through a long career without making one single mistake."

"I killed that little girl. Nothing will change that. It's hard enough to lose someone who's elderly—at least then you have the consolation of knowing perhaps no one could have saved them. But not this. Not an otherwise healthy eight-year-old girl."

"Michael, perhaps …"

"It was my fault, Shannon," he insisted, closing his eyes, swamped with an overwhelming sense of guilt. The pain of making a confession roiled in his stomach, yet he was compelled to get it out. "I got no more than two hours sleep last night," he whispered, then opened his eyes, glancing at her attentive brown eyes. "Two hours sleep the night before a heart surgery!" He could see in her expression a look of bewilderment. "You heard me. I was irresponsible enough to have stayed out all night before a complicated heart surgery. I guess I've gotten just that damned cocky."

She found herself perplexed by his confession. It had indeed been a mistake in judgment to stay out all night. And though she could not presume the right to know the private aspects of his social life, she did wonder what he might have been doing all night. Dr. Jacobs' words echoed in her mind. She sat for a moment in a fog of confusion, now concerned on a different level. "Michael, don't ever tell anyone else you only had two hours sleep before that operation," she said with the tone of a conspirator.

"Why not? It's the truth."

"Doctor Jacobs said you're facing a malpractice lawsuit."

He looked down at the table, then back up. "Of course I am. Wouldn't you sue the incompetent doctor who killed your daughter?"

"Oh, Michael. I'm worried. If that happens, they'll make me testify against you." A nervous tension came into her hands. There had been more than a few nights she had lain awake, allowing herself to imagine a number of paths their lives might take if Michael ever fell in love with her, but testifying against him in court was surely not one of them.

Michael stared at her, her short blonde hair sparkling from

the glare off the ocean behind her. They had become very good friends during the last few weeks, but the message he saw within her eyes seemed to be concern beyond what might be considered friendship. Suddenly apprehensive, he feared he may have mislead her somehow—this on top of his wretched failure as a doctor. Jody Anderson, his sister, had warned him. Her words began to ring in his ears.

Aside from being Michael's sister, Jody was also his best friend. She lived in the apartment next door to his on the sixth floor of a high-rise. Jody had accompanied Michael and Shannon one night for dinner the week before. That night she had stopped by his apartment after he had taken Shannon home. Though he simply discounted the possibility, Jody argued mightily to convince him that Shannon was falling in love with him. "Women know these things," she had said, and he had laughed it off. In his thirty-six years, he had been unable to imagine any woman falling in love with him. But before him now, within the eyes of this innocently beautiful nurse, the message was piercing his heart with arrows.

"Shannon …"

As she watched him, his demeanor seemed to have changed. He now seemed as vulnerable as she herself felt. This time, she interrupted him. "You've figured it out, haven't you? You know how I feel about you, that I have fallen in love with you."

"Oh, God!" he moaned. Overwhelmed with grief, he couldn't bear the weight of yet another guilt on this most tragic day of his life. The responsibility of breaking a wonderful woman's heart came into his chest like a physical pain. He had suffered depression on more than one occasion, but he had never felt so utterly worthless. It was as if his existence came at the expense of other's lives and emotions. Jody had been right about Shannon, this lovely lady, so caring, so vulnerable, and he now felt like a man about to punch her in the chest. If suicide had at that moment been a viable alternative to facing her, he would have chosen it.

Shannon had wondered for many years if she would ever meet the right man, what it might be like to tell him that she loved him, that the moment would find its way atop a lifetime of joyous memories. But this wasn't the reaction she had hoped for. Now, beyond vulnerable, she also felt embarrassed. She sat fidgeting, unable to find words that might ease this sudden tension.

Michael had no idea of how he might undo the damage he had caused, but the burden was upon him now to hurt her. She had become a true friend, someone that he also loved, but only in a different way. Oblivious to the salty breeze, the endless stream of joggers and skateboarders, the volleyball game nearby, he said, "Shannon, I guess I've always assumed my colleagues were all somehow aware of my private life. I know there are certain rumors at the hospital. I've never admitted it out right because of the complications that would crop up." He paused, looking at her solemnly. "But I surely regret not telling you about me now."

His heart ached with the sudden turmoil in Shannon's eyes. He had never said a word to anyone in his profession about his sexual orientation. Now he had no choice. He had withheld the disclosure throughout his career because it would have caused gossip and concern; but today it would have the additional effect of heartbreak, and he loathed himself all the more.

"I'm gay," he confessed quickly, to get it out before he found himself simply running away. The testimony continued to pour out of him as if his words might poison him if they stayed inside a moment longer. "That's what I was doing last night … all night. I went to a bathhouse and had sex with three men I didn't even know. I suppose a man who lives like I do doesn't realize that a woman could fall in love with him."

He couldn't stand looking at her face any longer, so he fixed his eyes on the table as he continued. "I love you too, Shannon. Your friendship has been one of the few normal things in my life, a source of nourishment for me. I've enjoyed our conversations and your company." He glanced at her, wincing at her expression. "I'm sorry. I just didn't know. But this is why I'm not fit to be a doctor, and now why I don't even deserve your friendship."

Stunned, she hardly knew how to respond. Her first instinct had been to get up and walk away, but something kept her from doing so. He might have told her sooner that he was gay, but she understood why he hadn't. There was simply no justification for holding him responsible for what had unfolded in her own heart. Sex with three men he didn't know? Her mind couldn't go there, but his confession of this did eliminate any further misunderstanding.

"Wow," she simply said.

He looked at her. "I'm expecting you to hate me."

"You're not the kind of man who's easy to hate, no matter how stupid you are."

A distorted half smile came to his lips.

"At least it explains why you never suggested we spend the night together, or even kissed me good night."

"I suppose it does. While you were puzzled about all of that,

I saw myself as your guardian angel; you know, a big brother intent in keeping you from getting mixed up with the wrong guy. But then I let you to get mixed up with the worst guy imaginable ... me."

"Well, for your information, I was dying to spend the night with you. I was plotting a way to suggest it."

"That's very flattering, Shannon. But I'm certain that the man who deserves to spend the night with you will not be patient enough to wait for you to make the suggestion."

She smiled. "Can we still be friends?"

"I'm quitting."

"What?" she gasped. *What does he mean, quitting? Quitting what?*

"You heard right. I'm quitting the medical profession. I'll never kill anyone again. I'll take the medicine I deserve, but I'll never risk doing it again."

Shannon again found herself dumbfounded.

"I'm going to leave San Diego ... for a while anyway."

"But, Michael, why?"

"Look at what I did last night. I'm revolted by the way I live. My life is inherently dysfunctional. I don't have enough character to be a doctor. There's something wrong with me and I have to figure out what it is."

Oh God, no, Michael! Don't leave me here alone. Please don't leave me here alone. Distraught, she looked down at the table, rubbing her temple with her fingertips. The conviction in his voice rang in her ears with alarming certainty, and there wasn't a single word she could think of to say.

CHAPTER 2

Jody looked over the railing and saw her brother's Jeep Cherokee pulling into the parking garage. She looked at her watch. It was just past noon. Michael rarely came home this time of day. Nude, she stood and slipped into her housecoat. She had been on the balcony to enjoy the sun on this uncommonly warm day for early February.

She stepped into the hallway to find out why he had come home. Watching the light above the elevator door, it popped on and the door opened. Michael stepped out, and she could see at once he was in some kind of a mood. He didn't make eye contact until he stopped in front of her. Now pressed for time since she had stayed longer on the balcony than she intended, she wasn't sure about getting into a long conversation about whatever might be bothering him.

"Why did you come home in the middle of the day?" she asked, her curiosity heightened by his solemn expression.

"I came home to pack a few things," he stated bluntly.

Most everyone knew Michael as a slightly eccentric, but brilliant surgeon. The gay community knew him as fun loving and hot. She knew him as the older brother who often needed to be looked after, who would never have a wife to do that job, and apparently, who would never even have a permanent male companion to console him in an hour of need. And since he came home out of the blue to pack and go off for some reason, this clearly appeared to be an hour of need.

She watched him pull his keys from his pocket, aware he was distraught, thinking she had never seen that level of sadness in his eyes. With his life a series of emotional highs and lows, she sometimes found him pouty, but it had been a long time since she had seen a tear roll down his cheek. Jody's need to hurry faded and evolved into concern for her brother. "What do you mean, *pack a few things*?"

"Sis, I killed a little girl today." He turned toward his front door and pushed his key into the lock.

She stared at the back of his head as the door swung open and he disappeared inside, leaving the door open behind him. Jody took the cell phone out of her pocket and dialed her associate's number to cancel their afternoon appointment. Concern for her brother superceded a meeting to discuss the graphic designs for a department store promotion and a potentially disgruntled client. She then trailed into his apartment and heard him rummaging in the bedroom closet. Stopping at the bedroom doorframe, she saw a canvas duffel bag fly out of the closet and land on the bed, followed by the re-emergence of her brother.

"Michael, would you please calm down a bit and tell me what you're talking about?"

"It's simple. I hung out in a bathhouse until four o'clock last night, knowing I had a surgery scheduled for seven this morning. The patient was a little girl, eight years old. I cut her open with less than two hours sleep. She's dead because of me." He flopped on the edge of the bed and buried his face in his hands.

Jody closed her eyes tight, well aware that this was the inevitable day she had dreaded from the moment he became a surgeon. She knew what something like this would do to him, and the circumstances that apparently caused it were more unfortunate than her worst fear. He was clearly wrong in staying out the night before an early surgery.

"I'm not sure what to say," she said, staring dumbly across the room. Normally, one of his moods would simply prompt one of her lectures. He might pout or carry on for a while, but in the end, she always found the right words to help redirect his perspective. This was clearly not the time for a lecture, even if he had been wrong, even if he deserved it more than ever. Now was the time to be more concerned for his sanity.

Jody walked softly toward the bed and sat down beside him, then reached out to stroke the side of his face.

"Eight years old. All she needed for a long life full of promise was a competent doctor. I wasn't alert enough to head that procedure. Now she's dead. She's dead because her pathetic doctor wanted to get himself fucked one more fucking time."

"Michael, please. You can't let this destroy you. You're far too good a doctor to let one tragic mistake overshadow the hundreds of successes you've had. It was a learning lesson. I know you won't ever let this happen again."

"That's for damn sure! I'm quitting."

Jody gasped. He had made the statement with the kind of conviction she knew to not take lightly. She had helped him suffer his problems in the past, but never anything like this. Now she was scared. In his present state of mind, she feared he might easily lapse into an abyss of self-destruction. She knew to choose her words carefully, but did such words exist? Things were moving too fast, spinning out of control. Before she could think of anything to say, she heard his voice again.

"And you were right about Shannon. She tried to make me feel better after the operation. We went to the beach to talk, and she told me she had fallen in love with me. Can you imagine what it feels like to hurt someone like her? You have all the answers. How can I reconcile that?"

"Oh God!" Jody murmured. This alone would have upset him, but it came on top of the worst tragedy he had ever faced. "Michael, you're going to have to give yourself some time to deal with all of this. I'm so worried right now I can't stand it. Please don't compound this problem by doing something irrational."

"You don't have to worry, Sis." He took a small vial from his shirt pocket and handed it to her.

"What's this?"

"It's my blood. I drew it in my office after the operation. I want you to take it to that gay clinic I use to get tested for HIV. I'll contact you in a few days to get the results."

"What!" She looked at him, incredulous. "You're scaring me, Michael. What do you mean contact me in a few days?"

"I'm quitting the medical profession and I'm quitting the insane lifestyle I've been living," he stated matter-of-factly. "If I ever have sex with another man, he will be someone I want to spend the rest of my life with."

She felt a sense of relief and the edge of apprehension at the same time: relief in that he might be actually serious about quitting what he had referred to as his insane lifestyle. That was hard to believe. She had worried about the way he lived for so long, she had grown almost numb. She had always found it difficult to be resigned to the fact that she might lose her brother to AIDS or violence long before his time. Her sudden apprehension revolved around his delusion about quitting the hospital, and in that she was truly concerned. He was certainly capable of saying something irrational while in a state of emotional turmoil, but could he actually follow through with this? Yes, if he was convinced that his patients couldn't trust him, he was indeed hardheaded enough to quit.

"That's why you don't have to worry," he went on to say. "It makes me sick that my life has been so shallow, that I've taken so many chances. I realized today that I'm too incompetent to be a surgeon, and I'm also a jerk. It's hard enough to face being incompetent, but I truly hate feeling like a jerk. So if I'm to go on, I have to figure out a way to become a person I don't loathe. I'm quitting the medical profession and I'm leaving San Diego for a while. I want to be alone to work this out."

She sat gaping at him, at a complete loss. Then half a dozen questions formed in her mind, all with an urge to leap off her tongue at the same time. "Leave San Diego? Where the hell are you planning to go?"

"I don't know." He turned his head and looked at the duffel bag. "I might just drive around the country for a few weeks."

"How can you just give up your lifestyle?"

"I'm revolted by it!" He bowed his head, his face twisted with angst, then looked back at her with a tear in his eye. "That way of life is like an addiction, an endless cycle that always left me feeling empty. Its only value was to keep my mind off the constant strain of my profession. But just look at what it caused. That little girl should be in a room eating ice cream right now. She should have lived. I think I've always been disgusted by the way I live and just didn't admit it."

"But you can't simply quit your practice at the hospital!"

"Yes I can."

"Michael, your office, your patients, your ties to the hospital."

"I need your help, Sis. I honestly can't walk back into that building. I hope you'll be willing to go over there as soon as possible and talk to Dr. Whitlow. Just explain it to him. He can transfer my patients to other doctors and terminate my relationship with the hospital. Clean out my office. I'm sure Shannon will help you do that." He looked toward the floor for a moment in thought. "There's one more thing. The little girl's family will sue me. I want you to contact my lawyer and explain what happened. Tell him I have no intention to testify in my own defense. Tell him I will state the truth in no uncertain terms if I'm put on the stand. There's no doubt the little girl's family deserves a settlement, but I don't want to be responsible for causing an inflated amount." He studied her pained, befuddled expression for a moment. "Will you do these things for me, Sis?"

"I'll talk to your lawyer. And I'll go to the hospital, but not to tell them you're quitting. I'll tell Dr. Whitlow you're suffering an emotional crisis, and I'll arrange for an extended leave-of-absence. You're not quitting, at least not until you've have time to think it through."

"Fair enough," he said.

"I'll also tell them you've left town, but Michael, you're breaking my heart." Jody wasn't the type who cried easily, but now she was fighting back tears. "So when are you planning to leave?"

"As soon as I pack."

"Shit!" She studied his odd demeanor for a moment, sort of a tight state of calm. She feared the underlying turmoil behind it.

A silence evolved. Michael stood and walked to his chest of drawers. He pulled open a drawer and then slipped off his jeans, confirming his complete lack of modesty and total absence of tan-lines. She tilted her head, directing her eyes to the floor, thinking of her many female acquaintances who have expressed regrets about his sexual orientation. She had one friend who once said that it was the well-formed rounds of Michael's buttocks that had established her standard by which all male butts were measured. Another of her colleagues had spotted him at Black's Beach, where he usually went to maintain his overall tan, and had told Jody that he was one of the few men she had ever seen that actually looked better nude than dressed.

Jody knew her brother was a beautiful man, his broad chest patterned with a masculine landscape of sun-bleached hair, as were his legs and forearms; she knew that Michelangelo would have happily used him as a model for one of those marvelous statues; and she knew it was also the source of her deepest anxiety in worrying about him. It was hard enough to accept the fact that she would never be an aunt, and all but impossible to accept the way he attracted other men when he went to those sordid places. Why he did it, she could never understand, for he almost always came home depressed.

"Sis, I also need you to pay my bills. There's a checkbook in the desk drawer," he said, looking at a pair of wrinkled shorts he had taken from the drawer.

She looked up and saw him digging through the drawer. *At*

least he doesn't have to worry about money. He had invested most of his significant income in mutual funds, which could provide for him the rest of his life. "So you're leaving immediately, and you don't know where you're going or how long you'll be gone?"

"Yes, immediately, and no, I don't know how long I'll be gone."

"Then make sure to keep your cell phone turned on so I can get in touch with you if I need to hear your voice."

He walked back across the room, carrying the shorts, and she averted her eyes again. He sat on the bed beside her. "Sis ... I'm scared."

"You're also naked, big brother."

"Oh ... sorry." He pulled the shorts up his legs and lifted himself to get them over his hips.

She took his hand after he buttoned them. "I'm scared too, Michael. I don't want you to go, not in this state of mind. After what you went through today I want you nearby so I can look after you."

"And I've realized something else," he said, ignoring the issue of his plans to leave. "I'm lonely."

She stared across the room for a moment. His loneliness was something she understood. They had counted on each other all of their lives, quite alone together in the world. "I guess we both are," she said regretfully. "But we have each other."

"And we'll have that forever. But will we ever have the other? Someone who is part of our lives and dreams? Someone to grow old with and hold while we sleep?"

"Michael, please wait a few days before you leave."

"I'll call you at least every other day, Sis. I'll be fine. I just have to think this through, find some answers, to learn how to become the man I want to be." He leaned forward and pulled on his sandals, then stood and zipped the fly, looking down at her. "Don't worry about me. I'll be all right. I'm actually relieved I'm going to face this challenge. I can't keep living the way I have been."

An hour later, the engine in his Cherokee was laboring up the steep, sweeping slopes of the Rocky Mountains, heading east on Interstate eight. Though his heart still beat with the weight of lead, a calm had settled in his hands as he steered through the winding mountain curves. Left behind was stress, that relentless phantom always whispering in his ear, reminding him of unending obligations, prodding his fast paced performance and long hours at the hospital; ahead were countless miles of highway and country he had never seen, and unlimited hours of discovery which might offer a fresh perspective.

Michael spent the first night in a small motel room in Yuma after eating a sack full of tacos. The room smelled musty with a hint of air freshener as he laid in bed, contemplating how long it might take to drive all the way to Key West, Florida. But then, was that really a good idea, Key West, a city known for its gay population, crowded, and perhaps much like San Diego? Or should he choose a destination that would provide a therapeutic solitude, someplace where he could spend hour upon hour in thought, and figure out what he should do with his life? He stared at the ceiling and smiled. It was something he might decide tomorrow.

He was back behind the wheel with a full tank of gas by dawn.

He had driven through the desert before, but this time he was actually seeing it. The window down, the air-conditioner off, he drove with the wind on his face, the feel of dry air on his skin. Long miles melted away behind him like an endless stream of fading memories, as the wonders of timeless creation unfolded ahead. He drove on, through panoramas so vast his imagination could not comprehend their limits, a ribbon of highway stretching beyond what the eye could see, so few cars and trucks the solitude lay over the land like quiet weight. Miles turned into lost hours as the sun journeyed across the sky, and it was all right with Michael if this drive through the desert went on forever.

In the late afternoon, growing weary, he pulled onto the shoulder at an exit near Fort Stockton, Texas. He got out to stretch. Staring back over the unending stretch of concrete behind him, he had never felt more alone or so utterly useless in his life. Why had it come down to this? Though he had won countless accolades for his accomplishments over the years, those seemed to belong to someone else. All of that now seemed like rewards with no real value, no more meaningful than an endless quest for glory. Why had there never been a sense of simply helping someone, simply rejoicing in his ability to do so? Had the politics and compromises and the clutter of rules led to his shallow choices, those countless, faceless men? Was he now paying the price? He wanted to live, to learn what it felt like to look forward to a new day. But to go on meant change, it meant finding a reason to exist, a meaning, but how? How does a man who has wasted half his life point himself in another direction?

He turned and found himself staring at a large brown highway sign. *Big Bend National Park, 80 miles.* A deep breath filled his lungs with warm dry air. Back inside the car, he unfolded a Texas map and ran his finger over the western part of the state until it landed on the Big Bend.

Jesus, that looks big. He looked back at the sign, deep in thought. *I know I've heard of it.* He thought about the vast barren stretches of land he had driven through all day, the blissful solitude. *It must be wilderness down there, too.* He looked back at the map, wondering what it might be like to camp out in the open air, miles from anything or anyone, to lay back at night and count stars, and make coffee on the coals of a campfire.

Staring at the map, he rubbed his lower lip with his index finger. It was something he had never done before, and it unfolded in his mind as a grand adventure. Camping in the wilderness, a challenge of self-reliance, something he had not experienced since college. He could exit here at Fort Stockton, stop and buy supplies and a small tent, and then head south toward the Big Bend. Folding the map, he looked back at the brown sign.

Why not?

He pulled the gearshift lever into drive and took the exit. Spotting a Wal-Mart, he pulled into the parking lot. After filling a cart with a small tent, a bedroll, a variety of utensils and gear, a couple of paperback novels and a few dozen bags of snacks and dried fruit, he found himself on a lonely asphalt two lane road that led across the desert like a country song. He had never contemplated territory so vast, a land of hearty American history, a barren desert landscape with horizons untold miles away. On it went, up a long gradual incline where he finally entered the park, and eventually came to a modern visitors center that seemed situated in the middle of nowhere. Inside, Michael looked over a few brochures, ignoring the half dozen tourists who were milling about.

Then a park ranger emerged from a hallway behind the counter. Michael looked up as he walked through the lobby, struck by the man's stature and rugged beauty. A man of African descent, he strode with confidence, his skin a rich honey black. A gleam of boyish innocence came from his coal colored eyes, his long lashes and full lips most alluring. Michael watched him cross the room, his lean body well defined and masculine in the brown uniform, a small cocker spaniel trotting happily ahead of him.

The ranger glanced Michael's way, his mind apparently elsewhere, and then he paused and turned his head at the door. He looked at Michael again, his eyes sweeping over him, and he nodded before walking out the door. Michael shifted his attention back to the display of brochures, and he discreetly picked up a map of the park and then used the men's room before going back outside.

He stood staring at the vista he had just driven through, across endless miles of arroyos and the hues and texture of sparse desert fauna. He had never seen the sun's glare so bright, or the sky quite that shade of pastel blue, and he paused. A peaceful tranquility lay over the land like a soundless poem heard only through one's eyes. Clean dry air passed through his nostrils as he watched the broad circle of a soaring hawk, recharging mind and soul, and all at once he couldn't imagine anywhere else he would rather be. It all came together in a timeless image, vibrant in all five senses, silently offering the promise of past and future, country so vast it had the power to make a man realize that he really could feel alive.

A SONG IN THE PARK

Back in the Cherokee, Michael opened a bottle of water and took a few drinks as he studied the map of Big Bend. Tracing an errant line with his finger along the southern perimeter of the park sparked his imagination. *Let's see ... hmm ... the River Road. Looks like a good bet.* He had chosen a primitive road to explore, one of the longest and most remote roads on the map.

CHAPTER 3

Justin Brooks woke up thinking about Christie—again. Though the early dawn filled his bedroom with crisp desert air, he was sweating. It had been more than three years since he had lived through the worst day of his life, and it still haunted him with the certainty of another sunrise. Each time he awoke thinking about her, as always, it was that last image of her stunned face that formed in his mind, and it crawled like an insect on his skin.

Justin had never figured out what had possessed him that day, their wedding day. He and Christie had been engaged for over a year. He remembered standing in that desperate trance at the alter, watching her proud father escort her down the aisle toward him, how each step they took plunged him deeper into unexplained panic. It must have been written all over his face. She had approached with a broad grin that slowly melted as she took notice of his dire expression. He had glanced at her father, who was watching him with incredulous concern. Gripped by torment, he took his last desperate look at her.

"I can't do this!" he had muttered, lightheaded with panic. His first steps toward the door seemed like they came in slow motion, faces in the congregation looking on aghast, gasps and spontaneous murmurs of disbelief. Then he broke into a run. Now, even his own mother shunned him.

No wonder. Everyone who knew Christie loved her, including himself. A gorgeous prospective bride, she came from a prominent family in Jasper, respected by both the white and black community, her father a banker in their small east Texas community. Now they all considered him a pariah. A month later he was still wandering around Texas, living in his van, trying to figure out what might be wrong with him.

Now on the federal payroll, he had been persistent with his application to the park service and he finally made it. It was a perfect job, a park ranger at Big Bend National Park. His job was patrolling a sixty-mile stretch of primitive ruts and rocks known as the River Road, a road through desert so rugged and isolated, so mysteriously beautiful, he still found himself awed. And best of all, his job provided long days of solitude on this land that so easily nourished his soul. He sometimes wondered if it had something to do with his ancestral roots, if perhaps generations before him had lived on land like this in Africa. He didn't know if being a black man had helped him or hurt him, but when all was said and done, he was glad he got the position whether politics had helped or not.

The wind-up alarm clock ran out of steam, its annoying clatter sputtered to a stop. It was after six o'clock and the small stone house had warmed a bit with the sun's first light. Justin threw back the sheet and sat up on the edge of the bed, stretching his arms with a broad yawn. Perk, his cocker spaniel, jumped up on the mattress beside him, looking at him with anticipation. Justin smiled and gave the dog a good head rub. "You're right, boy. I dreamed about her again. And I'm getting pretty tired of running out of that church." The dog's front paws upon his leg, he stretched his neck to lick Justin's chin. "Seems like I just got to sleep, Perk. Must have been a restless night."

He stood and walked barefoot across the ancient tile floor, into the front room, where the squeaky hand pump was mounted on the counter next to the old porcelain sink. The kitchen was not much more than a counter along the south wall of the room. He plugged in the percolator and then pumped a glass of water, squinting into the bright light of a new day through the dingy glass of the window over the sink. There wasn't another house or a structure for ten miles in any direction. Holding the glass up to the light, he then poured it down the drain.

"Perk, looks like we have a little sand in the water today."

He pumped more water into the drain before filling the next glass. The water was clear this time. He drank it down in one gulping swallow, then filled Perk's water bowl before pulling open a rough hewn cabinet door under the counter. The little dog watched him take out a bag of dog food, their same comfortable ritual that took place every morning.

Pushing open the heavy wooden back door, Justin walked some twenty paces into the desert, watching for rattlers. It was warm enough for them to migrate from their den, but not hot enough yet to keep them out of the sun. Lowering the waistband of his faded boxer shorts, he splattered the sand before him. He never bothered to walk all the way up to the outhouse just to pee. Perk had followed him and was sniffing for the lizard that had scurried into a clump of pointed dagger plants.

Justin had rigged a five-gallon water jug between two poles. Mounted about seven foot off the ground, the jug tilted by means of a dangling rope, and it was high enough for his six foot one frame to stand under. As close to duplicating a shower as he could get, he preferred bathing in the open air under the jug to pumping a cramped washtub full of water, and the runoff provided his pepper plants with plenty of water. In the winter, it wasn't often so cold as to make a quick shower unbearable, but when it was he simply postponed a bath.

He pulled off the boxer shorts and hung them on a creosote bush. Stepping under the jug, he pulled the rope. Standing naked in the morning sun, the water cascaded over his head and he lathered up quickly before the soap could dry on his body. After pulling the rope once more to wash off the soap, he tilted the jug again to fill a small washbasin. Placing it back on a weathered table next to the shower, he used it to brush his teeth and shave. He then pitched the water across the sand and stepped back into the boxer shorts. The color of coffee with light cream, his skin had dried by the time he pulled his uniform off the clothesline. Perk eagerly watched him zip up the fly, then button the shirt, for the little dog knew the uniform meant a long drive in the Jeep.

Justin went back into the house and filled his coffee mug, locking the rusty deadbolt when he stepped back outside. It was Friday. Another sunny day lay ahead, patrolling the River Road. He got behind the wheel of his official Jeep and looked across the barren land, always aware of his good fortune to live in paradise. It had become part of his soul, and he loved it, but sometimes, even with the companionship of his little dog, he felt lonely.

By ten o'clock, he had bounced over the rutted road for going on three hours. Earlier, he had stopped to give a couple of backpackers directions, and before that he had helped some middle-aged women change a flat tire. Like tourists often do, they had driven their SUV over a thorn. It had been the only vehicle he had seen all morning. Now, where the road veered close to the

Rio Grande, from the corner of his eye, he thought he had seen a glint of sun on metal. Justin pulled off what amounted to little more than a goat path and switched off the Jeep's ignition. Perk jumped out and followed him through the brush in the direction of the glint. A white Jeep Cherokee came into view.

He approached cautiously. Stepping around the Cherokee he came upon a small camp, nothing more than a two-man tent and a campfire, though here it was an illegal campfire. Beyond the camp, he saw a man sitting atop a rock formation gazing out over the rapids of the Rio Grande, apparently in deep thought. Perhaps in his mid thirties, the man sat perfectly still, his sandy brown hair in disarray, his bare shoulders tanned and muscular. Apparently alone, it appeared he had chosen this spot to find solace in its peace and solitude. Justin stepped forward, stopping some twenty feet away, the sound of his boots on the hard desert crust lost on the man's ears in the noisy swirl of fast water.

"Howdy, Mister," Justin called out to announce his presence.

Startled, Michael turned toward the voice. Other than an occasional river rafter, he hadn't seen another human being for four days. His heart began to settle immediately when he saw the brown uniform. He got to his feet and took a few steps toward the rather stoic looking ranger, nodding as he approached.

"Didn't mean to jump like that," said Michael. "I wasn't expecting someone to walk up behind me out here."

Justin studied him a moment. He remembered seeing him at the visitor's center a few days before. Strikingly handsome, he stood bare-chested in a pair of faded blue jeans. Almost stunned by the icy blue eyes, Justin sensed a city air about him. Wind blown sandy brown hair, a distinct jaw line peppered with three or four days of stubble, his disarming smile revealed perfectly straight white teeth. Justin's eyes fell over a well-tanned torso, a muscular chest scattered with fine blonde hairs, and a stomach uncommonly hard for a man of this age. He caught a fleeting glimpse of a distinctly masculine contour near the fly of the jeans before his eyes shifted back to the man's face.

There seemed something distant behind the man's smile, a weight of some kind, and Justin found himself regretting the responsibility of having to make him move on.

"Didn't I see you at the visitor's center the other day?" he said.

"I believe you did. That was the day I got here. You walked through with your dog when I went in for a map."

"It looks like you've been camping out here," Justin said with a ranger's straightforward manner.

"That's what I've been calling it."

"Did you get a camping permit while you were at the visitor's center?"

"I didn't know I was supposed to."

"You should have. They would have told you where to camp. You've put this tent right in the middle of a ravine. If there had been a cloudburst last night, you and everything here would have ended up in the river."

Michael glanced over the terrain, suddenly feeling a little stupid.

"That's one of the reasons this isn't a designated camping site."

"Oh," said Michael, "I didn't know." He fidgeted a bit, brushing his hand back over his hair. Dealing with the pain still stabbing his heart, he wasn't prepared for a problem to crop up.

"I'm afraid that campfire is illegal," Justin said matter-of-factly, pulling a citation book from his back pocket. "Sorry, it's a hundred dollar fine."

His eyes on the small leather binder, Michael's smile turned to a look of bewilderment. "You have to write me a ticket?" he muttered, drawn from the harmony of this dry paradise back to the nettlesome thorns of civilization. It drew his mind for the first time in four days to his pending lawsuit. *Guess if I'm going to get sued for a few million dollars, another hundred won't matter much.*

Justin paused, glancing back over the camp. A perfect circle of stones ringed the small fire. A feather of steam rose from the spout of a coffee pot resting atop the coals. Perk was sniffing out the area. This wasn't a part of his job that Justin relished; in fact he would have prefer a splinter under his fingernail to disturbing this man's retreat. Instead of one of the park's caretakers, he felt more like an intruder, aware the man before him had likely chosen this site for its proximity to the river and its solitude. Now he wondered if he had compounded the sadness in those blue eyes.

Michael's gaze shifted to the untold miles of desert beyond the tall ranger. His hair fluttered slightly with a fleeting breeze that came whispering out of the mountains. He had spent four days at this spot, soothed by the unending song of the rapids in watching a river with the power to ignite dreams. He had breathed dry desert air, and he had lain awake at night gazing at a black sky filled with countless stars, savoring every minute of being in this land of wonders that had revived his soul. It all came together right here: the river, the sky, the timeless mystery of the desert. And as the hours had drifted away, he had come to think of this ravine as his own.

His gaze still locked in wonder on the distant mountains, he said, "You know, I didn't know a place like this existed."

Justin looked off in the direction of Michael's gaze, and then he glanced at the citation book still unopened in his hand.

"That coffee is fresh," said Michael, nodding at the pot. "You got a few minutes to have a cup?"

Their eyes met for a moment, then Justin glanced at the citation book before he pushed it back into his pocket. He sighed, his sense of benevolence at odds with his position of responsibility. "I'm afraid you can't stay here. You can't camp anywhere in the park without a permit, and then you have to use a designated area."

"Can you give me a permit?"

"No. They're issued at the tourist center. But the campsites are all full now. Most people know to make reservations in advance."

Watching the cocker spaniel, Michael sat down on a large rock near the small fire. A look of melancholy washed over his face. His four days in the desert had brought him peace; the lonely calm a blissful therapy. He hadn't contemplated leaving the park anytime soon. He then turned his head and stared at the river.

A moment later he spoke, his voice somewhat distant. "I drove across this river coming through New Mexico. It didn't seem to have this much water in it back there."

Justin looked toward the river. "It gets a trickle from the Pecos upstream. But most of what you see here comes out of the Conchos in Mexico." He looked back at Michael.

It wasn't the first time Justin had come upon someone who had come to the Big Bend to resolve private issues. Not at all comfortable with the intrusion he had imposed, he sensed the weight on this man's shoulders and he wished he not noticed the Jeep.

Justin's sense of responsibility was losing the battle with his heart. "I'm sorry about this," he said. "Is there anything I can do for you?"

Michael's eyes swept over him, instinctively attracted to his lean masculine beauty, but these were among the thoughts this sojourn was meant to dispel. Beyond that, as attractive as the ranger might be, there wasn't a hint of mutual thinking on his stoic face. But there *was* something. Michael detected a certain mystery behind those no nonsense lines of his expression, something deep within those boyish but solemn dark eyes. And though he had stopped to instruct Michael to move on, he had done so with obvious reluctance. Michael had no desire to leave; yet, after four days of solitude he wouldn't have minded someone to talk to for a while.

"Is that your drug-sniffing dog?" he asked.

Justin finally allowed the hint of a smile to form on his full lips. "That's Perk. Even if he knew how to sniff out drugs, it wouldn't occur to him to do anything about it. His only job is to be my buddy."

"I like his name," said Michael, clapping his hands to draw the dog's attention. "Here boy, come here." The dog approached eagerly and Michael gave him a frisky head rub.

"I called him Perky when he was a pup, but that didn't seem appropriate when he grew up."

Michael glanced at the coffee pot. "How about that cup of coffee?"

Justin nodded. Michael got back to his feet and extended his hand. "I'm Michael Anderson."

"Justin Brooks," he said, taking a hold of his hand.

Michael kneeled near the pot, remembering he had bought just one tin coffee cup. He had not planned for visitors. "I'm afraid I have just one cup."

"I've got mine in my Jeep. I'll be right back."

Michael watched Perk prance along behind the tall ranger as he stepped around a prickly pear cactus and on up through the sparse scrub. He sighed, wondering where he might go since there were no available campsites. It felt like being displaced having to leave.

After Michael poured both cups full of coffee, they sat on the ground on opposite sides of the fire, folding their legs before them. "You didn't write that citation," he said. "I would understand if you're obligated to."

"I use my own discretion in writing citations. It's one of the things I like about this job. I'm supposed to, but it's not like working in an office with hidden cameras watching everything you do." Justin studied his sudden companion for a moment. Certainly personable enough, he wondered about the anxiety lurking just behind his eyes. "You're not from around here are you? Sounds like you have an eastern accent."

"Not eastern. California. I was born and raised in San Diego. Lived there all my life."

"You're here alone?"

"Yes."

Justin nodded. "A lot of tourists come down here these days. A good many who come to get away from something they've left at home. Looks to me like that's the category you're in."

Michael looked at him. The intuitive statement came with a hint of compassion. Unaware his tribulations were all that obvious, he said, "I've decided to leave my profession, and now I'm not sure what I'm going to do."

"Oh. I can understand that. I quit a job in my hometown before I came out here. I remember it left me feeling empty." As Justin watched him take a sip of coffee, he decided to further indulge his curiosity. "What did you do?"

"I was a surgeon."

Justin, amazed that someone with such a casual appearance was a doctor, glanced at Michael's hands. He had wondered about a surgeon's hands, their ability to perform such important and precise work. He wouldn't have guessed this man was a surgeon, but now that he knew, he could see the sophistication under the stubble and unruly hair. "A surgeon. That's pretty impressive. Count me among those in awe of people like you."

Michael knew the general population viewed doctors this way. He didn't want the attention. He wondered if it might be a good idea to make-up a different background for himself.

"Would you mind if I looked at your hands?"

Somewhat taken aback, Michael smiled and said, "No, I wouldn't mind."

He watched the ranger set his cup on the ground and approach, kneeling then before him. Michael put his cup aside and lifted his hands, and Justin took one of them, as if observing a delicate object of art, running his rough dark fingertips over the white, silky smooth skin. Michael watched the enchantment in the black man's eyes, suddenly aware that he had never experienced a moment of such undefined intimacy. Justin turned the white hand palm up and held his own beside it, the rough, calloused skin a remarkable contrast. "There's quite a difference, isn't there?"

"Yeah," said Michael in quiet awe, "I suppose there is."

Justin returned to his position and picked up his coffee. "It's none of my business, but I'm wondering why you decided to quit. I didn't know surgeons quit their jobs, not after all you go through to become one."

"I killed a little girl on the operating table." Saying it again revived the painful emotion. Michael looked down at the small fire.

It was almost like a slap, the statement so direct and blunt. *So that's it, the source of his trouble.* Justin sipped of his coffee. He wasn't sure what to say to a man who believed he had killed a little girl. Perk, having checked out the entire area, trotted over and curled up beside him. He decided it best not to pursue the subject, though he had a sudden urge to get to know this man, to find out what was so intriguing about him. And not only had his curiosity gotten the better of him, he couldn't remember the last time he had had the luxury of a thoughtful exchange with someone. "So you're not sure what you plan to do now?" he said, trying to avoid becoming too personal.

"Right now I'm wondering how often campsites become available around here."

"If we get your name on the list, it might not be all that long."

"What about in the meantime? The last motel I saw was in Fort Stockton."

Justin contemplated the problem for a moment. "There might be a room at the Badlands Hotel over in Lajitas. That's just a few miles west of the park, and they have a place to eat right next door."

Michael studied the ground. He didn't really want to spend time in a motel room, now that he had become so attached to the beckoning mystery of this desert.

At odds with the disappointment he had caused this man who just wanted peace, Justin considered walking away. He could pretend he had never come upon him, just tell him to move the tent to higher ground and then leave him alone. Yet he still had the strangest desire to get to know him. His thoughts a confusion of contradictions, he struggled for a solution.

"You could stay at my place," he said impulsively, adding, "that is, if you don't mind sleeping on a couch."

His invitation came out suddenly, surprising even himself; but then, why not? He had taken an immediate liking to this Californian, and a curiously uncommon interest in getting to know him. Though the promise of intelligent conversation for a few days seemed refreshing, he wasn't certain his forwardness had been entirely appropriate. His tone reflected the uncertainty of his social prowess when he added: "And I guess I should warn you before you decide, that my place is a little primitive."

Michael sat observing Justin's sudden change in demeanor. The tall ranger seemed a bit nervous and apprehensive. His eyes drawn back to the contours of a masculine body, the flawless black skin of his arms, and then back up to the alluring dark eyes,

Michael considered the ramifications of spending a few days in close proximity with such a beautiful man, a man whose appetites were opposite of his own. He too felt a little nervous, a perception of tension just beneath the surface. Caught off guard by the invitation, he wasn't quite sure of what to say. "Primitive? I'm not sure I know what you mean."

Justin broke into a full-blown grin. "You'll find out what I mean when you see it."

Michael nodded, intrigued. The possibility of getting to know a straight-laced park ranger, a personality unlike any he had ever encountered, suddenly seemed like a good way to spend a few days. Justin Brooks struck him as someone with a sensitive intellect; and if Michael's intuition was right, he might have come upon a neutral new friend who would be willing to lend a sympathetic ear, a chance to discuss his emotions with someone not personally involved or affected. And of course it might also satisfy his curiosity about the mystery behind this park ranger's dark eyes.

A grateful smile came to Michael's lips. "I appreciate the offer, and I accept."

Justin helped him break camp. They folded the small tent and put out the fire, destroying the evidence that it ever existed. With all of the gear packed into the Cherokee, Justin stood with his hands on his hips and surveyed the abandoned campsite.

He nodded up the incline. "My Jeep is up there. Pull out and follow me. It'll take about an hour to get there."

It was slow going back over the River Road, bouncing over eroded ruts, driving into and back out of creek beds and arroyos, climbing steep, near impassable cliffs, a route impossible for anything short of the mulish determination of four-wheel drive. Michael followed, shifting the transmission into its lowest gear on the steepest inclines, wondering what the next few days were to bring.

CHAPTER 4

When they reached the end of the River Road, they pulled back onto the asphalt two-lane that meandered toward the western parameters of Big Bend National Park. A few miles west of the park, Justin turned off onto a gravel road, where Michael followed in his dust for about six more miles. He pulled off this road and parked near a rather small stone house. When Michael moved the shift lever into park and got out, Justin was standing beside the Jeep, his thumbs hooked on his belt. Perk pranced around yapping, as if he was excited to have a visitor.

Mesmerized by the dramatic panorama, Michael scanned the mountains in the far distance. They lay along the horizon in every direction except to the north, where the land stretched in endless miles of desert, the hues shimmering with warm rays from the sun. The faded stone house stood like a solitary relic from the past, its tin roof rusting, its windowsills weathered from decades of exposure to sun and dry wind.

"What do you think?" asked Justin, reading the wonderment on Michael's face.

"I've never imagined anything like this. It looks like something out of an old western movie." He looked at Justin. "Don't you ever get lonely living out here by yourself?"

"Sometimes."

Though Michael had detected a remote dissonance in Justin's eyes, he had also detected a peace of mind. Now he knew why.

He couldn't imagine a life like this, and he hungered to know more. Contemplating a simpler, more meaningful life during his last four days on the river, he had wondered if such a existence was even possible. Obviously it was. Here, in the form of a house and a man with his dog was something most intriguing, and he was suddenly very glad that Justin had extended the invitation.

"Shit, it's hard to find a vacant lot in San Diego," he said, looking at the house. He looked back at Justin. "What do you do, I mean personally, when you're not on duty?"

"Read mostly. I get the *Wall Street Journal* and a couple of news magazines to keep up with what's going on in the world. Every couple of weeks or so I go up to the library in Alpine and pick up two or three novels I haven't read. I'll pickup supplies and sometimes take in a movie when I'm up there."

Michael thought about his own fast paced life. By comparison, this was hard to fathom. "So you've lived here three years?"

"Most of that. There's a community of houses for the rangers, but I decided to live out here early on. It's a ranch. The owner lives in Houston and he let me have this place for a hundred a month. It might be worth more, but we're friends and he likes the idea of having a ranger live on his property. It was a working ranch until the twenties. It goes all the way back to the days when the Comanches were raiding settlers out here. The house was for ranch hands, an outpost. I still find an arrowhead every now and then."

"This is unbelievable," said Michael, thinking about the freeways, the sprawling suburbs and shopping centers, the endless commercial clutter of the city; where here, for as far as the eye could see, there was nothing, a barren land dotted by sparse brush and sculpted in rock. "A hundred dollars a month rent! You must bank most of your income. It sure doesn't look like there's anything else to spend it on."

Justin smiled. "Well, the electric bill runs about twenty dollars a month."

Michael shook his head.

Turning, Justin said over his shoulder, "Come on, I'll show you inside the house."

Michael followed him around to the back of the house, where they ducked under a clothesline and stepped up onto a small porch. Justin unlocked the door and pushed it open. Michael walked in and stopped in the middle of the room. His gaze turned slowly as he took it all in: the Mexican tiled counter, the large porcelain sink chipped and rusting in spots, the old cast iron hand pump, a fifties era refrigerator and a small stove. On the rough hewn shelf over the counter were a few pots and pans and dishes. Under the counter were four cabinets and four drawers with porcelain knobs. There was a small, apparently handmade table in front of the counter and three mismatched chairs.

The other half of the room, some fifteen feet square, made up the living room, half its floor area covered with a threadbare rug. A leather sofa, dry and cracked with age, a handmade rocker, an overstuffed chair, a discount store floor lamp, one end table with a lamp, a coffee table scattered with newspapers and magazines and a pot-belly stove made up its furnishings.

"No TV?" said Michael.

"Afraid not," Justin shrugged. "The last time I watched a television my head started to feel soft." He nodded toward an old wooden door leaning half open. "That's my bedroom."

Michael stepped toward the door and noticed it wouldn't close any further than half way. He pushed it open and saw a rather solid looking metal frame bed, unmade, a nightstand with a lamp, a chest of drawers, a rack of clothes attached to the wall, another pot-belly stove and a good size fan.

"I did indulge in a good matress," said Justin.

Michael wondered what he'd look like laying on the bed in his underwear, propped against the headboard with one of his novels, and he immediately chastised himself for the thought. "Where's the bathroom?" he asked.

"I though I saw you looking at it before we came inside."

"So that was an outhouse!"

"That's right, the bathroom, but a better local word would be shithouse."

"What was that water jug hanging between two poles?"

"The shower."

"You shower outside!" Michael was fascinated. "What do you do in the winter, when it's too cold to shower outside?"

"Well, we do get some pretty frigid weather sometimes. I just skip the shower for a day or two."

Michael looked ambiguous. "Doesn't the cold weather ever drag on for more than a day or two?"

"That's when you have make the hard choice. You can get a little ripe sometimes before Spring, or you can fill the wash tub and take a bath in the kitchen if you start having a hard time living with yourself."

Michael remembered the hand pump on the counter. "Is the pump next to the sink in there where you get your water?"

"Yes. It's pretty simple here. There's no running water, but I

..ve electricity. I burn mesquite wood in the stoves to heat the house in winter. The stoves work well but I back them up with an electric heater when necessary. Clothes are washed by hand and hung on the clothesline outside. Music comes at the mercy of the Zenith radio in the other room. I shave in the wash basin outside. No air conditioner, but nights are cool here even in summer. I usually pick up groceries when I drive up to Alpine." He paused, looking at Michael. "At this point in my life, I can't imagine living any other way."

Michael looked around the room again, utterly amazed. Laundry for him was something to be left at the front desk, a sevice that included someone returning it to his drawers, all neatly folded, while he was away. He wasn't quite sure what it was, that pleasant shiver that came to the back of his neck, but it was much like entering a warm room from the cold. He felt all around him a clean, refreshing purity. He sensed a quality of life that came with an overwhelming desire to experience it, if only for a few days. Wondering how long it would be before a campsite opened up, he realized he was suddenly in no hurry to get back to the park.

He turned to look at Justin, who was staring at his left hand.

"What are you looking at?" he asked quizzically.

"You're not wearing a wedding ring," said Justin, looking back into Michael's eyes. "It seems a guy like you would be married?"

Michael considered for a moment how he might respond, but there wasn't but one possible reply, for he had already decided he would never hide his sexual orientation again. "Well, Justin, if you have a girlfriend, you won't have to worry about me trying to make a move on her. I'm gay."

Justin's eyes widened. His gaze swept down over Michael's bare chest and then dropped to the floor as if his mind had been transported a million miles away. An awkward silence suddenly displaced their casual ambience. Michael couldn't tell if Justin was put off or perhaps worse.

"If that bothers you, I'll leave right now if you want me to."

Justin looked up and stared at him, his gaze still distant.

Michael added, "If it's a problem, I mean, if you're worried someone might find out a gay man is staying at your ..."

"No ... uh, no. Sorry. I just didn't anticipate it." He laughed, adding, "I never expected to hear that stated so bluntly. Really ... I'm sorry for that reaction."

Relieved, Michael smiled. "No apology necessary. I had a feeling you were intellectually beyond homophobic. But let me pose the same question. You're obviously not married either."

Justin reached up and nervously pulled his collar away from his neck, again looking at Michael in thought. "Would you like a beer?" he finally said.

"Sure."

They went back into the other room. Michael sat down in the over-stuffed chair and watched him walk over to the refrigerator. Imposing in his light brown uniform, his stride graceful on long legs, Michael's eyes were drawn to the well formed contours of Justin's buttocks, certain such muscle would draw attention in a bathhouse. The uniform defined a lean body in a way civilian clothes never could: broad shoulders over the distinctive V of his back, a narrow waist that made his pronounced buttocks all the more enticing. As attractive as he was, Michael felt a sense of relief that he wasn't gay. It imposed circumstances that allowed him to relax, to focus on the purpose of his journey without being distracted by sex. Still, he could not avoid admiring Justin's physical beauty, enhanced by his uniquely masculine surroundings.

Michael watched him close the refrigerator, wondering what he was thinking, now that he knew the man he had invited to his house was gay. Would the visit be awkward, or would the diversity of their race and background and sexual orientation make it more interesting? He could see no reason any of this should jeopardize their opportunity to become friends. He had asked Justin why he wasn't married, and had received a reaction that left him itching with curiosity to find out.

Justin approached and handed Michael a can of beer, who couldn't remember the last time he drank beer out of a can. "While you're here, help yourself to anything you want," he said, glancing at the window behind the over-stuffed chair. "A little warm, isn't it." He stepped behind the chair and pushed open the window. The old screen was all but rusted out. "It's only about sixty degrees out there, but the sun beating on this tin roof heats up the house."

Michael watched him sit down on the rocker and take a swallow of beer. Positioned on the other side of the end table several feet away from the chair, Justin leaned back in the rocker and looked at Michael. "So you're gay?"

"Yes."

"No interest in women at all?"

"I like women, just not sexually."

"I have to confess," said Justin, "no man has ever looked me in the eyes and told me he's gay. It kinda surprised me. I always thought you guys kept that sort of thing a secret."

"Some do, but those who keep it a secret have little opportunity to meet other gay men."

"Well I'm not gay," Justin stated flatly.

"I figured the odds were in favor of that."

"I'm not sure I've ever known a gay man."

"You might be surprised about that. My guess is you have. You just didn't know it."

"Does it bother you talking about it?" asked Justin.

Michael adjusted his weight against the chair back and said, "No. Does it bother you?"

Justin took another swallow of beer in thought. "No," he said, wiping his mouth on the back of his hand. "I'm not bothered by it at all. I guess I'm just a little curious, I mean with your being so straight forward about it. It's not like I'm worried you're going to attack me or anything." He smiled and added, "You don't look dangerous."

Michael laughed. "You're right, you don't have to worry about that. But what you're talking about is intellectual curiosity, a rather common thing among straight men. After all, when you consider just the physical aspect of sex, we're all driven by the same thing—a climax. It's just that gay men are drawn to other men, and there may be a few emotional differences. Most of the straight men I've known who knew I'm gay were loaded with questions, so if you're curious, I really don't mind talking about it." Michael studied Justin's attentiveness. This man who lived a life of near total isolation seemed eager for conversation. "I'm curious, too," Michael went on to say. "I've never met a park ranger before, and it strikes me that a man like you would be married."

Justin's expression melted into a look of dismay. "I've never been married. Just close."

"Close?"

"Back home, in Jasper. Her name was Christie. She was beautiful. Came from a wealthy family. We had been engaged for a year. I got all the way to the altar, then got cold feet." Justin paused, as if for a few seconds his mind traveled back to that day. "It all seems like a crazy blur, but I ran out of that church like it was full of vampires. That's why I came out to west Texas. It's why I wanted to live alone on this ranch. I've never understood why I did something like that." He looked over at Michael. "But for some reason that I've never really figured out, I know it would have been a mistake to marry her."

Michael sat quietly. He hadn't expected his new friend to express such personal emotions. Now, even more than before, he felt drawn into getting to know him. "So today we've both heard something we haven't heard before. I've heard of cold feet, but nothing that dramatic."

Justin stretched his legs out before him. He looked up at the rough hewn ceiling with a sigh. "If you were a psychologist instead of a surgeon, perhaps some free therapy would help me figure it out."

Michael laughed. "Perhaps we both need a little free therapy." He thought for a moment, then asked, "Did you love her?"

"Of course … well, I thought I did. I sometimes think I still do."

"Were you sleeping with her?"

Justin looked at him stiffly. "Isn't that supposed to be a personal thing?"

"I suppose it is. I didn't mean to pry."

Justin often thought about those nights he and Christie had spent together, and the memory always led to the same question. Why had there been so many occassions he had failed to achieve an erection, when the girl he planned to marry was blessed with such heavenly curves? The question still haunted him.

"Don't apologize," he said. "It's me. I'm being defensive." He sighed, adding, "Yes … I went to bed with her. We spent the night together several times a month."

"Has there been anyone since?"

"No. I can't get involved with another woman until I figure out why I ran out on the first one. I can't go through that again, or put someone else through it. Besides, there's not a lot of opportunities to meet women out here, especially since I'm probably the only black man within a hundred miles."

Michael studied him as he spoke, with a sense there was something lurking in his mind left unsaid, but there wasn't a clue as to what it might be. Perk, curled on the floor near Justin's feet, jumped up, suddenly alert, then bolted outside through the back door.

"He must have smelled a jack rabbit," said Justin.

"He keeps you from feeling lonely, doesn't he?"

"Yeah. Nevertheless, I still do get a little lonely at times. But I haven't got to the point where I want to make a change. Sometimes I wonder if I'm going to live out my whole life alone, right here on this ranch."

"Maybe you want to." Michael looked around the sparse

room. "It's obvious your relationship with Christie was traumatic. It's not surprising you wouldn't want to risk it happening again. And you're right—living out here sure increases the odds against meeting another woman."

Justin let out a half-hearted laugh and looked toward the back door. "I suppose time will tell." He looked back at Michael. "What about you? Don't gay men form relationships similar to marriage?"

"That's one of the reasons I'm out here, too. I lived with a man a few years ago, but nothing close to a lifelong commitment. Mostly, I've lived like a fool, in an endless swirl of sex with men whose names I didn't even know. I left San Diego to get away from that."

Justin sat looking at him, dumbstruck. "An endless swirl of sex?"

"Yeah, bathhouses and gay bars, places men go looking for sex."

"Good lord! You might have AIDS."

"No, I don't. I gave my sister a vial of blood for testing before I left San Diego. I called her yesterday for the results. I don't have any disease, but I'm lucky I don't. I'll never live that way again."

Justin reached up and rubbed his forehead with his fingertips. Perk came prancing back into the room with a small dead animal in his mouth. Justin leaned forward to look at him. "So it was a chipmunk. Good boy." The dog laid the small creature at Justin's feet, wagging his tail with proud enthusiasm. Michael craned his neck to look at the small corpse, his nose wrinkled. Justin glanced at him and grinned. "He doesn't catch a chipmunk very often," he said reassuringly. "They're too quick." He looked at Michael with renewed curiosity, thinking about the subject they had been talking about. "I'm having a hard time with that bathhouse picture. What is it exactly?"

Michael wasn't sure if he felt comfortable talking about the activities in a bathouse with a straight man. Risking Justin's sensibilities, he decided to chance it. "They're usually unobtrusive, located in secluded areas. You wouldn't know what it was unless you knew. They have hot tubs of course, and showers. You can rent a small room or just a locker. Inside, the men walk around naked or wear a towel, and they check each other out. Those who rent a room usually lay on the bed with the door open, so others passing by can look in and decide if they want to go in. If the guy in the room … well, you know, likes taking it in the ass, he'll perch on his hands and knees with his ass pointing toward the door. There's usually men having sex everywhere you look, and there's a lounge room with a TV where you can go between interludes. The men consist of all shapes and sizes, all races and ages." He paused, then added, "That's about it, a typical bathouse."

Justin looked spellbound, as if for a moment he didn't know what to say. "That's incredible," he finally ventured. "I can't imagine it."

"I expect you didn't have one in Jasper."

Justin laughed. "You ever hear of tar and feathers?"

"That's what I figured."

"So you've never had a sexual encounter with a woman?"

"No. I've never even considered it. I've known with certainty since I was a boy that I'm gay."

"Are you curious about what it's like to sleep with a woman?"

Michael considered this question for a moment, then said, "I can see where this must be difficult to understand, but I'm not curious about it either. I'd probably go into shock if I reached between someone's legs I'm sleeping with and didn't find a cock. But I do think women are lovely creatures. I enjoy looking at them in the manner of looking at fine art. I have a beautiful sister. She's also my best friend."

"She's who you called to find out about your blood test."

"Yes."

"How did your parents take it when they found out?"

The question saddened Michael. He had no good childhood memories. "My mother died of breast cancer, and that might have been a blessing for her. When she found out she was sick, she refused treatment, and I still believe she saw it as a way to escape her thankless existence. She lived a life of heartache, being married to a man like my father. He's a commander at the Naval Shipyard in San Diego, a bastard." He laughed, recalling the memory. "I guess you could say he found out about me the hard way. It was during my second year of college. I knew a young lieutenant who I was visiting on base, an occasional lover. My father walked in and caught me sucking his dick. Talk about a trauma. Any hope for a relationship with my father ended that day." He paused, looking at the can of beer in his hand. "I never did find out how he knew I was in that apartment."

"That's a tough story," said Justin, adjusting his weight in the chair, glancing over Michael's bare chest and tight jeans. He wondered what might cause a man to be gay, thinking it might have something to do with the way he had been raised. "So your father was overbearing?" he asked.

"That's an understatement."

Justin nodded. "Think it might have something to do with why you're gay?"

Michael dismissed the notion with a slightly cynical laugh. "Don't kid yourself about things like that. Those theories are ridiculous, designed by people who want to believe homosexuality can be *cured*. Gays, men or women, are born gay. It's no more complicated than that."

"Your relationship with your father ended during your second year in college, but you managed to go on to become a surgeon."

"Yeah. I had a couple of scholarships, but mainly I had to work my ass off to get through medical school. My sister helped out, too. What I've put her though with my lifestyle is one of the things I regret." Michael watched Justin drain the last of his beer and set the empty can on the end table. "What about your family?" he asked. "Do you ever go back home to see them?"

"No. My father abandoned us when I was a baby. I don't have anything in common with my older brother. My mother worked two jobs raising us, but I'm still on her shit-list because of that wedding. She won't even accept the two hundred dollars a month I send, so it goes to my brother who pretends he's the one giving it to her. She's ashamed of what I did to Christie."

"Another reason why you're out here," said Michael.

"That's right."

Justin glanced at his watch, then came to his feet. "Well, I'm still on duty." He walked over to the stove and pulled open the oven door, bending over to look inside. The room filled with the delicious aroma of roasting meat. He looked back at Michael, who had leaned forward, his elbows propped on his knees.

"Pot Roast," said Justin. "I put it in last night. It'll make a half dozen meals. Sound good for dinner tonight?"

"Sounds great. I was wondering what that smell is."

Justin closed the oven. "I'll be gone the rest of the afternoon. Just make yourself at home."

Michael stood up. "I thought I'd drive over to the visitor's center and get my name on the waiting list for a campsite."

"You won't have to. That's where I'm going. I'll take care of it for you."

Michael smiled. "Okay. Then I'll just take a hike out in the desert while you're gone. How far are those mountains to the south?"

"That would be a little ambitious for an afternoon hike. They're further away than they look." Justin nodded at the refrigerator. "There's plenty of food in there, so find something to eat before you start." He lifted a canteen off a nail on the wall. "Take this with you, and be careful, city boy. This terrain is tricky. You can get disoriented before you realize it. The best thing to do is spot a couple of distant landmarks before you start out, then keep an eye on them to maintain your sense of direction. And keep in mind the rattlers start coming out of their dens this time of year, and they're always in a foul mood."

"I believe I'm having seconds thoughts about a hike."

"Don't let me discourage you. I just want you to use a little caution. It takes awhile to understand this part of the world. It's easy to fall in love with it at first sight, but the more you get out there and get to know it, the more you'll love it."

"I believe I've learned that already."

Michael followed him and Perk out to the Jeep, watching the

the trail of dust as the Jeep grew small in the distance. He went back in and opened the refrigerator. It was well stocked with food and Tecate. He reached in for a hard boiled egg and a small can of tomato juice. Back outside, he took a bite out of the egg and walked over to take a look at the five gallon jug mounted between two poles. It had been four days since he had showered. Though the way to use the contraption to wash off was obvious, he decided to wait.

CHAPTER 5

Justin pulled the Jeep to the side of the road where it intersected with the asphalt pavement. Perk jumped up on the front passenger seat and sat eagerly watching him, wondering if they were to get out of the Jeep. Justin let go the steering wheel and propped his arm on the door, leaning back into the seat. He stared out across the northern desert, thinking about Michael. An odd feeling lay over his skin, something more than the dry air or the sun's warmth. There was something tight within his chest. He reached over to pet his dog.

"Perk, we have a gay man staying with us at our house. What do you think about that?" He took a deep breath of the warm dry air. "Well, he's interesting and I like him, and it looks like you do, too." Perk stepped over into his lap and Justin rubbed his neck. "There's something about him that makes me a little nervous, though." He paused, thinking about how Michael looked sprawled out in the over-stuffed chair. "One thing about him, he makes you want to look at him, kinda like the way you keep looking at a beautiful woman. Now don't you think that's a little strange? I think he noticed me looking at his chest. Do you think there's something wrong with that, I mean me looking at his chest?" He looked down at the little dog. "It doesn't seem to bother me, you know, that I kept looking at his body, but I suppose it could have given him the wrong impression. It didn't seem to bother him either, if he noticed."

Justin rubbed his forearm. A sensation had flashed across his skin. It felt like tingles, and he remembered feeling it before. Thinking about those moments back in high school, in the showers after basketball practice. He remembered that myriad of male bodies interspersed in the steam, how his eyes were drawn below their navels, how he found himself catching glimpses of the variety of shapes and sizes of the other boys' genitals when they were washing their arms and hair. He had been discreetly fascinated by how the white boys' were dull red in color and the black boy's, like his own, were often darker than the rest of their body.

Intellectual curiosity Michael had called it. Was that why his eyes were tempted to explore the well defined lines of that sun bronzed chest, the distinctly masculine contours of those tight fitting jeans? They had shared a few moments of personal conversation, and more than once those tingles ran on his arms. He had even felt them on the flesh between his legs. Was all of this cause for concern? Were these sentiments reason to question his motive for inviting Michael to stay at his house? But then, what's the big deal? Wouldn't any thoughtful man find someone like Michael interesting to look at, or be curious about such an exotic lifestyle?

Perk let loose a yap. It brought Justin out of his contemplation. He remembered that he was on his way to work, and Perk jumped off his lap when he reached down to fire the ignition.

They turned into the parking lot of the visitor's center thirty minutes later. Perk ran ahead of him as he walked along the display of native desert landscape, stopping to sniff spots previously marked by visiting dogs. Justin entered the lobby and walked around the counter toward the back office. From behind a desk, his boss looked up when he opened the door and stepped into the office. The heavy-set man's eyes shifted to Perk.

"That damn dog better not shit on my floor again," he stated gruffly.

"Bernard, didn't you find it interesting he chose your office to take a shit the other day? Dogs have certain instincts, you know."

The man huffed and looked back down at some papers, saying, "Where have you been? I tried to get you on the radio awhile ago and got no answer."

"I turned my radio off for awhile. I had some personal business to take care of."

"Personal business!" the man growled, looking back up. "You're supposed to be on duty."

"I'm not surprised a shithead like you would come up with something like that. I've been on duty seven days a week for more than a year, and you make an issue over a couple of hours."

"What kind of personal business would the lone ranger have all of a sudden?"

God! Why was I cursed with something like this? Justin looked at the ruffled, overweight man behind the desk, his uniform obviously a size or two too small, and said, "Bernard, I've got a splitting headache and still I feel sorry for you. My headache will go away, but there's no cure for your stupidity. Personal business means it's personal."

"So why the hell are you here anyway? You're supposed to be on patrol."

"I ran out of maps of the park."

"Then get some damn maps and get back out there."

"I take it there's nothing going on."

"Not a damn thing," said Bernard.

"Then why did you try to call me on the radio?"

"Oh, yeah. A tourist called in on his cell phone. The damn fool tried to drive a mini van over the River Road. Seems he's gotten it stuck in the sand in a dry creek bed. If he hasn't already gotten it out, you'll probably run across him. Said he was about three miles in from the eastern entrance."

Justin shook his head and held the door open for Perk to run out. He grabbed a handfull of maps from a box under the counter, then strolled over to the desk where the reservation log was kept. Running his finger down the list of names and dates, it appeared a campsite would become available in three days. He picked up a pencil, then paused before writing Michael's name on the next blank line. He looked up and saw a retired couple looking at brochures on the wall rack, and his fingers tightened on the pencil. Terry, the young ranger attending the counter, looked over at him.

"Hey, Justin. How's it going today?"

"It was going pretty good until I ran into Bernard in the back room."

Terry laughed and looked at his hand on the reservation log. "Anything I can help you with there?"

Justin looked back down at the log and laid down the pencil. "Uh, no, had a few tourists asking me when there might be a campsite opening up. Thought I'd just check and see."

Terry nodded and looked back at the elderly tourists. "You folks finding everything you need?" he asked them.

Justin and Perk returned to the Jeep.

They entered the River Road from its eastern end. All the

way to the visitor's center, Justin had thought about the man staying at his house. Those thoughts had not been entirely distinct, but rather a vague contemplation of the man who had captured his undivided interest. They were fleeting images of him sitting atop that rock next to the river, and his forlorn expression when he learned he could not camp at that spot in the park. Justin couldn't explain why he had been compelled to invite him to the house, nor could he understand the elusive nuances that had passed between them when he knelt to look at his smooth white hands. Now, those same curious thoughts had entered his mind again.

He bounced along over the primitive road, the sun now in the western sky, intrigued by his own enchantment. Now there was the additional question of why he had not written Michael's name on the reservation log. But then, the answer really was perfectly clear. He simply wanted more than three days to get to know him. After all, with his self-imposed solitude, how long had it been since he had an opportunity to make a new friend, or a chance to get to know someone so fascinating?

It was a man and his teenage son who had driven their mini van into the creek bed. Justin stopped the Jeep and grinned. The sign at the entrance to the River Road clearly stated *Four Wheel Drive Vehicles Only*! He wondered how anyone could be so stupid, or if their four hour wait in the sun had taught them a lesson. Standard cars were obviously inappropriate for the River Road. He couldn't say how many of them he pulled out of ruts each month.

He looked at his watch. By the time he pulled the van free,

and then made his way over to the western end of the road, three hours would pass before he got back to the house.

CHAPTER 6

Sound could travel for miles through the thin desert air, especially sounds like the wheels of a vehicle crunching over a gravel road, but Michael had not heard Justin's return in the Jeep. He was downwind, laying on a towel behind the house, when Perk pranced over to lick his face. Startled, he quickly sat up and saw Justin standing near the corner of the house, staring at him. With no more than an hour's sunlight left, he sat on the towel in the soft light, the last rays golden on his skin. He was nude.

Also startled, Justin stood momentarily transfixed. His jaw had gaped. The man whose image had dominated his mind all afternoon was before him again, a vulnerable, masculine form not thirty feet from where he stood. His gaze dropped down over his chest and belly, the hint of pubic hair nearly hidden by his folded legs. So thoroughly distracted, he was not aware of the awkward stretch of time.

"Didn't hear you drive up," Michael said, feeling self conscious in Justin's prolonged gaze.

Justin nodded.

"Uh … I just assumed this would be all right. You know, with no neighbors and all." Michael paused for his reply, but none came. "Really, if you'd rather I didn't …"

"Michael," Justin interupted. "It's okay. You're fine. I want you to feel free to do whatever you like here." He smiled, adding, "But if it's something I wasn't expecting, you might have to give me a moment to adjust."

Michael let out a sigh, worried for a moment he had offended his magnanimous host. Perk stepped back when he got to his feet. He took a couple of steps and reached for the jeans he had thrown over a creosote bush.

Justin realized his heart had quickened. He had not considered seeing his new guest nude, but this sudden visual excluded all other conscious thought. He watched Michael shake out his jeans, gazing upon his masculine form in the golden light, not at all certain of just why the visual affected him so pleasantly. He thought of the exquisite statues created during the Renaissance, how this body was much like them. He saw skin glistening in the sun, intimate shadows and blonde hairs, a male symmetry seemingly punctuated by a lithe penis of unimposing size, and he closed his eyes for just a moment to gather his thoughts.

"No tan lines," said Justin, now watching him step into his jeans.

Michael glanced down at his body, then looked back up. "No shortage of nude beaches in California these days."

"I come across nudists over in the park all the time."

"I'm not surprised," Michael said, buttoning jeans. "I took that hike today." He nodded toward the southern horizon. "I know what you meant earlier. Walked for an hour toward those mountains and they never looked much closer." He gazed toward the mountains for a moment. "I know why you love this land. It grabs you by the heart. You can't really know by just driving through it. You have to get out and walk, feel the desert beneath your feet, weave through stands of cactus and scrub, and climb down into arroyos. That's when it starts to get into your blood."

Justin nodded. "Not a bad observation for a city boy. A lot of people come out here, but most never understand any of that."

"It's going to be hard to face going back," Michael said wistfully.

"No reason to think about that right now, is there?"

Michael smiled. "No, there's not." He looked at Justin for a moment. "But I would like to say how much I appreciate you asking me to stay at your place."

"It's my good fortune that you accepted. You've made me realize how starved I am for a little thoughtful conversation." Justin stepped toward the back door, saying, "Let's eat. Those bananas I had for lunch didn't stay with me very long. I'm famished."

Michael followed him into the house. "Anything I can do to help?"

Justin went to the counter and picked up the coffee pot. Dumping the old grounds into a can lined with plastic, he said, "You can set the table. I'm going to get some coffee going, then change. This uniform starts to get a little stifling by the end of the day."

Justin pumped a little water into the coffee pot as Micheal reached for a couple of plates on the shelf over the counter. He swished the water and poured it into the sink, saying, "Forks and knives are in that left drawer."

"My God!" Michael gasped when he turned and approached the table. "What on earth is that!" he said, holding the plates to his chest, looking at an insect crawling over the oilcloth on the table. Then he nearly jumped out of his skin when Justin's arm came smashing down from behind, squashing the insect with a rolled newspaper.

"A scorpion," he said, reaching up to massage Michael's collar bone. "Sorry I startled you, but I didn't want to see that little fellow in my bed tonight." He removed his hand from Michael's shoulder, amused by how his eyes were fixed on the squished creature. "You can start breathing again, any time."

"Are they common?" Michael asked anxiously, watching Justin pick up the insect with a waded paper towel.

"I see one from time to time, but I wouldn't say common. Just check your shoes before you stick your feet in them in the morning."

Michael rubbed his forehead with his fingertips and looked over at the couch, which looked like a perfect haven for such creatures, now wondering if he was going to be able to fall asleep.

Justin put fresh grind in the coffee filter and plugged in the pot. "It'll take me just a minute to change," he said, starting toward the bedroom.

Michael took flatware from the drawer, pumped two glasses full of water, and then found some napkins. He sat down at the table to wait. A few moments later Justin emerged from the bedroom wearing blue jeans and a white cotton shirt, the long sleeves rolled half way up, the tails out, the front of it unbuttoned and gaping open. There was not a lot of bulk in his chest, suggesting he didn't lift weights, and his belly looked relaxed though it was clearly not soft. The shirt allowed a hint of his nipples, the tight curls of hair around them which also ran down the center of his lean torso. When he opened the oven and leaned over to take out the pot roast, the loose fitting jeans tightened over the firm rounds of his haunches. Michael shifted his eyes to the oilcloth with a small sigh. He realized that he would be constantly aware of this magnificent black man's ingenuous allure.

Justin tossed a pot holder near the center of the table and sat the pot down upon it, placing the lid in the sink before he sat down. Steam rose from the roast and its juices, carrying the mouth-watering aroma of spices and simmering beef. "Hand me your plate," he said, extending his hand.

"The rest of your day go well?" Michael asked, watching him fill the plate with carrots, potatoes, and stringy, tender roast. "That's plenty."

"Yeah, except for a little run-in with my boss. I've never had a real pleasant relationship with the fat-ass bastard, and I think it got worse since Perk took a shit in his office the other day." He handed Michael the plate, bearing the mischieveous smile of a school boy.

Perk was sitting on the floor, looking up at the passing plate with mournful eyes. Justin glanced at the half eaten dog food in his bowl. He stood and went over to pick up the bowl, then spooned some beef broth from the pot onto the dog food and sat it back on the floor. This satisfied Perk just fine. He began crunching down the food like he had a sudden time limit to finish it.

"Those run-ins with your boss happen often?" asked Michael.

"Damn near every time I see him. It's a habit I suppose, but he knows I'm a good ranger, and I have to admit he's pretty good at his job, too. Just no people skills. I think he secretly likes me because I'm the only one who ever gives him a hard time."

"Any of the other rangers ever come out here?" Michael

asked, taking another bite of the pot roast.

"Almost never. One guy stayed with me a year ago for a few days when his wife kicked him out of the house. But I don't have much in common with any of them. I like to talk about Faulkner and Michelangelo, they like to talk about rodeos and football."

Taking a bite of potatoes, Michael said, "Sounds like you might make a good city boy." Getting no reply, he looked up to see Justin gazing at his chest. "Would you rather I wear a shirt when we're eating?"

Justin's eyes lifted. "What?"

"Would you like me to wear a shirt when we eat?"

He sighed. "No, Michael, I wouldn't. We're not out here for the rules." He turned his head and stared at the counter.

"What is it, Justin? What are you thinking?"

"I wish the hell I knew what I'm thinking. I feel unsettled about something, and don't have a clue what it might be."

"Maybe that run-in with your boss has affected you."

"Not likely," Justin laughed cynically.

"Think it's me? Maybe you shouldn't have invited me here."

"Oh God, no. Don't think that. I'm glad I ran across you out there today. I haven't had a chance to get to know someone worth knowing in …" He shrugged his shoulders. "Who knows how long? I'm actually relieved to find out I still have the capacity to want someone's company."

Michael remembered something that had occurred to him while he was walking through the desert. He smiled. "Today I thought about being here in your house. It's kind of like that fantasy of being stranded on a secluded beach with someone." He studied Justin's eyes, wondering about their unspoken message, wondering if Justin himself understood it. "Of course in our case, it's an intellectual fantasy as opposed to a sexual one." He still could not read Justin's eyes. There was something there, but what? "You know, we were talking about intellectual curiosity earlier. It's not uncommon for straight men to want to experiment a little, just to get an idea of what it's like."

Justin stared at him intently, his full lower lip between his teeth, his eyes, with their enduring wonder now lost in what appeared to be confused thought.

Michael wondered if he was considering what could have easily been interpreted as a proposal. "Do you understand what I mean by that?" he asked, captivated by the soft nuance of his eyes and their long beguiling lashes.

"Of course I do." Justin's mood had shifted to straight forward.

After a brief silence, Michael said, "Forgive me for saying this, but you're an extremely attractive man, and I think you know I'm not judgmental about any human response to personal sexuality."

"It's not for me. I'm not gay. My curiosity doesn't go that far," Justin said flatly.

Michael nodded, thinking Justin's conviction sounded somewhat less than resolute. "Well then, what I said should be considered a simple statement as opposed to a suggestion."

Justin took a bite of food, and said, "Don't worry, I'm not offended." He paused before adding, "But I am glad you're here."

Michael continued to eat. A few minutes later he reached down and placed his hand on his stomach. "I eat a small steak from time to time, but it's been years since I had a big meal like this. Hope you don't mind if I do a little groaning after dinner."

Justin laughed. "I cook a roast about once a month. Perk usually has to help me finish it off. Did you see the frozen dinners in the freezer?"

"Yeah. You have it packed full of them."

"They're those light dinners, which is what I usually eat, so I might join you in some of that groaning."

After dinner Justin stopped the sink and pumped it full of soapy water. Michael stood beside him and dried the dishes as he washed them. After sealing the left over roast in a plastic container and storing it in the refrigerator, they went to the living room. Justin turned on the lamps and stretched out on the couch, placing his hands behind his head. Michael sat in the over stuffed chair, setting a novel on the end table beside him.

"I know you're not anxious to go back, but have you thought about when you plan to return to San Diego?"

"No. It won't be any time soon."

"You spit that thought out like it was poison."

"I've got a lot of things to think about before I go back. And I want to be conspicuously absent when the lawyers start the lawsuit."

"Lawsuit?"

"The little girl I killed. Her parents are certain to sue me, and I can't think of a better place to be than out here. I'm not anxious to relive it in court."

"Good grief!"

Michael looked at him. "What do you mean?"

"You must have one hell of a complicated life," Justin said, sitting up. He studied his new friend for a moment, then asked,

"Michael, have you done a lot of operations over the years?"

"Yes, hundreds, sometimes three in one day."

"Were they mostly life or death situations?"

"A good many were," Michael replied. "Why do you ask?"

"Did you lose many of them?"

"A few of my elderly patients died."

"But never any of the younger ones, or children?"

Michael looked at him quizzically. "I was fortunate," he said. "They weren't meant to die."

"So you've saved hundreds of lives, and now you want to quit because you've lost one patient. That's hard to understand."

Michael recoiled. He couldn't bear to tell Justin the real reason losing *just one* patient was so significant, that he was lucky there had been just one, that his irresponsible behavior had certainly caused that death. He feared revealing the truth would not only taint Justin's opinion of him, but also his opinion of all gay men, when his own arrogant behavior was not representative of the average gay lifestyle.

"This is the one thing that's difficult for me to talk about."

"Then we won't talk about it. But if you decide you want to, I can be a pretty good listener."

Night had fallen over the desert. There came the howl of coyotes in the distance. The outside temperature had fallen sharply, and Justin got up to turn off the fan and close the window. He paused behind Michael's chair and reached over to massage his shoulders, aware this disconsolate man could well use the patience of a sympathetic friend. "At least you've found the right place to reflect on your future," Justin said, the tense muscle of the bronze shoulders feeling firm and warm under his rough palms. He looked down at Michael's sandy brown hair and closed his eyes. *And why do I suddenly feel you are somehow going to change mine?*

Their coffee mugs within arms reach, they began to read and sip coffee. From time to time each of them paused to silently contemplate the ambience of the evening. When Michael got up to go outside to relieve himself, Justin looked up from his magazine and watched him walk toward the back door.

"You going out to take a leak?"

"Yeah."

"Take the flashlight on the shelf over the door and walk slow. Rattlers don't necessarily rattle if you walk up on them too fast. They'll gladly get out of your way if you give them time."

Michael stood in thought for a moment. He had never had to imperil his life by just taking a pee. He felt a chill in the air the instant he opened the door. Stepping out and looking up at a pitch black sky, he scanned a splay of stars. He never realized there were so many while living in San Diego. Shining the flashlight on the ground a few feet ahead of him, he started his cautious steps into the desert. Just as he unbuttoned his fly the sudden alarming presence of a small animal startled him. He shined the light in a mad zigzag until the beam fell upon Perk.

"Perk! Goddammit! I didn't know you were coming out with me."

Retracing his steps back to the house, he took out a shirt from his suitcase and put it on, and the evening hours continued to pass with easy calm and conversation.

At ten o'clock, Justin stood up and arched his back, stretching his arms into the air with a yawn. "You ready to turn in for the night?" he asked.

Michael looked at the couch with apprehension. Why did it have to look like a perfect haven for scorpions?

Justin smiled. "Never saw a scorpion on the couch."

A sense of relief washed over Michael's face.

"Did see a centipede come out from under it once," Justin added, watching Michael's eyes drop to the floor around the couch. "Trick is, if you feel something crawling on you in the night, don't swat it or jump up. Just go still and brush it off quick as you can."

Michael nodded, his eyes still combing the area around the couch.

"I'll get you a pillow and some blankets," Justin said, turning toward the bedroom.

He returned with the bedding in his arms, tossing the pillow onto the couch and lifting each blanket one at a time to shake it out. That done, he smiled at Michael.

"You shook them out," Michael said with wonderment.

"Yes. Did you see anything fall on the floor?"

"No."

"Good."

Michael began to arrange the blankets into a bed. Justin sat down on the low table. "I'm thinking about taking the day off tomorrow," he said. "Have you made plans to do anything?"

Michael turned. "No."

"Would you like to spend the day on the river? One of the best swimming holes I know of is on the other side of those mountains south of the house. There's nothing like stripping down and sitting in the middle of the Rio Grande, letting the rapids flow around you."

"Sounds like you're talking about a little skinny dipping."

Justin thought for a moment, contemplating the ramifications of nude swimming with a gay man. He looked back at Michael, grinned and said, "Yeah, I guess I am."

"Sounds great," Michael said, turning again to adjust the blankets.

"Michael … how do you know you're gay, I mean, what does it feel like?"

Michael sat down on the edge of the couch, looking at him. "Uh … I …"

"I know you are attracted to other men. I know that. But do you feel different in other ways, too?"

"I'm not sure I understand what you're …"

Justin shook his head in frustration, interrupting, "I'm asking stupid questions. Never mind." He stood. "Guess I'm more tired than I thought."

Michael watched him turn and start toward the bedroom. The soft denim of his jeans had wedged inside the cleft of his buttocks. It clung to the fleshy contours, hinting at the most beguiling gluteal muscle Michael had ever seen. Then the tall ranger stopped in the door frame and turned, his brief gaze confused and warm. "Goodnight, doctor."

Michael smiled. "Goodnight, park ranger."

He stared at the low table, the ancient stone walls of the small room reflecting soft yellow light. The barren miles surrounding the house, black as tar in the night, lay in silence as if awaiting the morning sun, and it all made him feel like an insignificant speck in a vast scheme of land and time. He looked over at the bedroom door, wondering what dynamic might lay in store for him in this raw land, for through Justin's eyes it had come to him like a warm breath on his skin. Whatever this feeling, at least for now, it lay beyond what his mind could comprehend. The best thing to do was to try to avoid the thought, for it was far too easy to confuse fantasy for what might actually be in the air. Was Justin also attracted to him, or was this beautiful man at odds with having a gay man in his house? Slipping off his shirt and jeans, he tossed them on the low table and pushed his legs tentatively under the blankets.

Michael slept fitfully through the night, his eyes popping open with dreams of centipedes crawling on his skin and scorpions dropping from the ceiling and landing on his face. It was chilly, the room frigid. Pulling the blankets tight around his neck, he lay scrunched up, his legs together with his hands between them. And when his eyes refused to stay closed, he stared at the wall thinking about Justin. What were these strange emotions touching his mind with questions, these feelings he could not identify? It was not the first time he felt a hopeless physical attraction for a beautiful straight man, but this time was different. He knew he needed a friend, and so did Justin for reasons of his own. But what was this electricity that charged the air when they were together, this haunting mystery that lay somewhere beyond his grasp?

CHAPTER 7

Michael awoke to the creaking sound of Justin pumping water for coffee. When his head emerged from the blankets a moment later, he saw Justin standing near the couch, whose eyes moved from the crumpled jeans on the low table to the form of a male body under the blankets.

"Did you sleep well?" he asked.

Michael swiveled his legs and rested his feet on the floor and sat up, the blanket covering his waist. Yawning, he glanced over his tall lean host. He stood bare chested in his blue jeans. The early morning light lay golden and hazy in the room, the air sweet with the quality of Spring. It occurred to him how warm the night would have been had he slept engulfed in the heat of Justin's lean body who now stood close enough to reach out and touch.

"Uh … I don't think I slept all that well. The blankets weren't quite as effective as my sleeping bag. I think I'll bring it in tonight."

Justin glanced over his torso and legs. "I can't sleep in pajamas either." He had not slept well himself, but it wasn't images of scorpions that kept him awake. It had been Michael's sudden presence in his life that kept his eyes popping open, the image of his nude form in the evening sun, the thought of that same body under the blankets in this room. "Would you like bacon and eggs for breakfast?"

"Sounds good."

When Justin turned to walk toward the kitchen, Michael flipped off the blankets and reached for his jeans. He buckled his sandals and then went outside to pee. Returning, he joined Justin at the counter. "You'll have to tell me what to do until I get the hang of this," he said.

"You can shred some potatoes for hashbrowns. There's some potatoes and a shredder in the cabinet on the far left."

After Justin sliced off a few strips of bacon, he laid them out in a large cast iron skillet atop the stove. The sizzle and smoke made their mouths water, and Perk, his tail dusting the floor, sat watching every move they made. Michael placed bread in a small toaster-oven on the counter while Justin fried eggs and hashbrowns in the bacon fat. Before sitting down they squeezed a few oranges for juice. Michael glanced over the food when he sat down, suddenly aware he had never felt so alive this early in the morning. Justin handed Perk a crisp strip of bacon.

"You can't quit being a doctor you know," Justin said out of the blue. Dashing pepper on his eggs, Michael looked at him as he continued. "I thought about it last night. I know doctors make a lot of money, but that's not why people choose that life, at least not men like you. I can tell money isn't that important to you. You became a doctor because you were meant to be one. It's who you are."

Michael wasn't quite sure what to say. Justin was right about money—it was important only in the sense that Michael was glad he didn't have to worry about the rent. But he wasn't so sure he had been born to become a doctor, at least not a surgeon. "I haven't told you the whole story about that operation," he confessed with reservation.

The question formed on Justin's face as he swallowed a bite of eggs.

"I was reluctant to tell the whole story because I feared what I did would taint your opinion of all gay men. I …" Michael released a long breath. "I didn't want to lose a chance to get to know you, so I didn't tell you exactly why the girl died." He paused to gather the courage to go on. "I told you about bathhouses. Well, I was in one of them the night before the surgery until four o'clock. I didn't have enough sleep to perform a heart surgery. I wasn't alert enough to detect a ruptured vessel before I closed her up."

Justin considered this for a moment, then looked at him. "Did you feel alert at the time?"

It took Michael a moment to think back. He couldn't remember feeling groggy or that he dreaded to get out of bed that morning; nevertheless, it didn't really matter. "Whether I felt alert or not isn't the issue. It was simply irresponsible to stay out all night before an early surgery."

"So it was. But the fact remains, you've performed hundreds of surgeries and after all this time you've made one mistake in judgment."

"*The fact remains*, in my profession, a mistake in judgment equals the loss of a life that should not have happened."

"I'm thinking of the lives that might *not* be saved if you quit. I don't believe for a moment you'll ever allow a mistake like that to happen again." Observing the pain in Michael's eyes, Justin paused. He got to his feet and went over and stood behind him, massaging his shoulders. "I'm sorry. I'm not being very understanding about something that's troubling you a great deal." Combing his fingers through Michael's unruly morning hair, he added, "What is it about you that makes me care so much?" His distant tone seemed soft, as if this had been a private thought spoken aloud.

When Justin returned to his chair, he decided to make his own confession. "I didn't put your name on the campsite reservation log."

"You didn't?" Michael said, looking at him quizzically. "Why not?"

"Because I'd like you to stay here ... that is, if you want to. There'll be a few spots available in three days if you'd rather go back to the park. I guess you wouldn't have to suffer my opinions if you do decide to take one of them."

"I ..."

"I really would like you to stay here though," Justin added quickly. "There's a couple of knots in my head I think you can help me untie."

Michael smiled. "You think so?"

"Yeah, I do. Not only have you made me realize how desperate I was to have someone to talk to, I like being with you. I haven't enjoyed having a friend in years. Last night, when we were together, just sitting over there reading, I was almost overwhelmed with a contentment I don't remember ever having before. It's like you are someone I can really talk to for a change, express feelings that have been bottled up for a long time." He paused, looking at his new friend. "Maybe it's because you're gay, and I don't have to constantly keep up that macho image." Justin sighed, as if he were exasperated by his inner conflicts. "I don't know … I just feel comfortable around you. There you have it."

Michael was fidgeting with his napkin. He had never experienced being at the center of such sensitive emotions, nor had he been involved in a friendship where two men seemed so ready, even eager to pour out their hearts. And Michael couldn't help but wonder if these words had additional meaning that Justin could not state or understand, and it must have been for this reason that Michael's heart had quickened.

He smiled. "Then I think someone else should use those campsites."

After they washed the dishes, Justin came out of the bedroom with his cell phone. "I'm going to call in to let Bernard know I'm taking the day off." He pressed in the numbers and put the phone to his ear. "This is Justin. Let me speak to Bernard… Good morning, Bernard. I'm taking the day off… Get someone else to do that… Don't be a shithead, Bernard… Go ahead and write me up if you don't have anything better to do. Put in a request for about two thousand hours of overtime that I haven't been paid for while your at it… Forget it… No, my radio won't be turned on… Good-bye, Bernard. I'll listen to this tomorrow."

Justin pushed the off button and smiled at Michael. "My boss is a shithead. Are you ready to go to the river?"

They turned south on the gravel road in front of the house. Where the road ended, Justin veered west, steering the Jeep over the desert for another half mile. He turned south again on the gravel of a wide wash, following it a good distance until it ended at what appeared to be a sheer wall of rock some two hundred feet high. Then Michael saw a vertical crevice, a narrow canyon four or five feet wide. It divided the stone cliff as if it been purposefully cut by the elements to provide a natural passage to the other side. Trekking through, the floor was so deep in pebbles it was difficult to walk.

"I was down here one day when a big rain hit," said Justin. "You wouldn't believe how violently the water courses through there."

Michael craned his neck to look up. The canyon captivated him with the same enchantment as did all of the phenomena abundant in this part of the world. Its smooth stones walls loomed high overhead, their rims so near the sky it seemed his view of the heavens was from within the bowels of the earth. They walked on through the canyon, a route twisting and turning through solid rock, until they came to a stagnant pool of dark green water. Obstructing their path, it lay between the two walls like a confined swamp, stretching some fifteen feet before them. Wedged between the walls on the other side of the water, rested the result of a rock slide, a six foot high pile of boulders. The route looked impassable to Michael.

"The pussies turn around here," said Justin, smiling at Michael's bewildered expression.

Michael stood staring at the awful pool, grinning dumbly. "How do we get past this?"

"That water is only knee deep. You have to lower yourself in and then wade across it. Once we climb over those rocks on the other side, it just a few more yards to the river."

"Did you say *wade* across?"

"I'm afraid it's the only way. Here, I'll go first."

Michael watched Justin step down into the stagnant water, which swirled awfully about his knees as he began with cautious steps a slippery journey across to the boulders. Michael held his breath and lowered himself in, resolved to prove that he was not a pussy.

"You okay?" Justin said over his shoulder, half way to the other side.

"This is dreadful!" Michael protested.

"Don't forget to check your legs for leeches when we get to the other side," Justin mused.

"Oh, God," Michael cringed.

On the other side of the boulders, Michael looked down at his wet pants legs. "You were kidding about the leeches, right?"

"Yeah."

They finally emerged in a broad canyon cut by the river a million years before. They stood on a small sandy beach blocked on both sides by a dense growth of river foliage and scrub. The river was wide here, running in rapids and roiling around rock that jutted above the surface. Placid water lay some fifty feet upstream where the land beneath it was still flat. The other side of the river was contained by the other wall of the canyon, a towering rock wall that shadowed the river.

Michael stood turning his head, taking in the wonders of nature's beauty, wondering if there could be any place on Earth more remote than this. He took off his shirt and tossed it on the sand. Reaching for the buttons on his jeans, he felt the weight of Justin's gaze. Hesitating, he said, "Are you sure you feel comfortable doing this?"

"I was just thinking ..." He shook his head with a grin. "The gossip would be pretty damn hot around headquarters if they found out I got naked on the river with a gay man."

Michael looked around. "It seems about as private here as it can get."

"We'll see some rafters is about all. It's likely I might know one or two of the guides."

"We don't have to do it," Michael said, thinking about the rafters he had seen at his campsite downstream.

"Yes we do," said Justin, reaching for the buttons on his shirt. "I'm beyond giving a damn about what anyone might think."

A moment later his shirt was off. He went for the jeans: the belt unbuckled, the zipper down, his thumbs hooked on the waistband. He looked up just before pushing them down his legs. Michael was standing near the edge of the water, naked, watching him. The pants then came down the long black legs with just a hint of reluctance, and he kicked them aside.

Michael closed his eyes for a moment and smiled. *He's as beautiful as I thought he would be.* "Okay," he said, opening his eyes. "You know I'm gay, so do you mind if I just look at you for a minute?"

Feeling suddenly a little numb with modesty, Justin tilted his head forward and rubbed his eyes with his finger and thumb. The muscle of his lower body was more defined than his shoulders and chest. His hips flared slightly above firm muscled thighs. Like two halves of a melon, his buttocks rounded below the small of his back, the contours tantalizing within the shadows of the gluteal cleft. Scattered across his chest the landscape of tight curls narrowed into a strip that trailed down over of his belly, joining a thick bush of pubic hair below the indent of his navel. His cock, much darker than his body, glistened in the sun as it had been smeared with black oil, and lay over his testicles the length of a man's finger, the dark pliant sac drawn up tight to his body. What struck Michael as remarkably exotic was Justin's glans, resting in the shape of a tiny German helmet at the end of his penis, distractingly pink in color, a visual contrast protruding from the black sheath that set his imagination afire.

Justin had not anticipated Michael's overt request. Knowing they had planned to disrobe, he had assumed, as the day wore on, they might snatch discreet glimpses of each other, but nothing so openly sensual. He stood awkwardly in Michael's gaze, his heart pounded faster against his chest, and there came the sensation of gooseflesh flaring across his folded arms. Not remotely aware of his own masculine beauty, he stood feeling somewhat light-headed, though he found the sensations running through him were oddly pleasant. As Michael's eyes lingered, Justin saw a sensuous man standing near a rushing river in the morning sun, taking visual pleasure in his body. His toes curled tight in the soft warm sand; he took deep breaths to calm his heart, and found that he really didn't mind this at all, for no one had ever looked at him this way before.

Michael, privately overwhelmed by the intimacy, sat down in the sand. He was accustomed to being around men in two distinctly different environments: one, the harried, coldly professional rooms and offices of the hospital; the second being the emotionless, carnal haunts of bathhouses and men's clubs; neither as intimate as this canyon, and certainly with no one from whom he so desperately yearned for acceptance.

"This is kinda embarrassing," said Justin a short while later. He was beginning to think that Michael would have him stand there all day.

Michael drew a deep breath. "Sorry. Didn't mean to embarrass you. But you are a beautiful man. Thanks for sharing it with me."

It was a compliment Justin couldn't bring himself to return, but he was thinking it. He walked toward the river and stepped gingerly into the current. Michael got up and followed him, gasping at the first shock of cold water. The rapids swirled around their calves at a depth just below their knees, their footing tentative on the uneven rocky bottom. They waded out to the wide middle and sat down side by side, the frigid water now churning beneath their arms and pushing against their backs.

"I felt self-conscious when you looked at me like that," said Justin. "It's hard to believe anyone could think I'm attractive."

"You are, remarkably."

Justin had an unsettled feeling, a lightness in his hands. "No one has ever said that to me," he said, adding, "It's odd hearing it from another man."

"No doubt there's been more than a few who have thought it." Michael looked at him. He was more used to men who were cocky and vain. Justin's modesty did nothing but add to his appeal. He looked at his shoulders, the droplets of water glistening with sun on his rich black skin. Justin was more than just attractive, he was beautiful, and Michael knew it best to refrain from revealing the full extent of his thoughts.

"It's funny how comfortable you make me feel, especially about things I've never imagined doing before. It never occurred to me that I'd find myself standing naked on a beach, letting a man look at me."

"It's just a matter of appreciating natural beauty, Justin.

Looking at the human body is an inherent inclination for anyone, gay or straight. There may be many who refuse to admit it, but it's true."

A short silence passed as their bodies adjusted to the cold water. Michael stood and stepped over and sat down behind his companion, the rapids swirling around them, and he reached out to massage the tight tendons between Justin's neck and shoulders.

"I've spent hours sitting in this river, just like we are now," said Justin.

Michael looked up toward the high rock rims surrounding them. "I like this spot. It's the first time I've ever been in a canyon like this."

"Except maybe those made of concrete and steel."

"Yeah."

Justin turned to look at him. "What fascinates me about you is how different our lives have been, how different we are from each other. Think about it. Based on the lives we've lived, we don't have anything in common. Maybe that's why I enjoy your company so much." He paused, smiling, shaking his head. "Those bathhouses. Shit! That's something I've never dreamed even existed."

"It's something I'm trying to forget about."

"Sorry. Maybe I shouldn't bring it up."

"Don't worry about it. I don't mind talking about it really, but I think it's like breaking an addiction. There are actually psychologists who specialize in curing sexual addictions. It's a sorry way to live." Michael resumed the shoulder massage. "We have one thing in common though—we're both lonely."

Justin rolled his shoulders, taking pleasure in Michael's

hands. "It's hard to see how you were ever lonely, living in a city next door to your sister and working in a busy hospital."

"It's not uncommon for people to be lonely when they're surrounded by people. It might be the worst kind of loneliness. I've even had married men tell me they're lonely."

"I sure rather live alone than be married and lonely." Justin sighed and scanned the banks of the river. "Do you ever wonder if the whole world is searching for something they will never find?"

"Justin, is that what you feel like you're doing?"

He nodded absently, his thoughts somewhat distant. "Sometimes I do. Not about living in west Texas though. I know I wouldn't want to live anywhere else. And I like my job too, but I'm not sure I've ever known anyone who was fully content with his or her life." He looked at Michael. "So what do you suppose I might be looking for? Marriage? I think about that a lot, especially when I'm lonely. Then you read an article and learn that ninety-two percent of all married women find more understanding from their girl friends than they do from their own husbands. That's a bleak scenario. It would break my heart to be married to a woman who felt that way."

Michael kneaded the muscle between the shoulder blades with his thumbs. It was obvious that Justin was content with living alone in his house on the ranch, perhaps in part because he still had not resolved the traumatic end of his wedding plans; but if he knew he was lonely, why would he continue to live in such solitude, or make no attempt at all to meet someone? How did this add up if he knew something was missing in his life?

Looking at the strong, sinewy shoulders, Michael knew

something was troubling him. It was in his eyes, and Michael had detected it from almost the first moment he had looked into them. A possibility began to form in his mind. Could it be that Justin was grappling with his own sexuality? Michael looked at the back of Justin's head. Was that the subconscious reason he ran out on his bride? There had to be some basis for his questions concerning homosexuality. Was he just curious, or was he trying to enlighten his own feelings and emotions? Michael thought about how Justin had stared at him when he was nude on the towel behind the house. Was he just stunned to find a naked man when he came home, or had he found himself lost in the allure of another man's body? It was a complicated question, and perhaps premature, yet the question now loomed in his mind with increasing weight.

Michael wanted to lean forward and kiss the satiny black skin on the back of Justin's neck, but of course he could not. If this beautiful black man was gay, he didn't consciously realize it, and he was apparently not prepared to accept it if he did know. And living in isolation in the desert would have certainly made it much easier to ignore. *What can I do to help you, you beautiful man? If you're gay and not ready to face it, I'll tread lightly. I'll be thoughtful with what I might say. I won't risk your peace of mind, or risk losing a new friend, not now, not when being with you has brought me such calm.*

Michael responded to Justin's comment. "You wonder if people are searching for something they'll never find. I've seen exactly that all my life. So many think it's money or power or both. Material things. People actually believe they'll find meaning in status, even to the extent they'll sacrifice love or relationships for it, when those who live with no voids in their lives are those who've simply found the right person to share life with." He paused in thought, then added, "Maybe those of us who have not met the right person are even more aware of how important it is."

"Michael … don't you love sitting in this river?"

"Yeah, I do."

"That sure feels good. Your hands are so soft."

His legs crossed before him, his knees against Justin's hips beneath the cold, churning water, Michael leaned forward to continue the massage. Now dealing with the possibility that his new friend might be bisexual or gay, an unexpected element that could translate to a disquieting edge, he also had to deal with his own physical attraction to him.

Voices suddenly came on the breeze from upstream. Both men turned and saw a fairly large inflated raft emerge from around a bend on the calm surface upstream. As the craft came into clear view, its passengers consisted of six tourists and a young female guide who was maneuvering two long oars.

"Do you know her?" asked Michael, watching her bark orders to her passengers with their paddles.

"Yeah. Her name is Judy Houser. Lives over in Terlingua. You can't out-drink her or beat her arm wrestling."

The craft neared and Judy guided it masterfully around Michael and Justin, staring at them with a curious grin. "Hey there, Justin," she called out. "Not working today?"

"Day off," he called back.

The tourists were watching them as if they were another sight to see on the river, and Judy craned her neck as they passed. "Who's your friend?"

"A visitor from the city," Justin replied grimly.

Distracted from steering the raft in the rapids, it bounced off a large boulder protruding from the surface. Jolted, she turned and resumed working the oars as the boat grew smaller in the distance.

"What do you suppose she was grinning about?" Justin asked, looking after the raft.

"Let's hope it wasn't what it looked like."

"To hell with it," he declared and stood up.

Justin looked down at himself and shook his head. The cold water had shrunk his penis and caused his scrotum to retract defensively, drawing up almost entirely into his body. He pulled it discreetly to coax it back to normal size, the hapless attempt less effective than a few minutes in the warm air would be. Droplets of water trickled down his black skin, glistening in the early sun. Michael stood and followed him to the small beach, cold chills alive on his skin, his genitals also shriveled.

Looking down as they stood side by side in the sand, Michael groaned, "Good lord, they'll never hire me to pose for Playgirl magazine."

Justin glanced from Michael's retracted penis to his own. "Looks like we have something else in common—small dicks."

"That cold water sure has a devastating effect." He glanced at Justin and shrugged. "At least neither of us will end the day with an inferiority complex." Michael turned and looked downstrean. The raft had disappeared. "Are you worried about that girl seeing us together out here?"

He glanced in the direction the raft had disappeared. "She hangs out with a couple of the rangers at a bar over in Lajitas.

We've damn sure given them something to hoot about over a beer."

"I'm sorry, Justin. I shouldn't have been massaging your shoulders."

He looked at Michael. "Don't give it a second thought," he said, his tone no longer defensive. "That's something else no one has ever done for me before. I could have sat out there all day with you rubbing my shoulders. I liked the way it felt. To be honest with you, Michael, it's like you're breathing life into me again, and I like it." He stared out across the river. "Sitting out there with you, that cold water flowing over us, the way your hands felt on my shoulders, was one of the most pleasant sensations I've ever felt. Why apologize for something the small minds around here might conjure up?"

Justin glanced around the small beach, then leaned over to pick up the small bag he had brought with him. His eyes met Michael's again. He smiled. "There's something about you. I don't know what it is, but I've enjoyed every minute I've spent with you since the moment we met. Even last night, when we were sitting in the living room, reading and not saying a word. Like I said earlier, I enjoyed having you there. Even now. We've started a day on the river together, totally naked. Our balls are all shriveled up from the cold water. And you know what—I've never been more comfortable in my life." He took a tube of sun screen out of the bag and sat down in the wet sand near the edge of the river.

Michael sat beside him and watched as he spread lotion on his arms. The sentiment of Justin's words rang in his ears like a pleasant song, but he still couldn't be sure if Justin had meant more than he actually said? Was it really a message that he could-n't express in more certain terms? Michael found it all but impos-sible to read between the lines, but knew he could not make assumptions, so he would simply be a friend and continue to lis-ten, and perhaps eventually find a way to encourage him to empty his heart.

"Justin, what did you mean last night when you asked what it feels like to be gay?"

Gazing out across the river in thought, he said, "Well, for one thing, I was wondering if you ever feel guilty about being inti-mate with other men. You know, like there's something wrong with you by doing something like that."

Michael smiled. "That's not hard to answer. It's no. Being with a man came as naturally for me as being with a woman would for someone else. I've never even had a clear perception of making love to a woman. But I suppose a good many gay men do feel guilty, for reasons of family or social pressure. Some worry over how society will view their masculinity. You should know there's only one truth concerning gay men—none of us choose to be gay. We are born gay, and among gay men there's as many vari-ations of masculinity as there are among straight men. Homosexuality is simply another natural element of humanity. That a considerable segment of our society doesn't have the intel-lect to understand that is not something I can feel guilty about."

Justin had covered his chest and arms and was now smooth-ing the lotion over his legs. "And you've known since you were a boy?"

"Yes. It was always obvious to me. I think most gay men rec-ognize it early on, except for those affected by the social stigmas we have to live with. It takes some longer to deal with it, before they're able to go forward with who they are." He glanced over Justin's short hair, the distinctively African trait of his small ears, the smooth black skin of his neck. "Was that all you were curious about?"

"I was wondering about the sex. It's not too hard to visualize what men might do with each other, but I was wondering what it's like?"

Michael smiled again. "I guess I have to confess, the sex I've had at those bathhouses isn't exactly ideal. Male lust, plain and simple. Ideally, just as a man and woman do, two men who care for each other make love. It's a physical expression of their feelings for each other. I've always thought males lovers have at least one advantage: each being male, they know what theirs bodies respond to, so they know by experience what their lover enjoys and how he likes it done. There's no guess work." Michael glanced at his new friend, who was looking at his fingernails, listening. "But, Justin, to answer your question, it's quite a wonderful experience. It takes you to a place you can never imagine, and I think you have to go down that road to actually know what it's like, and then, from my own perspective, you'll be hard-pressed to find anything its equal."

Justin turned his head to look at him with a peaceful gaze in his eyes that drifted skyward, as if his thoughts had been drawn by the lone wispy cloud floating not all that far above the canyon rim. The sun had grown warm and glistened across the river's fast water, feeling warm and luxurious on their skin. His eyes drifted back down over the long shadows and sinews of rock, and his thoughts now seemed absorbed in the mighty canyon wall jutting skyward from the river's opposite shore.

When Michael glanced at him again, Justin's eyes were moving over the profile of his torso, and he quickly averted them as if he had been caught doing something wrong. "I don't mind you looking at me," Michael said softly.

"Of course you wouldn't mind. You're gay." His tone had found a defensive edge.

"Was it all that awful when I was looking at you earlier?"

Justin hesitated, as if for a moment he was struggling with something he couldn't admit. Then he said, "No."

Michael reached for the sun screen and began to smooth it on his arms. "I don't think being gay is the only reason men enjoy looking at other men. Don't you agree that it's not necessarily a sexual thing when you consider Michelangelo's work? Do you believe he created David just for gay men, or just to give women something to fantasize about? He knew the ultimate beauty found on Earth comes in the form of the human body, male or female. His work is a celebration of that knowledge. Why wouldn't it follow that what we see in his statues we would also see in its living form?"

Justin shook his head. "I hope my sanity never depends on winning an argument with you. You're right; I do agree."

Michael looked at him and smiled. "Okay then. So, tell me, do you enjoy looking at me or not?" He had already noticed Justin looking at him enough to believe that he was at least curious about the male body. And though bringing the issue into the open seemed a bit of a risk, he thought Justin might feel more comfortable if he admitted it.

"Michael! Jesus, what a question!"

"Just say it. Yes or no."

Justin looked back at the river and said, "Yes."

Michael let out a relieved sigh. He felt Justin's admission would bring them more in harmony with each other. He sensed that some underlying tension had been laid to rest. He finished covering himself with the sun screen and decided to take one more risk. "Lay down on your stomach and I'll put some of this on your back."

Justin changed his position with no sign of reluctance. Facing the river on his stomach, he folded his arms and rested his chin on his hands. Michael squeezed out a dab of lotion and began just below his neck. His eyes drifted over taut muscle and down the distinct spinal valley, resting then on the bold contour of an alluring male ass, a landscape of shadows and small curls of hairs mingled with sand.

Go slowly. Don't allow your hands to hurry, and if it's meant to be, it will come. Michael spread the lotion with broad, circular strokes over Justin's upper back and shoulders, allowing his fingers to venture into the hair of his underarms. Tension melted beneath his palms in their migration down the taut muscle of Justin's back. There came a slight but perceptive hesitation when his hands moved close to the flare of his hips. Now keenly alert to Justin's reaction, the circular motion of his hands approached the duel mounds of his buttocks, and Justin's muscular legs came together slightly in response. One more dab, and smooth white hands ventured forth, and there came a sudden flex of black gluteal flesh. He massaged in the lotion, now gritty with sand, in a lingering manner beyond the mere application of oil, his eyes following the movement of his own hands.

"All your muscles are tight," said Michael. "Just relax for a minute. Take a few deep breaths."

Now the timeless noise of the river began to deliver its soothing effect, and the gluteal tension receded as Justin released a sigh. He didn't know if Michael was being intentionally intimate, or if this was the manner of any average massage; but of one thing he was certain—he was laying nude on the sand in the presence of another man, and he had been drawn with no reservation into the rapport of this man's hands.

Kneading the receptive muscle firmly, Michael's thumbs came together, sliding cautiously just inside the cleft, parting it ever so slightly with each upward stroke. The muscle now more pliant, the massage ever more bold, there came brief glimpses of dark anal flesh. With a striking contrast of color, daring white thumbs ventured further into the two halves, the hues there the alluring color of black ink, kneading the fleshy muscle, exposing again those fleeting glimpses of damp hair swirling about the alluring but elusive aperture. Michael sighed, closed his eyes and willed himself to stop, for he feared the growing tension within his own loins.

"There," he said, giving Justin's ass a playful slap, "feel more relaxed?"

Justin rolled onto his side and propped himself up on his elbow, his smile alive in calm eyes. "There's magic in your hands."

Michael handed him the tube. "You're not the only one who can't reach his own back you know."

The smile Justin's in eyes came to his full lips. It was hard on Michael. He wanted to kiss them, taste them, feel their texture with his fingertips. He found himself more attracted to Justin than he had assumed he would, and it went beyond a physical attraction. The peace he had found in being with him, at times, made him feel almost weightless.

"Then lay down," said Justin, "and I'll take care of it for you."

Prone in the wet sand, his chin resting upon his forearms, Michael felt Justin brush away the sand on his back and buttocks and the back of his legs. He closed his eyes as the rough black hands came in contact with his sun-warmed skin. Perched on his knees at Michael's side, Justin leaned forward with the lotion. Though tentative at first, his hands slowly began to reflect more inquisitive thoughts, fingers learning that which was already known by eyes. Michael felt Justin's hands come down over his ribs and then back up the middle of his back, dropping a little lower with more confidence each time. The hands then came all the way down to his legs, then back up over his buttocks, learning for the first time the contours of another man's ass. Michael's hips lifted slightly, reflexively for the brief lingering of hands, for thumbs not nearly so bold as his own.

After his back was covered with lotion, Justin continued the massage in a manner much like a caress. Then he lifted his knee over Michael's body, lowering himself, and his weight came upon white hips, and he leaned forward to rub Michael's shoulders. Surprised by Justin's sudden weight, Michael closed his eyes in near disbelief, this seemingly innocuous closeness so far beyond anything he would have expected. Never had he been so aware of the heat of another man's loins, so utterly drawn into a dreamy state of tranquility. *Oh God, I like this.* He closed his eyes to the sun's glare across the river. *How is it I like this man so much?* His breath quickened with the warmth of Justin's weight. *What draws me to him so? What could be going through his mind?*

It seemed confusing and hard to fathom, this whole state of affairs, for it had all come over him so quickly, almost from that first moment on the river, when Justin had walked into his campsite, and he had turned and first set eyes on him. It came with no logic or rational reason, but whatever it was, it came with compelling and growing power.

Now, Michael was all but certain that Justin was driven by a physical attraction, its scope a question still unresolved; and within the heat of his intimate weight, he contemplated just how he might bring it to conscious thought. His optimism for life had never seemed so vibrant, nor his emotions for a man so acute, for this journey to escape his trials in California had brought him to Big Bend and it now owned his heart.

The sun dried his body as he watched the river coursing by, and he marveled that it was beyond anything he had ever expected to find. He thought of his long drive across the desert, that fateful stop along the interstate just outside of Fort Stockton. He thought about that brown sign, how it had beckoned him, how he took that exit and bought camping equipment and then found a place to camp. Now it seemed it all had some unknown purpose. He remembered those first breaths of dry air in the park, that first glimpse of its vast terrain. How the sky so defined its boundless limits, how the river with its surface glinting toward the horizon so looked like an endless silver thread. An arid paradise where a man could savor life with all five senses, it all came with a value no sum of money could equal, this land so vast, so quiet, that one could walk for miles and not hear a sound but the crunch of their own steps on the hard Earth. Here, a man could listen to the silence, contemplate his life with a clear mind, and he could open his eyes in the morning with no reason to agonize over the trials of a new day. And here, in an ancient stone house, lived a man like no other he had ever known, a man of radiant beauty whose mind and body had taken control of his every conscious thought.

Now, beneath the weight of this beautiful man, his imagination ran like a confusion of vivid color and fantasy. Had Justin taken this initiative to reveal his hidden thoughts? Did he mean to intentionally change the dynamic of their friendship? In a maddening swirl of speculation, Michael wondered if Justin had found a way to let his feelings be known?

His eyes still closed, Michael turned his head, resting it upon his forearms. With just one wish he would make time stand still and make this moment last forever. The massage continued. His breath began to come easier, his heart more still, as the sensations from Justin's hands melted into every fiber of his body. And then Justin reached up to stroke his hair. He leaned close to Michael's ear and said:

"I figured I owed you a shoulder rub."

Justin lifted his leg back off Michael and he sat down beside him.

Michael opened his eyes and looked at the man staring out across the river. He gazed over the calm handsome features, this enigma in the form of a man, and he said nothing.

A concern came over him that he did not want to contemplate. That Justin might have a physical attraction for him was one thing, that he himself could fall in love with this beautiful man was another. His trepidation revolved around that possibility, and he knew his heart could never be prepared for the potential damage. Even if Justin did have a physical attraction, it didn't necessarily include an inclination to love another man, not in a way that would redefine their lives and cause them to live forever as companions and lovers. But something clearly had sparked inside Michael. It stirred every time he looked at his new friend. And now, born in their intimate proximity on the river, these thoughts blossomed like Spring flowers. *Be careful, Michael. This is something that could really screw you up.*

They wiled away the hours in the sun, exchanging thoughts and ideas. They played with Perk and swam across the glassy surface upstream from the rapids, and they climbed atop big rocks just for the challenge. It was a day of calm and unspoken intimacy, and now, when Michael found himself in Justin's gaze, he was aware of eyes that no longer darted away.

They left their secluded paradise reluctantly in the late afternoon and rode across the desert back to the house.

Justin had never had a day he enjoyed more. Stopping at the back door, he turned toward his new friend. Scanning his chest once again, he saw clinging particles of sand and the oily residue of sun screen. He looked at Michael and smiled. "It looks like a good time for you to learn how to use the shower."

CHAPTER 8

Michael turned and looked at the jug between two poles while Justin unlocked the door. They went inside where Michael opened his suitcase to find his toothbrush and shampoo. A few minutes later, Justin emerged from the bedroom, a towel wrapped around his naked waist, another in his hand. He tossed the spare towel to Michael.

"We'll have to refill the jug first," he said.

They followed Perk outside where Justin climbed up the slats nailed to one of the poles. He unhooked the small chain that held the plastic bottle in place and handed the near empty jug down to Michael. Back in the kitchen, he took a hose from under the counter and attached it to the spout on the pump. With the other end of the hose inside the jug, he pumped it full of water.

Adept at replacing the heavy jug, Justin refastened the chain and looked down at Michael. "You can go first. Just pull that rope to tilt the jug. Stand right there," he said, pointing at a spot on the ground, "where the water will spill out. The trick is to not use too much water to get wet or rinse off. You don't want to run out before you're finished."

Michael surveyed the rig for a moment, then stipped off his jeans. Placing the bottle of shampoo on the sand near his feet, he took hold of the rope and tilted the jug over his head. The water poured out, plastering his hair to his head and drenching him.

"That's the idea," said Justin, smiling. "Now that you're wet, lather up quickly so the soap doesn't dry on your skin."

"I think I'll wash my hair first," said Michael, reaching for the shampoo.

Perk and Justin sat in the sand a few feet away as Michael lathered his hair with the shampoo. He watched suds run down through the golden hairs across his sun bronzed chest, on down over his belly and legs. He reflected on the day they had spent together, and still he had not grown tired of looking at him. As he watched the sensuous image of a man covered with wet rivulets of soap, he wondered why Michael had not said anything about the massage. He still didn't know how he had found the courage to straddle him that way, but he knew why he did it. Not only was it easier to rub his shoulders from that position, but he was also compelled to see what something like that felt like. He thought about the sensations that ran through him when he straddled that tanned body, about the erection it had given him. Certain that Michael had noticed it, he wondered why he never said anything about that either. So now, for whatever else might come, this was a day that would live forever in his memory. It was like he had let himself go, and then found he had enjoyed it, and found it intriguing that he had done it with another man.

Now, watching the soap run down his legs, those pleasant sensations again warmed his inner thighs, causing his legs to come together with his thoughts. He reached over to rub Perk's head, marveling again at this sudden and most agreeable inclination to watch a naked man. It was a dilemma he hadn't pondered since his days in the high school gym. But so what? Now was not the time to fret. In truth, he enjoyed the sensations that came like tingles across his skin, that caused his penis to take on increased weight, and in the private sovereignty of his own home, why not, for it came without a trace of guilt.

His hair thoroughly scrubbed, Michael pulled the rope and rinsed away the shampoo. He reached for the bar of soap in the dish nailed to one of the posts. Standing in the warmth of Justin's gaze, he was fully aware of the pleasant effect those dark eyes delivered, and he ached to know the thoughts just behind them. All day he avoided asking questions, nor had he made a single suggestion, though many had entered his mind. He was far too familiar with the numbing complexities a man could encounter when facing a predicament; and to reach the right conclusion, Justin had no choice but to muddle through.

Watching Michael lather his chest and arms, the late afternoon sun shimmering on his skin, Justin reached under the towel to adjust himself. He closed his eyes and released a long breath. Though the day had been thoroughly enjoyable, it had also unfolded with an underlying concern. His eyes drawn so irresistibly, he couldn't help but question this dilemma colliding with his masculine sensibilities, this struggle to understand an unadulterated attraction to another man. How could a man's sudden presence cause such emotion, raise questions that had never before entered his mind, and create so much conflict while bringing such calm at the same time? Why did he long to touch him again? And why did he dread the inevitable day that Michael would get into his car to return to California?

His entire body covered with a lather of soap, Michael tilted the jug again, and the soap began to run off his body onto the sand. "Pour it slower and there'll be enough left for me," Justin said, getting to his feet. Perk had lost interest and had begun selecting cactus on which to mark his territory.

Michael blotted his chest with the towel while Justin filled the wash bowl on the weathered table. "You can use this to brush your teeth," he said.

Perk suddenly started yapping and shot off into the desert, after a jack rabbit dashing in a terrified zigzag to escape the dog's wrath. Watching his dog, Justin slipped off the towel and drapped it over a bush. He stepped naked under the jug, his penis hard and jutting forth, and he saw Michael's eyes stop short when he noticed it.

Justin pulled the rope and water cascaded down over his head and glistened on his skin in the late afternoon sun. Michael had an urge to step forward to bathe him. Instead, he brushed his teeth, contemplating Justin's thoughts, aware those thoughts had no doubt caused his erection. He turned his head and saw white soap suds running down over Justin's chest, making his black skin look blacker. He watched hands washing away the grime of desert heat and the oily residue of sun lotion, over shoulders and arms and chest. The hands went down, one lifting his genitals while the other reached through his legs with the soap. He leaned forward, running the soap down his legs one at a time, lifting each one to wash toes and feet. One more pull on the rope emptied the jug and more soapy water ran across the sand.

They put on their jeans and walked barefoot into the kitchen. Michael stepped up to the Mexican tiled counter and rinsed out the coffee pot while Justin poked around in the old freezer. "Do you like beef tips and rice?" he asked, looking at the box in his hand.

"Anything would sound good right now. I'm famished." He

sloshed water inside the pot and poured it into the chipped porcelain sink, watching it run into the drain. "Where does this water go?" he asked, pumping the handle to refill the pot.

Justin had found a second box of beef tips. "It runs out a pipe through that wall. Keeps the tomato plants out there watered." He struck a match and leaned forward to light the oven. "You haven't said anything about it," he said, placing the frozen dinners on the oven rack.

"About what?" said Michael, looking over his shoulder.

"The erections I've had today."

Michael paused before responding. Justin's tone suggested this might be a sensitive subject. "Oh … well, I did notice it," he said with caution, "but I wouldn't give it much thought. It's natural. It just happens sometimes."

"Come on, Michael. I'm thirty-three years old. That hasn't *just* happened in ten years."

"Well, I guess it could mean you are horny as hell. After all, it's been a long time since you've had sex, hasn't it? We've been naked all day long, and seeing that much skin in any form could cause that kind of reaction."

Justin laughed. "Now that really is a stretch, Dr. Anderson."

"Then I'm not sure what you're getting at."

Justin stood up and looked at him, the soft glare from the kitchen window filtering through the room. "I think you do," he said.

Michael took a deep breath. "Are you saying that you're attracted to me?"

"Yes."

"I'm flattered."

"You're probably use to men being attracted to you."

"Well, right now we're talking about you." Michael turned and poured fresh grind into the coffee pot and plugged it in.

"But I'm not gay. Do things like this happen to men who aren't gay, or is there something odd about me?"

"There's nothing odd about you, Justin. It's pretty simple really. It has to do with that concept of intellectual curiosity we were talking about last night." Michael studied Justin's troubled expression for a moment. "How long has it been since you've had sex?"

Justin laughed. "Oh shit! I can't remember."

"There you are. You're a man who hasn't had a release in a long time. It's not unnatural or odd that my body turned you on. It just made you think of sex." He looked over at the refrigerator. "Isn't there more Tecate in there?"

The question jolted Justin's train of thought. "Uh … yeah. Why don't you slice one of those limes and I'll get out some beer?"

Michael sliced a lime and Justin took a couple of cans of beer to the table. Michael joined him, sucking one of the slices before taking a swallow.

"This was the most incredible day I've ever had in my life," Michael said casually. He wouldn't have traded the day for all his carnal experiences combined, especially the massage Justin had given him, those few moments when he laid in the sand beneath his weight. Such a simple, impulsive act it had been, but how it had so redefined his idea of sensuality. The day had passed with that magnificent black body in his gaze. They had wiled away the hours stretched out in the sun and they had swam and climbed rock. Michael had watched him from angles near and far, his body alternately wet from swimming and dry from the warm sun. Though Justin had been relaxed all day, he was now tense and grappling with confusing questions.

Michael noticed Perk looking into an empty water bowl and got up to refill it.

Justin leaned forward and rubbed his forhead with his fingers. He felt like he was about to explode.

"He still has food in his bowl," Michael said. "Do you wait until he finishes it before you give him more?"

"Yeah. We're going to have to get him another brand. He doesn't get too excited about that one anymore."

Michael noticed at once that Justin had used the term 'we' in reference to getting Perk's new brand of dog food. He sat back down at the table and said, "It bothers you that you're attracted to me, doesn't it?"

"Yes." He looked up. "I mean no ..." He slumped back into the chair in utter frustration. "I don't know if it bothers me or not."

"I'm not one of the other rangers you work with, Justin. You can say anything you want to me. And you don't have to worry that I'll be judgmental. It's one of the benefits of having a gay friend."

"Well, I would say it if I knew what it was. You already know I enjoy looking at you, that I'm attracted to you, and that *is* confusing. All of this has come out of the blue. I've never had these feelings before I met you."

"Have you ever caught yourself looking at another man, wondering what it would be like to ..."

"No." Justin turned his head, staring blankly toward the living room. His tone softened with an admission. "In high school," he said. "In the showers. I looked at the other boys. There's probably been a couple of times I've noticed tight blue jeans." He looked back at Michael and added, "Maybe there's something about me I've never admitted, or have had guts to face."

"I've heard that sort of thing before," said Michael.

"But how am I suppose to deal with it?"

"Are you hoping to have this problem resolved before you finish that can of beer?"

Justin rolled his eyes. "I know better than that."

"Then just give yourself some time. One way or the other, you'll eventually figure these emotions out. This confusion will go away or it'll lead you down another road. In the meantime, let's enjoy our time together. If you like looking at me, don't fret over it, just enjoy it. Who's going to know besides you and me?"

They both turned to look at the low table in the living room when Michael's cell phone rang. He got up and crossed the room to pick it up. It was Jody.
"Hello, Sis."

"Where are you, Michael?"

"I'm still in west Texas. I'll be staying here for awhile."

"Are you still camping in the desert?"

"No. I met a park ranger and we became friends. I'm staying at his place."

"What a surprise! It's amazing how you gay guys can sniff each other out even in the wilderness."

"It's not like that, Sis. He's a friend. His name is Justin."

"Bullshit!"

"Believe what you want."

"So how long will it be before you come home?"

"I'm staying here for awhile."

There was a short silence. "I see," Jody said. "Your lawyer has been contacted by the little girl's parent's attorney. They're going to file a suit, but your lawyer thinks it'll be settled rather quickly. The parents aren't being aggressive."

"Okay," said Michael.

"He said you'd eventually have to come back for a deposition."

"I was afraid of that. But maybe not if they settle."

"Don't count on that."

"How are you doing, Sis?"

"Everything is peachy, except I miss you, and I'm worried about you."

"No need to worry."

"You have no idea when you plan to come home?"

"No."

"Then I'm coming out there."

"Sis, you'd never find this place. It's a remote ranch in the middle of nowhere."

"I won't have to find it. You're picking me up at the airport in El Paso the day after tomorrow, at noon."

"What?"

"You heard me. Southwest Airlines. And don't be late. I hate waiting around in airports."

"Sis! I don't even know where you could stay."

"You have almost two days to figure that out. I'll see you the day after tomorrow."

Michael heard a click and the phone went dead. He stood staring at it a moment.

"She coming out here?" Justin asked.

Michael turned. "Yeah. I wonder if all females are that hard-headed."

Justin smiled at his loss for words. "I'm glad she's coming. It'll be fun meeting her."

"Be prepared for a woman who speaks her mind."

"I will. When does she get here?"

"Noon, day after tomorrow. I have to pick her up at the El Paso airport."

"I'll go with you. I know the way."

Michael nodded, wondering how long his sister's presence was going to disrupt the harmony of their desert calm.

"You and your sister are close, aren't you?"

"Yes," said Michael, looking over at him. "How did you know?"

"I could tell from your conversation. And she's coming out here because she's worried about you."

"That's what she said. We've been best friends all our lives. We live next door to each other."

"She's not married?"

"Never has been. She's too head-strong and independent. But you never know. She might meet someone who can handle her one of these days."

After dinner, Perk curled up on the couch next to Justin. Michael sprawled out in the over-stuffed chair. Dusk fell over the house with its late February chill and the room filled with the chirping of a cricket hidden somewhere inside the old house.

Contemplating the day's events, they fell into the serenity of the evening, reading and passing the time in thought. Michael was yawning by ten o'clock.

"I think I'm ready to turn in, too," said Justin, getting up off the couch. He watched Michael get up and pull his sleeping bag from behind the chair and begin to untie the knot that held it rolled tight. "It's warmer in the bedroom," he said with a hard swallow. "I mean … well, you get no effect from the electric heater all the way out here."

Michael looked up from the knotted string.

"There's plenty of room in the bed for both of us."

"You want me to sleep with you?"

"I figure nothing has to be read into it."

"No. Nothing does. I just wasn't expecting …"

"You won't get so cold in there."

"Okay." Somewhat astonished, Michael put the sleeping bag back behind the chair.

They walked into the bedroom together. Justin turned on the small table lamp next to the bed, then turned on the heater. He sat on the edge of the bed and watched Michael pull off his jeans. "You never wear underwear?"

"Never have," Michael said, standing nude in the soft light.

Justin took off his jeans, leaving on a pair of white cotton briefs. He lifted the crumpled sheet and scooted over to the other side of the bed. Michael joined him, pulling the sheet up to his belly. They lay on their backs staring up at the old wooden plank ceiling. The electric heater produced just enough heat to take the chill out of the room.

"Beats the couch, doesn't it?"

"Sure does. You do have a good mattress."

"Michael … thanks."

Michael turned his head to look at him. "Thanks for what?"

"For being understanding. I know my behavior was a little strange before dinner. I hope you don't think I've been impossible to put up with."

"No. After all, you're putting up with my emotional baggage, too." He looked back at the ceiling.

"You'll work it out in time. I'm just not sure I will."

"You will. I don't think your behavior is all that strange, and you certainly don't have have a problem just because you got an erection. I'd say the opposite is true."

"That's just it. That was one of my problems when I was engaged. Can you imagine being in bed with a beautiful woman, and being unable to get a hard-on?"

"You're asking the wrong guy."

Justin spoke again after a short silence. "Are you thinking my curiosity goes beyond just looking at you?"

"I'm not making any assumptions about that. But I don't see that as a huge problem, either." Michael turned to look at him again. "You must know I'm attracted to you, too."

"You've hidden that very well, except a couple of times on the river today." He smiled. "This morning, when you were putting that lotion on me, you were getting pretty intimate."

Michael glanced down over the outline of his form, one knee bent and lifting the sheet, the other leg stretched toward the end of the bed. "I tried to not be obvious," said Michael. "The truth is, you have a great ass."

Justin remembered all too well the electricity that ran

through him when Michael's thumbs came up between the two halves of his buttocks. "I didn't want you to stop," he said, almost submissively. "I didn't know how to encourage you, but I had a feeling about what you were doing." He turned his head to look at Michael. "It might surprise you, but I liked it. I wanted you to ask me to put the lotion on your back. I wanted find out what it's like to touch you."

"Is that why you straddled me? You wanted to see what that was like?"

Justin released a kind of befuddled half laugh and shook his head. "It sure feels odd talking about these things."

"It's okay. Remember, you don't have to worry about what you're saying around me."

"Well, I couldn't believe I actually did that, but yes. It was a sudden urge to get close to you, so I just did it without thinking about it."

Michael sensed where their conversation was heading. Beside him lay a man who was tense, whose eyes couldn't settle, whose thoughts had become obvious. He proceeded with sensitivity, his voice calm and reassuring. "And you enjoyed that too?"

"Yes."

"Do you want to touch me now?"

"Yes."

"Okay, then there's no reason not to."

Justin swallowed hard. "You know how to go about this, don't you?"

Michael rolled onto his side and looked into his eyes. "Justin, if you decided you would like to make love with me, it would likely be the most wondrous thing I've ever experienced, but you have to be the one who makes that decision. It shouldn't happen unless you're certain. We can't do anything that will end up making either one of us feel guilty."

"I thought about it all day," Justin said. He looked up at the ceiling as if he were contemplating how much it had been on his mind. "Actually, I didn't think about much of anything else." He looked back at Michael pensively. "I'm just not sure how to go about it."

Michael smiled at him and said, "Give me your hand."

Justin's hand came forth from behind his head. Michael took it gently, caressing the rough skin of his palms and fingers. A plea of anticipation came into his gaze as he lifted the black hand and placed it aside his face. He closed his eyes and the tension melted away when Justin's fingertips moved across his lips.

"Now," Michael whispered, "just take your time and relax. Think about what you would like to do."

Justin shifted his weight and came up on his knees, and he lowered the sheet down over Michael's legs. His eyes swept slowly down over the sun browned body. He closed his eyes and released a long sigh, and then he lifted his leg to straddle Michael again. Leaning forward, he reached up and his fingertips again found the smooth texture of Michael's lips, tracing lightly their outline. He studied the warm glow on the calm white face and his fingertips explored its proportions.

From beneath him came the heat of Michael's erect cock and his hips flexed in response. His eyes then followed the masculine lines of his body. A sweet tension charged the air as Michael felt the fingertips pass over his neck, brushing lightly over his chest to his nipples, and a circular caress made them hard.

"I can't believe I'm doing this," said Justin.

Michael tilted his head and he looked down at the outline of Justin's hard cock in the briefs. "Looks like it agrees with you."

"I think it does. More than I could have imagined." He laughed. "If those boys I work with saw me now."

"I'm afraid what what we're doing might be over their heads."

Justin gently pinched and pulled on his nipples. "Do you like this?"

Michael's cock twitched beneath the heat of Justin's ass. "Can't you tell?"

Justin ground his hips a bit on the cock. "Yes, I can tell."

Warm black hands slid over awaiting pectoral muscle, a massaging grip, moving then down over his stomach. His hips slid back over Michael's legs, his redish-brown penis now jutting forth. Together they found the natural harmony of like minds, two men drawn from the throes of their lonely lives, submissive with their bodies and increasingly daring with their hands. Black fingertips brushed the blonde pubic hair and passed tentatively over an erect cock. A new and distinct feeling came over Justin, a freedom. He found he could dwell upon and look at Michael's body from the perspective of a lover. Now with less reserve, he could gaze at his cock, behold its shape and dark fleshy red color, its veins, the walnut shaped glans divided atop the end with a small slit. He had entered a sensuous world of discovery that made him feel alive in a way he had never known. How Michael's cock beckoned with its throbbing and twitching. How it brought alive fantasies he had not known existed, yet must have and had remained buried all these years. He yearned to know its texture and feel, and by taking it gingerly into his hand, he learned. Firm and warm on his palm, his hand slid further down and tightened its grip. Squeezing harder, he marveled at the way it felt, its heat, its quivering response, the intimate texture of its pliant sheathe.

Tingles of gooseflesh raced across Michael's skin as he felt the cautious lift of his testicles, his hips twisting in response, and the rough hand closed warmly on the vulnerable sac.

"God!" Michael whispered, "I've never been turned on this much in my life."

Captivated, Justin pulled and kneaded the supple male pouch, the testicles rolling back and forth between his fingers and thumb. A pearl of pre-cum appeared at the tiny slit and Justin touched it with his fingertip, circling the slippery fluid atop the swollen glans. He sighed, his eyes captured by the engorged veins running the length of the shaft, and he took it again in his hand with a confident grip. Sliding easily, the loose skin moved up and down, the throbbing intense on his palm. Drawn by Michael's writhing and moans, he found himself lost in this most intimate act.

Losing all doubt to passion, he gripped harder and quickened the pace of his strokes. He saw surrender, and muscle and sinew grow tight as Michael's whole body tensed. Born within Michael's inner thighs and belly, spasms welled and spread through him in waves of pleasure. Then, spewing from the tiny slit came quick streams of white fluid, falling randomly over legs and belly and sheets, and as the convulsions slowly abated, the last rivulet of semen trickled down over fist and scrotum. Justin squeezed out the final drop, hypnotically lost in the aura of Michael's climax.

Michael's eyes eventually opened in a mystified gaze. He found the strength to sit up, and he took Justin's hand and licked from it a remnant of semen. He reached up and stroked the side of his face and said, "Would you like to see what that feels like?"

"Yes," he whispered.

"Lay down on the pillow and close your eyes and relax."

The bouquet of sweat and semen laden with pheremones, Justin felt lightheaded as he lay back. Michael straddled him, his back to his lover's face. He lowered his hips, allowing a slight weight to rest atop a nervous lover's chest. Reaching forward, he brought his hands up along Justin's legs, brushing lightly the tight curls of hair. He massaged tense thighs, coming ever closer to the bulge in Justin's briefs. He ran his fingernails over the bold outline of a hard cock that strained against the white cotton fibers. His thumbs hooked under the waistband, he pushed down the briefs and the black cock sprang free. Justin lifted his hips as Michael pushed the briefs down over his thighs, exposing testicles warm and low between his legs. Michael's fingertips came brushing up over them, then lightly over the veined shaft. The cock twitched involuntarily and soft moans came from Justin's throat.

Michael teased the pink glans with his finger, caressing and pushing at the tiny hole, tracing lightly the inflamed ridge. Justin squirmed and tensed, his hands turned into fists as Michael gripped his firm shaft and pulled the loose skin up over the glans, and then began to slide it up and down, falling into a masterful rhythm. His hips rose in response. His whole body taut, he strained against the weight atop his chest as agonizing seconds brought him closer to the inevitable. It swept through him like a summer storm. He groaned and gripped the sheet, his toes curled tight, and the unbridled spewing seemed to have no end, spurting and running in rivulets down knuckles and legs and belly. Michael leaned forward and passed his tongue over the swollen pink glans, licking the last pearl from the slit. He then lifted his leg back off the heaving chest. Repositioned beside him, Michael held his novice lover close, engulfing him with his arm and leg.

Still breathing hard, Justin's arm came up under him, pulling him in tight, and they lay quietly for a few moments entwined in their embrace, the earthy scent of semen mingled between their bodies. Justin reached over once more to touch Michael's lips.

"Did we make love?" he asked softly.

Michael smiled. "That's what I would call it."

"It didn't last long."

"It will next time."

"You're not surprised, are you?"

"I'm happy."

"Am I gay?" asked Justin.

"You're human. We don't know yet if you're gay. But you're off to a damn good start if you are."

"I can't believe it. All these years and it comes down to this."

"Do you feel guilty?" asked Michael.

"That's what surprises me. I don't. Not a bit. I liked it more than I thought I would. I like laying here with you like this."

"Perk doesn't seem to think anything unusual is going on."

Justin tilted his head to look at the dog curled nonchalantly at their feet.

"If you liked it more than you thought," Michael added, "seems to mean you must have been thinking about going to bed with me."

"I admit, I was. Actually, I couldn't stop thinking about it.

Even last night, when you were out there on the couch. I debated inviting you in here then." Justin stared at the old wooden ceiling, reflecting on the moments of passion he had shared with the man in his arms. "When you started to climax, I felt you pulsing in my hand. I liked the way that made me feel. Then I realized your semen has a distinct smell. It made me so light-headed I thought I was going to faint. I liked that, too."

"And you like talking about it, it seems."

Justin's head snapped toward him. "Is that okay?"

"Of course it is."

Michael was delighted with Justin's new-found enchantment with male sex. He had never shared such wondrous moments with another man. Still, he knew he must leave control of its direction in his new lover's hands. And he worried, for his heart was now at further risk. It was entirely possible that Justin could wake up regretting what he had done. He could wake up lost in a muddle of guilt and attempt to deny that something wonderful had happened, and their world would lapse into a state of tension. He knew all too well these were the risks suffered by a man in conflict with his sexual identity.

"You were right," he said, "it is warmer in here, but not necessarily because of that electric heater."

"I like this, Michael."

"Me too."

"But it's nothing new for you."

"Yes, I'm afraid it is."

Justin turned his head to look at him. "What do you mean? You've had countless experiences with men."

"Experiences? Maybe so. But never anything of value. I've

never known a man who I have ached for, and have ached for him to want me. My entire life has been no more than an endless cycle of meaningless encounters." He paused and sighed, rubbing his hand over Justin's chest. "This is the first time I've been in bed with a man who is important to me. And it was important that you were mentally ready." Michael got up on his elbow and looked into Justin's perplexed eyes. "I think you were."

"This must be why I ran out on my wedding."

"It might be. If you are gay, you knew subconsciously the marriage was wrong."

"It's amazing," Justin mused. "It seems like the world is suddenly a different place."

"Did you feel that way when you made love to Christie?"

"No. I remember looking forward to spending the night with her, but I didn't feel like this. You already know there were even a few times it was frustrating."

Michael ran his hand down over Justin's stomach and on down between his legs. There wasn't the slightest sign of impotence. It was far from the first time his hand had closed on a man's erection, but it never came with such unspoken reverence. He was beginning to believe that Justin might indeed be gay. If so, it would change their dynamic. Michael knew it could be the best thing that had ever happened to him; but at the same time, though he was in no hurry to go back to California, with this revelation he might never want to go back.

"Well," said Justin, "I'm thirty-three, and in all those years it never occurred to me that I'd end up laying in bed naked with another man." He turned his head. "What are we going to tell your sister?"

"Whatever you want to tell her," said Michael, aware Justin had used the term 'we' again.

"She knows you're gay?"

"Of course."

"Then, even if she knew the truth, it wouldn't bother her?"

"She'd assume it, even if we lied to her."

"Tomorrow, I'll tell Bernard I'm taking off again."

"I don't want you to risk your job," said Michael, caressing Justin's testicles, now flaccid and moist and low between his legs.

Justin sighed. "That's not a worry," he said, his words labored in reaction to Michael's hand. "I have accrued enough time-off to just about retire on." He parted his legs a bit to allow Michael's hand more access. "God, that feels good."

"Justin … I think something might be happening between us that I haven't quite figured out yet."

"I know. Nothing for me will ever be the same."

"Does it scare you a little?"

"Yes."

"Me too."

Michael reached over and turned off the light. "You ready to get some sleep?"

"I might be able to go to sleep."

Michael stroked the side of his face. "Good night, you beautiful man."

"Good night, Michael."

CHAPTER 9

Justin awoke at daybreak. The first rays of sun had just spilled in through the window, already warming the room. Michael was still asleep, his head resting atop Justin's damp chest. The distinct bouquet of their sex still lingered in the air. He ran his fingers through Michael's sandy brown hair, contemplating their sensual day on the river, and a night that had changed his life, and now, awaking next to the man with whom he had shared it all. Justin realized that he had never awakened feeling such pure joy, nor had he faced a morning charged with such truth.

He slipped out from under Michael's head and stepped into his jeans. The early Spring air lay on his skin like a pleasant spell. Perk followed him into the kitchen where he started the coffee. He looked at the iron griddle hanging from a hook on the stone wall behind the stove, and thought of pancakes. Checking the cabinet to see if he had a box of mix, he heard Michael's voice.

"Good morning."

Turning and seeing him near the bedroom door, his eyes puffy and still groggy from sleep, his sandy hair in disarray, Justin stood upright and gazed at his nude lover. He remained motionless as Michael approached and leaned forward to kiss the smooth skin below his ear.

"Mornin'," said Justin, his heart light and full of joy, his eyes implying they had fallen upon the best thing that had ever come into his life.

Michael looked at him and smiled. "Remember what happened last night?"

"I'll never forget it. You could say I feel reborn."

Perk was looking up at them, tail wagging.

Michael reached out and touched Justin's lips. "I'm almost disoriented by what's happening to us. It's going to take awhile for it to soak in."

He looked around the room in wonder, the low wood plank ceiling just above his head, the iron skillets and pots that hung in disarray on the ancient stone wall, the old sink and pump. The dull clay tiles comprising the floor felt like hard earth under his bare feet. The old stone house with its silent, secret history, no more than another tiny speck in this vast land, seemed to Michael more significant than any palace could ever be. Justin's world had surrounded and embraced him, and filled his chest with joy. And it had surfaced upon his heart, that somehow, standing before him in the form of a beautiful and sensitive man, was the unspoken promise of a magnificent future. That long cluttered life in California already seemed like the distant past, for in so short a time he already felt more a part of this world than that left behind. He was alive, and it came to him every minute of every day through sight and smell and touch. And the possibility of sharing it all with Justin was beyond anything he would have ever hoped.

Though he felt he could go out into the desert and throw his fists into the air in celebration, shout to the blue sky his pure joy, and jump high in unending elation, he would keep his heart calm and allow destiny its own wise course. He opened the cabinet door under the sink and reach in for the metal pail he had seen there the night before.

Justin watched him pump the pail full of water and carry it out the back door, Perk tagging along behind him. Puzzled, Justin took the mixing bowl off the shelf and dumped in some pancake mix. Stirring water into the mix, he noticed through the window Perk following Michael to the outhouse. Michael set the pail on the ground and went inside the small structure, closing the door behind him. Perk lapped a drink out of the pail and then sat watching the outhouse door. Moments later, Michael stepped out and squat down over the pail. Justin, his curiosity acute, laid down the spoon and walked out and on up toward them. Michael was splashing himself with the water.

"An audience—just what I needed for this," said Michael.

"What are you doing?" asked Justin.

"Well, if it's not obvious, I just took a crap and I'm cleaning up."

"You find toilet tissue unsatisfactory?"

"As a matter of fact, I do, and we have no bidet in the out-house."

"I see," said Justin, watching him a moment longer. "Guess we ought to keep that bucket handy then."

"Good idea," said Michael, coming to his feet and pitching the water out over the desert.

"Do you like pancakes?"

"I love 'um."

They walked together back to the house.

"I think I'll wear my sandals next time I come out here," said Michael, stepping tentatively over the crunchy hard earth.

Justin glanced down at Michael's bare feet, and then his eyes then drifted up his muscled blonde legs. Protruding from under a scant swatch of near blonde pubic hair, his cock tended to point outward, bobbing from side to side with each step, his testicles drawn tight in response to the crisp morning air. Delighted Michael's casual nudity, it seemed refreshingly natural for a man like him. Though he may have come to Big Bend country wound with tension from the burdensome trials left behind, Justin hoped that he would eventually feel as much at home in the desert as he obviously felt in his own body.

Justin smiled and wrapped his arm around Michael's shoulders, pulling him close as they walked toward the house. "Good thing we don't have to fret over what neighbors might think."

Back in the kitchen, Michael poured two cups of coffee and set them on the table. He got some oranges out of the refrigerator and took them to the counter. Justin, standing beside him, opened a can of apple sauce and poured it into the batter. "I'd like to take a couple of weeks off and do nothing but watch you walk around naked," he said, reaching down to adjust the physical reaction in his jeans.

"So it didn't bother you waking up with a man in your arms?" asked Michael as he sliced the oranges.

"Bother me? Hardly. The only thing that bothered me about it was thinking about the day you go home, and then *not* waking up with you in my arms."

Michael glanced at him and noticed the bulge. "Justin, you're showing some obvious signs here. I mean it's beginning to look like more than a casual curiosity. Thing is, if you are gay, it's amazing you weren't more aware of it than you were." He started squeezing the juice from the orange halves into a jar.

"Maybe our minds are powerful enough to repress even something like that. Fact is, right now … and I feel a little silly saying it, but I'm downright giddy about it."

Michael's brows lifted with his smile. "That could be every gay man's fantasy—a tall, handsome park ranger who feels giddy," he said, returning to the oranges. "Of course it's still possible you're just uncommonly horny after your long dry spell."

"Possible?"

Michael looked at him and grinned. "Well, okay, you *are* horny. What I meant is, maybe that's what motivated you last night. Maybe you just needed a release."

"Maybe," said Justin, stirring the batter.

"I didn't know pancakes had applesauce in them."

"It's my personal recipe. Adds flavor and keeps them moist." He carried the bowl of batter to the hot griddle on the stove and ladled out a half dozen pancakes.

"How much orange juice do you want?"

Justin looked over his shoulder at the jar. "About half of that."

Michael filled two small glasses and took them to the table. He then set the table with plates, flatware and a dish of butter. Justin joined him a few minutes later with maple syrup and a plate stacked with pancakes.

"Looks like it's going to be a warm day," said Justin.

"I still can't believe this wonderful weather out here."

"What are you going to do today?"

"I was looking at the map last night. Thought I might take a drive over to Lajitas."

Justin smiled. "Going to check out a little of the local flavor?"

"Yeah."

"They had to elect a mayor over there awhile back. There were three candidates: a goat that eats beer cans, a wooden Indian, and a human being from Houston."

Michael shook his head with amusement.

"I thought the wooden Indian was best for the job, but the human won by ten thousand votes. They figured the election was rigged since Lajitas has only a few hundred people eligible to vote."

Fascinated by the contrasts of this part of the world compared to the busy sophistication of San Diego, Michael found the story about Lajitas refreshing. He buttered his pancakes and poured maple syrup over them, aware it was increasingly hard to comtemplate going back. He looked across the table at Justin, knowing his new lover would find it difficult to ever consider going back with him. He was a man who could never leave Big Bend.

"Any reservations about what happened last night?" he asked.

His mouth full, Justin said, "No. I woke up in the middle of the night wanting to do it again. Feeling your body next to mine ... I don't know. I can't explain it. I couldn't resist touching you. I took some liberties with my hands while you were sleeping."

"So that wasn't a dream."

"No, it was me. You responded by putting your leg over mine. I could smell your hair and your underarms. I wanted to wake you up."

"I wouldn't have minded."

"I can't wait to go to bed with you tonight." Justin paused in thought, toying with his food with a fork. "Michael, I want you to teach me. I want to learn how to make love to you."

Michael felt a pleasant shiver on the back of his neck. He took another bite of pancakes, thinking about a myriad of ways he wanted to be initmate with his new lover. That he would be his teacher at the same time made the fantasies all the more compelling, and he too was most anxious to get back into bed with him. But he felt comfortable with their pace the night before, allowing Justin's first knowledge of male sex to come in the form of masturbation. Tonight, his lover would be prepared to enter another world, a world of abandon and passion and pain. Now, there was little doubt, that which beckoned from within Justin's loins had lay in wait for years.

"We can teach each other then," he proposed. "You're teaching me how to live, and I'll teach you how to make love, and I promise, we'll go to heights you've never imagined existed."

A soft glaze of anticipation came over Justin's face as he continued his breakfast, regretting that within the hour he would have to leave, that he could not go with Michael to Lajitas. He would spend his day on the River Road with Perk, the long hours passing slowly, contemplating the promise of another night with this beautiful lover. It would indeed be a long day, and regrettably, it had to start with a visit to Bernard's office.

Justin parked his Jeep in front of the visitor's center and drew a deep breath, psyching-up for confrontation. Perk followed him into the building. He walked behind the counter, nodding at the two rangers coming toward him down the hall from Bernard's office. Staring at him inquisitively, they nodded back, their grins indiscreet. Justin looked past them and noticed Bernard's office door open. Before starting down the hall, he felt the sensation of being stared at, and he turned toward the lobby and saw the two rangers still watching him. He shrugged and started toward Bernard's door.

Perk shot into the room ahead of him.

"Get that damn dog outta here!" came Bernard's booming voice.

Justin stepped into the room and Bernard's eyes moved from Perk to him. The large man nodded toward the dog. "What's he sniffing around over there for?" he grunted.

"He was constipated this morning, Bernard. I thought if I brought him to your office, it might inspire a bowel movement."

"Very funny." He nodded at the chair in front of his desk. "Sit down for a minute, Justin. There's something I want to know."

Justin sat down in anticipation of something he wasn't expecting. As Bernard stared at him a moment, a dopey kind of a grin formed on his fleshy face.

"Are you a queer?" he stated bluntly.

"What the hell are you talking about now?"

"I know all about that little rendezvous on the river with a man no one has ever seen around here before. Heard you two were naked together."

Justin lowered his head and rubbed his eyes with his fingers.

"'Course if you are, you don't have to worry. We can't discriminate against queers either."

"Bernard," Justin sighed with exasperation, "it's your nature to discriminate against the whole damn human race. Nevertheless, I'm not going to explain my personal affairs to you; it's none of your damn business."

"Well, okay, so you won't tell me what's going on. That's fine. Just watch yourself in the men's room. I don't want to hear about you making a move on any of the other rangers."

"You're having yourself some grand fun this morning, aren't you, Bernard?"

"If it's true, you haven't heard nothing yet."

Justin closed his eyes and shook his head.

"What are you doing over here anyway?" Bernard asked, coming back around to his usual self. "You're supposed to be over on the River Road."

"I came in to let you know I'm taking some more time off. Two days."

"What!"

"The next two days."

"Are you out of your mind?"

"Come on, Bernard. You can't remember the last time I took off. I've bailed you out every time someone has turned up sick. Now I'm asking for a little cooperation in return."

"This have anything to do with that man you were with yesterday? Who is he anyway?"

"He's a friend from California."

"Where's he staying?"

"At my place."

"Oh! Well, now. I'm beginning to understand why you live all the way out in the middle of nowhere."

"Bernard, I know you're not completely brain-dead, so why don't you just get off that line of thinking and show a little respect for my privacy?"

Bernard's face reddened a bit. "Okay, okay, you're right. But you better be prepared to take some ribbing about that little river scene of yours. Seems you've sparked a pretty good source for fresh gossip."

"I'll live with it."

Bernard pulled the employee log over from the side of his desk. "This two days off you're talking about," he said. "Want me to set it up for sick pay?"

"That's fine with me."

"Should I expect more of this any time soon?"

"No plans at the moment," said Justin.

Bernard looked at his desk calender. "That'll put you back on duty Friday morning. Check in with me for any possible change in assignments."

"I'll see you Friday morning."

Justin got up and walked out of the office, followed by Perk. He walked directly through the lobby and on out into the parking lot. He crawled in behind the wheel of his Jeep and stared at the tourist center landscape deep in thought, his mind spinning with these sudden revelations in his life. The entire staff was now assuming he was gay, and it didn't seem to bother him. Actually, it didn't bother him a bit. Everyone he knew was now certain to have heard about that event on the river. Bernard had ribbed him about being gay. Why did he not get defensive and deny it? He gripped the steering wheel, staring into space, and he felt the pleasant muscular contraction of a broad smile on his face.

When Michael returned from Lajitas, he parked the Cherokee next to Justin's Jeep, stepped out from behind the wheel and reached down to rub Perk's head. "Is he inside the house, boy?" he said to the frisky dog. Following Perk to the back of the house, Michael saw Justin taking a shower. He sat down on the ground a few feet away, his eyes falling into a gaze upon a fine landscape of black skin glistening with late afternoon sun and water.

Justin let go of the rope, stopping the flow of water, and he reached up and ran his hands over his face. His eyes opened and he smiled. "It's been a long day."

"I know," said Michael.

"What did you think of Lajitas?"

"I got lost in the suburbs."

Justin laughed and reached for his towel. "Hope you missed the rush-hour traffic."

"I figured that grill over there works so I picked up some steaks. Got some beer and cigars, too." He watched Justin blot his legs, then sling the towel over his shoulder. "You're beautiful."

"Guess what," said Justin, his face alive with an unually animated smile. "There's no doubt. I know for sure."

Michael turned his head curiously. "You know *what* for sure?"

"I'm gay. I'm dead certain. And it looks like I won't be spending any time in the closet, whether I want to or not."

Michael reached up and scratched the top of his head. "I'm a little overwhelmed. This is rather sudden, isn't it?"

"Just like we suspected: that river guide, Judy Houser, made an issue of seeing us in the river. Apparently, the whole staff has heard about it already. Bernard couldn't wait to ask me about being queer. That's why I know. None of this bothers me. I'm actually relieved they know."

Michael's eyes widened. "You admitted it to Bernard?"

"I didn't deny it. I'll just let them make their assumptions and let them figure out whether it's true or not. But I know, and I've never felt better about anything in my life. It answers all the questions that have been piling up since I was in high school. And I have you to share it with." He started toward the house.

Michael took a deep breath and wrapped his arms around his knees. With Justin yielding to his long buried disposition, his validation came like the sweetest kind of music to Michael's ears. It also brought on complications promising to change both of their lives.

"Justin ... there's something I think you should know." Justin stopped and turned back toward him to hear what he had to say. "I'm falling in love with you. I know I am. It's never happened to me before, but I can feel it in every fiber of my body. I've never been happier, or more scared."

Justin went and knelt before him and reached out to stroke

his hair. "You don't have to be scared. I know your life is rooted in another world twelve hundred miles away, and that scares me too. But right now, I'm not thinking about that. I can't. I can't face the thought of you leaving. Right now I'm just taking it one day at a time. That's what we both have to do. Things have fallen into place for us so far, and I have to believe they will in the end."

He looked at the paper sack resting on the ground beside Michael. "Right now we have some steaks to grill and some cigars to smoke. In a little while, we'll have a sunset to watch. Tonight …" He closed his eyes and and drew in a deep breath, then he looked back into Michael's eyes. "Tonight I'm going to follow you to those heights you were talking about. I know it's a place that's been in my dreams for a long time, and it's been in my heart and soul. I've just never realized it until now."

Justin stood and looked west, out across the desert toward the western horizon. The sky touching the mountains had taken on the pale blue of a day coming to an end. It all seemed just a little different, his private kingdom, perhaps because he was looking at it with different eyes, eyes which all at once seemed to perceive things with a new-found underlying joy. He turned and saw Michael staring at the ground with what looked like lost sorrow, and it touched his heart. He wrapped the towel around his waist and knotted it, and then sat down beside him.

"What is it, Michael?" The compassion in his voice was as soothing as the guiet that lay across the land.

Michael's expression lightened as if he were about to respond, but then it seemed he couldn't find the words. It had come over him suddenly, all those years of searching, of trying to understand, of struggling for something and never knowing exactly what it might be. His thoughts took form on his lips much like a plea.

"All my life I've managed to just barely keep my head above water, and when it seemed like I was going under, I don't think I would have made it if Jody had not been there. I'd see people who seemed happy, you know, walking together on the beach or talking and laughing in a restaurant; but I never really believed I would ever find anything like that. I was convinced I didn't deserve it for some reason, that it was for others and not for me. It was so often those kinds of people who came to me with their problems, a tumor or diseased heart or something that threatened to take their happiness away, and I'd lay in bed at night worried that I might screw up, make some mistake when I cut them open, that I'd be the one who took from the wife or husband something I would never have myself."

Michael's eyes narrowed on the ground in front of his feet, his jaw tightened. "That's why I went out. I couldn't burden Jody with with what's inside me. I had no one else to talk to about it. You can't worry about what you have to do tomorrow at the places I went, or feel lonely, at least on the surface. In those places, you can't spend every waking minute wondering why you can't have your own slice of happiness. But they leave you feeling so lonely."

Justin took his hand and placed the back of it aside his face, and from it he could almost feel Michael's pain. He thought about the things Michael had told him: the shifting from place to place while he was growing up, the disastrous relationship with his overbearing father. Surely that had affected him, perhaps like he himself had been affected when his own father abandoned his family. He kissed the back of Michael's hand and looked at him.

"You have someone to talk to now, Michael. Someone who believes you deserve every happiness life can bestow on you. Someone who would like to be part of it."

As Michael glanced over him, his plea seemed to move into his eyes. "Is it any wonder that I falling in love with a man like you?"

A pleasant glimmering came from within Justin's smile. "Go ahead and fall, Michael. Fall in love with me deeply. That's something that would be so easy to return, and it might prevent you from ever leaving me."

They were distracted by Perk sniffing the paper bag.

"He must smell those steaks," said Justin.

"I got him one, too." The little dog brought back Michael's smile.

"You bought Perk his own steak!"

"Of course. Otherwise I wouldn't have been able to eat one in front of him."

Justin looked at the dog. "He won't know how to act."

"I'm betting he'll like his steak rare."

They got to their feet and started toward the house. Justin stopped to light the grill before he went inside. With preparations for dinner under way, they stood side by side slicing lettuce for salad, mixing marinate for the steaks and slicing yellow squash into strips for grilling. Michael found himself continually distracted by the shadows and light over Justin's body. Still wearing the towel around his waist, he hadn't bothered to put on his jeans after the shower.

"This was an excellent idea," said Justin, turning the steaks over in the marinate.

"Damn, you turn me on!" Michael stated suddenly. "Do you have any idea of how enticing your ass is? It's hard to think about anything else with you standing there in that towel."

Justin looked at him, his eyes soft and submissive. He relished having someone to share such intimacy with. "That you think so is all I care about." He turned his back toward his lover, and said, "Tell me, is this something a gay man would do?" He abruptly leaned forward, bending over and flipping the the towel up over his hips.

"Oh Lord!" Michael sighed, his eyes drawn to a visual on which they could never tire. Ever so lightly, his fingertips reached out and followed the contour of his lover's gluteal halves for a brief but intimate encounter. "God, Justin. I'm not sure just how much you have to learn," Michael said. "I think you might be a natural."

Justin straightened his back and looked at him. "Whew! Uh … so is it?"

"Yes. A gay man would do something like that."

"I'm telling you, I'm gay. I've known it all along. I just didn't know that I knew … if you know what I mean. I also realize that it's why I ran away from getting married. But that was then, and this is now, and it feels like pretty comfortable skin to be in to me."

Thirty minutes later, they sat down at the table to eat. Justin placed the rare steak on a plate and sat it on the floor. Perk zeroed in on it for a moment. His tail stopped wagging as if he were dazed. He suddenly snatched it up in his mouth and went prancing quickly out the back door. Justin and Michael looked at each other.

"What was that?" said Michael.

"I don't know. He must have thought I put it down there by mistake, and he wanted to get it out of here before I could take it back."

Michael laughed. "That's priceless. I've never heard of such a smart dog."

A few minutes later, Perk trotted back in, happily licking his chops.

Sunset wasn't more than an hour away by the time the dinner dishes were put away. They refilled the water jug so Michael could take a shower. Perk curled up on the ground next to Justin and they sat watching the changing colors in the western sky while Michael lathered his hair. After his shower, Michael sat on the ground beside them.

"We ought to pick up a couple of outdoor chairs tomorrow," he said.

"Why don't we pick up some redwood instead, and make our own chairs?"

"Of course. I didn't think of that," said Michael, the concept of making chairs so foreign to him he would *never* have thought of it.

"I'm serious," said Justin.

"I know, and that's what I mean? You're teaching me how to live."

"We'll stop in El Paso for the materials after we pick up your sister." That reminded Justin of how soon Jody would be there. He was worried about how her visit was going to go. "I have to say, I'm a little nervous about meeting her. I hope she'll like me."

"She will. But be prepared to listen to her pressure me into going back home."

"Could she talk you into it?"

"No," said Michael. He didn't see Justin's eyes close with relief.

"How long do you think she'll stay?"

"I don't know. If she's coming out here with an agenda, it wouldn't surprise me if she got mad and simply stormed back home. She'll try to make me feel guilty. Some women seemed to have a well developed skill for doing that. She'll argue that I'm wasting my talent as a doctor."

Justin picked up a small rock and examined it. "You are, if you don't find a way to use it."

"Don't team up with her, Justin. It may never happen. I feel utterly incompetent as a doctor. I'm not sure I could ever practice again. For all I know, I could be barred from it after all the inquiries are made."

"I'm sorry, Michael. I don't mean to add more weight on your shoulders, but I guess the people who care about you can't lose their confidence in your ability as a doctor. But it doesn't matter. Right now all you need to think about is what's happening in your life in this desert. Beyond that, we'll find a way to make your sister understand."

They watched in silence a great ball of fiery orange touch the peaks on the far western horizon. Those few light clouds across the sky took on a thousand shades of crimson, and the last remnants of light fell across the desert in golds and yellows like a silent poem that lay quietly over the earth. And soon the shadows melted into a vast black void as stars seemed suddenly born in the sky, and when the first howls from the coyotes came mournfully across the land, two men got back to their feet and walked into the house.

CHAPTER 10

The antique Zenith came to life with a sudden burst of static a few seconds after Justin switched it on. He stood patiently, moving the dial back and forth until the old radio picked up some distant station. The static had turned into the beautiful voice of Roy Orbison singing *In Dreams*. Justin turned his head and smiled. Michael watched him go to a kitchen drawer and take out a candle, and they walked together into the bedroom.

Justin placed the candle atop the chest of drawers and lit it, filling the room with flickerng yellow light. He turned, his back now toward the chest of drawers, his desire for Michael now a pleasant ache, and he reached down and loosened the towel, letting it fall to the floor, and took his own testicles into his hand. Perk had curled up on the floor near the electric heater. Michael had sat down on the edge of the bed, his eyes vital with desire. Justin stepped slowly forward and stood before him, the natural oils and perspiration on his chest alive with dancing candle light. Warm air still fragrant with their sex from the night before lay on their skin, and from the old Zenith in the front room came the elusive sound of Jimmy Reed.

Michael placed his hands on his lover's hips and pulled him closer. He leaned forward slightly, his lips so close they brushed swollen glans. On his next breath came the light scent of male musk. To his tongue came that distinct taste. His lips parted and slipped over the glans, his tongue exploring its shape. His lips then moved down the shaft and his hands came forward, taking the vulnerable egg-shaped organs between finger and thumb, kneading and pressing their meat, setting black flesh afire and broad nostrils flaring.

Justin's head fell back with a moan, his muscles seemed to go limp, and Michael maneuvered him onto the bed before his knees no longer allowed him to stand.

"Lay back," whispered Michael, and his lover obeyed like a small boy, and before him now was the fine definition of a male lover in submission. He sat on the bed beside him as his hand slid over the firm meat of Justin's leg. "We don't have to hurry," he said softly. "Your eyes and hands and mind have only a fleeting knowledge of my body. You know who you are now. You can love me with no inhibition. You can make love to me with all of your senses. What you know in your heart and your mind, you can now know with touch and taste and smell. Just relax my beautiful man, and let it all unfold."

Justin closed his eyes with a sigh, his hand resting upon his own chest. It rose and fell with each breath as his fingertips found a nipple. He stroked the small brown peak ever so lightly, and his docile eyes opened with a glaze of euphoria. "Michael, I *have* fantasized all day. I want to suck you. I fantasized about what it would feel like in my mouth, what it would taste like," he said, his breathless tone reflecting a new born carnal need. His raised arms drew Michael over him, both men lucid with anticipation.

Michael straddled his lover's chest and lowered his hips, allowing his cock to rest on full lips, feeling then a warm wet mouth. The sucking began tenuously, the tongue a bit shy, but the full lips soon released their years of denial, sucking with profound intensity. How he savored the presence of his lover's cock in his mouth, its push at the back of his throat. There came long sighs and grinding hips and wave after wave of pleasure. When he finally allowed the cock to spring free, he sucked Michael's testicles into his mouth, his tongue still hungry and lapping at the male taste. And then Michael pulled back, placing his hands aside Justin's face, staring into the depth of helpless dark eyes. Leaning forward, his tongue found the texture of full moist lips, and their passion grew with a long, probing and devouring kiss.

Michael moved closer to his ear. "We have to slow down a little," he whispered. "You almost made me come a minute ago."

"I wanted that to happen."

"Me too, but maybe a little later," Michael said, shifting his weight to sit beside him. "Wow. I still can't believe what you do to me."

Justin smiled. He enjoyed bringing such pleasure to the man he cared so much for. He laid back on the pillow, entwining his fingers behind his head, and asked: "Have you had any fantasies about what you'd like to do with me?"

"Are you kidding!"

"Then there's no time like the present."

Michael leaned into his neck to kiss the smooth black skin, the stubble coarse and prickly. His lips moved down over his chest and nibbled at the soft flesh and damp hair of his underarm, his passion inflamed by the scent and pheremones of male sweat.

Moving down over ribs and hips, his lips leaving a wake across his lover's radiant skin, his tongue aware of its taste. Michael reached down and the black cock filled his hand. Its full warmth in his grip brought a pleasant shiver to the back of his neck. A pearl of pre-cum appeared at the tiny hole and formed a rivulet down over Michael's fist, and he squeezed a second drip from the meaty shaft as his thumb caressed the slippery glans. When his lips came down over the pink glans and his mouth engulfed the tar colored shaft, Michael felt the warm glans deep in his throat, found himself lost in a state of floating.

The moment stretched, and Michael realized his lover's body had tensed. So quickly the black cock pulsed between his lips, so intently came the salty taste of semen spurting within his mouth. He swallowed and sucked harder and heard a loud groan as black fingers grabbed desperately at the sheet. He sucked from it all it had to give, and then Michael lifted his head and looked at the sweet agony on his lover's face, aching for him now more than ever.

"Roll over on your belly and spread your legs," he said, his tone hinting a sense of urgency.

Justin released a long, easy sigh, wondering if he had the strength to roll over, and of course he did. He knew what Michael wanted to do, and he was ready. He had thought about it all day, wondering if it was going to happen tonight. His body thoroughly exhausted and docile, he could only imagine that which would heighten this moment of pleasure, the feel of his lover inside him, and right now there was nothing he could possibly want more.

On his knees between Justin's legs, Michael eyes followed the thin spinal rift that ran down the middle of his back, and fell on two muscular rounds of gluteal flesh. His gaze lingered as his eyes absorbed the sensual mystery within the shadowy void. He saw resting on the sheet in the intimate shadows between Justin's legs the undying allure of male organs now spent. Michael's hands ventured over the textures of hairs and flesh, and through his fingers came the message that defined what compelled him to lay with a man. His hands gripped the firm meat, his thumbs pried open the void, and his eyes found and dwelled upon the inky black flesh; and there, centered within the damp heat and musk, flexing in anticipation, Justin's anus beckoned.

Leaning forward, Michael felt the damp heat come upon his face. Drawing his next breath, his nostrils flared as the sour male odor passed through his nose, igniting potent chemistry. With the power of ambrosia, the sensation streaked through him like tiny electrical pulses, sending tingles down his arms to turn his fingers into fists, and down his legs to curl his toes into tight knots. He licked at the dark flesh with unyielding desire, his nostrils drawing breaths of the musky drug, his tongue pushing hard to breach the impossibly small hole.

"Oh, Michael," came the soft tone of Justin's passive voice. He reached over and pulled open the night stand drawer, taking from it a small jar of vaseline, which he placed it on the bed.

Michael took a final deep breath, and a moment later there was a dab of vaseline on the tip of his finger.

"Oh God!" Justin groaned when he felt the first small push, the fingertip just barely inside. He felt a circular movement, a gentle stretching of the tight inner rim, and then a small stab. They were sensations far better than any pleasant dream or fantasy, and it took effort to keep his legs from coming together in response. His hips writhed as the finger entered him and he grasped again at the sheet, pulling it absently to his face as a pleasant warmth spread throughout his body, the finger probing deeper and deeper, now stroking the sensitive inner flesh of his rectum.

His own pleasure heightened by Justin's reaction, Michael felt the anal muscle begin to relax, as he knew it would. Then, ever so slowly, he backed his finger out, and Justin's hips lifted as if to encourage more. When his finger disappeared again, no more than the knuckle that joined it to his hand remained exposed. He paused, his finger as deeply inside his lover as it would go, withdrawing then again slowly. Struck by how different the sensations were in having sex with a man he loved, Michael realized he had never made love this way before: so carefully and affectionately, so utterly carried away, so much more aware of what he wanted to give as opposed to what he might receive. Now with a rhythm of in and out, with responsive black hips in sync, Justin's head turned from side to side as his anal muscle flexed hard again. From him came a long guttural moan when Michael pushed in two fingers at once. And eventually, with the gentle inner caress, just as it had with one finger, Justin's anus mellowed around two, gaping slightly and awaiting an altogether different, but imminent kind of violation.

The heat and odors of two men making love filled the room. They didn't plan it, nor had they expected it, nor could they believe it was happening to them, but they were falling in love. They were coming to know each other in a way only such intimacy would permit, their hearts growing interdependent. They had contemplated this night during most of their preceding day; and now, with each one of them in harmony with the other, the candlelight flickered on their moist skin, and their island of solitude was alive with hazy melodies wafting in from the front room. Justin continued to lay on his belly, keenly aware of the feel of Michael's fingers inside him. He felt within his bowels a yearning when the fingers withdrew. He knew he was ready and he rolled onto his back, lifting his legs and resting them on strong shoulders when Michael positioned himself between them.

His breath stopped when he felt the first nudge. He winced and grit his teeth when a sudden sharp pain seared through him. Michael's glans had pushed through. It came slowly, tenderly, filling him, the pain soon fading away like a chorus at the end of a song. His tight muscle relaxed as the cock pushed further into his bowels, its firm warm diameter sending such waves of pleasure that he felt light-headed. It came with a meaning he had not anticipated, this coupling, this giving himself to another man, a man who had entered his life and who now so intimately demonstrated his love. A light sweat lay over his face, and a pleasant calm shimmered in his eyes as Justin watched desire come into the glow on Micael's face.

There came a slow, wondrous rhythm, coupled with closed eyes, labored breaths and hearts beating hard. Michael wrapped his arms tightly around Justin's legs, pulling them closer to his chest, tilting his head and resting it against Justin's calf, lost in the sensations of discovery, this slow thrusting, this joy of making love to the man he wanted to spend the rest of his life with.

It formed in Michael's loins like a gust of unexplained summer wind. It swept through him, turning so quickly into a fury of passion. His thrusts became more urgent, his body in want of nothing short of that one inevitable end. Now pounding harder and harder, there came boundless waves of pleasure, tensing every muscle and fiber and sinew. His head fell back and with spasms spreading through his stomach and legs, from his throat came the sound of a guttural sigh. Aching for that moment which nothing else on Earth equaled, pushing harder and harder against Justin's haunches, his cock pulsed and ached for release. Michael tensed, clinging fast to Justin's legs, his body shuddering. The anus tightened upon the cock as it spurt forth its creamy white fluids deep inside his lover's warm bowels.

The spasms subsided as surely as they began, and Michael found his muscles drained. When Justin's legs came down, Michael crawled over and collapsed in exhaustion beside him. The effect had been their bonding. With the certainty of the sun rising at early dawn, two men were now one with their thoughts, their hearts and their souls and their bodies.

They lay in the heat of each others' arms, their minds in sync with all that lay before them. Their future would come with more passion and the tranquility of warm desert nights, a lifetime of dreams and long days on the river, a life free of superficial ambition, but filled with endless wonder. It was all so very simple— Justin had not blinked, nor had he been looking in another direction that day his eye caught the metallic glint off Michael's Jeep, that moment their wayward paths crossed. Yes, it was so abundantly clear, the answer to lost hope born for them from the unknown mysteries of fate.

By six o'clock the next morning, they were in the Cherokee on their way to the El Paso airport. They had had less than two hours sleep. Perk had protested mightily at being locked in the house, but Justin didn't want to leave him in the car while they were in the airport. The sky had turned from black to light gray and the sun's appearance was moments away in the east. Justin yawned.

"We sure didn't get much sleep," said Michael.

"I thought we weren't going to get any at all there for awhile."

"Think you could have gone one more time?"

Justin shifted his weight in the seat, squirming a little. "Whew! I don't know."

Michael looked over at him. "Are you still sore down there?"

Justin smiled. "Superbly sore. I hope it lasts all day."

"It all came pretty natural for you, didn't it?"

"It's hard to believe that was in me all these years and I didn't know it. Or maybe I knew and never understood it. I went to a bar a few weeks ago with a couple of the other rangers. A good looking Mexican girl came onto me pretty strong and I declined her invitation to go to her place. I laid awake most of that night trying to figure it out. I thought there was something wrong with me. In truth, I think I knew then. But now it seems it hit me like a ton of bricks the moment I walked up on you camping by the river that day."

"You tried to make out like a hard-nose ranger for awhile," said Michael, smiling at what already seemed like a distant memory. "But I felt the sparks too. There was something under the surface, something that was coming through your eyes, and I had the strongest urge to get to know you."

"Michael, last night, I felt it when you climaxed inside me. I never imagined anything could feel so wonderful. You pushed against me so hard I could hardly breath. I didn't know I could feel so close to someone. Is it so because that was my first time to know a man?"

"No. It was much more than that, Justin. It was everything you felt in your heart. You could sleep with a hundred men and not come close to what we shared last night, what we have together. And I envy you, because you don't have the burden of so much to forget as I do." He reached up to stroke the back of Justin's head. "I've wondered all my life what love feels like, and envied those who obviously have it. Now I know. I now know the peace of mind that comes when you truly understand the essence of life. Its power makes nothing else matter."

"Everything takes on a new perspective when you realize you have something to lose. I fear the day I wake up and not have you next to me."

Michael turned to look him. To prevent that day from coming was to abandon his life in California, a choice that seemed perfectly clear. "Don't fear that day, Justin. Can you imagine it possible that I could leave you? If you can, you can also imagine that I could stop breathing."

They sat in silent contemplation, turning north on the isolated two lane highway that would take them to Alpine. Miles of desert solitude fell behind as a new day spread over the earth, and on the console between them a black hand rested upon white. The windows down, fertile hints of Spring whispered over their faces on the wind, their shirts aflutter, their hearts calm. They had lived through a night of physical expression, a bonding of hearts and minds, of warm flesh and emotion that both knew very few ever find. It had been a perfect union of human chemistry, a merger in its rarest form, for they were synchronized in everything that mattered. They had begun a journey, their destination not yet clear; but they knew that wherever this road might lead, it would be traveled side by side. Neither could explain how it all happened so fast, for their instincts had led them and in their hearts they knew, that their promises had unfolded without question or doubt. They had set their stride toward the distant horizon, and they would discover together whatever might lay beyond that.

They drove into short term parking at the El Paso airport at eleven o'clock. By twelve noon, they had finished a casual lunch and were waiting near the base of an escalator, upon which Jody would descend. Then, among a sudden throng of passengers, she appeared, spotting them immediately with a broad smile and a small bag under her arm. She crossed the upper balustrade, heading with the others toward the escalator.

"She's a beautiful woman, Michael."

"I know."

"I'm surprised she's not married," Justin said, watching her descent. Her eyes were on him, and by the time she reached the ground floor, he felt that her analysis of him had already begun.

She laid down her bag and threw her arms around Michael. "I've missed you, big brother." She took one step back and glanced him over, and smiled. "So you still look fit. Evidently you've been taking care of yourself."

"It's the good clean air out here," he said.

Then her eyes returned to Justin.

"Sis, this is my friend, Justin Brooks."

She extended her hand. "Glad to know you, Justin. I'm Jody Anderson." She looked back at Michael. "Friends, huh. I'm not surprised, Michael. You've always had a weakness for chocolate."

Michael shook his head.

Justin had taken her hand. "And I a weakness for vanilla," he said in return. "And I've been looking forward to meeting the dynamic woman Michael has told me so much about."

She stepped forward and gave him a hug. "I have to warn you, Justin. I'm a hard person to get to like."

"I disagree. I like you already."

"Has my brother given you any indication of when he plans to return to California?" she asked directly.

"Sis, do we have to plow into all of that so soon?"

"I'm just curious," she said, then looked back at Justin. "Has he?"

Justin reached up and rubbed his jaw. "He hasn't mentioned it to me."

"Then that answers the question of when I plan to go home—when I find out when he's going back."

"Sis, that should give you plenty of time to get to know this part of the world. Now all we need to know is how long you can go without taking a shower."

She looked at him quizzically. "What on earth do you mean by that?"

Michael looked at Justin and smiled, then looked back at Jody. "You'll find out in good time."

They walked through the airport to the baggage claim area, where they stood watching the conveyor. Among the approaching luggage, Michael recognized his medical bags. He lifted them off the belt and looked at Jody. "Why did you bring these?" he demanded.

Her eyes were following the bags on the conveyor. "Justin, will you grab that black canvas bag? It's mine."

"Answer me, Sis."

"You forgot them," she shrugged.

"I did *not* forget them!"

"Oh. Well, now they're here."

Of course he knew she brought them to remind him that he was a doctor, but he decided it useless to make an issue of it.

They walked out of the airport and on to the Cherokee and loaded the bags. Justin sat in the back seat behind Michael. A few minutes later they were maneuvering back through El Paso traffic. Jody turned to look at Justin.

"So you work in a national park?"

"Yes. I'm a park ranger."

"And that's how you met my brother?"

"Afraid so. I had to run him off an illegal campsite."

"Then policy, of course, is to provide illegal campers with free room and board at your own residence."

"I told you she's blunt," Michael said over his shoulder.

Her grilling off to a good start, she proceeded with more. "Did he tell you he was gay before you offered him a place to sleep?"

Michael interrupted before Justin had time to think of a response. Jody looked at him as he spoke. "He found me camping where I wasn't supposed to be camping. We had a cup of coffee and some conversation. We got to be friends and since there were no campsites available in the park, he invited me to stay with him for awhile. Why would it matter if I'm gay?"

"It didn't matter," said Justin.

"I see," she said, turning back to him. "Then you're a straight liberal, like me. That's interesting, because you're cute as hell. You are straight, aren't you? Michael told me over the phone that you two are just friends."

Michael interrupted again. "Jody, for chrissake! Why do you have to be so damn nosey? Take a breath. Check out the scenery. We're driving through a city you've never seen before. Don't you want to see what it looks like?"

"No, because I want to get the picture between the two of you." She looked out the window for a moment. "I see a lot of cars, very few trees and no grass. Are you happy now?" She turned to Justin and winked. "I seem to have a habit of getting on his nerves."

"I bet you didn't know the city of El Paso has paid its residents to convert their grass lawns to desert-scapes," said Michael.

She looked at him incredulous. "That's very interesting, Michael." She turned to Justin. "Okay, to be fair, we'll start with me. I'm twenty-nine, maybe a little bitchy, hotter than hell in bed, well paid, independent, and I haven't found a fucking husband yet." She glanced between them, then looked squarely at Justin. "Now my cards are on the table. It's your turn, Justin. The question before you is: Are you straight?"

"I thought I was," he said.

"What?"

"I thought I was until recently."

She sat upright and stared out through the windshield. "Boy!" she said in exasperation. "Sometimes getting a simple answer is like pulling teeth." She turned back to Justin. "You thought you were straight until recently, and now what? You think you are gay?"

"Yes."

"I see. Did this revelation have anything to do with my brother's cute little ass?"

"That was part of it. But I don't think I'm gay, I know I am. I know now that I've been gay all my life and didn't realize it."

"And where does Michael fit in?"

Michael was tempted to jump in, but he realized Justin was doing well in holding his own.

"I love him," Justin said simply.

She released a long breath. "I guess now all the cards are on the table." Her voice had softened.

"Jody, that approach was pretty thoughtless."

"I'm sorry, Michael. I think it's because I've never been so worried about you. I'm getting a dozen calls a day from people wondering when you're coming home."

"Those people aren't really concerned about me," he said.

"Some of them are."

"Maybe. I suppose there are a few on staff who would like to see me happy, even if it meant I didn't return to San Diego."

They were entering the outskirts of El Paso. Justin pointed out a large home improvement center and Michael pulled into the parking lot. Inside the store, they began to gather the materials needed to construct two new chairs. By the time they got to the section stocked with redwood, their cart was half full with glue, screws, sandpaper, weather resistant stain, and Justin had thoughtfully selected two or three new woodworking tools. Jody and Michael stood back and watched him study the various cuts of redwood, staring at certain pieces as if he were visualizing it as part of the chair. They were both amazed by how meticulous he had been in everything they had purchased.

An hour later they were back on the highway.

Jody's curiosity was running amuck in her mind, but she knew it was a good time to back off, to not press further. She was in a car with a man who had just said he loved her brother. The word *love* had never been uttered in connection to any relationship he had ever been involved in. Now she ached to know exactly what that meant. Michael had clearly heard the statement and had not responded, and she feared something had taken place in his life that had enormous influence on him. Both men were silent, even a bit somber. She sensed they were reluctant to talk about what was going on, that they might be involved in something far more emotional than a quick sexual fling.

"It's kind of bleak here," she said, gazing out across the unfolding desert.

"Bleak might be one word you could use," said Michael, "but once you walk across that sand and rock, once you feel the sensation of sun and dry air on your skin, and sleep in a quiet you never knew existed, it's likely you'll choose another word to describe it."

The long miles passed with Jody and Justin in continuous conversation. Justin spoke of his childhood in Jasper, his drunken father who had abandoned the family when he was a boy. As if he were realizing some of his own history for the first time, he spoke of the continual tension he had felt while in school, those failed romances and confused attractions for other boys. He described in detail his long relationship with Christie, the awkward moments, which at the time he couldn't explain, and Jody was aware of the pain he still suffered in talking about what he had lived through on his wedding day, especially the part of how guilty he still felt by putting such a delightful young lady like Christie through that ordeal.

"Speaking of old girlfriends," she said, turning to Michael. "Shannon is one of those who have called me a few times to inquire about you."

"She hasn't decided that she hates me?" he said, glancing from the road.

"Hardly. She misses you. Considers you a friend. I think she's miserable in San Diego, but she can't bring herself to go back home. I'm supposed to call her as soon as I get back."

"I'm glad she doesn't hate me," said Michael.

Jody turned to face Justin again, and their conversation resumed.

She talked about her and Michael's father, a man limited by a rigid narrow mind, who saw the world in military black and white. Mostly, without a word about the little girl who had died on the operating table, she spoke of Michael's career. Justin had already assumed the dynamic of any surgeon's accomplishments, but in hearing the details that Michael himself had not wanted to talk about, he was beginning to understand Michael's unique status in the medical world. He also understood Jody's position that his career should not be abandoned. And because of this, he worried. He knew, no matter what Michael's frame of mind might be at present, that he would eventually be torn over his decision to abandon his medical practice. It was more than apparent he and his lover had embarked on a path that promised to be strewn with obstacles.

Jody glanced at her watch. They had been on the road for just over four hours and it had seemed like just one. She had been watching the amazing scenery they were passing through, on a road that ran up and down hills in hairpin turns along side the Rio Grande.

"This highway ranks among America's ten most scenic," Justin said. "The vast majority of the people in this country don't even realize it's here."

Contemplating her conversation with Justin, she already knew why Michael was attracted to him. She couldn't remember the last time she had met a man so sensitive, so quietly intelligent, and gay or not, so masculine. Beyond his flawless black skin and rugged good looks, she was fascinated by the air of mystery about him. She sensed an intellect that allowed him to reduce life to its simplest terms, that for him the superficial aspects of modern life had no value. Though he was a national park ranger on the surface, he also appeared to be a man who could look down on society's misguided aspirations with pity.

"Justin," she said, "I like you. I hope you like me, in spite of the way I came across when you first met me. I realize I was thoughtless. Truth is, I came here with a purpose, and that got in the way of my civility. Please accept my apology."

"Apology accepted."

"What purpose, Sis?" Michael asked.

"Let's talk about that later, big brother," she said. "Right now I'm getting anxious to see where you've been living these last few days."

"It's not far now," he said, glancing at her with a brother's enduring love.

A few miles before reaching the river town of Lajitas, Michael turned off the blacktop, onto the dusty gravel road that would take them to the old stone house. When he pulled off the road in front of it, Jody's eyes filled with enchantment. She stepped out the Cherokee in a near trance.

"This is incredible. There's nothing around it, not for miles. I can't believe this is where you live, Justin."

He wanted to amend her statement by saying this is where *we* live, but he refrained. He knew all too well her agenda.

Nor did Michael respond. He knew, if she found herself amazed by where they live, she was soon to be utterly shocked by *how* they lived.

They started toward the back of the house at the sound of Perk's muffled yapping. Rounding the southeast corner, Michael stopped and nodded toward a small wooden structure. "That's the outhouse, Sis. There's a few things you'll need to know before you go out to use it, especially at night."

Her eyes drifted from the structure to his face, and she smiled. "Go ahead, have a little fun with me. I can tell the house isn't big enough to have more than one bathroom, but don't try to convince me that I'll wake up in the morning with rattlesnakes in my hair."

She noticed Justin was looking casually at the ground.

Stopping again around the southwest corner, Michael said, "I know my credibility is in question, but for what it's worth, that's the shower."

She studied for a moment the water jug hung between two poles. She saw the soap dish nailed to one of the poles, the dangling rope, and the wash basin atop the weathered table. She turned back to him, her eyes wide with trepidation, and he smiled and nodded.

By now Justin had unbolted the back door. Perk exploded out in a frenzy of excitement, running circles around everyone's legs. "Don't you just love dogs," he said with a broad grin.

"He's wonderful," Jody blurted, dropping to her knees and slapping her thighs. Panting, his tail in furious motion, Perk's front paws were upon her lap in a split second. "I love him," she said, rubbing the dog with both hands. "So there's three males living in this tiny house." Perk had rolled onto his back, now enjoying a belly rub, all four paws straight up in the air. "I bet this one's not gay, are you boy? We'll have to stick together, you and I. We can't have these men ganging up on us, can we?"

"He's not gay," said Justin. "I saw him going after a female coyote a couple of weeks ago."

Michael laughed.

"See what I mean, Perk?" she said. "They'll give us a hard time if we don't watch out."

A few moments later, she took her first step into the house, stopping just beyond the threshold. Starting from one side of the room, her head slowly turned, her eyes taking account of every object in their wake. Enthralled, her survey ended in the kitchen. Her voice an almost unnatural calm, she said, "There's no bathroom, is there?"

"Everything you need is here, Sis. Just not all inside the house."

Justin walked over to look at Perk's food bowl. Half of the dry dog food he had poured into the bowl had gone uneaten. "I think I'll get him some canned dog food next time. He might like that better."

Michael had taken three cans of Tecate out of the refrigerator and placed them on the table. Jody took a seat and watched him slice a small plate of limes at the counter. After refilling Perk's water bowl, Justin joined her, taking a slice of lime when Michael set the plate in front of him.

"Your brother was also a little stupified when he first saw the house," said Justin. "Just so you're better oriented, there's two rooms, this one and the bedroom back there. No bathroom. That was the shower out there, just like Michael said. Unless you prefer going behind a creosote bush, you'll have to pee in the outhouse. There's no running water on the property, maybe never will be. We pump water from an underground well. No central air or heat. Other than a small electric heater in the bedroom, we use pot belly stoves to heat the house, but this time of year we're past those nights cold enough to inspire us to tote wood. The kitchen may look a little primitive, but there's not much worth eating we can't prepare right here. If you brought an electric hair dryer, there's probably enough electricity to run it, as long as there aren't too many lights on. Our gas comes from that propane tank out by the outhouse. The man who delivers the gas wanted me to put it there so it would be convenient in case he wanted to take a shit when he comes out to refill the tank. There's a pretty good supermarket in Alpine, and that's not much more than a hundred miles north of here." He smiled and added, "This place might be a lot more ostentatious than you were expecting, but I think you'll like it anyway."

Michael had never seen Jody listen to someone talk with her jaw open. Whatever it might be, he was confident her agenda was destined to be overwhelmed by what she was about to learn during the next few days.

CHAPTER 11

"Maybe I won't have to pee while I'm here," Jody said helplessly.

"Better not drink that Tecate then, Sis."

"There's only one bed?" she said.

"Yes," said Justin.

"And I assume you two have been sleeping in it together."

They looked at each other, then Justin answered, "For the last two nights we have. Now I can't imagine sleeping without him."

She glanced over her shoulder. "Well, that's pretty clear. Then I'll sleep on that couch."

Michael reached up to scratch the top of his head.

Justin spoke: "I've thought about this, and there's only one practical solution. We have one bed and one electric heater. The bed is large enough for all three of us." He looked down at Perk. "I mean all four of us."

Jody and Michael sat looking at him, somewhat stunned.

"Wouldn't that interfere a bit with your budding romance with my brother?" Jody said lightheartedly.

"Sis, don't be so damn flip about that."

"I really don't mind sleeping on the couch," she said.

"It's cold at night," said Justin. "And the fuse in here is too small for the electric heater."

"I'm okay with all of us using the bed," said Michael.

"Or Michael and I could sleep on the floor," said Justin.

"No," said Jody. "Let's try the bed. Actually, in thinking about it, I'm a little intrigued. Are you sure you two can restrain your carnal instincts."

"Sis!" Michael protested.

"That won't be easy," said Justin, "but I can always get up and take a cold shower if necessary."

"Why don't we change the subject to dinner," Michael suggested.

Justin glanced over at Perk's bowl again. "That's it! That's why he didn't eat much of that dog food today. He's hoping for another steak." He looked at Jody. "Michael is spoiling my dog. He gave him a steak last night."

She reached down and ruffled Perk's head. "He deserves it."

"He'll just have to live without steak tonight," said Justin. "I took a package of ground beef out of the freezer this morning. Anybody object to grilling some hamburgers?"

Everyone agreed. When Justin went out to light the grill, Michael got a tomato and onion out of the refrigerator and took them to the counter for slicing. Jody strolled casually around the room, absorbing the furnishings of what in her mind was pioneer living. She emerged from the bedroom a few moments later and joined Michael at the counter. He was forming the ground beef into patties.

"I didn't know you knew how to cook," she said.

"It's one of the things I'm learning."

She caught a glimpse of Justin walking out into the desert through the window. "What's he doing out there?" she asked.

Michael looked out the window. "Looks like he's taking a leak behind an ocatillo."

"Oh! Of course he is. Silly me."

"Well, Sis, what do you think?"

"Of what? This house or Justin?"

"Both."

"I like Justin. He's quite a package. It's not hard to see why you are attracted to him. But Jesus, Michael, it's all but impossible to imagine you living in an environment like this. But I guess I can see why it might be good for you for awhile. You can certainly get a lot of thinking done out here."

"I've been doing a lot of thinking," he said.

She looked at him with concern. His tone implied that he had also reached some conclusions. "What does that mean?" she asked.

"You'll see for yourself in time," he said, nodding at the plate of condiments. "Put that plate on the table."

She set the sliced onions and tomatoes on the table, watching him reach for dinner plates on the shelf over the counter. She had never seen him so calm. Aware her brother had found a world of mysterious and alluring fascination, she wondered what effect it all might have had on him. Why did he seem somehow different from the man she knew, so relaxed, so contented by slicing a tomato? Her agenda to get a commitment from him to come home suddenly seemed to be on very thin ice.

Justin entered the house a few minutes later, his arms full. He set her luggage and Michael's medical bags on the living room floor near the low table.

"Everything's ready to go," said Michael.

Justin picked up the plate of patties and they all went outside. Jody walked over to examine the jug and two poles while Justin placed the burgers on the grill.

"How do you fill the jug?" she asked.

Justin turned the meat and then turned to look at her. "We attach a hose to the pump in the kitchen."

She placed her hand on one of the poles and stepped under the jug, looking up at it. She then looked back over at the two men who were standing side by side, watching the hamburgers. She couldn't hear what they were saying to each other, but there was a clear magic between them. It was in their body language or something, she wasn't sure, but it was clearly there. Justin lifted one of the patties off the grill with a spatula, and their heads tilted in unison to smell the aroma of the meat.

A few minutes later, they were at the table customizing their burgers, and on their second round of Tecate.

"I have to admit, this seems like an enchanting way to live," said Jody. "One might even consider it romantic. But alas, I'm a city girl."

"Well, it's not for everyone," Justin said.

"So Justin, do you have plans for your future, long term plans?"

"I do. It has to do with this ranch. The man who owns it is a friend. He has fifty thousand acres in this parcel. I have a deal with him to buy a thousand acres of it, as soon as I put together the money. Two hundred, fifty thousand dollars." Michael as well as Jody listened with interest as Justin continued. "My property will include this house and run along that road out front and on down to the river." He looked at Michael. "I'll own that spot you and I went swimming at the other day." He took a bite of his hamburger and continued after a hard swallow. "That's why I haven't fixed the place up a little. I'm saving as much of my salary as I can."

Then Michael said, "I didn't know you were planning to do that, Justin."

"Do you like the idea?"

"It's the best idea I ever heard," said Michael, excited.

Jody glanced between them, a little astounded by Michael's enthusiasm. "I agree," she said. "It does sound like a wonderful goal. But what would you do with that much land?"

"Walk on it."

"Oh," she said dumbly.

The sun had set by the time they finished dinner. While Michael and Justin washed the dishes, Jody went into the bedroom to change into a pair of black silk pajamas. They went into the living room; Justin on the couch, his feet propped up on the low table, Michael in the over-stuffed chair, Perk curled up on his lap, and Jody took a seat in the hand made rocker.

"I never really thought about it before, but the desert is a beautiful place in a unique sort of a way," she said.

"I believe more so here in the Big Bend. I think it's because of the way the desert comes together with the river and mountains and sky. One time I was sitting on a rock formation just off the River Road, kind of like Michael was doing the first time I saw him. I was looking at a distant mountain range, daydreaming or something. I heard a song. It sounded like it came across the desert from those distant mountains, something like an ancient Indian flute whistling into the wind. I just sat there for a long time and listened to it." He paused in thought, as if his mind had traveled back to that day. "This country can give you chills. If you look close, the colors are never the same. The sun seems to find ways to cast a slightly different light each day, and the sky knows a thousand shades of blue. And the sunsets out here are so magnificent they can stop your breath."

Jody was still watching them closely, the way they looked at each other, the obvious nuances between them. She realized that what had taken place in this desert was far more substantial than what she had expected. She could no longer wait to find out exactly what was going on. "Justin," she said, her tone direct, "do you think you have fallen in love with my brother?"

"Yes," he said.

"How can you be certain," she asked.

Justin closed his eyes for a moment, then opened them with Michael in his gaze. Her question pertained to what he had already been thinking about almost constantly, and it would have been constantly had her arrival not been a distraction. He felt he had a pretty good idea of her personality, that she could handle the unedited version of how he was certain he was falling in love with Michael.

"I'm certain because for the first time in my life I don't feel lonely. It's finding someone who makes you feel alive. It's finding someone who helps you discover who you are, who makes you feel good about it, where you otherwise might have had a severe problem in dealing with it. Last night, he made love to me. It was an experience that answered a lifetime of questions. When I felt him inside me, I knew nothing could ever equal that moment. I just laid there, locked in his arms, wondering how something so wonderful could have happened to me. And it goes far beyond just that. It's having him beside me when I wake up in the morning. It's the scent of his skin in the sun. It's having him close by, even if he's just reading one of his novels in that chair over there. It's discovering finally that my life has a purpose, and what it's like to have a dream. It's looking forward to another new day."

Jody's mouth had fallen open. Her head turned slowly and she looked at Michael, who sat there with his head against the high chair back, his eyes softly closed. She felt a bit awkward in the intimate quiet that fell over the room, and then her words stumbled out. "Well … uh, I'd say we're getting to know each other quite well." She hesitated and looked back at Justin. "So tell me, Justin, are there any other single rangers like you over there, straight ones I mean?"

"I know one single guy. He likes drag-racing, and he's pretty good at cutting a wart off your toe in a bar if he's had enough to drink, but I don't really think you'd have much in common with him."

"Okay then, never mind." She looked at her brother. "I believe I understand it now, Michael. You're not planning to go back to California, are you?"

He opened his eyes and looked at her. "No."

"You really are in love with Justin?"

"Yes."

"I believe you. I've often wondered if something like this would ever happen to you, and it certainly seems like it has. I'm happy for you, big brother. But I have to say, this has come on so fast it must have felt like a slap in the face."

"I can't explain why it's happened so fast," said Michael, "but I think I knew on some level ten minutes after I met him."

"What are you going to do out here in this desert?" she asked.

His eyes shifted to Justin. "Right now, I'm thinking I'd like to help Justin buy this land." He watched Justin's eyes widen with these words, and then he asked, "How much do you have saved?"

Justin thought for a moment. "Well, I was lucky the last couple of years. Made a couple of investments that really paid big. Most of it's in mutual funds right now, mostly small cap stocks, and they've been pretty good, too. I have a little more than half the purchase price."

"How long will it take to save the other half?" asked Michael.

"I don't expect the mutual funds to keep paying so well, so five years or more if they don't hold up."

"If I put in the other half you could buy it right away," Michael said.

"That's a hard thing to ask you to do," said Justin.

"You don't have to decide now. Take your time. Think it over and decide later."

"Now that that's settled," said Jody, "what I meant, Michael, is that you're a surgeon. More than a surgeon, you're a miracle worker, and my guess is there's not too many hospitals down this way. So I'm asking, what are you going to do with your time out here?"

"I don't know. I haven't thought about it. But I *have* thought about what I left behind, and there's not much about my life back there I'll miss very much. Think about how you'd feel spending most of your time in meetings arguing with colleagues or insurance companies, or hoping you'll be able to pay next year's malpractice insurance. You're in some kind of a battle every time you turn around. Every now and then, worn out and demoralized, you find yourself in the operating room.

"You can no longer look at your patients as human beings—they're potential law suits. Doctors are getting sued into obivion, not because they screwed up a procedure, but because they didn't perform the miracle their patient expected. And then comes the day you really do screw up. You kill someone." Michael looked down at the floor, wiping away a tear with the back of his hand. He looked back up a moment later, and continued. "And if you live the life I did, you go out at night like a vampire on the prowl, but instead of blood, you're looking for sex." He looked at Jody. "You know what, Sis; I didn't go out for the pleasure of it; it was to keep my mind off the career you think I'm making a mistake in leaving behind."

She was almost too stunned to respond. Michael had never described his life as so helplessly lost. It was obvious to her now that these sentiments would have been difficult, if not impossible for him to face in California. It would have meant admitting that his life and future held no hope for happiness. Here, where he had had time to reflect, where the future seemed pure and full of promise, he had realized how disenfranchised he had been back home. When she finally responded, her tone was quiet and remorseful. "I'm sorry, Michael. I feel so guilty I wasn't there for you. All these years and I didn't know what was buried in your heart."

"Don't feel bad about that, Sis. Neither did I. Not really. I just knew something was wrong, but I never got to the point I could admit what it was."

"I came out here thinking I knew what's best for you, and this desert has absorbed it like a drop of water in the sand. I suspected the friend you described over the phone had become someone significant to you, so I was even brazen enough to believe I could convince him to return to California with you."

"You would have had better luck convincing one of these mountains to move to California," Michael replied.

She laughed. "Of course I understand that now." She sighed. "Oh Michael, I wish you had become an artist. You could have inspired people instead of heal their bodies, and not have suffered all that pain."

"Artists suffer pain in their own way," said Justin.

"Indeed," said Jody. "I suppose we all do in our own way. Mine now includes losing my brother. He's all I have."

"You haven't lost me, Sis. When things settle down, I'll come home on occasion. And you can always come back out here, for weeks on end if you like."

She couldn't help the tears. "I can't go weeks on end without a shower," she said, sniffling.

Perk jumped to the floor when Michael scooted forward to get up. Michael approached and got down on his knee before her. He took her hand and said, "I hate making you unhappy, Sis."

"You're not making me unhappy." She reached out and stroked his hair. "I love you, Michael. You've found a wonderful man and your lives together hold more promise than anything you'd ever find in California. I know you can be happy here. I just also know how much I'm going to miss you."

"I believe you'll eventually meet someone, too," he said.

"Eventually."

"You will, Sis. Keep your heart open to it."

"Let's change the subject."

"Okay. I'm glad you came. It's good you and Justin have had

a chance to get to know each other. But now that your agenda has been put to rest, I hope you're not going to turn around and go back home right away, just because I'm not going back."

"Not a chance. I made arrangements to be gone for at least a week."

Michael smiled. He stood and leaned forward to hug her. "I think I'll get us some more coffee." She watched him walk to the kitchen.

She looked at Justin and said, "I know you'll take care of him."

He smiled. "I will, and I'll never forget what he's done for me."

Justin had made the statement with such gratitude, Jody was intrigued. "I know of many things he has done for others, but you haven't told what he's done for you."

"Well, I guess I came out here with the state of mind Michael did, trying to figure things out. It seemed my whole life had been something of a challenge. I grew up facing the obstacles of being a black man in a small Texas town, where another word for black man is *nigger*. But for me, there was one more little problem— I'm gay. Even if I didn't know that at the time, it affected me subconsciously and kept me from having a normal life. Now another word for gay in a good many parts of Texas is *deviant*. Though I couldn't very well suppress my color, I did somehow manage to suppress my sexual orientation, even to myself, but the consequence was a constant underlying desperation.

"Then I met a man, your brother, who freed me from all of that. Every question festering in my soul was suddenly answered. What are the odds of that happening to me in this wilderness?"

Shaking his head, he added, "All I know is, I never want to face a another day without him."

"I must say, I love the way you express yourself, Justin," said Jody. "You have a way of getting through my hard head. I'm happy for you and Michael. I really am."

"Thanks, Jody. That's important. You don't know how much your support means to me, to both of us."

Michael refilled all three cups with what remained in the pot. Returning to the kitchen with the empty pot, he noticed Perk staring at the back door and he let him out.

"Perk's not the only one with the call of nature," said Jody, coming to her feet.

Justin stood up. "I'll walk her up," he said.

He reached for the flashlight as they walked through the door. She stopped just past the threshold, staring up into the black sky. "Oh my God!" she gasped.

"Beautiful, isn't it?"

"Where did all those stars come from, and how did they get so bright?"

"They're over San Diego as well. You just can't see them there."

She looked at him a moment, then turned her gaze across the immense void of the desert, eerily illuminated by the brightest partial moon she had ever seen. "I'm glad you're going to own this land. Michael was sincere when he said he wanted to help you buy it. Has he told you that he's wealthy?"

"No. He's never mentioned anything he owns, but I've had a feeling he isn't worried about money."

"What are you planning to do to the house?"

Justin's eyes lit up as his thoughts turned to his dreams. "I want to build a covered porch all the way across this back wall, a place to watch sunsets and watch the desert when it rains."

"That's a wonderful idea," she said, looking over her shoulder at the outhouse. "Have you considered adding a bathroom?"

"I will if you're planning to spend much time with us."

"No, I'll adjust. You watch me."

"Are you ready for your first adventure?"

"Let's go."

He pointed the beam of light on the ground where their steps would begin. "Walk behind me," he said, starting slowly. Perk pranced along in front of them. "When you come out here at night, walk slow. If there's a rattler in your path, a slow pace gives him time to get away."

"I knew that," she said, her hand locked onto his belt, her eyes glued to the path illuminated by the beam.

They reached the outhouse. Creaking when it opened, Justin held the door and looked inside, shining the light over every square inch. He then held the door open for her.

"Why did you look in there first?"

"No reason."

"Yeah, sure."

He handed her the flashlight when she stepped past him, then knelt to rub Perk's head while he waited.

The door creaked open and she stepped back out. "I believe I'll be able to handle this next time without an escort," she said, handing him the flashlight.

Justin went into the bedroom when they got back inside the house, re-emerging a few moments later with his arms full of soiled sheets. "Time to give these a little scrubbing," he said, walking toward the sink.

Jody looked at Michael. "I don't doubt that for a minute," she said, looking back at Justin. "Where do you keep the clean sheets?"

"In the chest, bottom drawer."

She went into the bedroom to remake the bed. Michael joined Justin in the kitchen.

Pumping the sink full of water, he said, "I sure like your sister. She's something."

"I was worried how she was going to take the news."

"I know," Justin said, swirling some detergent into the water with his hand. "Her concern about what you're going to do isn't misguided. It may be more difficult to leave your profession than you realize."

"Maybe."

"But you don't think so, do you?" Justin said, taking the sheets from the counter and pushing them down into the water.

"Is that how we wash our clothes?"

"Yeah. Here, try it. Keep pushing them down and turning them."

Justin stepped aside while Michael resumed the washing. "So you don't think it's going to be hard to quit?"

"No. I don't have a choice. I'm afraid of it. I don't think I could ever trust someone's life in my hands again."

"I think I can understand that. And there's certainly no reason to feel pressured to find an alternative. Maybe Jody was onto something a while ago. I could see you studying art."

"Or helping you do the things you'd like to do with this

place?"

Justin smiled. "I like that idea." He looked at the sudsy water. "Let the water out and we'll rinse them."

"Could take years."

"What?"

"Fixing up the place," said Michael.

"Okay, now you can pump fresh water while I squeeze out the soap." He continued while Michael pumped the handle. "It *will* take years. When the time comes, I'm planning to tell Bernard I want a four day week so I'll have more time to work on it."

Justin turned and squeezed the lump of sheets as fresh water ran through them. When the water ran clear, he wrung them out and they went outside to hang them on the line, Perk, as usual, watching with interest. "They'll be dry by morning," Justin said, looking at the moonlight on his lover's face. "You ready to turn in?"

Michael looked back through the door and saw Jody examining the rocking chair. "Looks like it's going to be a few days before we can …"

"I know," said Justin. "I'd say the anticipation will be acute by the time she's ready to go back home."

"Maybe we'll find an opportunity to sneak into Lajitas and get a room at the Badlands Hotel."

"Or disappear down on the river for an hour or so."

Michael laughed. "I can see it already. I'm sucking your balls and someone else you know floats by."

Justin shook his head, amused, and they went back inside.

"This is a great rocker," said Jody, looking up at them. "I've never seen one like it."

"He made it," said Michael.

"I'm certainly impressed," she said. "Something like this in a San Diego store would sell for two or three hundred dollars."

"Well, except for the mattress you just put clean sheets on, there's nothing in this house that cost more than twenty dollars. The couch and easy chair were already here. I made the coffee table and the table in the kitchen. Everything else came out of junk yards and salvage shops. That chest in the bedroom wasn't much more than a jumble of splintered wood when I found it, and I glued it back together. It cost six dollars, counting the glue."

"I like it all," said Jody. "It's perfect, in a masculine sort of way."

"You ready to turn in, Sis? You already know we didn't get much sleep last night."

She glanced between them, reminded of how Justin had described their nights together. "I feel like an intruder," she said.

"It's no big deal, Sis. Were you going to sleep in those pajamas, or do you want to go in and change before we come in?"

"Give me just a minute." She picked up her bag and disappeared into the bedroom, calling out a few minutes later. "You two can come in now."

They entered the room, Jody sitting on the edge of the bed in a flannel night shirt. They disrobed, hanging their clothes on wall hooks. Justin pulled on a pair of pajama bottoms over his white cotton briefs. He crawled into the bed and scooted to the far side by the window. Michael got in beside him, nude.

"Justin, don't you have extra pair of pajamas for Michael?"

Jody asked.

Michael looked at her, aghast. "You're kidding, right, Sis? You know I can't sleep in pajamas."

Jody shook her head. "Yeah, I guess I am kidding," she said, reclining on the pillow she had propped against the iron head-rail.

"Do you guys mind if I read awhile," she said, reaching for a novel she had placed on the nightstand.

"Won't bother me," said Justin, turning on his side to face the window.

"Me either," said Michael, on his side facing the same direction. His arm came from under the sheet and draped over his lover's waist. They shared the same pillow.

As much as she had always been a part of his life, she had never seen Michael even remotely intimate with another man. She never even tried to visualize it. Now, struck by the contrasting color of their skin, she couldn't help but stare for a moment. They lay quietly together, a closer proximity not possible, and she was surprised to find the visual quite beautiful. There seemed to be an innocuous purity to it, two men hopelessly lost in their attraction to each other, all in the face of condemnation by so much of society at large. No wonder they found solace in this remote place, for it provided them a haven far away from the torment of small minds.

By the time she had read the first few pages of the novel, they were asleep. Though she still felt the pangs of guilt, she was glad they had asked her to share the bed. She kept glancing at them, relieved to see her brother resting with such peace. She would take this moment back home as a memory, and it would comfort her when she thought of him, when she found herself worrying about him, when his absence descended over her like an ache in her heart.

She looked at him again, his sandy brown hair askew on the pillow, his nose pressed into the back of his lover's neck, their shoulders side by side. It was easy enough to understand his excitement in beginning a new life with Justin, that his excitement had displaced his love for healing the sick; but she knew, beyond all those elements of the medical world he despised, that in his heart he still loved it. She knew the day would come that he would wake up and find something missing, and that he and Justin could suffer a dilemma. For a man like Michael, the power to heal was a formidable and undeniable calling.

When her weary eyes fluttered, she reached over and turned off the light and nestled down into the bed, aware at once of the utter quiet in this desert of which Michael had spoken. It lay upon her face and calmed her soul, and the mad pace of a hectic life suddenly seemed a million miles away. Drifting toward her peaceful sleep, she was coming to know the same weightless peace that rested in the souls of the two men asleep beside her.

CHAPTER 12

Dawn broke with rays of morning sun warming Jody's face. The smell of frying bacon wafted in from the other room. She changed into a pair of jeans and cotton blouse and went in to find Michael whipping a bowl of eggs at the counter. Bacon sizzled in a large iron skillet on the stove, and a wisp of steam rose from the coffee pot spout. There were several pieces of bread spread on a cookie sheet and five or six oranges cut in half on the counter. The smell made her mouth water.

"You've learned to cook already?" she said, coming up behind him.

He turned. "Morning, Sis. Sleep well?"

"I don't think I've ever slept that well." She glanced over the preparations. "I have to say, I'm impressed."

"This isn't that difficult. It's timing. For instance, it's time to put that bread in the oven. Then you can squeeze those oranges while I cook the eggs."

She slid the pan in the oven and stepped back up to the counter. When she looked out the window, she saw Justin out by the outhouse, squatting over a bucket and splashing himself with water. Perk sat on the ground a few feet away, staring at him.

"My God! What's he doing out there?"

Michael looked out and grinned. "That's our bidet. I'm afraid he learned that from me."

"Looks like I might have a few more surprises in store this

week," she said, squeezing the oranges into a jar and watching Justin stand up to pull his jeans back on.

Michael put a small slab of butter into the smaller skillet next to the bacon, then poured in the eggs. Justin entered the room behind Perk.

"Good morning, Justin," said Jody. "You must feel fresh as a daisy."

He looked at Michael. "What does she mean by that?"

Michael shrugged. "I wouldn't know."

Justin stepped up beside her. "Good morning, pretty lady," he said, looking at an orange she had squeezed and set aside. "You're doing good, but you have to get all the juice out of them." He picked up the orange to demonstrate.

"Easy enough with those big strong hands," she said.

"You can set the table then and I'll finish this."

When she reached for the plates on the overhead shelf, he noticed her bare breasts against the soft cotton of her blouse. Aware of their feminine form and beauty, it was yet another confirmation of his orientation. The soft delectable shapes had no impact in a sexual sense, for it was firmer shapes and textures that bore stronger odors that did.

They were seated at the table a few minutes later.

"Well gentlemen, what are we going to do today?" Jody asked as she buttered her toast.

"We're going to build those outdoor chairs," said Michael.

"Another new experience for you," she replied.

"He'll be a natural born wood-worker by the end of the day," said Justin.

After breakfast, they washed the dishes, then unloaded the

assortment of redwood from the Cherokee. Justin sorted out the various sizes of wood on the hard desert ground and stood studying them for a moment, as if they were taking shape in his mind in the form of two chairs. Jody was folding the sheets she had taken off the line. Perk didn't seem to know who to watch. Michael looked at the pieces of wood with bewilderment, as if they were about to embark upon something far more complicated than heart surgery.

Justin unlocked an old wooden bin against the house, where his collection of tools were stored. Digging through it, he took out an electric drill, an extension cord, a small saw and some wood chisels. They proceeded with shaping the various boards into pieces which would fit together, sanding and sawing and chiseling holes for the joints, Michael looking on and following Justin's lead. The morning passed with the fine poetry of hands upon wood and the satisfaction of achieving a perfect fit. As the sun began to inch into the noon sky, Michael noticed Jody staring at the shower.

"You ready to give it a try, Sis?" he asked.

"Are you asking me if I want to take a shower?"

"Yes. I'll fill the jug if you're ready to try it."

Running her hand along her gritty forearm, she stared at the contraption with apprehension. Justin glanced up and smiled at her hesitation.

"I know you want to wash off, Sis, and it's unlike you not to step up to a challenge." Michael got up off his knees, then went over and climbed up the pole to take down the jug. Back on the ground, the jug under his arm, he looked at his sister. "Are you ready?"

"What are you and Justin going to do if I try it?"

"Well, Sis, we'll be right over there, working on those chairs. You can't fret about modesty out here in the desert."

A look of resignation washed over her face. "Go ahead, fill up the damn jug."

Ten minutes later the jug was back in place. Before going back to rejoin Justin and their project, he showed her how to work the rope. She sucked in a deep breath and began to unfasten the buttons of her blouse. Slipping it off her shoulders, she drapped it over the creosote bush next to the pole. With obvious reluctance she unfastened the jeans and pushed them down her legs, looking back up to see both men staring at her.

"I knew it!" she protested, standing naked with her arms folded over her breasts, still doubtful of her will to proceed. "I knew you guys wouldn't let me bathe in peace."

"You have to admit, Sis, this is pretty good entertainment."

"She *is* a looker," said Justin.

"Yeah, she is," said Michael, taking delight in his sister's modesty. "And with a body like that, I've never figured out why it's been so hard to get her married off."

"Go ahead," Jody seethed, stepping under the jug and taking a hold of the rope. "Go ahead and have your fun."

She pulled the rope, chilled instantly the moment cold water splashed over her head. She gasped and let go of the rope and ran her hands back over her short sandy blonde hair. Water ran down her shoulders and over her full breasts, rivulets glistening with sun down her belly and legs, streaming to the ground from the wet curls of her pubic hair. They were still watching when she opened her eyes.

"Okay," she said. "If you have to watch me do this, tell me what gay men see in looking at a naked woman. What is it you think about?"

"A guy doesn't think about anything when he looks at his sister, naked or otherwise," said Michael.

"What about you, Justin?"

"I see one of nature's great wonders. I think about my mother."

"Well good. If that's the case, maybe I can finish this." She grabbed the bar of soap and began to lather herself.

Michael and Justin went back to their work. By late afternoon, all three stood looking at two perfectly matched chairs. The high fan backs and wide wooden arm rests angled back slightly, to give their occupants a feeling of being reclined. They looked much like those popular wooden beach chairs of days gone by, inviting and in sync with the human form.

"I think Jody should be the first to try one out," said Justin.

She had watched in wonder as they fit the pieces together, using small screws and glue to hold them in place. As the form of a chair took place, she realized the unique reward a person could find in a world so uncomplicated as this west Texas desert. She stepped forward and sat down, and found the chair to be possibly the most comfortable she had ever sat in. It may have been because of their makers, their crafting in the sun, and so much that added to their significance. The chairs seemed to define the pure joy that had come to her brother's life.

"These are wonderful, Justin. I can see them on that porch you told me about last night." She looked up at him, now convinced he could do anything. "I can't wait to see what you do with this place."

"The main project will be a barn." He pointed at a spot about fifty feet behind the house. "Right over there. I want it to match the house, but the stone used to build the house came off the river bed, or at least that's the only place I've been able to find it."

"The river bed?" said Michael. "You mean the Rio Grande river bed?"

"Yes. You remember, when we walked across it, all those stones that were so hard to walk over. They're the same stones the house is made of. Same size and colors. I figure whoever built the house used an oxcart to bring them up from the river."

Michael pictured unending hours of lifting stones off the river bottom, lugging them ashore and getting them back through that narrow canyon, in which lay that stagnant pool of water and that rock formation they had had to climb over. "How will we get the stone through the canyon?"

"In back-packs," said Justin. "We'd have to build a ramp over that standing water."

Michael could picture it. Though it might take long days on end, he could picture warm sun on their shoulders as they took stones one by one from the river bed, toiling all day long with the promise of another night together. At once it became his dream, too.

Jody got out of the chair and said, "It's your turn, gentlemen."

Michael sat down first, satisfied with its solid feel and fine sanded wood. He leaned back, his hand gliding over the smooth surface atop the wide arm, and he thought about watching sunsets and hours of reading his favorite authors. When had anything that he ever owned equaled the value of these chairs? What material possession had ever provided such delight? His eyes followed Justin's form as he sat down in the chair beside him, and Michael could not resist reaching for his hand.

"We could start that barn pretty quick if you want me to help you buy this land," he said.

Justin looked at his lover, falling back into near disbelief of Michael's offer. That his dream could come to pass that suddenly was still too much to comprehend.

"If you want to own it by yourself it's not a problem," Michael added. "You could pay me back anytime you'd like."

"If we do it, I think we'd enjoy it more if we owned it together." He looked at the ground in thought, then looked back at Michael. "We would be making a commitment to each other."

"I know."

Justin hesitated, looking at his fingertips, a bit nervous. "So much has happened that seems too good to be true. I'm in love with you, Michael. I've found great comfort in having you in my life. You've given me the only truly important reason a man can have for living. How I feel when I look at you or hold you is beyond anything I thought I'd ever have. Is it really possible you feel the same way?"

"I think you already know. I think you know how much I would value making that commitment with you."

Justin drew a deep breath and smiled. "Then we should buy this land together. I'll contact the owner tomorrow."

"Just let me know when to write the check," said Michael.

Jody had collected the tools and returned them to the bin. She turned to see the two men stand and take each other in an embrace. She had listened to their conversation and her heart had filled with both joy and sadness: joy for the happiness her brother had finally found, sadness that she would miss him so.

An hour later they gathered at the kitchen table for dinner. The menu consisted of a salad and left-over pot roast. Perk happily devoured his share from a plate on the floor near the table.

"I believe this roast is actually better the second time," Michael said.

Toward the end of the meal Justin cocked his head as if he had heard something.

"What is it, Justin?" Jody said, laying down her fork.

"Someone is coming down the road. Sounds like they're maybe a mile away."

They sat quietly and listened. The outside air perfectly still, it was one of those nights the sound of tires crunching over a gravel road could drift across the desert for miles. After a few moments all three of them heard the distinct sound.

"Could be a tourist," said Justin. "Every now and then one of them will ignore the *Private Road* sign, curious to see where this road leads."

"Do they ever stop here?" Jody asked.

"Sometimes. Usually to ask directions."

A few moments later, they heard the car pull off the road in front of the house. Perk started yapping at the back door. Justin got up and walked toward it just as the room echoed with insistant knocking. Pulling the door open, Justin recognized Juan Gutierrez, a Mexican caretaker from the next ranch over, his face contorted with despair.

Concerned at once, Justin stepped forward and placed his

hand on the man's shoulder. "Juan, something is wrong. What is it?"

Standing perhaps five foot six in the crumpled clothes of a ranch hand, his thick hands fidgeting, he had difficulty with his words. Trembling, his words came in a plea of broken English. "My son, Señor, is terrible sick." Panic rang in his troubled voice.

Michael and Jody had moved from the table and were standing behind Justin. Perk was sniffing Juan's pants leg.

"Calm down just a little, Juan," said Justin. "Does he need a doctor? Do we need to take him up to Alpine?"

Juan closed his eyes, distraught. "My son has much pain and fever."

"Where is he?"

Juan nodded toward the front of the house. "With my wife in the truck."

Justin turned to Michael. "Let's go out and see what we can do."

The group hurried around the corner of the house and approached the battered old pick-up truck. Mrs. Gutierrez sat inside, their son curled in agony on the tattered seat, his head upon her lap. Justin opened the door and saw the boys' knees drawn toward his chest, his face sweating and twisted in pain, his mother stroking his hair and fraught with worry. Momentarily at a loss, Justin stared at the boy, his mind groping for something to do.

Jody pushed past him. The boy lay groaning in a tight curl, clutching with both hands his right side. She looked up at Mrs. Gutierrez. "How long has he had this pain?"

The woman's worried eyes shifted up to her. "He told me his

side hurt three days ago." She bit her lower lip, then added, "It got worse yesterday. Now this."

Jody reached forward and pushed the area just below the boys' stomach. The boy winced in agony and held his breath as if to suppress a scream. She looked over her shoulder, "Michael, I hope this isn't what it looks like, not way out here so far from a hospital."

Michael stepped forward and looked at the boy's hands. He placed his palm on the boy's damp forehead and felt the fever, then gently prodded the lower abdominal area with his fingertips, getting the same painful reaction as Jody had seen. He closed his eyes and stood up, suddenly alarmed by his own fear.

"What is it, Michael?" Jody demanded.

"Appendicitis," Michael whispered.

"We better get him on up to Alpine," said Justin.

Jody looked at her brother. "Is that what we should do, Michael?"

He stood staring at the boy, oblivious to her question.

"Michael!" she said sternly. "Should we take the boy to Alpine?"

"I don't think there's time for that," he muttered.

"Justin, help me get him into the bed." She ducked her head into the truck. "Mrs. Gutierrez, we're going to move your son into the house. Please don't worry. My brother is a doctor. He knows how to help him."

These words soaked into Michael's mind like a headache. A light sweat came over his face. At once, he felt helpless to care for this boy.

Jody and Justin had gotten the boy out of the old truck.

Justin carried him toward the house. Jody rushed ahead of him to turn on the light and prepare the bed. Justin lowered the boy, a tight little mass of agony, onto the cool sheet and Mrs. Gutierrez sat down beside him.

Standing just beyond the bedroom door frame, Juan looked up at Michael. "You can help my son, Señor?" he said. "You are a doctor?"

Michael looked down at him in a stupor, his eyes glazed with fear, and this made Juan feel anxious.

Jody stepped up and stood in front of him. "Michael, you know what you have to do, now get on with it."

His hands came up before his eyes. They were shaking. Staring at them, he muttered, "I can't … I can't do it."

"Oh for chrissake!" She turned and called for Justin. "Help me move the table in next to the bed."

Each of them on one end of the kitchen table, they maneuvered it into the bedroom and set it beside the bed. Now and then the boy writhed and cried out with a stab of pain. Jody went into the front room for Michael's medical bags, ignoring him momentarily in the process. She spread the surgical instuments on the oil cloth and then opened the bag containing drugs and supplies. She placed an array of bottles in neat rows along the back of the table, anaseptics, antibiotics and pain killers. She found a bottle of ether, glad there would be an anesthetic. After laying out an assortment of bandages, she looked around.

"He'll need more light," she said.

"I'll run the extension cord from the front room and use that lamp out there," Justin said.

"That'll have to do," she said.

When Justin went out to rig the lamp, Jody looked again at Michael, exasperated. He stood like a small boy who couldn't swim, who was about to be thrown into a lake. Mrs. Gutierrez was sobbing, holding her little son's head to her breast, the boy still clutching his side. Jody stepped up and stood before her brother again.

"There's no time to waste here, big brother. His appendix needs to come out, now! This is a piece of cake for you, and we have no choice."

He looked over her shoulder at the boy folded in his mother's arms, his eyes alive with grief.

"I said *now*, Michael!"

He took in a deep breath and released it. "Boil some water," he said.

He stepped forward and sat down beside Mrs. Gutierrez. "Ma'am, your son has appendicitis. His appendix is infected and there's a danger of the infection spreading if it doesn't come out. It's a common operation and if we don't do it, it's possible your son could die. But I need your permission to perform the operation."

Her eyes full of fear, she glanced at the instruments spread across the table. Though they frightened her, they also suggested the knowledge and skill of a doctor. She looked back at Michael and nodded.

"Then I want you to undress him while I get ready." He pulled the blanket off the bed and then went over to turn the electric heater all the way up. Sorting out the instuments he would need for the operation, he returned the others to the bag. "Boil these," he said to Jody. "This isn't exactly a sterile environment, but we'll take what precautions we can."

Justin guided Juan to the couch and sat down beside him. Jody gathered the instruments and Michael picked up a bar of antiseptic soap. In the kitchen, she dropped the instruments into the pot of boiling water. Michael took a pair of tongs from the drawer. "Use these to get them out. Put them on a plate and take them back to the bedroom. Right now, I want you to pump water over my hands while I wash them."

Back in the bedroom, Michael bathed his hands with alcohol. He soaked some gauze with ether and leaned over the boy, covering his nose and mouth. Seconds later the boy lay unconscious.

"Mrs. Gutierrez," he said, "your husband is waiting for you in the other room."

She looked down at her son with apprehension and came reluctantly to her feet, then walked out of the room. While Michael swabbed the the boy's stomach with alcohol, Jody returned with the instruments. Then Justin appeared in the door frame.

"Anything I can do?" he said.

"Watch after his parents," said Michael. "This shouldn't take more than thirty minutes."

Michael picked up a scalpel off the plate and looked at the boy, now quietly asleep and laying flat on his back. He placed the sharp edge on the brown skin below the boy's belly, exactly over the appendix, and let out a hesitant sigh. Then, with his well refined skill, he made the short incision. A trickle of blood ran from the cut, and for the next thirty minutes every movement of his hands came with mechanical precision. When he finally placed the last suture, he felt his heart beating once again, for this simple procedure seemed to have drained him more than any surgery he had ever performed.

He looked at Jody, who beamed at him with pride, and he released another long sigh. "Hand me that penicillin and one of those disposable hypodermic needles," he said.

"How long will it take him to recover?" she asked, watching him inject the boy's hip.

"He'll have forgotten all about it in two days."

"I'm proud of you, Michael."

"Thanks, Sis. I'm sorry I put you through that awhile ago. I just wasn't prepared for something like this to happen out here. I'm not sure if I could have done it if you weren't here."

She looked back at the boy. "This makes me wonder if there might be a shortage of doctors around here."

He looked at her.

"Word of this is going to get out: how you saved this boy's life. You'll have to be prepared for people who'll seek you out when they need help. It would be a good idea to decide on what you're going to do when they come."

He looked down at the floor. Jody was right. He felt a sudden, unwanted weight of responsibility, and he wasn't at all sure how he planned to deal with it.

"You're a doctor, Michael. You will be until the day you die. I have complete faith in your love for Justin, and you may find yourself suited for a life in this desert, but I'm not sure I'm ready to believe you can walk away from your true purpose. If you are indeed suited for this part of the world, if you truly need what you've found here, you might find it needs you too."

"Sis, please, I don't want to talk about this right now."

"Just one more thing and I'll shut up."

"What is it?"

"Justin might be thinking the same thing."

"Has he said something?"

"No. But don't you think it would be natural for anyone to consider it a regrettable loss if you don't use your incredible talent? Call it a woman's intuition, but I bet Justin is as worried about you as I am. There are some things you can't bury, or just walk away from. I suspect Justin knows that, too."

"Are you trying to convince me I can't be happy out here?"

"Lord no. You've convinced me of just the opposite. I envy what you've found out here. I've never seen two people more perfectly suited for each other than you and Justin. I watched you two making those chairs. I've never seen anything like it—the way you looked at each other. Shit! There were a couple of times it was like time had stopped for a moment. I saw a interaction so vibrant it seemed to fill this entire desert. What I'm telling you is: that you'll never be completely happy if you try to abandon your medical practice. You might not feel it now, but eventually it'll start to gnaw in your gut." She looked again at the little boy. His eyes had started to flutter. "Look at him. You've become one of the most important people who ever touched his life. He has a future because of you. And you know there'll be others out here who'll find themselves in similar predicaments."

Michael stepped over and sat on the bed beside the boy. "Did you find out what his name is?" he asked.

"Julian."

"He's a beautiful boy, isn't he?" Michael said, examining the sutures. Then he reached up to check his forehead for fever.

"He looks like his mother," Jody said.

"Hand me that stethoscope." Michael put on the ear piece and listened to the boy's heart. "He's strong." Julian's eyes fluttered open and he stared at Michael, slightly dazed. "Call in Mrs. Gutierrez. I want her to give him a pain killer. Get him a glass of water while your out there."

The boy's mother rushed into the room. She stood in amazement for a moment as her son looked at her, a calm smile forming on his innocent lips. Michael moved out of the way when she came forward to sit down beside him. She examined the small body in disbelief. Julian lay perfectly still, his pain miraculously gone. Her eyes dwelled for a moment on the small sutured incision, then shifted back to Michael, as if her eyes had fallen upon a holy saint. He smiled with a touch of humility and handed her the pill. Jody stepped forward with the glass of water.

"We don't want to move him tonight," said Michael as Julian swallowed the pill. Then his mother lifted his head so he could take a swallow of water. "He can sleep right there. I'll move a chair in from the other room if you want to stay with him. Help him stand up if he has to urinate. We'll bring in a jar for that. I'll come in later to check his vital signs. You can take him home tomorrow, but he'll have to take it easy for a couple of days. He'll be back to normal after that."

Michael turned when he heard the thick Spanish accent of Juan's voice. "Señor ... you have performed a miracle for my son." Staring at him in awe, the weary ranch hand stepped forward and took his hand and kissed it.

He had received gratitude from his patients and their families many times before, but this time it struck a raw nerve. Then he thought of the little girl's parents in California, of the loathing they must feel for him.

Justin had been watching from just inside the door. He approached as Juan joined his wife. He leaned close to Michael's ear and whispered, "He's right, you do perform miracles. You're an incredible man, and I'm getting anxious to have you alone for awhile."

A pleasant chill came to the back of Michael's neck as he watched Justin scan with interest the instruments that lay spread across the table. Jody had stacked the bloody instruments on the plate. She was repacking the supplies into the medical bag. Juan turned and abruptly walked out of the room, and they heard the back door close when he left the house.

"He'll come back in a little while," said Mrs. Gutierrez, observing their bewilderment.

Jody took the soiled instruments into the kitchen for boiling while Michael and Justin returned the table to its place. Then Michael sat down. Justin joined him a moment later with three cans of Tecate.

"How do you feel?" he asked.

"I'm fine."

"I was a little worried about you there for a while."

"I wish I could explain it," said Michael, taking a sip of beer.

"You don't have to explain anything. Fact is, you were able to do it. What else matters?"

After moving the rocker into the bedroom for Mrs. Gutierrez, Jody sliced a lime and joined the men. Perk was standing in the bedroom door looking at the strangers on his bed.

"Juan left rather suddenly," she said.

"They have other children," said Justin. "He might have gone home to check on them."

Michael looked at Justin. "Hope you don't mind giving up the bed tonight. I didn't want to chance letting Julian go home yet."

"Of course not. We can sleep on the floor in here."

Jody looked across the room, at the floor. "Well, if it's all the same to you boys, I think I'll sleep on the couch."

Justin noticed Michael staring at the wall, a distant look in his eyes. "Are you sure you're all right?" he asked.

Michael looked back at him as if he had rejoined the group. "Yeah, sure. I'm fine."

"You had a hard time cutting the boy open, didn't you?"

"Yeah, I did."

Justin wanted to take him into his arms; instead, he reached out and took his hand. He held the soft hand delicately in his own hands, caressing the palm with his thumbs. He leaned forward, lifting his lover's hand to the side of his face, closing his eyes. "Heaven help me, Michael, I wish to God there was something I could do to help you heal. Your anxiety is an ache in my chest."

"If I could just understand why I've lost confidence in myself. When I put the ether to that little face, all I could think about is he won't ever wake up again. It was like having to ignore a never-ending nightmare while I was taking the appendix out. It was a battle to keep pushing it out of my mind."

They sat quietly for awhile, finishing the first round of Tecate. Jody got up to let Perk out the back door, then brought three more cans to the table. A few minutes later, they heard

Juan's truck come to a stop in the front of the house. When Justin opened the door, he smiled and moved aside as the Mexican stepped just over the threshold with a goat tethered to a rope.

Perk rushed back inside, not at all happy with a goat inside his house. He barked somewhat half-heartedly, as if he wasn't quite sure what this business meant. There was also a rather heavy quilt draped over Juan's shoulder. Michael got up and stood at Justin's side. Juan looked up at him, handing him the blanket and the end of the rope.

"For you, Señor," said Juan.

Dumbstruck, Michael looked at Justin.

"He's paying his doctor bill," said Justin.

Michael's reaction was to take the blanket. He stood staring at it, his mouth open.

"My mother made the quilt before she died," said Juan.

At a loss, Michael's instinct was to give it back, but before he could do anything, Juan was trying to get him to take possession of the goat by handing him the rope.

"I … uh … "

Justin saw at once that Michael didn't know what to do. "Hang on to the blanket," he said, tilting his head to look at the goat's underside. "But the goat. That's one of his milk goats." Justin put his hand on Juan's shoulder. "How many of these goats do you have, Juan?"

"Three … now two."

"You'll have to pay with something else. The doctor won't take a goat that's used for milk for your children."

A look of concern washed over Juan's face. He seemed to be considering his possessions, trying to decide what might be appropreiate compensation.

"Don't you have any money, Juan?" said Justin.

The hard-working man dug into the pocket of his faded over-alls and pulled out three crumpled one dollar bills. He looked at the money, then extended it to Michael.

"That ought to be about right, don't you think, Michael?"

Michael looked at the money and smiled. It was the first time he'd ever felt such emotion as a doctor. He nodded, and took the money and pushed it into his own pocket, and a huge smile of relief spread across Juan's face.

Perk had crept up close to the goat, his neck strained as he ventured his nose toward the goat's haunches, careful not to get too close.

"Would you like a Tecate, Juan?" Justin asked.

"No, Señor. I must return the goat and see to my children."

Justin nodded and Juan pulled the goat back out of the house, much to Perk's satisfaction. The dog went straight to his food dish to make sure no ungodly creature had dared mess with it. Justin closed the door and returned to the table. Michael walked in a daze to the couch, sitting down, staring at the quilt in his arms.

"Since we're sleeping on the floor, it's a good thing he paid you with that quilt," Justin said. "The only one I have is on the bed."

"That's a first, huh, big brother? No insurance forms, no endless itemized billing. I'd say without all of that, a doctor could afford to work for less."

Staring at the quilt, Michael said, "I've never been paid so well in my life." He looked over at them. "I can't believe he was going to give up his goat."

"He'll feel guilty for cheating you, but he'll get over it," said Justin.

Jody watched her brother, struck by how the quilt had affected him. It dawned on her that the quilt had more power to bring him back into his medical practice than any of her arguments could ever have.

Michael laid the quilt on the couch as if it were the golden fleece. He then joined them at the table. When they finished their second Tecate, Michael went back into the bedroom to check on Julian. Mrs. Gutierrez sat in the rocker beside the bed, holding the boy's hand while he peacefully slept. She watched the doctor step forward and stare into the boy's face for a long while, saying another silent prayer for the benefit of having this man here when she so needed him. The he looked at her with a nod of reassurance and smiled, and it was all she could do to hold back her tears.

CHAPTER 13

Justin had pulled the low table aside by the time Michael returned to front room. He had spread the sleeping bag over the thread-bare rug, and was now standing with chin between finger and thumb, looking down at the makeshift bed with apprehension. Jody had spread Michael's new quilt over the couch.

"Sorry, big brother, but I'm going to use this blanket. I figure you two can keep each other warm."

"It's okay, Sis."

Justin looked at him. "At least we'll have the rug and sleeping bag between us and the floor. Is it all right if I go in there and get a sheet and one of the pillows?"

"Sure," said Michael. He noticed Jody's portable alarm clock on the end table near the lamp. "Sis, set your alarm to go off at two o'clock. I want to go in and check on Julian before tomorrow morning."

Moments later, Justin returned with the pillow and sheet. Michael sat on the floor and pulled off his sandals and shirt, tossing them on the over-stuffed chair. Jody had stripped down to her panties. Standing with her back to them, she picked up her night shirt and pulled it over her head. She turned and sat down on the sofa, pulling on now a pair of heavy wool socks. They were a pattern of colorful stipes that went nearly to her knees. She noticed Justin looking at her.

"Sexy, huh?" she said, rubbing them smooth on her calves.

Yes, very, he thought, though he knew meant the socks. He smiled. Living in a city inhabited by God knows how many men, he still couldn't understand why one of them had not snapped her off the market.

"My feet got cold last night," she said, sitting rather unlady-like in the short nightshirt with her legs parted. "They won't tonight. Not with these socks on."

Justin averted his eyes, glad she felt so comfortable around him. Both of the Andersons in his house seemed immodest to him, his upbringing having been fairly narrow, but he found their lack of inhibition refreshing. He found it made the household more comfortable, and he liked it. He slipped out of his jeans and got under the sheet beside Michael, not bothering with the paja-ma bottoms.

At odds with the sleeping arrangements, Perk had gone back to the bedroom door frame and stared a while longer at the strangers in his bedroom. The room was quiet, except for the radio. The old Zenith had picked up a strong signal out of Alpine, so Justin had left it on low volume so they could listen to some static free music while it lasted. Jody had resumed where she left off in her novel. Michael seemed deep in thought. Laying on his back, Justin propped his hands behind his head and stared at the ceiling. He knew what Michael was thinking about, the Gutierrez boy, and the fact he had cut into him tonight; and Justin wondered what perspective would come of it in Michael's mind.

A break for the news interrupted the music on the radio. As the static began to creep back into the speaker—Justin figured it had something to do with atmospheric conditions—they listened to the weather report, which was to be a duplicate of the day that had just ended; and then the announcer relayed a story about a convict who had eluded the police in Alpine, a convicted serial killer. The state police and highway patrol were on high alert and had set up roadblocks in an effort to recapture the killer.

"That's all we need out here," said Justin, getting up to turn off the radio.

Back in bed, he lay beside Michael. They turned onto their sides and lay back to back, their heads on the pillow, both men aware of their proximity and body heat, both wondering if there was any credible possibility of falling asleep. They lay quietly in thought—it had been remarkably eventful day.

Justin thought of new chairs. Though he had always enjoyed the gratification of crafting his own furniture, he never knew the pure satisfaction he found in making the chairs with Michael. They were at once his most prized possession; and in that he shared them with someone he loved endeared him all the more. Laying close so he could savor Michael's warm body against his back, his heart beat with awe for the miracle Michael had performed for little Julian Gutierrez. That this amazing man had come into his life was beyond good fortune, that he had now touched someone else's would serve to make him a saint to the folks around Big Bend.

Michael still felt tense. The bedroom had not been all that warm when Michael first picked up the scalpel, yet his forehead had broken into a sweat at that exact moment. Jody had blotted his face several times during the brief procedure; and now, in just thinking about it, his face felt wet again. Much like that first time his hand directed a knife through those few layers of living flesh, this time with Julian Gutierrez it was even more unnerving. Back then, he had been nervous, but he was also self-assured. He had picked up the thin blade with the conviction of a cocky young physician who had set out to conquer the medical world. Tonight, he had felt like a coward, and he lay desperately wondering if this haunting emotion would ever subside.

They lay close into the night, and after awhile the warmth of Justin's body began to have its soothing effect. Michael's teeth were no longer so tightly clenched. His breath again came soft and easy, the phantoms had finally melted from his mind. He had relaxed and the pillow felt good against his cheek, and his thoughts began to unfold like dreams. What else really mattered now that he and Justin were together? It almost frightened him to think about the small decisions he had made that led to their crossing paths: that beckoning sign on Interstate Ten, choosing the River Road, finding a campsite not so remote that Justin had spotted him on the river; for any other direction he might have taken would have been most certainly a lonely road. Now they lay together on the floor a few feet from his sister. Though he loved her more than he could describe, just this moment he would have paid any price to not have her there.

She reached up and turned off the light an hour later. Both men lay in silence, still wide awake, their thoughts on the same path. It was pitch dark when they heard the light sound of her snoring. Another half hour had passed.

Aware of his lover's shifting of weight, Michael opened his eyes, seeing little more than when they were closed. He felt the rough texture of Justin's hand running from his shoulder down his arm, and his eyes closed again. Laying perfectly still, he felt the hand move from his arm to his hip, and then came the warm breath of a whisper on his ear.

"She's asleep, Michael. I've lain here for almost two hours thinking of nothing but how much I love you. Let's take this sleeping bag outside for a little while."

Gooseflesh spread across Michael's forearm.

They got quietly to their feet. Justin lifted the sleeping bag from the floor and they crept toward the door, Perk dashing ahead of them when Justin opened it. Hand-in-hand, two men walked together in the moonlight, stepping tentatively some fifty yards into the desert, where Justin spread the sleeping bag on the crusty earth.

As Perk explored and sniffed out the area, they sat down together. Justin's hand came up behind Michael's head, drawing it close. Their lips came together in a long, lingering kiss, and then Michael reclined.

He felt Justin's hand travel down his leg, brushing lightly over the fine golden hairs, then back up through the heat of his inner thighs. His thigh muscle tightened as the hand came up between his legs, his fingers finding the recess of damp anal flesh. There came sensations from just behind Michael's balls, a light caress of the fine hairs and sensitive skin. He knew instinctively what Justin wanted. He rolled over, his stomach now flat on the sleeping bag, his legs acquiescently parted. He shuddered, the intimacy so charged with pleasure. Bathed in the fresh cool air and moonlight of a desert night, how he yearned to give himself in any way to this man he loved, and in doing so receive pleasure he had never known, these intimate moments between two men. He drifted with the lingering caress as it neared and then stroked the small hole. His anal muscle tightened and his hips lifted slightly in reflexive response.

In the tranquil sphere of lovers so close, Michael lay calm and stress free, his tight muscle now relaxed, and he squirmed as the finger began to find its way inside him. It felt slippery, and Michael wasn't sure just how, but he assumed Justin had produced and found a use for a drop of his own semen. A warm feeling spread through his bowels and belly with this slow breach, as his lover's finger found new depths. Michael closed his eyes, letting go a soft gasp, and the sweet scent of the desert mingled with male sweat came to him like notes dancing from the strings of a fine harp. He knew it had been just a matter of time before Justin would find himself drawn to the mystery of anal sex, and so it was to happen between them now. The finger had found his prostate gland, stroking as it might the head of a small bird, confirming the fact that Justin was born with the instincts of a most sensual lover.

The sweet ache between Justin's legs became acute as Michael's heat engulfed his finger. The muscle flexed as he pushed it deeper. Forbidden by those who could never know or understand the essence of men with like minds, Justin felt his lover's anus dilate around his finger, his body's entrancing, unspoken reply. How he relished the pleasure it gave them both. His finger slipped in and out, probing and exploring the fleshy walls, so warm, so moist and slippery his lover felt inside, so anxious were his yeilding hips. Justin's lips neared the sinews of his lover's neck, imparting kisses alive with adoration and lust. Slowly he withdrew his finger, passing his hand before his face, his nostrils flaring as the scent of Michael's bowels leapt into his nose.

Beguiling, the anal scent beckoned like vapors of a carnal ghost, setting sleeping cells afire, and sending shivers across a full landscape of black flesh.

Under the endless void of a black desert sky and a perfect dreamlike quiet, Michael came up on his knees. Through loving hands came messages from the man mounting him from behind. Gone was the trepidation of a harrowing night. Gone was all awareness of tomorrow. Again the warm breath came to his ear, a whisper so soft it passed through his thoughts like a fleeting dream. "Michael … I love you so. You make me feel like I own all the world's riches. Relax and stay as you are. Let yourself go. I want you more than you can possibly know."

Every fiber of his body now alive with tingles of desire, Michael felt a gentle nudge. He held his breath and bit down on his lower lip. He felt the breach, the warmth filling him, his lover's arms coming around him and holding him tight, and the stabbing pain soon melted into a wonderful contentment. There came that natural motion to Justin's hips, that growing state of tension, that resolution that neither of them would ever again have to deny. And finally, locked in tight embrace, they found themselves laying side by side in the cool of night with no need of spoken words, contemplating yet another discovery.

Jody's eyes opened with the morning's first light. She cast her sleepy gaze toward the two men asleep on the floor. She sat up, amazed as ever that two men could love each other so, their arms and legs entwined; and she reached for the night shirt she had taken off in the middle of the night and had draped over the back of the couch.

Laying on the floor near the men's feet, Perk lifted his head when she stood. The dog stopped at the back door as they approached the kitchen, and Jody opened it to let him go outside. Stepping toward the other side of the room, she peeked through the bedroom door. Their guests were both still peacefully asleep: Mrs. Gutierrez slumped in the rocker, Julian sprawled upon Justin's bed.

Still amused by the practical simplicity of the kitchen, she prepared the coffee pot for the morning's first brew and plugged it in. The creaking handle on the water pump and the smell of fresh coffee failed to wake anyone up. After finding a jar of powdered creamer in the cabinet, she poured a cup of coffee and went outside to sit in one of the new chairs.

The sun, still a fiery yellow ball, had just topped the mountain peaks on the eastern horizon, and a soft morning light had fallen across the vast land. Perk trotted a broad circle behind the house, sniffing the ground for recent intruders and lifting his leg from time to time on clumps of agave plants. She took a sip of coffee, savoring its agreeable effect, aware once again of the reflective sentiment inspired by this mystical land. Scanning the distant terrain, she listened to the quiet, for it lay over the barren earth like a silent song. Though she soon had to go back to California, she knew it would be easy to return, and she also knew that Michael would never go back home. At least now, when she missed him, she could visualize he and Justin waking to mornings such as this, and knowing that he was happy might serve to lessen the heartache of his absence.

When the coffee in her cup was half gone, the sound of a distant car wafted across the land. She listened as it grew nearer on the gravel road. How it carried across the stillness as if it were the only sound being made on the face of the Earth, unfettered by time and space, dissolving finally so far away. How she marveled at being aware of such a small thing, that her imagination could conjure a thousand stories as to why a solitary car might venture down this road. She took another sip, and it dawned on her that this was the finest coffee she had ever tasted in her life.

The car continued its approach. Startled, Jody heard it pull off the road in front of the house. Frozen in her position in the chair, she heard a car door slam, followed by heavy footfall crunching over the hard earth. A few feet away, Perk stood alert, his eyes locked in the direction of the sound, a restrained huffing woof blew from under his chops.

"That damned dog!" came the impatient growl of a man's voice as he rounded the corner of the house.

Jody, unnerved, attempted to come to her feet but found her knees locked. Staring wide-eyed at the man, she set the coffee mug on the arm of the chair.

The man, rotund in size, spotted her and stopped abruptly in his tracks. His eyes swept over her in bewilderment.

Her heart calmed with quick perception of his innocuous demeanor and befuddled eyes, a man in a rumpled uniform, the overhang of his belly stressing his belt. Perk's alert stance had turned to tail-wagging anticipation as he stared at this obvious acquaintance. The man lifted his hat and ran his hand back over his thin hair, looking for something to say.

"Hello," Jody said calmly.

"Uh … didn't mean to walk up on you that way, Ma'am. Sorry. Just stopped by to see Justin."

She had already assumed that.

He stepped toward her, nodding as he passed, and continued toward the back door. "I suppose he's inside the house," he said, reaching for the door handle.

Instantly alarmed by the man's intention to enter the house without knocking, the image of the entwined bodies of two men on the floor flashed through Jody's mind. She came quickly to her feet, groping for words to stop the intrusion. It was too late. The door swung open and the man stepped inside, again stopped in his tracks. Staring in disbelief at what he had walked in on, his face twisted into a combined expression of stunned indignation and embarrassment. Jody stepped in behind him and peeked around his ample girth, and there lie those contrasting colors of male flesh.

Apparently the sound of the car had awaken Mrs. Gutierrez. She stood in the bedroom doorway, also staring with a similar befuddled expression. The man looked over at her, then back at the men on the floor.

Now resigned to a world of utter mortification, Jody took a deep breath and slammed the door to awaken Michael and Justin. She crept over to the kitchen table and slumped into a chair, watching two bodies stir to consciousness. They untangled themselves and Justin sat up first, yawning. At once his eyes widened on their visitor. Speechless, he glanced over at Mrs. Gutierrez, then down at Michael, who still lay semiconcious with sleep. Michael's hand came up and stroked the back of his head, just as Justin blurted:

"Bernard! What are you doing here!"

Michael stiffened. Instantly alert, his head popped up and his eyes darted about the room. It took only a moment for it all to sink in. He scrambled clumsily for his jeans, exposing his nudity for a split second before jerking the sheet back over his waist.

Now Jody knew who the man was: Bernard, Justin's boss. Feeling responsible for this predicament, she looked helplessly at the chief ranger, his shock still etched on his face as he glanced from the men on the floor, to her—the unknown woman at the kitchen table, to the Mexican woman he knew to be Mrs. Gutierrez, as if he were trying to make some sense of what his eyes were telling him.

"Goddamn you, Bernard! Just walk into my house like you own the fucking place. I told you I was coming in today. What's the matter, didn't you believe it?"

Mrs. Gutierrez glanced at Jody with a meek smile, then shrank back into the bedroom. Jody considered joining her in there, but decided this situation might end up needing a referee.

Michael struggled to get into his jeans beneath the sheet, wondering how in the world the morning had brought on such a god-awful predicament.

"Uh …" said Bernard awkwardly, still at a complete loss.

Out of frustration, Justin flipped off the sheet and came to his feet. He stood in his white cotton briefs, looking about the floor for his jeans. Exposed again, Michael lifted his hips and pulled up his jeans as quickly as he could. Justin snatched up his jeans off the floor, and while stepping into them, he looked back up at Bernard.

"Okay, so now you know. You've seen me in bed with a man

with your own two eyes. I suppose you're ready to make an ass out of yourself with a few asinine comments." He looked down at Michael who was now sitting on the floor, and shrugged his shoulders. "And by the way," he said, looking back at Bernard, "this is Michael Anderson and that's his sister, Jody, at the kitchen table. You know Mrs. Gutierrez, who last night slept in my … correction, *our* bedroom. It's where Michael and I usually sleep together. I guess Mrs. Gutierrez heard enough of my foul language and went back in there. So, everyone … this is Bernard, my boss."

"Uh …" Bernard said again.

"Give him a minute or two and he'll think of plenty to say," Justin said sardonically. He looked at Jody. "If you wouldn't mind pouring some of that coffee I smell, I'm going to step outside and take a leak."

Perk shot through the door as soon as Justin opened it, none too happy that he had been left out of the action. When Justin closed the door behind him, Michael leaned forward to put on his sandals. Jody went to the counter and poured four cups of coffee, which emptied the pot. Rinsing it out to make another round, she said over her shoulder:

"Have a seat at the table, Bernard. Do you like cream or sugar with your coffee?"

"Uh … no. Just black." He walked over and sat down at the table, rubbing the side of his nose with his finger, staring at Michael.

Jody placed a cup in front of him, then carried one in for Mrs. Gutierrez. It quickened her heart to see little Julian still sleeping peacefully under the sheet. Mrs. Gutierrez took the cup graciously, with the same meek smile. Nothing in the front room made any sense to her, so she contentedly watched Jody leave the room from her comfortable position in the rocker.

Michael had gotten to his feet. He stood in the middle of the room, looking down at the floor, scratching his head through a knot of unruly hair.

"Care to join us, big brother," said Jody, returning to the table to sit across from Bernard.

As there were only three chairs around the table, he took the stool from beside the stove and perched on it next to Jody. An awkward silence unfolded as they sipped their coffee. Jody realized that she might have been able to stop Bernard from walking into the house, and she still felt guilty; though now there was nothing to do but try to make the best of it. She was the first to speak.

"Justin has told us about his relationship with you," she said. "He seems to really like you, in an odd sort of way."

Bernard looked at her. "I bet."

"Of course he hasn't come right out and admitted that he likes you, but I can tell."

Michael's teeth began to hurt. He couldn't believe she had jumped immediately into difficulties between Justin and his boss. He wanted her to shut up.

"It sounds like you two have one of those love/hate relationships," she went on to say. "But I think he's amazingly interesting, don't you?"

Bernard studied his coffee for a moment. "Well, he's smart," he said, adding, "But I've never admitted that to him."

Jody smiled and said, "See there, just like he's never admitted that he likes you."

Justin came back in and joined them. He took his first swallow of coffee before his eyes again acknowledged Bernard's presence. "Shit!" he said in frustration, his gaze shifting toward the wall, uncertain of the ramifications that would come with Bernard's unexpected visit. He let out a long sigh, then said, "Let's just get the whole picture right out into the open, right now, up front. Bernard," he said looking straight into the man's eyes, "Michael and I are lovers. We're gay. He's the man Judy Houser saw me with in the river the other day. Michael lives in this house with me. When it's not occupied by someone else, we sleep in that bed in there together. It's as simple as that."

Bernard's lips pursed to avoid a grin.

"That's what I thought," said Justin, his frustration oozing from every pore. "Go ahead, spit it out. I know you're dying to make a comment."

"Just one question. Which one of you is the girl?"

Justin stared at him for a moment, his eyes shooting daggers. The others fidgeted.

"That does it," said Justin. "I'm going to contact the publishers of *Webster's Dictionary* to let them know they have to redefine the word *stupid*. It's not broad enough to fit you, Bernard."

"Wouldn't you call that insubordination?" asked Bernard, looking at Jody. She shrugged and then the big man's eyes shifted to their other visitor. "Why is Mrs. Gutierrez here?"

"Because her son is here, recovering from an operation Michael performed on him last night."

"What!" Bernard blurted, his gaze shooting back toward what looked like a bedraggled misfit sitting across from him.

Michael had spilled some of his coffee and was wiping it up with a napkin.

"You heard right. He's a surgeon. The Gutierrez boy had an infected appendix. Michael took it out last night. Probably saved the boy's life."

A silence passed as Bernard gazed at Michael. Then he said, "You operated on that boy here, last night?"

Michael looked down at the table.

"That's right," said Justin. "Right here, last night. The boy was crumpled in pain and we had no choice." He took another sip of coffee. "So now you know. Now tell me, what sort of grief is this going to mean for me?"

Bernard gave the question some thought as Jody got up for the second pot of coffee. As she refilled the cups, Bernard offered his response. "I know you think I'm a narrow minded redneck, but I don't think I am. I just never figured you to be a … uh, well, you know what I mean." He looked at Jody, rubbing the side of his face as if he were contemplating what he might say.

"Justin, you may never hear me get mushy again, but I think this might be a good time to be honest with you, just like you were a minute ago when you described your relationship with this oddball looking doctor. This pretty little lady was talking about how interesting you are when you were outside. Well, by God you are. I ain't never met a man with the kind of guts it must take to come out and admit he's queer, especially with the rigid circumstances you live with out here in west Texas. Truth is, you're the best man I got, and I think you already knew it, but I've always liked you and it don't make a damn bit of difference to me if you're queer. But you best be prepared for the shit to hit the fan when word gets out that you're shacking up out here with a another man."

Justin sat looking at him, speechless.

"Well now," said Jody, "how things can change right before our very eyes. And by the way, Bernard, you might consider using the word gay instead of queer. It rolls off the tongue better."

"Are you moving here, too?" the big man asked of Jody.

"Oh no. I'm afraid I'm entrenched in the city, though I do love this country. I'll have to be going back to San Diego in a few days, especially since Justin has outlined a girl's bleak prospects of finding a husband out here."

Bernard's eyes swept down over her breasts. "Didn't he tell you I'm single?" he said, somewhat distracted. He lifted his gaze and grinned. "The little woman left me eight years ago."

Her smile was contained within her eyes. "Bernard, I'm looking for a man much older than you."

"I see. And rich I suppose."

"That wouldn't be counted against him."

Then Julian appeared suddenly from the bedroom, his mother close behind. Michael got to his feet immediately, and went over to kneel in front of the boy. He lifted his t-shirt and inspected the incision. He then checked his forehead for fever. The boy was doing well. Michael pulled him into a careful, but emotional embrace, almost as if he were grateful to see the boy alive. A tear formed in the corner of Jody's eye.

"Are you my doctor?" came the innocent voice when Michael released him.

Michael nodded. "Yes I am, son."

"My mother said you took away my pain."

"I suppose I did," Michael said, holding onto the boy's small shoulders. "Do you think you're ready to go home?"

Julian nodded.

"You know you can't play outside just yet. I want you to rest for two more days. You can stay out of school, but I want you to stay in bed or sit up in a chair. Do you have any story books?"

Julian nodded again.

"Good. Then you can read your books or color, okay?"

"Yes," said Julian.

"Are you hungry?"

Another nod, this time eager.

"Then we'll have some pancakes."

Jody got to her feet. Scooting the chair back under the table, she looked at Bernard. "Have you had breakfast?"

"Well, not exactly. I was going to pick up one of those lousy burritos over at Haddie's General Store."

"I would imagine Haddie can live without your sixty-nine cents this morning. You're going to have breakfast with us."

Michael joined her at the counter. When Justin backed out his chair to get up, Jody told him to stay seated, that she and Michael could handle the pancakes. "So have you lived in the Big Bend a good while, Bernard?" she asked as she reached into the cabinet for the box of pancake mix.

"Yeah, I have. Twenty years. Got transferred down here from Yosemite. I sure was pissed off about that for awhile, until I realized they had moved me to paradise. Weren't near as many tourists back then. The Big Bend can find its way into your soul right quick. I reckon I'll never leave it now."

"Sounds like you've been with the park service for a long

time."

"Long enough. Just three years away from retirement, and glad of it. It's gotten to where I have to spend too much time behind a desk. That's why I'm jealous of these young bucks who get to spend all their time out in the park. It ain't that much fun for me any more."

Justin was watching him with great interest. He had never seen this far more human side of his persona. And it had floored him when Bernard took the discovery of his gay lifestyle with a grain of salt. Buried somewhere inside, he always had a soft spot for his impertinent boss, but now he thought he might actually outright like him, though he knew they would probably be bickering before the morning passed.

"So why did you drive all the way out here, Bernard?"

"Oh yeah. I damn near forgot. We have a problem over in the park. I tried to call but you have your cell phone turned off and I wasn't sure if you planned to come in today."

"What problem?" asked Justin.

"A man phoned me in a panic late yesterday afternoon. He was using his cell phone from a campsite in your area on the River Road. Seems their son disappeared. Walked off and got lost or something. The man sounded fit to be tied. I told him to stay at their campsite in case the boy found his way back. He was worried the kid would freeze to death out in the wilderness overnight, but of course it ain't that cold right now. I told him you'd be by this morning to check on them. If the boy hasn't found his way back, you can radio in and we'll get a search party down there."

"Bernard, how in the hell did you forget something like

that?"

The big man puffed up a bit. "You have to damn well admit that things were pretty distracting around here."

"What campsite are they using?"

Bernard didn't remember the site number, but remembered it as one of the sites out near Comanche Wash.

Justin didn't hear what Bernard mumbled after that. He looked down at the table in thought. He then turned his head and said, "Michael, I'm going to have to skip breakfast."

Michael turned and watched him hurry into the bedroom, emerging a few moments later in his uniform. He breezed into the kitchen, grabbing an apple from the fruit bowl on the end of the counter, pausing a moment to lean his head close to his lover. "I'll never forget last night," he whispered with a tone that couldn't have carried beyond Michael's ear. He turned to look at Jody as he neared the back door. "Try some applesauce in that batter," he said, taking his hat from a nail on the wall. He then looked over at Bernard. "I'll radio in as soon as I find out what's going on out there."

Bernard nodded, obviously not about to leave the table without a belly full of pancakes.

Justin opened the door and held it for Perk, and the two of them were speeding away in the Jeep moments later.

"God he's handsome in that uniform," said Jody, and she noticed Michael had closed his eyes, most likely with the same thought. "You ready for a little more coffee, Bernard?"

"I believe so, little lady." Watching her bring over the coffee pot, he leaned back into the chair and said, "Got to admit, you could spoil a man pretty fast, pouring him this good coffee and all."

She looked at her brother with a cunning smile. "Michael, you must be pretty excited, getting this chance to meet one of your fellow west Texans."

He shot her a discreet knowing glance, then cleared his throat, saying, "Yes, of course. I'm sure glad you came by, Bernard. Been looking forward to meeting you."

"We don't get many of your kind moving down this way ... I mean the doctor part, not the queer, uh ... gay part."

"Well, I thought that was a very nice thing you said to Justin awhile ago," said Jody as she watched Michael pour a can of applesauce into the batter. "I'm sure he thought you were going to give him a hard time about it."

"I intend to. But the fact is, he's still the best ranger in Big Bend. You saw how he lit out when he heard some folks were having a problem over on the River Road. He's like that. Any of the others would have waited until they got some of those pancakes. He don't know it, but I've put a half dozens commendations in his file. Problem is, and I didn't think about it before, but that could land him my job when I retire."

Michael turned. "He wouldn't have to take that job if he didn't want it, would he?"

The big man shrugged his shoulders and smiled at Mrs. Gutierrez, who had taken a seat across the table from him. She had no clue as to what this conversation was about, but that didn't seem to concern her at all. She was simply happy that her son was well.

"You going to be doing any doctoring around here?" asked Bernard, leaning forward to raise his pants leg. "I got this red blotch on my leg that itches from time to time."

Michael glanced at the white hairless calf. "Uh, Bernard, have your physician take a look at that. I've retired from the medical profession."

"I just thought since you operated on the boy …"

"That was an emergency and there was no choice," Michael said abruptly.

"Also, Bernard, you should know," said Jody, "he charged two hundred dollars for looking at red blotches in San Diego. And besides that, he's a surgeon. If your doctor tells you your leg has to be amputated, that's when you come to see Michael."

Bernard lowered his pants leg and adjusted himself in the chair.

Michael stood over the stove, the smoke from sizzling bacon wafting up about his face. Turning the long strips from time to time in the grease, he thought about Justin. He had departed in such an urgent hurry, Michael couldn't help but be concerned. With any luck, the lost boy had already found his way back to the camp; but if not, Justin would be fraught with worry and faced with the task of trying to find him.

After breakfast they all walked outside. Bernard had to get on to the office. Michael and Jody planned to take Julian and his mother back home. Bernard crawled into his officially painted Suburban and started down the road. They stood watching the dust kick up as the truck grew smaller in the distance.

Her feet planted wide on the ground, her hands on her hips, Jody said, "There goes one big hunk of west Texas manhood."

Michael nodded. "Yeah. It sure explains why Justin chose to live way out here with his library books, doesn't it?"

They turned and Michael held open the rear door to the Cherokee for Mrs. Gutierrez and Julian.

CHAPTER 14

Justin covered distance over the River Road faster than he ever had, slowing down only after a jarring rut had bounced Perk from the passenger seat onto the floor board. The dog looked at him with indignation. He swerved around deep erosion and large protruding rock, gripping the wheel over jarring bumps. It normally took two hours to get to Comanche Wash—he made it this time in forty-five minutes.

There weren't that many campsites in the area. The first one he came to was occupied by a retired couple, waving happily as he drove by. A small troup of Boy Scouts had made camp in the next site. The third site, five minutes from the others and the most remote, was occupied by the boy's parents. Justin stopped the Jeep and jumped out. The mother was sitting in a folding camp chair, sobbing. The father was pacing. A teenage girl stood near the mother.

"We thought you were never going to get here," said the anxious father, rushing toward Justin.

"Sorry it took so long, Sir."

"We need to do something fast. My boy was out there somewhere all night long. Can't we get a search party out here?"

"That's exactly what we're going to do. Just give me a few minutes to get some details." Justin looked in all directions. To the north, mountains formed an endless range not more than a mile beyond the camp. There was rugged terrain in every other direction. Many ravines and rock formations. It was terrain that Justin knew could easily disorient a grown man, let alone a ten year old boy. How often had someone hiked a couple hundred yards and found themselves turned around, and often lost for hours? He looked back at the man.

"When did you first notice the boy missing?"

"Yesterday, about two in the afternoon. We were going to take a short nap before hiking down to the river. When we woke up, Timmy was gone."

"And you have no idea what direction he may have gone?"

"No idea. All I know is we planned to hike to the river, but Timmy wanted to hike up into the mountains instead. I told him we'd do that next and he seemed to be satisfied with that."

Justin looked toward the mountains again. The boy might have set out in that direction in defiance of his parents, or he might have decided to try to beat the family to the river, the opposite direction. Justin took a deep breath, surveying the campsite. They were obviously a well-to-do yuppie family, dressed in safari style khaki. Everything in their camp was brand new, including every conceivable convenience. They had arrived in one of those over priced, over sized SUVs. The mother had stepped forward and was standing next to her husband, gripping his arm, her solemn face begging for help in finding their son. There was no doubt they needed a search party.

Justin went back to the Jeep and called Bernard on the radio.

"It's not a good picture, Bernard."

"I was afraid of that. Well, okay, I've got six men on standby. I'll send them over there right away. I phoned the state police. They're ready to bring some bloodhounds down from Alpine."

Bernard paused, then asked, "Any clues at all?"

"Nothing yet. As soon as we get off, I'm going to circle the camp to see if I can spot some tracks."

"A good trail would sure be a blessing. See what you can do, Justin. Give them boys a couple of hours to get there."

"I'll call in if anything turns up."

"Justin … by the way, a state police report came in yesterday. I didn't think much about it then. Seems a convict escaped in transit up in Alpine the other day. They were taking him to Huntsville. A serial killer."

"I heard that on the radio last night," said Justin.

"Well, I telling you now because another report came in before I got here this morning. They've traced him to a gas station in Marathon where he used a stolen credit card they know to be in his possession. He was heading south when he got to Marathon, so they think the park might be his destination. Keep an eye out, but if you see any suspicious characters, don't do anything. Phone in and we'll let the state boys handle it."

"I understand."

Justin returned the receiver to the dash and looked down at the ground. *A serial killer in Big Bend. Good God!. But why not? There's a million places for a man to hide forever down here if he had a good source for food.* He looked back at the family, now haunted by the news of the fugitive as he walked back over to the father. "The search party is on the way," he said. "We'll have some bloodhounds here sometime after lunch."

"Thank God," said the mother.

"Where are you all from?" Justin asked.

"I'm a real estate broker in Dallas. This is our first trip out here."

Justin nodded. "While we're waiting, I'm going to try to find your son's tracks leading out of camp. Do you see any footprints around us now that may have been made by his shoes?"

The father began to seach the ground. A few moments later he called out, "Here, this is his print."

Justin went down on his knee and studied the print for a moment, thinking about what he might say to ease the parent's apprehension. In this terrain he was glad Bernard thought to arrange for Bloodhounds. He stood up and said, "Looks like he was wearing new hiking boots of some kind."

"That's right," said the father.

He glanced at the teenage girl who didn't look all that worried. She seemed more upset because her parents had dragged her here. Looking back at the father, Justin said, "People get lost out here on a fairly regular basis. Most of them stumble around and find their way back. We've never had much trouble finding those who don't. In this terrain, it's good we have the bloodhounds coming in. All they have to do is pick up the scent, and they'll lead us right to your son. That is, if we don't find him first."

Both parents nodded with a look of relief.

Perk trotted along in front of him as he began a zigzag search of the ground around the camp. He spotted the foot print several times, but each time the trail indicated the boy had ventured outside the camp and then circled back in.

When the six man team arrived, Justin took charge. They grouped in the camp, including Mr. Johnson, the boy's father. Justin filled them in on the situation and told them what he had found so far. "Now I've circled the camp a hundred yards out and couldn't find any tracks leading out beyond that. The ground is pretty hard in most places, so it's entirely possible the boy walked away without leaving many tracks. So let's start with the 'broken ankle theory'. He might have fallen into a ravine and broken a bone. There's eight of us counting Mr. Johnson. I want each of you to start in a different direction, like spokes in a wheel, and walk straight out about a thousand yards. Then turn to your right and walk at a ninety degree angle from your spoke for two hundred yards. From there, turn again and walk directly back to this campsite. Veer off only to check ravines and arroyos. That way we'll have covered just about everything within a half mile from camp." He thought for a moment, then added, "By then, if we don't find him, the hounds will be here. And make sure you have a full bottle of water before you start."

Within five minutes, all eight men were starting out in their separate directions. Half way out, they started calling the boy's name. An hour passed before the last man walked back into the camp. None of them had seen a trace of the boy. But the hounds had arrived and they appeared anxious to start tracking.

The dog's trainer approached the boy's father. "We're ready, Mr. Johnson. I'll need something with your son's scent on it. Clothes work well."

"How about my son's sleeping bag?"

"Anyone else sleep in it recently?"

"It's brand new. Only my son has used it."

"That's perfect."

The dogs gathered around the sleeping bag, pushing their noses into it eagerly. They immediately started sniffing the ground and pulling the trainer out of the camp. Each direction they went circled back around to camp just as Justin had learned by following the available foot prints, except one. The dogs followed the scent in one direction for about three hundred yards, then stopped in abrupt confusion. The trainer unleashed them, but all they did was circle, sniffing the ground, apparently unable to pick up the scent any further out, or a return route. The trail simply ended. And strangely, this being the longest distance the boy had wandered from camp, there were none of his foot prints found along the entire distance.

The dog trainer approached Justin. "It don't look good," he said.

"What do you mean?" said Justin. "It doesn't look to me like he even came out this far."

"He was out here all right," the trainer assured him, scanning the area. He looked back at Justin, adding, "These dogs know he was here. I'd say it was possible he doubled back and took exactly the same path back to camp, if we had see some foot prints."

"That's what I mean—we didn't see a single foot print."

The trainer shook his head. "We didn't see the boy's foot prints, but we saw others. A grown man's print. That boy was carried out here."

"What? Then where is he? Why does his trail just simply end?"

The trainer nodded toward the ground a few feet away. "Come with me."

They walked some twenty feet and the trainer pointed at the ground. "There was a vehicle right here. It's easy enough to see." He pointed in the direction the vague tire tracks led. "He drove off in that direction. These are fresh tracks. That boy was carried from where we last saw his prints outside of camp and put in a vehicle right here. There ain't no question about it."

Justin's heart sank. He looked over at Mr. Johnson, who was still searching the ground for his son's foot prints.

"Guess you'll have to be the one to tell him," said the trainer.

Staring at the desperate father, Justin nodded. Far more ominous questions now loomed in his mind, the answers coming darkly from his imagination. How would they find the boy if he had been kidnapped? And even if they found him, could they hope that he would still be alive? Watching the bloodhound's futile circles, Justin cringed, thinking about a possible link between the boy and that fugitive killer.

The father fell into a stunned trance as Justin's words formed meaning in his mind. He started shaking his head as if he did not—could not—believe it. "There's some other explanation," he muttered.

"Sir, we know for sure the boy didn't walk away from your campsite. We'd be on his trail by now if he had. There may be some other explanation, but it's pretty clear your son has been kidnapped." Justin refrained from telling the distraught father about the fugitive killer known to be somewhere in the area.

"How will I tell Nancy?" he said blankly. Then he looked at Justin. "This will kill her." His hands began to tremble. "It'll kill her!"

"If you want me to, I'll talk to her," Justin said with helpless compassion. It was clearly the worse day his job had ever provided, a day that promised only to get much, much worse.

"No," said the father. "I'll have to tell her myself." There was more grief in his tone than Justin had ever heard in a man's voice, grief so heavy as to not allow the additional weight of anger. But Justin knew that would come too. This man would eventually have blood in his eyes, and he would want to kill. He would want nothing more than to get his hands on the criminal who took his son.

They walked solemnly together back to the campsite. Justin was standing alone with Perk beside his Jeep when he heard the mother's scream. She was immediately hysterical. The awful sound carried across the desert like a howl of death, causing pain in his hands from fists so tightly clenched.

The dog trainer approached Justin.

"I called in the initial report. They're mobilizing a tactical search. They're also contacting the FBI since a kidnapping is involved. Looks like they're assuming this might be linked to a fugitive killer known to be in this area."

Justin looked out across the desert. "Yeah, I heard that report this morning. So the state police or the FBI will be taking over?"

"Yeah. Out of Alpine. They'll set up a command center somewhere here in the park. All you have to do right now is get the parents up to speed. I reckon they'll want to stay somewhere in the area while we're looking for their son."

Justin gave them a few minutes together before he approached the father again. He informed Mr. Johnson of the preliminary steps under way. Aware the father would eventually learn about the fugitive, Justin decided to not withhold that information.

"There's no reason to assume this is related, but just so you know, we're aware of a fugitive in this area."

The man looked at Justin in horror. "A fugitive?"

"Yes, but it'll work to our advantage in finding your son. They'll be prepared to mobilize more man-power, just in case there's a link. We can also expect the FBI to get involved."

The father's distraught gaze fell to the ground. "Oh God … none of this seems real. I can't believe it's happening to us."

Justin looked over at the mother. She had collapsed into the folding chair, her face wet with tears and contorted with grief. The teenage daughter stood beside her and now seemed focused on the reality of the family's problem.

"Do you have any idea of what you'd like to do while this investigation gets under way?"

He looked over at his wife. "I'm going to call her sister. Get her to come down here and take my wife and daughter home. I'll stay." He looked at Justin. "Is there a motel nearby?"

"The lodge here in the park is booked full, but there might be a room available at the Badlands Hotel over in Lajitas this time of year. That'd be one of the closest."

The man nodded.

Justin took out a pencil and a pad of paper. He wrote a telephone number on it and handed it to the father. "This is the number to the visitor's center. You can find out what's going on by calling there. Is there anything I can do for you right now?"

The man was staring at his wife. He shook his head and muttered, "No, uh, but thanks." He looked at Justin. "Thanks for your help."

Justin reached out and squeezed the man's shoulder. The search party had gotten back into their vehicle and were leaving. The dog trainer had loaded the bloodhounds and he waved before getting inside the truck to drive away. Perk followed Justin back to the spot where the little boy's trail ended.

Thirty minutes later he had found no clues whatsoever, no sign of a struggle, no spot of blood, no shred of clothing. He followed the vague tire imprints several hundred yards, to the campsite road where they then merged with countless other tracks. Frustrated, he returned to his Jeep, where Perk jumped up into the passenger seat beside him. He got Bernard on the radio.

"This is big," said Bernard. "There's going to be a lot of action first thing in the morning. State police and FBI. They think it's that fugitive."

Justin's heart sank. He let out a long breath and said, "There's nothing more I can do down here."

"Go on home. Report here in the morning. Maybe we'll find out where we're going to fit into the investigation by then."

Justin signed off and started the Jeep. Heading back over the River Road, he pulled off where the road veered close to the river. He got out of the Jeep and made his way through scrub and cactus to the river bank, and crawled atop a rock formation overlooking the rapids. Angry, he felt the Big Bend had been contaminated. Some animal had violated the poetry and natural harmony of one of few places on Earth where the elements came together to lift a man's soul, a paradise now invaded by evil. Consumed with helpless rage, he watched the timeless flow of rushing water, and several minutes passed before his rage settled, for he resolved to do everything he could to rid the park of this menace.

Justin's thoughts drifted to the night before and a bit of calm began to settle over him. He had again lay unashamed with his male lover. Gazing out over the river, he pondered his sexuality. Beyond a radical change in his lifelong mindset, for him, it also brought on a source of fascination. He loved it. A peace of mind, something like a long awaited liberation, had settled over him like a pleasant summer rain. Yet he was still mystified by how a man could be so disattracted by another, and he was especially mystified by the intense techniques of physical male love; one reason, he was certain, that caused him to almost constantly think about Michael. Under the spell of another night, their world together the night before had continued to expand, and now another memory felt warm in his heart. He looked at his hands, thinking of the intimacy they had encountered, the sensations that had come in the black of night through his palms and fingertips, those contours and textures of Michael's skin; and the tingles came alive on his arms again.

He closed his eyes, his mind adrift with the memory. What was this miracle that had come into his life, that had come to him like a song born in the mystery of this haunting land? How could his heart and mind fall so helplessly into the possession of another man? It seemed such a complicated question, resolved by such an uncommon, yet resolute answer. The image of his lover formed in his mind as he listened to the music of fast water: the innocence and intensity of his sky blue eyes, the sandy brown hair always in disarray atop his head. And all the myriad answers really didn't matter, for it had come as naturally as a bird takes flight, and for the very first time ever, he was able to cherish his own life.

A hawk circled on the warm thermals overhead, and as Justin gazed up at it, he thought of his lips brushing the stubble of his lover's firm jaw, the sinew of his neck. He pictured tanned shoulders and taut chest, the mesmeric allure of those small brown nipples. How he loved to pinch and caress them, turn them into hard pebbles and see Michael's legs come together in response. As he watched the hawk's effortless flight, the images continued to unfold like a dream. How quickly he had surrendered to the temptations of male flesh; how easily he had succumbed to those odors born within male loins and damp skin, those tantalizing elements with the power to ignite a man's primordial desire and draw forth his eyes and lips and tongue. He closed his eyes, lost in the timeless voice of the river. What lay in wait within his fibers that could spark such passion; that, at long last, caused this celebration of life? What else on God's green earth could cause such a state of helpless euphoria?

He opened his eyes, staring blankly into the swirling water before him. *So this is who I am. And these are the measures that nourish my soul. I'm gay. I have fallen in love with a man as naturally as I breathe air, and it's given me more contentment than I knew was possible.*

He knew. As surely as the hawk soars in a cloudless sky, he knew he was born to love and be loved by a man. So compelled by this need, it came with a tingle of life within the pores of his skin. And along this path would come cool nights in the heat of each other's arms, coffee together in the first light of thousands of new days, and countless sunsets as they sat side by side. And with it came the knowledge of love, the essence of life, and the boundless contentment and joy of walking side-by-side with his lover.

Perk had given up on trying to climb up on the rock. He was sniffing cautiously near the edge of the water. Justin smiled, thinking of the bloodhounds, how they had largely ignored the playful cocker spaniel as he tried mightily to get their attention. He drew a deep breath, filling his lungs with fresh dry air, looking about him at a landscape of rock and river and banks of ever-changing wet sand, wondering how long it would take to capture the fugitive, wondering if there was hope of finding the boy still alive. It was time to go home, time to return to the comfort of his lover's close proximity.

Sunset was still two hours away when Justin pulled the Jeep to a stop in front of the house. He rounded the corner at the back of the house and saw Michael bending over between the two poles, blotting drops of water from his legs with a towel. He stopped, allowing his weary eyes the pleasure of his lover's form.

Jody was sitting in one of the new chairs, reading a novel. She looked up and saw Justin staring at her brother, and she lowered the novel to her lap. "You guys just can't seem to get enough of each other," she mused.

Michael wrapped the towel around his waist as Justin approached. "I've been worried about you all day," he said, placing his hands aside his lover's face and leaning forward for a light kiss, which surely would have lingered had Jody not been watching them.

"It wasn't good," said Justin, his eyes drifting down Michael's chest. "I'm ready for some beer."

Jody followed them into the house and told them to go ahead and sit down, that she would get the beer. The men pulled out chairs at the kitchen table while she filled three glasses with Tecate and sliced a saucer of lime. Justin looked up at her as she set the glass in front of him.

"Try it out of a glass for a change," she said, taking her seat.

Michael could see by the sadness in Justin's eyes it had not been a good day. "The boy is still lost, isn't he?"

"He's been kidnapped," said Justin.

Jody gasped.

"Kidnapped?" said Michael.

"There's no doubt about it. And that fugitive we heard about on the radio last night is in the area. It's scary. We learn a serial killer is heading this way, and then a boy turns up missing. Looks like we have no choice but to assume there's a connection."

"My God!" said Jody. "We can't get away from that sort of thing, not even out here."

Michael felt immediate dismay. He knew Justin shouldered a self-imposed responsibility for the boy's fate, perhaps similar to what he himself had suffered when that little girl's life had been in his hands.

"I hate it," said Justin. "The first thing I thought about when I found out the boy was kidnapped was guilt. I took the day off. The River Road is my watch. What if I'd been out there, maybe at the right place at the right time. I might have seen something. I might have seen the boy trying to get away from his abductor. Or that animal might have seen me and been discouraged from going through with it. I might have saved that boy from this grief."

Jody was put off. "What are you saying, Justin, that you should work every day of the week for the rest of your life?"

"Sis, I can understand why he feels that way," Michael said.

"It's ridiculous for Justin to feel responsible for that boy's kidnapping," she retorted.

"She's right, Justin," Michael said with compassion, reaching for his hand. "That area is so vast it isn't likely anyone could have prevented it."

"Maybe not, but I am out there for a reason," said Justin, his tone bitter.

Michael lowered his head. He felt a sense of despair that he couldn't console the man he loved.

"I'm sorry," said Justin. "I hated even bringing this up. It just shouldn't have happened. Not here. People come here to get away from crime and the problems of society. I'd like to kill that son-of-a-bitch."

Jody realized that Justin wanted no consolation, that he was suffering the pent-up emotion of a dismal day, and that he might need no more than to get it off his chest. She remained silent.

Justin took a swallow of beer, then reached down to stroke Perk's head. He cleared his throat and began to relate the details of the day's events. He told them about the boy's family and how their lives had been so suddenly changed. He told them how they determined the facts by using the bloodhounds, that the state police and FBI would be taking over the investigation. Then finally, he took another swallow of beer and leaned back in his chair, and a calm began to come back over his face.

"With those other agencies involved you might be making short work of that kidnapper," said Michael.

"We'll find that creep, I promise. I'll find out what the game plan is in the morning. If they don't intend to include the park rangers, I'm going to go out there and start my own search."

Michael closed his eyes. A nervous fear swelled inside his chest. He couldn't bear to think about the possibility of Justin coming face to face with a serial killer.

"Well," said Jody, "are you two ready to start thinking about dinner? I thought I might use some of that ground beef to make some spaghetti."

Justin smiled. "Come to think of it, I missed lunch."

"Want some help, Sis?"

"Not tonight. I thought you guys might want to watch the sunset from your new chairs while I make your dinner. You've both been through an ordeal during the last twenty-four hours."

Later that evening, Jody was already in bed when the two men returned from their walk in the desert. She looked up over her reading glasses when they walked into the room. They seemed uncommonly quiet and calm as they readied themselves for bed; Justin stepping into his pajama bottoms; Michael shirt-less and deep in thought, staring at the floor, unconsciously scratching an itch between his legs. Justin picked up his shirt from the floor and sniffed the underarms before he carefully hung it on the cross-bar of the wall rack.

"Ahhh, these intimate moments in the private quarters of two men," said Jody.

They both looked at her, at a complete loss as to what might be in her mind.

"You boys see any rattlesnakes out there tonight?"

"Nary a one," said Michael, now crawling over her. He pulled off his jeans before slipping under the sheet.

Justin stepped around the bed and got in beside him. They both lay on their backs side-by-side, both staring peacefully at the ceiling.

Jody pushed the glasses back up her nose.

"Looks like those walks in the desert at night have a real soothing effect on you two," she said, lifting the novel back up to eye level.

"Great spaghetti tonight, Sis," said Michael.

"Hit the spot with me too," added Justin.

She smiled and turned the page. Perk jumped up on the bed and stepped between the confusion of legs until he found a spot large enough to curl up for the night.

CHAPTER 15

The next morning Justin was in Bernard's office by six o'clock. FBI agents from San Antonio were there in addition to a team of ATF agents from El Paso. By seven o'clock a plan was in place from what for awhile seemed like chaos. The ATF team brought in a helicopter, which put them in charge of the air search. The FBI agents planned to accompany state police in calling on every campsite in the park to interview visitors. State troopers also had every road leading out of Big Bend blocked. The park rangers were to perform their routine patrols and stay alert for anything suspicious. Justin remained seated while the other rangers filed out of the office. He looked at Bernard when they were alone.

"Looks like those boys are serious about finding that guy," said Bernard.

"I'm impressed, and I'm also relieved. If that serial killer hadn't turned up in Marathon, we wouldn't be getting this kind of action." He noticed Bernard was unconsciously stroking Perk's head. "Did you hear the FBI profile on that killer?"

"No," said Bernard.

"They've got him linked to a dozen murders. Sex crimes. All of the victims are kids under thirteen years old, boys and girls. He's struck as far away as Phoenix."

Bernard shook his head. "I hope they kill him." He opened his desk drawer and took out a box of Milk Bones and handed one to Perk.

Justin was amused. "Where did those come from?" he asked.

"I picked them up at the grocery store. Figured if I could make friends with this mutt, he wouldn't shit in my office again."

"You know, Bernard, you're not really the asshole everyone says you are. Not as narrow-minded either. You floored me with that casual attitude when you found out I'm gay."

Bernard looked at him and shrugged. "I don't understand things like that, never will. But shit, I don't understand women either. Every woman I ever met thinks I'm a jerk. The last time I got any pussy, I had to drive over to Ojinaga and pay for it." He paused and his expression turned more serious. "I know I've always given you a hard time, but you're smart enough to know that's just the way I am. I'm glad you and me get along. Like I said yesterday morning, you're the best man on my crew. That's why I put up with your crap … but I wouldn't push it too far."

Justin smiled and nodded. "Thanks, Bernard. And I'll try not to push it too far." Then his smile turned into a grin. "But, uh, you say you went to a whorehouse? That's hard to picture."

Bernard paused in thought. His face took on a bit of a glow, as if he were visualizing the memory. "A little Mexican girl," he said as his gaze moved toward the ceiling. "She didn't look a day over eighteen years old. Prettiest little thing I ever set my eyes on. Those big brown eyes looked at me with the innocence of a child. Now she might have looked innocent, but she had some incredible talent. I couldn't believe it. Damn near gave this horny old fart a heartattack. I almost shot my load before I could get my money's worth." He closed his eyes for a moment, then added, "I'm thinking I'll go back down there after we catch this kidnapper." He looked back at Justin. "Maybe you ought to go with me. I bet she'd get you thinking straight again."

"I am thinking straight, Bernard. I'm gay. There's no two sides to the coin."

"Well, whatever." He paused in thought again, then asked, "So have you got any plans for your patrol today?"

"Those tire tracks we found were too vague to make out clear tread imprints, so I thought I'd start checking all the tracks that veer off the River Road. I know it's a shot in the dark, but I might stumble on something."

"Just remember, if you do, call in. Don't try to be the hero."

Justin got to his feet. Perk was licking the last crumbs from the Milk Bone off the floor. "Let's go, boy," said Justin, patting his thigh, and the dog followed him back out to the Jeep.

By two o'clock, Justin had lost count of how many tire tracks he had followed off the River Road, all of them eventually circling back toward the road. At four o'clock, he was wading back through a thick stand of scrub a few yards from the Jeep when the helicopter passed overhead in the direction of the visitor's center. Making his way back to the Jeep, he heard a call on the radio. It was Bernard.

"They found the boy's body," came the scratchy voice.

Justin slumped against the Jeep. Perk looked up at him quizzically.

"We're dealing with a bastard who picks children. The boy's rectum had been torn."

"Has his father been informed?"

"Yeah. He's already made arrangements to get the boy's body back to Dallas."

Stunned, Justin stared at the ground at a complete loss. His teeth clenched, he closed his eyes and shook his head.

"You still there?" came the voice.

"Yeah. I'm here."

"Half the campsites in the park have been vacated. No doubt most of the campers will move on when they get the news."

Justin didn't reply.

"Listen, there ain't nothing more you can do today. Head home and get some rest. Tomorrow I want you to check every campsite along the River Road. Inform anyone who's down there of what's going on. I want every visitor in the park alert to the risk of staying."

"Okay," Justin said, despondent.

They signed off and Justin climbed back into the Jeep. It took an hour to get home.

Michael was reading a magazine in one of the new chairs when he heard the distant approach of Justin's Jeep. He looked up when Justin rounded the corner of the house, instantly concerned by his somber expression. Justin sat down beside him, still almost too emotional to speak.

"What's happened?" asked Michael.

"The boy was found dead … raped and murdered."

Michael lowered his head in dismay. He closed his eyes and rubbed his forehead with his fingertips. There seemed nothing to say or do, other than to let the silence begin its healing effect.

Jody approached. She had been stretching her legs, walking among the Ocotillo and cactus, marveling at the rugged endurance inherent in desert plants. She saw at once the mood and looked at Michael with the question in her eyes.

"They found the little boy murdered," he said.

She let out a sad sigh and looked at Justin for a moment. No appropriate words came to her mind as she fideted for something to say. "I think I'll make a fresh pot of coffee," she finally said, turning toward the back door.

Perk followed her inside, trotting over to his water bowl to lap up a quick drink. He sniffed what remained of his dog food and began to crunch down a few bites while Jody made the coffee. She pulled the rocker out next to the two men while the pot percolated. After checking the coffee a few minutes later, she returned with three full mugs, taking a seat beside them. They were staring silently at the western horizon.

"That creep is still out there somewhere," said Justin. "The park has provided his sanctuary. He's found a place to hide and find new victims."

"Maybe he fled after he murdered that boy," said Michael.

"No. The state police put up road blocks yesterday, right after I radioed Bernard the boy was missing. I believe the killer thinks he's safe, at least for now. I believe he thinks he's found the perfect hunting ground, right here in Big Bend."

Michael cringed with the horror of such a creepy scenario. That another innocent life could be lost at the hands of a brutal killer, that the man he loved might find himself in confrontation with such a criminal, was more than he could stand to think about.

"Well, they know what the killer looks like," said Jody. "If they distributed pictures in the park, maybe someone would spot him and turn him in."

"By this time tomorrow, there's not likely going to be anyone left in the park," said Justin. "Would you want to camp out over there knowing that guy is running around?"

"Do they know anything else about him?" asked Michael.

"They know that his last victim was a little girl. He took her right out of her bedroom in the middle of the night. Stole her father's credit cards in the process. That's how they traced him to Marathon. Obviously he's not too bright, or else he's desperate. Either way, it'll help us catch him. He'll make another mistake."

There were low clouds on the western horizon that took on myriad shades of red and orange as the sun moved down behind them. By the time the great ball of fire dipped below the earth, the whole western sky was aflame in brilliant color. And when the golden hues across the desert turned bronze and began to darken, three somber souls went inside the house to warm up frozen dinners for the evening's meal.

Jody was the last to take a seat at the table. "We're getting low on beer and groceries," she said to no one in particular.

"You and I can drive up to Alpine in the morning when Justin leaves for the park," said Michael. He looked at Justin, wondering if a more upbeat subject might take his mind off finding that kidnapper. "Think we ought to get in touch with that guy who owns this property? I'm kind of anxious to get started on building the barn."

A smile formed in Justin's eyes.

Jody's mind was elsewhere. Her visit would come to an end in a few days, and so far, she had refrained from talking about a couple of things that were on her mind.

It had to do with their future together. Now they were planning to buy this property, and though she had been reluctant to say anything, she decided to not put it off any longer. She looked up from her half eaten dinner. "Justin, you were pretty emotionally involved in finding that boy. It made me wonder about something." She hesitated and looked at Michael. "Forgive me Michael, for bringing this up, but you guys are so carried away with romance I'm worried about how much thought has gone into the long term ramifications."

Michael's expression slumped. "Sis, what on earth are you getting at?"

She held her hand up. "Just hear me out for a minute. Right now you believe that you can walk away from one lifestyle, into one completely different from what you've left behind. Okay, that's that, but what about Justin? I mean, he didn't realize he was gay until he met you for chrissake." She looked back at Justin.

"You felt something in your heart for that boy. Have you thought about never having your own son? Do you fully realize that will never be a part of your life in making this commitment with my brother? His philosophy on having children is simple— he's just glad someone else is willing to do it, but what about you? Have you really considered never being a father?"

Michael released a frustrated sigh and shook his head. "For Christ's sake, Jody."

"It's okay, Michael," said Justin. "I don't want her to go home worried about us. This is as good a time as any to talk about it."

Justin looked down at the table in thought for a long while, then looked up at her. "I think I have, even before I met Michael, before I realized I was gay. Even though I haven't been around them much, I've always liked children. I love to watch them play and listen to their antics, but I've never pictured myself in the role of a parent. I have no strong need to leave behind a legacy, nor have I felt a burning desire to have and raise my own child. If I was twenty there might be some doubts, but I've always known that children are not in the cards for me."

"Satisfied, Sis?"

"Michael, I said I was sorry. But I love you. Actually, I love you both. That's why I care."

"It's all right, Jody," said Justin. "I don't want you to ever hold back anything that's on your mind. I realize it seems strange since I just discoved I'm gay, but I've known on some level for a long time. I don't feel like I'm giving up being a father for Michael, because if I had never met him, if I had never consciously admitted that I'm gay, even then, I would have never gotten involved with another woman. Like I say, I've always known on some level.

"I knew in high school, in the gym showers, where my eyes wandered to places they shouldn't have." He laughed. "You wouldn't believe how angry I got with myself when I couldn't stop those urges to look. I've known all my life, by noticing the way a man's clothes fit his body, by allowing my imagination to visualize him naked. Then along comes denial, and those mental interludes would melt back into the darkness of my subconscious. But how could I have not known? It wasn't a lack of awareness, but rather a lack of understanding that stood in the way.

"And there was the weight of angry frustration when I was in bed with the girl I almost married, when I looked at her beautiful body and found myself impotent. I thought I must really be screwed up. You can probably imagine what I fantasized about during those few times I managed to achieve a climax, but then actually allow myself to believe she had been the cause.

"I knew the moment I set eyes on Michael, when I walked up on him in the park. He was sitting calmly next to the river on a rock ledge, day dreaming, wearing nothing but a pair of jeans. His image quickened my heart and stopped my breath, and I found it almost impossible to approach him with my duties as a park ranger. Then he turned when I called out and it felt like I melted within his eyes. He spoke, and the sound of his voice crawled over my skin like electricity. He was sad, and I had an overwhelming urge to comfort him, to figure out a way to help him find peace. I tried to play the role of a ranger, but I was most anxious to cast that aside and get to know him. I wanted to stay there with him all day, and when we talked about where he might stay, I knew I had never wanted anything in my life more than I wanted him to come to my house. I was compelled to ask him to do just that, and thrilled when he accepted.

"I know our hearts have taken control of our common sense, that we've cast our destiny on the wind. But for me, it's nothing short of a miracle."

Her elbows upon the table, her chin resting upon interlocked fingers, Jody sat staring at him, absorbing every word. She looked at Michael at the sound of his voice.

"I saw much of that in his eyes within fifteen minutes of knowing him."

Her gaze returned to Justin. A silence settled over the room as she stared at him. Then she said:

"Well … Justin … okay. I guess it's time for me to put to rest my little concerns about what has happened between you two."

"There are times I'd like to shout it from a roof top," said

Justin.

The silence stretched again. Jody sat looking at the table. She looked back up. "You know, Justin, you're real good at explaining what's in your heart. And now I don't know if I feel sad or what. I have nothing, no posession or dream that I wouldn't give to have someone feel that way about me."

"I've told you, Sis, open your heart and your eyes, and it will happen for you sooner or later. For now, give us your blessing to buy this land together."

"You have my blessing, Michael."

Justin and Michael exchanged smiles.

"I'll call and make arrangements with the property owner in the morning," said Justin.

After they washed the dishes, Michael and Justin took another walk in the desert moonlight. Jody, joined by Perk, changed into her nightshirt and took her novel and a can of Tecate into the livingroom.

She turned to look at the two men when they returned thirty minutes later.

"I feel guilty about this," she said from the sofa.

"What are you talking about, Sis?" Michael asked as he reached into the refrigerator for two cans of beer, handing one to Justin.

"You know what I'm talking about. You two wouldn't be taking so many walks in the desert if I wasn't sleeping with you."

Michael crossed the room and sat down in the over-stuffed chair. "Don't worry about that, Sis."

"It's not just this visit, Michael. I love being here with you and Justin. Hard as it is to believe, I love this desert. I want to come back every time I get a chance, but it's uncomfortable feeling like an intruder."

"I've been thinking about that," said Justin from the rocker. He looked at Michael. "I enjoy having her here. I want her to come back as much as she wants and feel comfortable when she's here. I think we should reconsider the barn project. Make some changes to the house first. I'm ready for a bathroom myself."

Michael looked at him, surprised, not to mention the concept of building a bathroom was completely beyond his imagination.

"Need to remember to do laundry tomorrow," Justin mumbled, sniffing his armpit.

"You don't have to move out of nineteenth century just for me, Justin," Jody said.

He turned to look at her, lifting his brow at her sardonic mood and wit. "I can't think of a better reason to move out of the nineteenth century. I *do* want you to be comfortable here. I'll look forward to your visits from now on, but I am ready for the convenience of a bathroom and I'm sure Michael is, too. We could add a bedroom at the same time. It won't be that difficult. We'll also need to increase the electical supply and install a septic tank and an electric pump on the well."

Michael was fascinated. "Where would we build it?" he asked.

"On the north side. There it wouldn't interfere with the view from the kitchen window, and it would give the house good proportion. We could put the door to the new rooms where that window is behind your chair and maybe add a window over the couch, a large window that would give us a good view of the western horizon. If we're careful it won't affect the personality of the house at all."

"I love the idea," said Michael, taking a sip of beer.

"Can I make a suggestion?" asked Jody.

"Of course you can," said Justin.

"What would you think of a fireplace right there in that corner," she said, nodded toward the corner nearest the couch.

Staring at the corner as if envisioning a fireplace, Justin's eyes took on a satisfied glow. "That would be perfect!" he said, reaching down to stroke Perk's head. The little dog had curled up near his feet. He looked over at Michael, who sat with his feet propped up on the low table. "Do you like the idea?"

"I love it," Michael repeated, trying to grasp the magnitude of such a project. Though the structural concepts were foreign to him, he knew he could learn; and as far as he was concerned, starting the project tomorrow would not be soon enough. He closed his eyes, contemplating long days of toil and construction, and with it the promise of contentment in its purest form.

The cool night air had settled over the room from the opened window. Scratchy tunes, the likes of Johnny Cash and Merle Haggard, wafted from the old Zenith on the wall shelf. And three very close friends spent the rest of the evening turning a few more pages of the books they had not finished reading.

Justin awoke the next morning haunted by thoughts of the kidnapper. Not sure in what direction the state police and FBI had decided to take in their manhunt, he still felt his own time best served in exploring the vehicle tracks off the River Road. He set out right after breakfast, planning to start where he had left off the day before. Jody and Michael walked out of the house with him, planning to drive into Alpine for groceries and supplies.

After three days, Justin had found no leads whatsoever, nor had any of the agencies involved. The park was all but deserted. It seemed the kidnapper had disappeared, that perhaps he had found some way to vacate the park. The state police had closed down the road blocks and the FBI had returned to San Antonio. Justin reluctantly accepted the fact that the killer had eluded them, at least for now.

That night Mr. Kirkland, the owner of the property, was to meet them at the house at six o'clock. Justin and Michael would own the property by the time the meeting concluded. Much of the documentation already existed. Justin had in his possession a copy of the contract and survey, so all that remained were a few closing documents and the transfer of funds.

Justin swung open the door when Mr. Kirkland arrived. With his amiable demeanor, he stood dressed casually next to a well dressed young lawyer with briefcase in hand. They stepped inside and Justin introduced Mr. Kirkland, a sophisticated gentleman perhaps sixty years of age, who in turn introduced the young lawyer, Brian Espina, a dapper professional type with an olive complexion and coal black hair. Apparently of Spanish ancestry, his facial features were distinct and his jaw had darkened during the course of the day with the masculine shadow of a heavy beard.

Michael stepped forward to shake the young man's hand. He noticed Brian seemed immediately distracted by his sister. Still standing near the doorway, the young man lifted his hand absentmindedly as he craned his neck a bit to look at her over Michael's shoulder. His eyes seemed fixed as he shook Michael's hand.

Jody's demeanor had turned somewhat coy as she sat observing all of this from the kitchen table in her white t-shirt and jeans, her radiant beauty not lost in her casual apparel.

Michael maintained his subtle observation as Justin and Mr. Kirkland proceeded toward the kitchen, the lawyer still caught for a moment in his tracks by the door. Justin walked to the counter to plug in the coffee pot. He turned and noticed the lawyer still standing there, staring across the room at Jody. His eyes shifted from Brian to Jody and then to Michael. He gave Michael a discreet wink.

Aware of the sudden tension, Mr. Kirkland scanned the faces about the room. He shrugged his shoulders and sat down at the table.

Brian swept across the room and stood beside Jody, his gaze still locked. "It's a pleasure to meet you, Miss Anderson."

She extended her hand and replied, "And my pleasure too, Mr. Espina."

He took her hand and instead of the expected handshake, he drew it to his lips and kissed it. "Are you from around here?" he asked.

Michael noticed then how busty she looked in the tight cotton shirt. And she was obviously enchanted. He looked back at the young man who also apparently noticed these same things.

"No," Jody replied. "I live in San Diego. I'm visiting Justin and my brother for a while."

Brian glanced back and forth between the two men, as if an obvious conclusion had formed in his mind. Then Jody stood up.

"Please sit here, Mr. Espina. I have nothing to do with the

purpose of this meeting. I think I'll just sit in that rocker over there."

Something in her tone told Michael she was smitten. He looked back at Brian to size him up, watching the young man's dark eyes sweep over his sister's form as she walked toward the rocker. It wasn't the first time he had noticed a man's eyes drawn to her shapely hips.

They were all aware of Brian's sudden and obvious attraction to Jody. As Justin placed four cans of Tecate and four glasses on the table, Mr. Kirkland broke the silence.

"Justin, I'm delighted you're going to be able to buy this property this much sooner than you were expecting to."

Mr. Kirkland's train of thought was interrupted when Brian suddenly stood up. The young man had poured a glass of beer and was taking it to Jody. Standing in front of the refrigerator, Justin looked at the can of beer in his hand he had taken out for her. He went to the table and sat down, replacing Brian's beer with it instead.

"Do you like Tecate, Miss Anderson?" the young man asked.

"My friends call me Jody," she said.

"I'm honored, and my friends call me Brian," he said, extending the glass.

"Why thank you, Brian," she said, reaching for the glass.

Brian returned to the table, his eyes still drawn to the girl in the rocker as if no one else was in the room. Watching him with interest, Michael got the stool from beside the stove and joined the men. Mr. Kirkland cleared his throat and attempted to get the meeting on course.

"Brian, uh, do you think you remember why we're here?"

Brian glanced at him. "Yes, sir, I do."

"Good. Then we can proceed." With the awkwardness of Brian's behavior behind them, Mr. Kirkland looked at Justin. "I assume Michael here is the man you told me over the phone who will be your partner in this transaction."

"Yes. We'll be equal partners."

"All right then, we'll get this started." He nodded at Brian. "Mr. Espina isn't my lawyer, but I know him quite well. He knows everything there is to know about real estate. I hired him to represent all of us with no partiality; that is, if there's no objections. If not, half his fee will be covered by your part of the closing costs."

Both Michael and Justin agreed.

Then Brian spoke. "Mr. Kirkland assured me that his only interest is in conveying the land to you, unimpaired by any self-interests that might be detrimental to you. I've read over all the documents and since the purchase price is well below what the land appraised for, I'm convinced the integrity of his offer is sincere."

"I appreciate your assurance," said Justin, "but I've always trusted him."

The transaction took less than thirty minutes to complete. Just as Michael took out his check to fill in the amount for his share, Jody stepped outside to watch the sunset. Michael noticed that Brian had taken an interest in her exit. The young lawyer quickly tucked all the documents back into his briefcase. He abruptly stood up and walked out the back door, closing it behind him.

The three men still at the table looked at each other.

"Now if that ain't the damnedest thing," said Mr. Kirkland in his old traditional Texas drawl.

"Think we ought to send Perk out there to keep an eye on them?" Justin mused.

Michael reached up to scratch the top of his head.

"I wouldn't worry," said Mr. Kirkland. "I know that boy to be a fine gentleman. Damned successful too." He reached over and slapped Justin on the shoulder. "Looks like you own a thousand acres of this ranch, son. Congratulations." He studied the two men for a moment, their excited faces, their fleeting glimpses at each other, then said, "You fellows seem awfully close. Is this what it looks like it is?"

"I guess it's pretty obvious, isn't it?" said Justin.

"I reckon it is," said the old gentleman. "Two men living together alone out here, buying land together. I suppose things like that are viewed differently these days. I know age has enlightened me to many things I once misunderstood."

Justin smiled and nodded, then got up to get another round of Tecate. Mr. Kirkland poured himself another glass and said, "That business about the kidnapping over in the park made a pretty good splash in the Houston newspapers. I hear they didn't catch that guy yet."

Justin let out an angry breath of frustration. He filled Mr. Kirkland in on the details of the crime, of how he planned to continue his own private search for the kidnapper, and hoped to at least uncover some clues. They sipped the Tecate and continued their casual conversation. Mr. Kirkland, having related the details of a couple of interesting business ventures he was involved in, took an immediate interest in hearing more about

Michael's medical career. Michael spoke of it briefly, with no fanfare, concluding with his last fateful heart surgery.

"That little girl died," said Justin. "That's why he quit and came out here."

"That's when you two met?" said Mr. Kirkland.

Justin looked at Michael and nodded.

"It's a raw deal, something like that happening to a man who has good intentions. You came to the right place though. The Big Bend will help you put it to rest."

Michael looked at his watch, then looked at the back door. It had been forty-five minutes since Brian joined his sister outside. He got up and cleared the table of empty beer cans. Before he had set out another round, Jody came bursting through the door and went straight into the bedroom. Brian stepped in right behind her, his hands in his pockets, his eyes in her direction.

She called out for Michael, who looked at Brian for a moment before he went into the back room. Justin had repaired the door, so now it closed all the way. She looked nervous as a cat stepping over a sleeping dog.

"Michael, my heart is pounding so hard it almost hurts! I can't think straight!"

"Sis, what's wrong? Did something happen out there?" He didn't know whether to be angry or just concerned.

"Just looking at him drives me crazy, just hearing his voice."

"Uh, well, I wouldn't worry about it. He's going to be gone in a few minutes."

"No! You don't get it, Michael. That's not what I'm trying to tell you."

"Well what is it then?"

"He wants me to go to Houston for a few days," she said anxiously.

"To his place!" Michael blurted.

She looked at him, incredulous. "No, Michael, of course not. He'd get me a hotel room downtown."

"Oh."

"I told him I had to talk to you about it. I don't know what to do."

"You sure were out there with him a long time."

"Did you notice how incredibly handsome he is?" she asked. Her face comprised a mixture of panic, extreme excitement and doubt. She seemed unable to stand still, or decide what to do with her hands.

"Actually, I did notice," he said, at a loss for a way to calm her.

"Well that's not the best of it. It's that he doesn't know it himself, or at least he doesn't act like he does. Do you know how refreshing it is to talk to a man who doesn't spend the whole time talking about himself?"

"I do now."

"I let him kiss me."

"You weren't out there *that* long!"

"That's exactly the problem—we were. We were sitting in the new chairs, talking. He leaned toward me just a little, and when I looked at him I could tell what he was thinking. I never wanted to do anything more in my life than to kiss him. It's never happened to me like that before. It's never been so absolutely fucking perfect."

"There must be something in the air out here."

"So what am I going to do? I didn't bring anything to wear on a date with someone in Houston. That's not California down there. Did you see how he was dressed? He's wearing the most beauitful Armani suit I've ever seen."

"They don't wear blue jeans in Houston?"

"I don't know. But you'd think they do, at least some of them. After all, it is in Texas." She paced nervously, looking at the floor. "He wants me to go back in Mr. Kirkland's jet with them. They flew into Alpine."

"Sis, do you want to go?"

She swallowed hard, her throat and lips as dry as cotton. "Oh Michael … I've never wanted anything more than this chance to get to know him better. I've never met anyone like him. I'm just scared."

"Well, Mr. Kirkland is just about the nicest man I ever met. I can't imagine he'd allow you to go if there was something to be afraid of."

"That's not what I mean." She closed her eyes, lifting her hand to her chest, as if she was trying to hold down her pounding heart. "What if …"

"You can't allow '*What ifs*' to rule your life, Sis." He approached and wrapped his arms around her. "I'll tell you what you're going to do. You're going to Houston. In the morning, after you figure out what they wear down there, you're going to get out one of your credit cards and go shopping for some new clothes. Then, my guess is, you're going to have a couple of the longest dinners you've ever had in your life."

She tilted her head back to look at him. "I love you, big

brother."

"Get packed," he said, giving her a quick slap on the ass. "I'll go out and tell them you'll be out in a few minutes."

She went straight for her travel case as Michael turned toward the door. He closed the door behind him and looked at Brian, who was sitting anxiously on the arm of the couch.

Brian stood up and said, "I hope you don't think I'm being too forward with your sister."

"No. Actually I'm accustomed to men being taken by her. I'm just not used to seeing her being swept off her feet by any of them." Michael looked over at Mr. Kirkland. "sir, you said you know Brian quite well."

"Yes. Quite well indeed. He's not my lawyer because he's more like the son I've never had. He went to work for me when he was in college. I loaned him the money to get through law school. Your sister will be in the hands of a remarkable young gentleman. That I can assure you."

Michael looked back at Brian, his lips pursed, and he nodded, saying, "She'll be out as soon as she packs a few things."

They all walked out of the house together thirty minutes later. Michael and Mr. Kirkland paused a few yards from the car while Justin followed Jody and Brian with her luggage. Jody got into the back seat, then Brian got in beside her.

"Looks like I'm going to play the roll of chauffeur tonight," said Mr. Kirkland. He looked at Michael and extended his hand. "I have to say I'm very happy for Justin. I met him when he first came out here and signed on as a park ranger, up in that wonderful dining room at the Gage Hotel in Marathon. He was at a table next to mine, and we got to talking. I liked him right away. One of the most interesting young men I've ever met. Well, they have pretty good rockers on the front porch at that hotel. I remember it like it was yesterday. It was one of those warm summer nights out here, when the sky is black and full of stars. We took a couple of cigars out with us and spent most of the night rocking on that porch, talking about all the things that really matter in life. Every now and then a train streaked though that lonely town on the tracks just across the street from the hotel, and we just sat there and listened to it go by. I knew he was starving for something." He paused, squinting into Michael's eyes, and added, "Now I know what it was."

Michael nodded. "We both appreciate your selling us this land. It's been Justin's dream for a long time now."

"Well, Doctor, it's been my pleasure to meet you. I think I can imagine how you felt when you lost that little girl, but that wound will heal. I've always admired doctors as special people. I believe you've answered a calling. Now you're living in a part of the world where your calling could do some real good."

"I've been told that," said Michael.

Justin approached and stood beside them.

"I'm sure you have," said Mr. Kirkland. He glanced at the car. "Looks like those two are ready for their chauffeur. Listen, Michael, don't worry about your sister. She'll be fine." He turned and reached for Justin's hand. "I'm glad you've bought this land, Justin. It suits you. And it's good you have someone to share it with."

"Thanks, Mr. Kirkland. You'll never know how much I appreciate your friendship."

"I'll be stopping by one day to see what you're doing with this place."

"Any time," said Justin. "We'll see you soon."

Mr. Kirkland walked over and got behind the wheel of the car. Jody leaned out the window to wave goodbye as the car started down the road. Justin and Michael stood side-by-side, watching the tail lights grow small in the dust.

"Are you worried about her?" asked Justin.

"Yeah. I've never seen her act like a giddy school girl before. Not even when she was a school girl. She's supposed to call me every day she's down there."

"Well she may be a little giddy over that guy, but I've never met a woman more capable of taking care of herself."

"What did you think of him? Wasn't he almost too pretty to be straight?" said Michael.

"That same thought crossed my mind." said Justin. "Other than that, I didn't get much of a chance to get to know him, but he seemed like an average nice guy."

They watched the car awhile longer, then Justin leaned over and picked up a handful of dirt. "Looks like we own a thousand acres of this," he said, looking at the sand in his hand by the light of the moon.

"Yeah it does," Michael said wistfully, looking back at the house. "And it looks like we have the place all to ourselves again."

Justin leaned toward Michael's neck and drew a deep breath, and his lips lingered a moment on the taste of his skin. He reached up to unfasten the buttons of Michael's shirt. "I believe there's a bottle of wine in the back of the refrigerator."

Michael's shirt fell open. He smiled, watching Justin unbutton his own shirt, and then they walked together back into the house.

CHAPTER 16

Twenty minutes after Jody had departed with Brian, Justin and Michael had gotten out of their clothes and lay relaxed atop the sheets on the bed, each with a glass of California blush. They had poured Perk a dish full of the wine and placed it next to the bed. The little dog happily lapped up every drop.

Justin lifted his leg and draped it over Michael's and he scooted a bit closer. "You know what amazes me about making love to you?" he said. "It's the way you smell. You turn me on when I think about you, when I see you, when I taste you, and when I touch you; but when I breathe the odors of your body, I'm lost to the rest of the world. Your hair, your breath, your neck, your underarms, those little drops that trickle out of you when you're aroused, it all drives me crazy. But what makes my whole body feel like it's on fire is right down here." Justin pushed his fingertips under Michael's testicles and stroked the sensitive skin around his anus. "The way you smell down here. God, Michael, it's like a drug. I knew the minute I saw you that you were a turn-on, but I never imagined how the way you smell would affect me."

Michael shivered with the caress. He looked at his lover and smiled.

"You've always known how that affects a man, haven't you?"

"I know how *you* affect me," Michael said, turning his face toward Justin's neck and drawing a deep breath. "You're talking about pheromones. They're unique in every individual. You might have a completely different reaction with someone else. You can find yourself put off by the way a man smells, even if he's attractive. You and I, my friend, are amazingly compatible." His smile broadened. "It's why we may never get enough."

Justin took a sip of wine, then adjusted his weight and rested his head atop Michael's chest. Michael's arm came down over his shoulder, his fingertips stroking across the scattered hairs of his chest. The sound of Willie Nelson's voice drifted in from the radio in the front room, and warm air from an early Spring day still lingered in the night. The heat from their bodies so close made their skin feel damp and supple.

"Tomorrow afternoon I'm going to talk to Bernard and make arrangements for some vacation time. A week. We can get started on our building project."

"Have you got our game plan?"

"Pretty much. There's an old deserted house and barn over on the Gordon ranch that Mr. Gordon said I could have. He's the rancher Juan Gutierrez works for and a good friend. You'll meet him sooner or later. We'll salvage the timber we need from there. Then there's the stone. I'm curious how much of it we can haul up from the river in a day. When we find that out, we'll be able to calculate how long it'll take to bring up enough for the walls."

"How will we haul it up here?"

"Bernard has a flatbed trailer we can borrow. We can pull it behind your Cherokee." Justin ran his hand down over Michael's thigh. "I was thinking, if we build the bathroom on the westside, we can put in a large window with a view of the setting sun, and a bath with room for two."

"Two men in a bathtub. Is that kind of thinking typical among you park rangers?"

Justin laughed. "Hardly."

"So the day after tomorrow we're going to start bringing up the stone?"

"I think that'd be a good starting place."

They finished the wine in their glasses and poured another round. When the bottle was empty, they settled into the easy calm of music and the oncoming chill of night air. Unhurried in the soft light cast from the lamp, their eyes and hands and lips began another adventure. So tender their love, their mingling tongues and lips, fingertips bringing tingles across skin, each whisper and caress came as long moments grew mellow into the night. They lay in an entanglement of white and black legs, of fast beating hearts and warm breath and long sighs, of closed eyes and mutual stroking of pliant skin. And finally, in the dark hours of late night, damp bodies united, came the gentle calm of sleep.

Justin finished the next day by exploring the meandering tracks of yet another vehicle leading off into the desert, tracks that ended like all the others, merging back on the River Road. He had taken the Cherokee so that he could stop by Bernard's aparment to pick up the trailer.

"So you two bought that thousand acres," Bernard said as they walked together down his driveway to where the trailer was parked.

"Yes. We're planning to add a bathroom and another bed-room to the house."

"And that's why you want a week off, to start that project?"

"That's right, Bernard. You any good with a shovel?"

"I'm not quite ready for my first heart attack," Bernard said, checking the trailer. "You might have to put a little air in these tires."

Justin hooked up the trailer and was home forty-five minutes later.

Right after bacon and eggs and coffee the next morning, Justin and Michael drove the trailer over to the abandoned house on Mr. Gordon's ranch. It was a dilapidated wooden structure that had survived the elements and many years of neglect. They entered through the front door, all but its top hinge pulled from the weathered door frame.

"Looks like we could use this door," said Justin, running his hand over its flaking green paint.

Stopping half way through the front room, Michael looked around the ghostly surroundings. The wall paper had long since fallen away from walls made of wooden planks. He stepped across a creaking wooden floor, looking up at ancient boards that were falling away from the rafters.

"There's our window for the bathroom," Justin said.

Michael looked at a large wooden window that overlooked the eastern horizon, its paint long gone and most of its glass panes shattered. Justin stepped toward it and managed to raise the lower section about twelve inches. "Needs work," he said. He reached up and pulled down a ceiling board, then shone his flashlight up into the rafters, studying the structure for a moment. "It's all hardwood up there, plenty enough for our roof and back porch. That old wood is difficult to work with, but it'll last forever."

"It already has," said Michael.

One doorway led to the bedroom. Another led to what was left of a 1930s era kitchen, the varnish long gone from the thick wooden counter top, the broken cabinet doors scattered about broken glass strewn on the floor.

They walked into the kitchen. Justin scanned the walls and ceiling and his eyes fell upon the counter. "Ah, that's what we need to build a ramp over that standing water in the canyon," he said, stepping forward to examine the heavy planks. "They don't manufacture stuff like this anymore," he said, leaning over planks some fifteen inches wide and twelve feet long. "We can get them up with the crow bar."

By noon they had erected a ramp over the stagnant water that blocked their route through the narrow canyon. Built with a slight incline, they fixed it to the rock formation that they would have to crawl over to get to the river. It would be a slow labor, but their most plentiful asset was time.

Justin looked at his watch. "Looks like we have half the day left to see how much stone we can haul out."

"I'm ready," said Michael.

"Why don't we start with one of those sandwiches you made this morning? I'm hungry."

They went back out of the canyon and sat on the back end of the trailer to eat the sandwiches. As he chewed the last bite, Justin picked up one of the canvas backpacks that Michael had found at the general store in Lajitas the day before, which they would use to pack out the stones. They strapped them on and made their way to the river. Wearing cut-off blue jeans and sandals, they waded into the rapids, the river bed under their feet littered with countless smooth stones. Justin leaned over and reached into the water, its power swirling about his arms and shoulders. He brought up the first stone and grinned.

"A couple thousand like this one ought to do it," he said.

They went about pulling the stones from the river bed with deliberate intent, the sun sparkling in their eyes from the water's fast surface. They each packed out some two dozen stones at a time. Ranging in size from an orange to a small mellon, their color a variety of earthy browns, the stones lay heavy in the back packs as they trekked back through the canyon. As the hours of a warm afternoon passed, they labored in harmony with the river, content in their isolation from a hectic world, and satisfied by the progress of their slow task. A half hour before sunset, they stood near the house, looking at three handsome piles of stone they had placed near where the new walls were to be built. Perk lifted his leg to pee on one of the piles.

"That's to let the coyotes know these rocks belong to us," said Justin.

Michael smiled, kneeling to call the dog over, giving him a good head rub when he trotted up.

Justin looked at his watch again. "We brought up more than I thought we could in six hours."

"Think we'll have enough if we spend the rest of the week on it?" Michael asked.

"Yes, I do, and that's a good idea. We'd have that part behind us. Then we'd be ready to prepare the foundation and install the plumbing." He studied the piles. "But it might not take all week to bring up enough stones."

Michael rubbed his stomach. "I don't think I've ever been this exhausted or hungry. You ready to eat?"

"Let's heat up some frozen dinners. I don't feel like cooking."

Michael's cell phone rang just as they finished eating. It was Jody.

"How's it going, Sis?"

"Oh Michael, I've never had so much fun." There was a level of excitement in her voice Michael had never heard before. She went on. "We went to Galveston. There's a wonderful historical downtown area called the Strand. We spent all afternoon browsing antique shops and galleries. We held hands and talked endlessly."

Michael looked at Justin and shrugged his shoulders, saying into the phone, "Sounds like a fun day, Sis."

"Brian is picking me up in an hour for dinner. Michael, I don't know what to say, I'm almost breathless."

"Uh, well …"

"I've never met anyone like him, Michael. He got me a suite in a downtown hotel, three hundred dollars a night. It's full of fresh cut roses. He even rented a Porsche. It's parked in the garage in case I need a car for some reason. The concierge called a minute ago to see if I wanted a masseuse or manicurist sent to my room."

"You've never let a man pick up the tab for your expenses before."

"I know," she said happily.

"Sis, you haven't lost control of yourself, have you?"

She laughed. "Let me just say that I haven't understood how things happened so fast between you and Justin, until now."

"Oh shit!"

"But I don't have time to talk. I've got to get ready."

"Did you buy a new outfit for tonight?"

"Wait until you see it. It's a strapless red satin gown, cut low in front and back and form fitting. If Brian is a breast man, I intend to drive him crazy tonight."

"Where are you having dinner? I think I'll call Mr. Kirkland and see if he'll join you two."

"Forget it, big brother. I haven't got a clue where he's going to take me for dinner. Goodbye."

He heard a click and then he held the phone out, staring at it.

"You look dumbfounded," said Justin.

He looked over at his lover with a kind of disoriented half smile, nodding blankly, and said, "I am dumbfounded. Brian is wining and dining her with both barrels. It sounded like she's morphed into a completely different female. I sure hope we don't have to go down there and bring her back with a broken heart."

Justin laughed. "Judging by what I saw, it would be Brian at risk of a broken heart. Nevertheless, Jody is a tough lady. She'll survive whatever happens."

Perk trotted over and sat on his haunches near the table, looking up at them and licking his chops. Justin looked over at his empty bowl. "Looks like he likes that canned dog food you bought him."

Michael reached down to scratch the dog's chest. "Yeah. Don't care much for that dry stuff, do you boy?" He got up and cleared the disposable plates from the table.

Justin had gone into the bedroom and had returned with some file folders, a legal pad and a portable calculator. He sat down at the table and turned on the calculator. Michael brought him a can of Tecate. Standing beside him, Michael looked down at his own chest and ran his hand over the oils and grit of a day's work. He lifted his elbow and sniffed his underarm.

"I think I'll go out and rinse off," Michael said.

Justin looked up at him. "Guess we got a little sweaty hauling that stone, didn't we?" His eyes swept over him.

Michael noticed his suggestive gaze. "Yeah, I guess we did."

"Why don't we skip the shower tonight?"

Michael stared at him a moment. Justin's unspoken thoughts were clear. "Maybe I'll just sit down and read for awhile in the living room."

Justin's gaze lifted from the contours of Michael's cut-off jeans. His gaze reflected anticipation of entering a garden or male odors. "This shouldn't take too long," he said he said somewhat distantly, looking down at the table in deep thought. His eyes shifted to the folder and his expression changed, as if he suddenly remembered what he had intended to do. "I thought I'd make a list of the materials we're going to have to buy to finish the project. Get an idea of how much it's going to cost."

He watched Michael walk into the living room and unbutton his shorts, then step out of them and fling them into the bedroom. Momentarily distracted again by the flex of Michael's buttocks with each step, Justin watched his nude lover walk over to recline in the over-stuffed chair. When Michael picked up a magazine, Justin's eyes drifted back to the legal pad and he reached for a pencil.

Michael propped his feet upon the low table and began to read an article about the Middle East. Five minutes later he fell asleep, Perk curled casually in his lap.

The creaking sound of the water pump handle awoke him an hour later. Justin was getting a glass of water. Michael joined him at the table.

"This is a list of the materials we'll have to buy," Justin said, "things like the septic tank and lines, plumbing fixtures, mortar mix, tiles and brick. We'll have to lay in all the preliminary plumbing before we start on the structure." He handed Michael the list and then picked up a stack of files, leafing through them. "I added up what I had left in mutual funds, and if I sold them all, it wouldn't be enough to cover that list." Michael looked at the files and said, "I'd prefer you not sell any of them."

"It's the only money I have left. We have to buy the plumbing material right away and I'd have to sell them to pay for it."

"Not if I write a check for this stuff. Shit, the whole list only comes to eight thousand dollars."

"Only if we can find a used septic tank. It could go over ten thousand, and it probably will anyway, when you figure what I'm forgetting to add in."

"That doesn't matter. I doubt you could replace a commode in San Diego for this amount. We're talking about a new bathroom and bedroom. I'm amazed at what little this is going to cost."

"Still," Justin argued, "it wouldn't be fair if you paid for all of it."

Michael pondered the concern in his lover's eyes for a moment. "I'd rather you not spend your last penny on our project, Justin. The way I look at it is you gave up almost everything you saved to buy this land, while I gave up just a fraction of what

I have, and since I couldn't do any of this without you, I'd feel a whole lot better if you'd let me kick in a little more money."

Justin looked down in thought at the files on the table. Michael stood and came up behind him, placing his fingertips aside his temples and massaging them gently. Justin's head tilted back and rested on Michael's stomach, his eyes closed with the soothing feel. The fingertips caressed the lines of his face, moving over forehead and brows, down over eyelids, exploring the round shape of his eyes, over cheeks and nose, then lingered so lightly on the smooth texture of Justin's lips that chills came to the back of his neck.

"You know," said Justin, his tone relaxed, "I'm looking forward to sleeping with a man who worked all day in the sun. You smell sweaty and it's turning me on."

"Now that's far more interesting to think about than that budget."

"Are you ready to go to bed?"

"I was ready at two o'clock this afternoon, when I looked up and saw you bending over in the river."

Both weary, they walked together to the bedroom, their shoulders and backs sore from toting heavy packs of stone. Justin placed his hands on Michael's hips as they stood beside the bed. He leaned forward and his lips neared Michael's neck, kissing the salty taste of male flesh. He lifted Michael's arm and his kisses found their way into the damp hollow and his nostrils flared with the odor of a man's full day of labor. The scent spread through him with the effect of a powerful aphrodisiac, its message inexplicably clear. Drawing another long breath, his tongue came forth and swathed over the silky hair, lapping at the bitter taste as if it nourished him, the ache in his lower back now forgotten.

"I could lick every inch of you," he whispered, his lips again close to Michael's ear.

Michael looked down. His penis now erect, twitching with those sensations still alive in the hollow of his underarm. He watched a black hand come forth and take his swollen glans between forefinger and thumb, caressing and pressing its warm meaty shape. His cock flexed out a drop of semen, a slippery lubricant for Justin's lingering caress that caused Michael's knees to go weak.

"Will I ever believe I really found you?" Justin whispered. He looked into Michael's eyes. "I've had a fantasy all day today."

Michael swallowed and cleared his throat. "What would you like me to do?" he asked passively.

Justin closed his eyes and took in a deep breath. It took a moment to summon the courage to make his request, but then he knew that Michael would respond to anything he wanted with no reservation or second thought. "When I lay down, I want you to straddle my head and squat over my face."

Michael had detected his hesitation. He smiled. "Just now, I can't think of anything I'd rather do."

Justin sat on the edge of the bed and pulled off his shorts, tossing them across the room. He lay back on the sheet, watching his lover with a glow of anticipation. Michael crawled upon the bed and lifted his leg up over Justin's face, straddling him on hands and knees. He paused as Justin's hands came up the sides of his legs, allowing dark eyes to linger on the intimate visual of what was to come. He looked down at a pulsing black cock, and saw a rivulet of semen materialize from the tiny hole and streak toward the tangle of course black hairs. He leaned down and licked it away, and then leaned further until his nose pressed into the pliant sac, the musk quick with spell-like magic.

Captivated by what could never be explained, Justin watched his lover's leg come down beside his head, his heart racing. Inhaling the odors born in a long day's work, the intimate minutia of a man's body unfolded before his eyes: the distended fleshy sac, the soft mound of skin just behind it, the darker, always damp, always hidden anal flesh scattered with fine hair. His eyes followed the crease where Michael's legs joined his body, and over the two muscular rounds of his buttocks, dwelling there, the gluteal crease as deep as his second knuckle. The small pucker flexed and then dilated slightly, which quickened his heart and increased his growing hunger. Bewitched with the perfect decadence of male contours and textures and heat, his hands rested on muscled legs. That Michael gave himself this way, that they shared such intimate fantasy, defined profoundly the essence that drew them together.

As he lay within the intimate air between his lover's legs, the aphrodisia crawled through his nose, spreading like beguiling vapors through helpless limbs. "Oh Michael," he sighed as the heat came nearer his face.

His lover's testicles now lay upon his lips, his nose so near that allusive rift, and his hands rested upon Michael's hips in their slow rhythm. His body felt liquid, weak, alive with the sensation of floating, his mind adrift in an erotic realm of pleasure. The hunger that warmed his loins soon haunted his tongue. He grasped tight Michael's hips, pulling desperately his weight upon his face, lapping anxiously at the fine sweat of a compliant lover.

He took a testicle into his mouth, sucking it between his lips, kneading the egg-shaped organ with his tongue. From Michael he heard a long moan, he saw the small hole pinch tight, and he felt his cock engulfed within a warm wet mouth.

Lost in the vast quiet of the desert, they made love. Michael on his knees and impaled by his lover, they collapsed together on the bed, their bodies damp on the cool sheet. From the Zenith came country songs mingled with static hum. From the window came wispy night air. They lay spooned together in the heavenly quiet, Justin behind and still coupled, in contemplation of the seamless passion of men with like minds.

Michael's anal muscle flexed. "That sure feels good. It's fine with me if you leave it in all night."

"Think it can stay hard that long?"

"It might if you don't think about it."

"I can't help but think about it," said Justin.

"Was it different getting into bed with a sweaty lover?"

"Yes. I didn't know a man could get that turned on. Those pheromones you were talking about. Pretty potent stuff. It felt like I was breathing fire there for awhile."

"God! That feels good."

Perk jumped up on the bed and started licking Justin's face.

"Dammit, Perk!"

"What's he doing?" Michael asked, unable to see with his head turned.

"He's licking my face!"

"He's probably ready to go to sleep. Can you reach the light?"

"No."

"Leave it on then."

Perk curled up beside them and Justin pressed in closer. He reached for a pillow and folded it under his head, the fragrance of Michael's hair near his nose. He rested his hand on Michael's shoulder and closed his eyes, and fell asleep with his lover's warm back against his chest.

Justin woke up at first light alone in the bed. He sat up on the edge of the mattress, rubbing his eyes, then noticed Perk standing in the doorway looking at him.

"Where's Michael, boy?"

The dog looked back over his tail toward the kitchen.

Michael was at the table, on his second cup of coffee when Justin walked into the room, apparently brooding about something. So deep in thought, Michael failed to look up as Justin passed on his way to the coffee pot. Placing a full cup on the table, Justin stood behind Michael and ran his hands down over his shoulders, reaching down for the distinct pectoral muscle of his chest. He kneaded the muscle with both hands, his thoughts shifting from their encounter the night before to unease.

Justin sat down and took a sip of coffee, looking at Michael over the rim of the cup. "What are you thinking about this morning?"

"Nothing much," Michael said, looking over at him, the faint hint of a smile on his lips unconvincing.

Watching him, Justin nodded and took another sip of coffee. "Well, I'd assume you're worried about Jody, but I don't really think you are. We both know she can look after herself."

"I'm not worried about her. I've wanted someone like Brian to come along for a long time now." He glanced at Justin and added, "It's nothing, really."

"How long have you been sitting out here?"

Michael looked at his watch. "Three hours."

"What!"

"I woke up and couldn't get back to sleep." He looked at Justin. "I would have never left California if that little girl hadn't died," he said soberly.

Justin squinted, instantly concerned. "Maybe not. But why would that be bothering you?"

"Don't you see? I've found great happiness with you. You came into my life because I left San Diego and I wouldn't have left if she hadn't died. I found happiness because she died. I can't quit thinking about that. Every time I think about how good my life is out here, that operation starts haunting me."

Justin looked down at the table. *Oh God, Michael! Don't do this to yourself ... to us.* He looked back up and saw a tear trickle down Michael's face. His lover had been up half the night suffering this awful stress and it was like a stab in his own heart.

"Michael, it's two different things: what happened to the little girl and us finding each other. I can't stand to see you torture yourself this way. Think about Julian Gutierrez. He could have died. He's alive because you left San Diego. If the girl's death had something to do with your fate, maybe it was because of Julian and others like him. You left San Diego where there are countless doctors to care for people, to come to a place where many people are in desperate need. Don't you think that's a better explanation of that unfortunate day?"

Michael stared down at the table.

"You know, when I look at you, I see an incredible man. I see my lover, a man I want to spend the rest of my life with. I also see Doctor Anderson."

Michael looked at him.

"That's the real basis for what's troubling you, isn't it?" said Justin. "You're torn about giving up your medical practice."

"Maybe it is. Even Mr. Kirkland made a comment about it the other night. Same thing you and Jody have said, about how much another doctor is needed down here."

"He was right, you are needed here."

"But how can I, Justin? How can I practice medicine when I've lost confidence in my judgment as a doctor?"

"Well, I'm not so sure you really have lost confidence in yourself."

Michael looked at him. "You just don't understand, do you?"

"I'm trying to. But it is hard to understand how one mistake can wipe out who you are." Justin took another sip of coffee. He could see that Michael's perspective was still painful, that he himself could not find the right words to help him. "Maybe it's just not in the cards, at least any time soon. But there's no reason to feel pressured by it today. Give yourself time to settle into your new life in the desert. If you are to ever put on that white coat, it'll be a day you'll feel comfortable wearing it."

Perk lifted his front paws off the floor and rested them on Michael's thigh. Michael stroked his head.

"Looks like he wants you to give him his breakfast. He thinks I'll put that dry dog food in his bowl."

After Michael opened a can of dog food, they prepared oatmeal for breakfast. By noon, they were back up from the river with the first trailer load of stones. The piles were growing. Though Michael had been rather quiet most of the morning, he had started to come out of his depression. He had begun to envision the new walls, and the tranquility of watching sunsets from the new back porch. Justin had suggested they call it a veranda, since it was to sweep along the full length of the back of the house and extend out some ten feet.

They took a break after unloading the trailer, taking some cold cuts and cheese and cold beer out behind the house to relax a few minutes in their new chairs. It was high noon. With the sun casting its warm bright light from directly overhead, the desert seemed more vibrant with the subtle changes of Spring.

"Seems there's more plants blooming everyday," Michael said as he gazed out over the terrain.

"If we could get one good rain, you'd really see a difference. The Ocatillos are especially beautiful in full bloom."

"I don't feel as sore as I did yesterday," said Michael, tilting the can for another swallow of beer.

Justin glanced at him. "You didn't look sore last night," he said, his lips pursed.

Michael looked at him and smiled.

"I never imagined," Justin said, closing his eyes and tilting his head back. "I never dreamed I could be so overwhelmed, so consumed by someone. Last night it hit me just like I thought it would, you coming to bed after working in the sun all day. You have a distinct smell even after you take a shower, but last night, God, last night I felt like a whore in a barrel of dicks."

Michael laughed. "That must be a Texas analogy."

"Whatever. All I know is I can't seem to get enough of it."

Michael cocked his head. "Do you hear a car coming?"

Justin listened for a moment. "Yes. Sounds like it's about a mile away."

They listened to the car's approach. It stopped in front of the house. They waited a moment and Scott Baker, one of the park rangers, came around the corner of the house. He was a tall thin lad in his early twenties, fair complexion and coal black wavy hair, a rookie from Mississippi. He approached somewhat hesitantly.

"Hello, Scott," said Justin. "What brings you all the way out here?"

"It's my day off," said Scott, looking back over his shoulder at the piles of stone. "Bernard told me you were adding on to your house."

"Yeah, we're just now starting. A bedroom and bathroom. We're sitting where the veranda is going to be."

"Sounds great," said Scott, glancing between the two men. He shoved his hands into this back pockets and looked around, this way and that, though his survey of the property didn't fit his distant expression. Michael and Justin glanced at each other. Scott seemed nervous to them. It was obvious the reason for his visit lurked in his thoughts behind the pretense of his interest in the house.

Justin saw right away the young man had something on his mind. "By the way, this is Michael Anderson … Michael, Scott Baker. Scott has been with the service about a year now."

Michael nodded and extended his hand. The young man stepped forward and took it, his eyes reflecting an unusually intense interest in Michael.

"Would you like a beer, Scott?" Justin asked.

His gaze shifted from Michael as he responded. "Sure.

Sounds good."

Justin nodded toward the back door. "There's some in the refrigerator. Help yourself. Bring out one of those chairs in the kitchen."

The young man walked into the house and Justin looked at Michael. "I wonder what he's up to."

Scott came back out with a can of beer and a chair. He plopped it down across from them and took a seat. Perk stood a few feet away, staring at him. Scott glanced between Michael and Justin and smiled.

"So what's going on, Scott?" asked Justin.

He thought for a moment, then said, "That murder made a pretty big splash in the national news. The park is still nearly empty."

"It may take awhile for that to settle down," said Justin. He rubbed his chin with his forefinger and thumb. Scott appeared to be avoiding what was on his mind. "Any other news?"

Scott's eyes drifted up over their heads, resting in thought on the rock surface of the wall. "Well," he finally said, "I'm leaving my wife."

Justin's eyes widened. "It doesn't seem like you've been married long enough to even get to know her yet."

"It didn't work out."

Justin studied him a moment. "What happened? Was she unfaithful or something?"

"No, nothing like that. It just didn't work out."

Justin nodded. Whatever the reason for his failed marriage, he was sure it was the reason for this visit. Maybe he just wanted to talk. The young man was definitely troubled by this unexplained turn of events. "Are you two separated now?"

"Yes. I rented a room over in Lajitas until she can make arrangements to get back to Mississippi."

"I see," said Justin. "Does she want to leave you, too?"

"I guess so."

Justin was puzzled. The young man's emotions were so acute both he and Michael felt drawn into his situation, but getting him to speak his mind was beginning to be akin to pulling teeth. "Uh, Scott, it doesn't sound like you're certain about all of this. It might be no more than a case of newlywed jitters."

"I'm certain."

Justin reached up to scratch the top of his head, looking at Michael, who was studying the young man. He looked back at Scott. "Well, okay. Would you like to talk about it?"

Scott drew in a breath. "Word is you are gay."

Justin's mouth dropped. He had assumed Scott had come by to talk to someone about his marriage, but evidently not. He adjusted his weight in the chair. "That's right, Scott. I am gay. Michael and I live here together." He looked at the young man a moment longer, then asked, "Are you curious about that? Did you come by today to find out for yourself?"

Scott leaned forward, his elbows propped on his knees, looking down at the ground. His hands were loosely clasped, his fingers fidgeting. He still seemed reluctant to state exactly what was on his mind.

Michael spoke: "Scott, how long have you been married?"

"Six months," he said, looking up at him.

"And there's no clear reason why your marriage is ending?"

"It didn't work out."

"I know. That's what you said before. And you've heard that Justin is gay, so you wanted to ask him about it?"

"Well, I wanted to know how he knew." He glanced at Justin, then back at Michael. "He never seemed gay to me. How did he know?"

Justin and Michael glanced at each other again, this time both immediately suspecting the same thing. Scott was at odds with his own sexuality. They looked back at the young man, who was again staring at the ground.

"I almost married a girl three years ago, Scott," said Justin. "That was before I admitted or even realized I was gay. I knew deep down inside though. It was rather obvious actually. Things like being impotent when I was in bed with her." He watched Scott's reaction before venturing further, then asked, "Have you had that problem with your wife?"

"Is that where you can't get a hard-on?" asked Scott.

"Yes, exactly."

Scott nodded. "That happened a few times." He thought for a moment. "A lot more lately," he added.

"It was a long road for me," Justin went on to say. "In high school I found I enjoyed looking at the other boys in the shower. I had fantasies about things like that when I masturbated."

Scott was listening with interest.

Justin continued: "Sometimes I caught myself wondering what attractive men would look like with their clothes off. I never knew these were signs that I was gay. And even if I had, I would have been afraid to admit it. You know, I would've worried about what other people thought." Scott watched Justin's hand move over and rest on Michael's leg as he listened. "That all changed when I met Michael. All I cared about then was having him in my life."

Scott stared at the hand on Michael's leg.

"Scott … do you think you might be gay?"

He sat up and glanced at them, then turned his head and gazed out across the desert, his eyes glazed and forlorn.

"You can talk openly to us, Scott," said Michael. "We're not judgmental."

He turned to look at Michael. "My father would disown me."

"That's something many gay men face," said Michael.

He closed his eyes. "Yes … it's like it's been welling up inside me for a long time. I know what it is now. I realized it when I heard about Justin. I like looking at men, and I don't know what to do about it."

"You have to tell your wife," said Michael.

A look of horror spread across Scott's face. "Why?"

"You can't let her go on wondering what happened to her marriage. She'll suffer the guilt and blame for your separation if you don't tell her. And if you're lucky, you both might still be friends when it's all over."

"I didn't think about her feeling guilty about this. I thought she was just angry." He thought for a moment. "God, I have no idea how to tell her."

"Just tell her," Michael said reproachfully. "Scott, I've known men who have turned being gay into a lifelong pity party when in reality, it's something to celebrate. Don't fall into that trap. If you're gay, you're gay. Find someone to share it with. Don't mope around feeling sorry for yourself. Tell your wife, then deal with it. If you have trouble finding a friend around here, get on the internet. There might be someone in Alpine who would love to meet you."

A sense of relief washed over Scott's face. He tilted his can of beer and emptied its contents, then he looked at Michael and a smile formed on his lips.

"Thanks," he said. "I'm glad I came by. Thanks for talking to me about this." He came to his feet.

Michael looked up at him. "What are you going to do now?"

"I'm going to go talk to my wife."

Michael nodded his approval.

They walked with Scott back to his car, watching as he backed out onto the road.

"It makes you wonder how many gay men are out there," said Justin, watching the car head toward the main road.

"Who knows," Michael sighed.

"I'm glad you were here. I wouldn't have known what to say to him."

"Well, I've always been irked by those guys who slink around feeling sorry for themselves because they're gay."

"Let's just hope that his wife doesn't shoot him when he confesses," said Justin.

Michael's eyes widened with horror. "Don't say that! Don't even put those vibes in the air! I'm not sure I could handle something like that."

Justin reached over and squeezed the tendons between Michael's shoulder and neck. "Just kidding, handsome. But you did give him the lift he needed. Maybe that's what you should do—start a gay therapy clinic. Could be we could use one out here in west Texas."

"I'd rather go get another load of rock," Michael said, looking at the empty trailer.

By five o'clock, they had unloaded a second trailer of stones. The task finally completed, they sat on the back end of the trailer for a moment, exhausted.

"We need a break from this," said Justin. "I feel like an old man." He looked at Michael. "Why don't we go up to Alpine tomorrow and round up that list of supplies?"

"That's fine with me. I was beginning to worry I might not be able to keep up with you."

"I think the hardest part is climbing over that damn pile of rocks in the canyon with all that weight on our backs."

"Not for me. It's that last hundred yards in the canyon. Trudging over those ankle deep pebbles."

Michael lifted his arm and sniffed his underarm, wrinkling his nose when he lowered his arm. "You know, it's a whole different thing after the second day without a shower."

Justin lifted his own arm for a sniff. He looked at Michael and smiled. "Whew! You're right about that. Why don't you go first, and I'll start dinner."

CHAPTER 17

Jody called just as Michael was about to step under the water jug to take a shower. Justin came out of the house with the phone. Naked, Michael stepped gingerly over the rocky ground to take a seat in one of the new chairs.

Brian had just brought her back to her hotel. Michael inquired about last night's dinner date.

"I didn't get back to the suite until four o'clock this morning," she replied.

"You've only been there a couple of days, Sis. Did you spend the night with him already?"

"He didn't suggest it. God knows I wanted to, but I think he's waiting for me to make the first move."

"Are you planning to?"

"Yes. Tonight."

"Well, I suppose it's been awhile since you've been laid."

"That's what I like about these Texas men, Michael: they're not as crude as you California boys."

"I bet! He's just putting his best foot forward. Wait until you get to know him and he'll be belching as loud as the rest of us."

"My brother—the romantic."

"So do you guys have other plans for tonight, or are you just going to jump under the sheets with him?"

"We're going out for dinner again tonight. We went horse-back riding today. The senior partner at his firm owns a horse ranch outside of Houston."

"Of course he does. Isn't that a perquisite for any ostentatious Texan?"

"Don't be sarcastic. He is a nice man, and his ranch is charming, huge but charming." She paused, then said, "Listen Michael, I called my secretary and made arrangements to be gone another week. Brian wants to take me to New York to see a few Broadway plays. I told him I'd go." She paused again, then added, "I think he's going to ask me to move to Houston."

"Boy! That's fast! You'd better give that one some good hard thought."

"You know I will, but for now I have to go. I just have an hour to get ready."

"I love you, Sis."

He heard a click, then looked up at Justin, who was standing beside him.

"She's a goner," he said.

"It's beginning to sound a little like one of those white knight fairy tales, where prince charming rides up on a big white horse and sweeps the princess off her feet."

Michael ran his hand over his chest. The oils and grit from two days of labor in the sun had accumulated on his skin. He looked up at his lover.

Justin smiled, his tongue pushed against the inside of his cheek. "Could be interesting," he said.

Michael shook his head and came to his feet. "Not that interesting," he said, walking over to stand beneath the jug.

He pulled the rope, dowsing his head and body with water warmed from the day's sun. Justin stripped off his clothes and joined him and they took turns washing each other. Their bodies lathered, Justin moved up close to Michael's back, wrapping his arms around his lover's waist, lathering his hands a bit more before dropping the soap. Justin couldn't resist. He took the growing weight of Michael's cock into his slippery hand. Moments later, with the long squeezing strokes, Michael's head fell back on Justin's shoulder. His testicles drawn tight, the spasms came flashing through his legs, and streams of white fluid spurted from him and dotted the wet sand. Now spent, he felt warm and limp, and his erection began to recede as the loving hand milked it a moment longer.

"There," Justin whispered in his ear, "I think you're completely clean."

Michael opened his eyes and saw Perk.

"Did you know Perk is watching us?" he asked.

"Yeah."

"Have you noticed he seems curious when he watches us make love?"

"I've noticed."

"I wonder if he knows the human coupling is a little different at this house." Michael looked down at the little dog. "Too bad he doesn't have his own lover."

"Well, it's not likely he'll ever make it with any of those coyotes he likes to chase."

Michael pulled the rope and they rinsed off the soap. He then picked up a towel and blotted Justin's back. They walked together into the house.

Justin had used the last of the leftover potroast to make beef stew. The pot had simmered on low heat in the oven all day. After they filled their bowls, there was enough left for Perk to have a small portion. His mouth full of stew, Michael read over the list of material they would be picking up the next day in Alpine. Sitting across the table, Justin watched him.

"Do you ever miss that fast-paced lifestyle you left behind?" he asked.

Michael looked up from the list. "Lord no. It already seems like such a long time ago. It seems like that was someone else, a man I don't even know any more." He paused in thought, then continued, "Funny, I didn't realize fully how lost and unhappy I was. I don't even want to go back to San Diego to get rid of my stuff. I hope Jody will sell it all for me, if she ever goes back herself."

"I'd like to see where you lived."

Michael looked at him quizzically. He reached up to scratch his ear and said, "I guess we could take a drive over there one of these days. You've never seen California, have you?"

"No."

"I'd like to take you to San Francisco. We could spend a couple of days in the Castro. You and I are normal there. You won't believe your eyes. You get a sense that the whole world is gay."

"I'd like that. I'd like to travel with you."

Michael smiled, watching his lover take a bite of stew. They sat quietly for awhile, another of those many silent moments with Justin when his heart felt light with the promise of a thousand new dawns. He looked back down at the list of materials.

Another medical emergency came Michael's way three days later. He and Justin were outside laying out the parameters of the new rooms with stakes and string. Piles of stone lie waiting to be used to erect the walls. All the plumbing supplies and building materials they would need were stacked in various places around the yard. Perk stood barking at a shiny new oversized pickup truck as it turned off the gravel road.

It was Collin Gordon, the man who owned the next ranch over. One of his ranch hands, a middleaged Mexican whose face was contorted in pain, had fallen off a windmill while making repairs. Mr. Gordon helped the man out of the truck. He had broken his arm in the fall and was now clutching it as if it might fall off.

"Dang bit of bad luck this afternoon, Justin," said Mr. Gordon, helping the Mexican along in their approach. "Knew your friend here is a doctor and figured he might be willing to give us a hand."

Michael stepped forward to look at the arm. "What's your name?" Michael asked, gingerly trying to determine just where the bone was broken.

The Mexican looked at his boss, his expression blank. The old rancher translated Michael's question into Spanish.

"Fernando," replied the Mexican.

Michael nodded, then said, "It's his forearm."

"Can you help him, Michael?" asked Justin.

"I can set the bone using splints, but he'll have to see a doctor immediately. His arm needs to be set properly in a cast."

"What do you want me to do?" said Justin.

Michael scratched the back of his neck. "Splints," he said.

"Two boards, two or three inches wide, fifteen inches long. If you'll cut those, I'll take Fernando into the house and give him a pain killer."

Justin sorted through a stack of lumber they had piled near the house while Michael and Mr. Gordon helped Fernando into the house. Michael had him sit down in one of the kitchen chairs, then went into the bedroom for his medical bag, thankful he had a vial of thorzine. He injected Fernando's arm with the potent drug. Justin hurried into the house moments later with the splints. Michael gave the thorzine a couple of minutes to take effect, and he then went about manipulating the broken arm. When he felt the bone realigned, he used tape to hold the splints firmly to Fernando's forearm, wrapping it around and around until the spints restricted any possible movement.

Collin Gordon had watched the entire proceedure with great interest. When Michael finished wrapping the arm, Mr. Gordon stepped forward and stood before him. Creased with lines of time, the stoic, no nonsense expression of a west Texas rancher lay etched on his face.

"I know all about what you did for Juan Gutierrez's little son the other night. I'm mighty grateful for it too. Now you've helped Fernando here. I reckon you'll be opening up shop when you and Justin get that work done on the house."

Michael looked over at Fernando.

Justin took the initiative to respond for Michael. "He hasn't decided to practice medicine out here, Mr. Gordon."

"Be a dang waste if he didn't," the rancher stated bluntly.

Michael looked back at him. "That arm needs to be set properly tonight."

Collin Gordon nodded. "I'll have my foreman drive him into Alpine as soon as I get him back to the ranch. What do we owe you for this?"

"Owe me?"

"What does the bill come to, Doc?"

"You've all ready paid it," said Michael.

"What do you mean?"

"You gave us that old house on your property. That's where we got all that lumber you saw out there."

"That ain't nothing," said the old rancher, argumentatively.

"It meant a lot to us."

Mr. Gordon reached up and rubbed his jaw. "Justin," he snapped, "is this man always this bull-headed?"

"He's right, Mr. Gordon. That old house did mean a lot to us. We're grateful to have you for a neighbor. You don't charge for favors—neither do we."

He eyed Michael a moment longer then said, "I reckon you ought to open up that doctor's office, son. You're too young to let your talent go to waste. You think about it awhile, and we'll talk again, soon."

He turned and said something to Fernando in Spanish. The Mexican stood up and followed him out the door, neither of them saying another word.

Michael dropped into the chair Fernando was in, staring at the door. They heard the truck's engine fire, its wheels grinding over the gravel road.

"It sounds like Mr. Gordon is a man used to getting his way," said Michael.

"He is. He's richer than Midas. He owns oil wells up around

Midland and real estate in Dallas. He's a personal friend to half the politicians in Washington." Justin looked at Michael for a moment. "I hope you're not feeling uneasy with that pressure he put on you."

"Naw. I'm okay."

"People out here speak their minds. You'll probably hear that sort of thing again."

"I guess I can't blame them. I'd probably have the same opinion if I was looking at it from their point of view."

The setting sun had turned the light inside the house orange. It was too late to get anything else done outside.

"We can finish staking out the walls in the morning," said Justin. "The fun part comes next—digging."

"What all do we have to dig?"

"The foundation for the walls. We'll go down about two feet, pour in some concrete, then start the walls just above ground level. We'll also have to dig out trenches to lay in the plumbing. A hole big enough for the septic tank is going to be the real challenge."

"When are you going back to work?"

"Monday. That'll give us three more days. We can get a lot of it done by then."

By Sunday night they had finished digging the foundation and the trenches for the plumbing, and they were half way through digging out the hole for the septic tank. The monotony of digging a hole had been broken earlier that day when Perk had chased out after a overly curious coyote, regretting it dearly when the creature stopped abruptly and turned on him, snarling and bearing its teeth. Scared to death, the little dog turned and shot back toward the house, his tail buried between his legs, yapping frantically as if Satan himself had poked his rear end with a pitch-fork.

Jody called shortly after that. She was back in Houston with Brian, the young man now feeling right at home spending the night in her suite.

After hanging up, Michael went into the bedroom. He sat down on the edge of the bed trying to arch the soreness out of his lower back. Justin entered the room with two cans of Tecate, handing Michael one of them.

"You know," said Michael, "if we had that tub right now, I'd fill it up with hot water and sit in it for two hours without moving a muscle."

"I'd be in there right next to you."

"If I've learned anything these last two days, it's the injustice that ditch diggers are not the highest paid people on earth."

Justin's expression changed, as if he had been struck by a thought. "Uh, you said *hot water*."

Now laying back on the bed, his fingers entwined behind his head, Michael looked at him, puzzled. "Yeah, I did. I'd like to be sitting in some right now."

"I knew I would forget something." Justin sighed. "I didn't plan for a hot water heater, and we didn't get one in Alpine."

"Can't we just work that in?"

Justin looked at him and smiled, enchanted that Michael seemed to think he could do anything. Standing in the mellow light near the dresser, Justin took a drink from his can and looked down at the floor. It had been a long day, and several times during the course of it, as now, he had thought of his good fortune. His eyes shifted to the man awaiting him in bed. An easy calm rested in his neck and shoulders. All the lonely years and doubt passed through his mind, now as if it had been somebody else who had lived through them. But it had been him, that shell of a man feeling himself apart from the rest of the world. The calm spread down his back and legs. He had suffered no more of those dreams since that first night he slept with Michael, his lover, the man he would hold through the night and be held by, the man he would breakfast and life's chores and intimate moments he had never imagined, and moments like this. He stepped toward the bed.

"Yeah, we can," he said as if his thoughts passed beyond the hot water heater, His eyes swept down over Michael's body. "Roll over on your stomach and I'll give you a massage." He set his beer on the night stand. The damp towel fell from his waist when he moved to the foot of the bed. As Michael got into position, Justin's eyes rested on the serenity of his lover and the agony of sore shoulders left his conscious thought, displaced by the calm and a pleasant reverence. Michael lay with arms folded under his chin, his legs slightly parted, his breath coming soft and easy in the yellow glow of light. Justin paused. His eyes drifted over the contours and shadows of male shoulders, the bronze skin of his back that narrowed over the duel mounds of his buttocks, joined there by muscular legs and their landsacape of blonde hair, his testicles compressed on the sheet in the void between them.

He sighed, moving forward on his knees to straddle his lover, and he lowered his weight atop the back of Michael's legs. He thought about their first day on the river, when he had attempted that first tenuous massage and a smile came to his lips. Now it was different, for there were no limits in how he might enjoy this man. As he looked down at the man beneath him, it was as if he had come into possession of his own private work of art, a masterpiece upon which his eyes could dwell for as long as he might wish. But so much more than fine art, he also had a lover, and their joy of being together surpassed all the world's great wealth. And more still than a lover, he had a companion, a man with whom he could share his tasks and dreams, someone who understood the complexities and nuances of his mind, who loved him in spite of the flaws; the man he yearned to help, to protect, to so give completely his heart. There were no elements missing from their bond, no wanting more, no voids, for their two half-worlds had come together to make one.

Justin leaned forward, his knees upon the cool sheets astride his lover's hips, and he gripped the muscle of Michael's shoulders. How he loved the remarkable contrast of their skin, this chestnut and raven, that when united always brought the inevitable chills across his forearms. He kneaded the taut muscle, feeling the tension melt away beneath the magic of his fingers, and he then drew his hands down over the warm flesh of his lover's back. How he savored this new dimension in his life, these nourishing, intimate moments of physical love. He lowered his weight, guiding himself within the mingling warmth of their bodies, nudging with the heat of his stiff penis the unbearably small hole.

Michael closed his eyes, gripping the sheet, his thoughts drifting like lucid clouds. He felt Justin's breath and kisses near his ear. His heart quickened with the perception of Justin's intent, and his hips rose reflexively. Welling within him all day, the hunger now swept through him like a sudden tidal wave. The side of his face resting against the sheet, Michael felt a tentative breach, and his's hands thightened their grip of the sheet. A shiver of desire turned into an urgent need, its center deep within his bowels and belly. *Push it in!*, his mind pleaded, and his back arched with this plea. "Oh, Justin!" he whispered, clutching the sheet, the pain searing through his anal muscle with its initial defiance. He gasped, then held his breath, his lower lip tight between his teeth as he bore the unmistakable pain of entry. How it so beautifully defined what he wanted to give and to receive; how it came with the promise of pure bliss. The forgiving muscle slowly relaxed and a fine sweat now lay over his body.

"Oh yes …" came words on a long release of breath, "push it all the way in," Michael sighed, his words and agony melting into a dreamy state of pleasure. "Fuck me," he moaned as if he were speaking from within a dream, his fists now gripping tighter the sheets. "Fuck me, you beautiful man… fuck me hard."

His desire heightened by Michael's reaction, Justin had not yet seen this level of intensity in his lover's response. That he had caused it flooded him with joy. They fell into a growing fury of motion, of flexing muscle and perspiring bodies, of fire raging across skin, of sensations born within male loins, spreading heat and shivers through arms and legs and curling toes. And then, as Justin's body tensed, he wrapped his arms tightly around Michael's chest, pushing against his lover's hips with the urgency of a man who could not get deep enough.

Within the moist heat of his lover's bowels there came the

final contraction, leaving him thoroughly spent, and his weight melted atop Michael's body. They lay in quiet reflection, their hearts racing down, and Perk jumped up on the bed to curl up beside them. The black of night had fallen over the desert, and as the creatures of the night began to venture out, the moon and countless stars cast muted light across the land. The house sat in quiet solitude with nothing more than barren desert for miles in any direction, and moments later, two men and one dog were alseep.

They awoke when the first rays of the sun began to warm the room, in the same position in which their eyes had closed. Justin stroked the side of Michael's face and leaned in to kiss the back of his neck, more than ever aware of the pure essence of being in love. He had awakened thinking about the night before, how charged with passion Michael had been, and he found great satisfaction in having taken his lover to such a sensuous state. He no longer felt like a student, but instead, an equal lover. Inching closer, the heat of his chest against Michael's back, he breathed the scent of unruly sandy brown hair. His hand slid down over Michael's stomach and he stirred awake.

"Good morning," Justin whispered, his lips near Michael's ear.

Michael tilted his cheek toward the side of his face. "Morning."

"Did you sleep well?" asked Justin, nuzzling his lover's ear.

"Umm … this feels so good, I could lay here with you all morning."

"Michael … you sure got turned on last night. It was the first time I've seen you get that carried away."

"I know," said Michael, his mind floating on the memory.

"I liked it … a lot," said Justin.

"That's never happened to me before. You made me feel like the most fortunate man on Earth to be gay."

"Really?"

"Yes. I've never been able to let myself go the way I can with you. In the past, it was always like being involved in a competing performance, or something mechanical. It wasn't making love. What we have is as new for me as it is for you."

"I'm glad," said Justin, sliding his hand further down Michael's belly. His fist closed on Michael's cock. It was warm and stiff in his hand. "Something going on down here?" he asked.

"Yeah. I've got to pee."

Justin felt the same urge. He leaned and kissed Michael's neck and reluctantly let go of him. Michael scooted over to sit on the edge of the bed. The morning sun through the window lay warm on his back. He leaned forward and strapped on his sandals. Passing through the kitchen, he took the nearly full jar from the table they had used for a urinal during the night to avoid going outside, and then he walked out a few paces behind the house. After pouring out the jar he relieved himself, then he turned and looked at the abandoned shovels protruding from the mound of sand next to the half finished septic tank hole. Still a bit sore with remnants of pain in his lower back, he hoped to finish digging the hole by the time Justin returned from the park.

Bernard pulled open the desk drawer the moment he looked

up and saw Perk trotting down the hall toward his office. Justin was a few paces behind the dog. He sat in the chair in front of Bernard's desk and watched the big man fish a Milk Bone out of the box.

"It's been pretty quiet around here the last few days," he said, handing Perk one of the crunchy treats. "Everyone is still a little melancholy over what happened to that boy. The FBI has some sort of an investigation going on, but they're not down here anymore. I think the state police are waiting for the killer to surface somewhere. They think he's cleared out."

Justin didn't think so. He had a feeling the killer had found refuge somewhere in Big Bend.

Bernard continued as he watched Perk crunch on the dog biscuit. "Anyway, we're out of the loop." He looked over at Justin. "And that's okay by me. I'd rather spend my time worrying about illegal campfires."

Justin thought about the little boy's parents. He had been the one to face them the day they found out. He remembered well the agony etched on their faces, and he still felt a tremendous grief for them. "I just hope the bastard gets caught, wherever he is."

Bernard nodded in thought, and looked back down at Perk. "I think this pooch likes me." He leaned back in the chair. "Make any headway on your project over at the house?"

"We have the materials, and the foundation and plumbing are dug out. I dropped the trailer off at your place on the way over here this morning. Thanks for letting us use it."

"No problem." Bernard took a sip of his coffee, then said, "The park is still all but deserted. Ain't nothing going on, so I looked into how much vacation time you've accumulated. You never took any time off, did you?"

"No."

"Well, if you want another week, this would be a good time to take it."

Justin smiled. "I'll take you up on that, Bernard."

"Then go on and get out of here. You're still officially on vacation."

When Justin got out to his Jeep, he took out his cell phone and got Collin Gordon on the line and told him that he was going to spend another week working on the house, that they were going to pour some concrete, concluding with, "So I was wondering if I could borrow that portable mixer you keep in your barn."

"Sure you can. When are you going to be ready to pour?"

"We've got to put up a few forms and lay some rebar. I figured we'll be ready to pour first thing in the morning."

"Okay, son. Don't come after the mixer. I'll send it over there first thing tomorrow."

"Thank you, sir."

"Has that doctor friend of yours changed his mind yet about opening an office?"

"Not yet, Mr. Gordon."

"Why don't you work on him some?"

"Well, I think it best if we let him make up his own mind."

Collin Gordon hung up. When Justin heard the click, he smiled, aware a high powered Dallas banker probably couldn't have gotten the old rancher to come to the phone. He started the engine and drove home.

When he walked around to the back of the house, he saw the top of Michael's hair protruding from the top of the septic tank hole. A shovel full of sand flew out onto the slow growing pile. Perk ran ahead of him with a bark of excitement and stood looking down from the rim of the hole.

Michael looked up with a weary smile as Justin appoached, his bare shoulders glistening and gritty with grains of sand. He stabbed the shovel into the loose sand near his feet and turned to climb up the ladder.

"Bernard gave me another week off," Justin said, extending his hand to help brace Michael as he stepped off the ladder up onto ground level.

Brushing the sand from the hairs across his chest, Michael said, "Good! That'll give us time to make some more progress here."

Justin shifted his gaze from Michael's chest to the sprawling desert behind him. The morning sun had warmed the land and the fresh scent of a desert in bloom lay in the air. A half dozen vultures soared on rising thermals to the south, circling some poor creature that had not survived the night. Justin's eyes followed the mountains in the distant haze along the western horizon. A view alive with poetry and texture and limited only by imagination. Such vistas had inspired dreams for generations, but never had it so warmed his heart as it did in sharing it with his lover. "That's one great view we'll have from the veranda and the new bathroom," he said, nodding toward it.

Michael turned. "Yeah. I sat out here earlier with a cup of coffee, just looking at it. The colors change as the sun gets higher in the sky."

Justin scanned the stacks of material laying about their small construction site. It all seemed but a speck amid such a vast land. "We need to spend the rest of the day wiring in the rebar," he said. "We also have to set forms for the floor and rough in the plumbing." He walked over to look at the trenches they had dug for the foundation. "Mr. Gordon is sending over his portable cement mixer in the morning."

Michael stepped up beside him, invigorated by having another full week to work on the project together. Though lost on upcoming procedure, he could imagine the creative progression. He saw tile floors within the parameters of the trenches, and walls rising one stone at a time, and he could easily anticipate the luxury of submerging his body in the warm water of their new bath.

"Well, I have no idea what rebar is, but I'm ready to give that digging a rest," he said, arching his back. "I think I'm out of shape."

You sure don't look out of shape, Justin thought as his eyes swept over Michael's torso and arms. "I thought we might setup a weight station on the veranda. A few routine bench presses wouldn't hurt me any."

Michael pictured him reclined on a bench, the sinews of his chest strained under the weight of a barbell. "Good idea," he said, looking back at the trenches. "So where do we start?"

"The forms. We'll start with the main wall on the north side."

After Justin changed into a pair of jeans, he measured the outside wall and they began cutting boards for the forms. They followed the same procedure for all of the walls, laying out the boards where they were to be nailed into place. Taking turns on the saw while the other held the end of the board, they completed this task in less than an hour. Justin showed Michael how to pound stakes into the ground using a sledge hammer, and they took turns on this chore as well. They toiled methodically in the sun, using a level to make sure the forms were perfectly straight when they nailed them to the stakes. The forms were in place within two hours.

Changing his mind-set to plumbing, Justin layed out the PVC pipe in an organized fashion on the ground, Perk sniffing each piece to make sure it hadn't been tampered with in the night. Justin stepped back, scratching the side of his face, surveying the material in relation to the job at hand.

"If we drain the bathroom sink and the bathtub right there," he said, nodding at the ground next to the north side foundation, "we could use all this ground to plant some vegetables. The bath water would keep them irrigated instead of being wasted in the septic tank."

Michael nodded, still in awe of Justin's ability to bring all of this together.

"All we'd have to do is build the bath on a platform a few inches above ground level and it'll drain right out."

He proceeded to lay out pipe in the areas where it would to be installed, and then one by one they cut the pieces to fit. Using various shapes and sizes of connectors, they cemented the pipes together. This job took three hours. Then, while taking a break to drink some beer in their new chairs, Michael's cell phone rang.

It was Jody. She was so excited Michael wasn't certain just what she was trying to tell him.

"Slow down, Sis. You said you were going to go to San Diego?"

"Yes. I told Brian I had to go back and dispose of the furnishings at your apartment before your lease ends. He arranged for a month long leave of absence to go out and help me."

"That won't take a month, Sis."

"I know. We're going to get rid of my stuff too, Michael. I'm moving to Houston. We've talked about it for hours. We're going to live together in his apartment for six months, and if it goes the way we think it will, we'll get married and buy a house."

"Uh, well ..." he muttered, looking over at Justin, perplexed. "What about your career?"

"That's just one more of the exciting things about this. You wouldn't believe Houston, Michael. There's a dynamic here. This city reeks with money and opportunity. I'm looking forward to the change."

"It still won't take you and Brian thirty days to finish that business in San Diego."

"I figure about a week, give or take. Then we want to come back out there and help you and Justin finish the house."

He was dumbstruck for a moment. "You're making my head spin, Jody. You're talking about moving to Houston, living with a guy I hardly know, and even marriage. Good grief."

"Exactly. That's one of the reasons we want to spend some time in Big Bend. Brian wants to get to know you, and Justin too. And I want to help you guys finish the spare bedroom so we'll have a place to sleep when we come out to visit."

He looked again at Justin. "They want to come out and help us finish the house."

Justin tilted his head, his expression amused.

"What did he say? Is it all right with him?" Jody asked.

He looked at Justin again. "She wants to know if that's okay with you?"

"I don't know why not. Sounds like fun."

"It's fine with him, Sis," Michael said into the phone.

"Give us a week to ten days." She paused, then said, "Oh, yeah, is there anything other than some of your clothes you want out of your apartment?"

He thought for a moment. There wasn't much that he wanted from the material possessions he had left behind. "Just my books and my laptop and that metal filing cabinet."

"All right. Then what I can't sell, I'll give away."

"Fine with me."

"See you soon, big brother."

He heard a click, then he laid the phone on the arm of his chair, looking at Justin.

"She's moving to Houston. They're talking marriage."

Justin leaned forward and propped his elbows on his knees. "It might be a good thing we get to know him a little bit then."

"A fucking lawyer!"

Justin laughed. "Don't hold that against him, Michael. It's not like he's out there suing doctors."

Michael tilted his can for a swallow of beer, then looked at Justin and retracted grudgingly. "I suppose you're right."

They resumed their work, sorting through long lengths of rebar. Cutting the long steel rods with a hacksaw and wiring the pieces into place was a time consuming, arduous task, but they managed to finish it by sundown. Side by side they stood admiring their work. They had completed the forms that would contain the concrete for this new section of their house, the grids of rebar that would keep it together, and the network of PVC pipe that would bring running water into the house for the first time in its long history.

Justin noticed Michael rubbing his hands. He reached for one of them and turned the sore white palm up to where he could see it. "You got blisters from all that sawing today," he said with concern.

"I'll live."

Justin ran his thumb lightly over the blisters. "Goddammit!" He looked at Michael. "I want you to wear gloves next time we do that kind of work."

During the late afternoon, a breeze had come across the desert out of the mountains in the northwest. Now it was gusting, here and there swirling up curls of dust and sand. The haze across the western horizon had thickened and the air was gritty and felt like it had lost ten degrees in an hour.

Justin looked out over the desert, at the darkened low clouds moving in from the northwest. "Must be a cold front moving in."

Michael rotated his bare shoulders and folded his arms over his chest. "It's gotten a little chilly in the last few minutes and I need to shower off this grit. Can't say I'm looking forward to that."

Justin ran his rough hand over the gritty texture of Michael's arm. "I've got an idea. Let's take the washtub into the kitchen and take turns soaking in some hot water."

Michael smiled and followed him to the south side of the house, where an oversized washtub hung on the wall, big enough for a man to sit in as long as his knees were drawn up. They hauled it into the kitchen and pumped their three largest cook pots full of water, placing them then atop the stove. When the water began to boil he poured it into the tub, topping it off with cool water from the pump.

He swirled his hand in the water, testing the temperature, looking over at Michael with a smile. "It's just about right. Are you ready?"

Michael stepped out of his jeans while Justin went outside for the bar of soap. His eyes closed, his head resting on folded arms atop his knees, Michael was already in the tub by the time Justin got back. He laid the soap on the floor next to the tub and began refilling the pots for his own bath, taking a seat at the table with a can of Tecate when the full pots were simmering on the stove. He sipped the beer while Michael leaned back to relax. Perk lifted his front paws up on the rim of the tub. He looked over into the water and lapped up a sample, apparently delighted with this strange event.

Michael leaned forward, cupping his hand together to bring some of the hot water up to his sooth face. "Damn, this feels good." He reached down for the soap.

Justin stepped over and came down on his knees, taking the soap from Michael's hand. He splashed water over white shoulders and began to lather them. Michael propped his forearms on his knees in thought.

"I wish I had gotten to know Brian a little better that night. Could you tell anything about him?"

Justin ran his soapy hands down over Michael's arms, coming back underneath to his armpits. "You mean besides the fact he was hypnotized by your sister?" He had submerged the soap and was lathering Michael's underarms.

"Yeah, besides that."

"Only that Mr. Kirkland seemed to think the world of him. And I got the impression he's a nice guy. A little stuffy maybe."

"Doesn't it seem they're moving a little too fast with all of this?"

"Looks like that runs in your family. You spend a third of your lives wondering if you'll ever fall in love, then bingo, you suddenly meet the right one."

Michael laughed. "Yeah, and it happens when we least expect it, in the wilderness, *where* we least expect it."

"That's perfectly understandable to me, that is if you run across the right person out here. Have you ever been anyplace where the moon and stars shine so bright? Or have you ever drawn a breath in a place where songs from the past still linger in the air? Have you ever set eyes on sunsets like those we have here?"

"Maybe not, but I have gotten a headache breathing carbon monoxide."

"Get up on your knees, city boy."

Michael came to his knees. Soapy hands swirled over his back and then came up his ribs and on through to lather his chest. The soapy hands moved in sync down his belly, then on down over his thighs. Michael felt warm breath on the back of his neck as the hands came back up between his legs, lifting his testicles and rubbing the soap into the recess behind them. He drifted on the sensations as Justin continued.

"You read stories about people falling in love in Paris and Rome, but places like that have nothing on Big Bend country. In Rome they have statues—we have mountains alive with color and poetic texture. In Paris they have fountains—we have moonlight so bright it bathes your skin with golden light and inspires thought free of clutter. The days are so warm and lazy that dreams are born and mingle with those ancient songs. The quiet lays over the land with such tranquility that it frees your soul from stress, and all five senses come alive with what really matters." His soapy hands moved down over Michael's buttocks and the back of his upper legs, and back up between the two fleshy mounds. "It's not hard to fall in love out here. All it takes is the right chemistry and two people who can understand the gifts this land has to offer."

Caressed by his words as well as his hands, Michael leaned forward, his hands bracing his weight with a grip on the rim of the tub. He felt a unique sense of security as soapy hands swirled over his skin. With the agony that tormented his muscle melting away, he cherished these moments with his lover. How it kindled the essence of being in love and calmed him and made him certain all is well, for nothing else ever brought him such joy.

"I like bathing you," said Justin.

"I like it too."

"We're kinda eat up with it, aren't we? This physical stuff we do together. I would have never imagined myself doing something like this."

Michael reached out and ran his hand over the top of Justin's head. "Doesn't everybody do these things when they fall in love, stay preoccupied with each other's bodies? I doubt we're inventing it."

"Will it ever settle down?"

"Doesn't seem so now, does it?"

Justin splashed the soap from Michael's upper body, then said, "Are you ready to stand up?" His tone was serene, his thoughts had merged with the beauty of a bronze body vibrant with soft light and water and soap.

So relaxed, Michael found it took effort to come to his feet. He looked down and watched Justin's soapy hands slide up and down his legs, captivated by the sensuality of being bathed. After Justin splashed away the soap, Michael stepped out of the tub and toweled off.

They dipped out the cloudy water and refilled the tub with fresh. Justin pulled off his jeans and got into the tub. Michael knelt to wash his lover's body. Still enchanted by the contrast of white suds on the rich black texture of Justin's skin, Michael bathed him with the same abandon and care. He knew, had they not exhausted themselves with a full day's labor, had every fiber in their bodies not been thoroughly spent, this sensual bath would have drawn them into another passionate coupling.

Justin looked down at himself. With the caress of Michael's soapy hands sparking such wonderful sensations, he was surprised when he lifted and felt no more than a slight increase of phallic weight.

"Must be a sign of age," he said, stepping out of the tub yawning.

"We're tired. I don't think you'll need to rush out for some Viagra anytime soon." Michael glanced at the stove. "Got any ideas for dinner?"

"We could heat up a can of chili."

"Canned chili? You must have seen that on the cooking channel."

"The what?"

"Never mind."

"Well, I'm hungry but I think we're both too tired to cook anything."

Michael took the towel and blotted the drops of water from Justin's back, responding to his contagious yawn with one of his own. "I'm not sure we have the energy to get the can open." He slung the towel over his shoulder and pulled open a drawer, reaching in for the can opener.

They labored through the motions of warming and eating a can of chili and were in bed within thirty minutes. Michael's arm draped over Justin's chest, they were sound asleep moments later. The early hours of dusk grew dark with increasing howls of wind. Lost on their semiconscious dreams came a few drum rolls of distant thunder. Perk lifted his head and stared out the window, occasionally glancing at the two sleeping men. Braced against the gathering storm, the desert awaited, and as fast moving clouds passed over the house, the creatures of the night hunkered down to endure whatever might come. Entwined in the comfort of body heat, their peaceful sleep extended into the small hours of the night. The distant thunder now came from the east. Unaware of the storm's threat, it had passed over the house with not so much as a drop of rain, and the desert once again lay calm and luminescent with moonlight.

The rude noise of a large truck jarred them awake just after sunup.

CHAPTER 18

Startled, Justin's head jerked toward the figure of a man he didn't know, peeking in and tapping upon the window. An obnoxious clutter of noise rattled the tin roof from the powerful diesel engine just outside the front of the house. The man's eyes widened when Michael sat up and he became aware of two men sleeping in the same bed. He slunk away from the window.

"What the hell … " Justin muttered, weaving wearily to the kitchen to find his jeans that he had left on the floor. Still disconcerted, he forgot to shake them out in case a crawling night creature had found refuse within the legs during the night. Michael was right behind him and Perk was already waiting at the door, his throaty growl reflecting his displeasure with all the noise and the gall of that stranger walking right up to the bedroom window.

The man seemed a bit awkward in manner when Justin swung open the door. He glanced over Justin's shoulder, at Michael, as if to confirm his perception of strange bed fellows. He finally spoke.

"Uh, this has to be the right place. Mr. Gordon ordered a load of cement to be delivered here."

Justin and Michael glanced at each other.

"Ya'll were expectin' it, weren't ya'?"

Justin nodded blankly. "Yeah. Give us a few minutes and we'll be out." He slammed the door.

"I'll be damned. Mr. Gordon knew we were working on the foundation. He sent a whole load of concrete. Looks like he found a way to pay you for wrapping up Fernando's arm the other night."

"Then I'll tell him he wasn't obligated to do it."

"Forget it. Just thank him if you want to, but since he's your neighbor too, it's best you know he doesn't need to be *told* anything. I've seen him irritated and it ain't pretty." Justin stuck his finger into his mouth, back over his teeth. "Damn, I'd gotten up early enough to brush my teeth if I had known that truck was going to arrive this soon."

"Brush them now."

"I will after we finish pouring the concrete. I don't want to tie that truck up any longer than we have to." Justin nodded toward the counter. "Why don't you put on some coffee while I go out there and get him started."

Justin went out and told the driver where to back the truck. He stood near the forms and held up his hand when the truck inched close enough. By the time the driver had the slue rigged, Michael walked out with three mugs of coffee. Pausing for a moment to sip his coffee, the driver glanced furtively between the two men. Justin was too busy checking the rebar to notice, but Michael noticed. Thinking it likely this west Texas good ol' boy had never seen two men in bed together, he found it amusing.

A few minutes later concrete came pouring down the slue. Justin guided the flow to distribute the concrete evenly across the foundation, stopping from time to time to shovel the heavy wet material into places the slue couldn't reach. Within thirty minutes, the grid of rebar could no longer be seen, the foundation now comprised a thick mass of gray slush staining against the wooden forms. While the driver hosed off the slue, Justin took off his sandals and rolled up the legs of his jeans. He laid a long two by four board across the concrete on the west side of the foundation.

"We have to level it," he said stepping into the wet mix, his bare feet quickly swallowed. He looked at Michael. "You pull that end of the board across the top of the forms while I pull this end," he said, bending over next to the house. He had attached a temporary guide made of angle iron the full length of that side of the house. The iron was at a height the exact depth of the foundation and provided a ledge upon which he could pull the board. A few minutes later, the glistening surface was perfectly level. Before the driver put away the hose, Justin asked him to spray off his feet, which he did, and then got back into his truck.

After watching the heavy truck lumber back onto the road, they turned to look at the pad and plumbing pipe jutting from its surface.

"Well, that saved us about two days of back-breaking work," said Justin.

Michael studied the foundation, quite pleased with their progress so far.

Justin leaned forward to buckle his sandals. "I think I'll brush my teeth now."

"I was thinking about baking some of those cinnamon rolls I bought the other day."

Justin looked at him and smiled, placing his hand on the back of his head. "That noise was nerve-racking. Sorry if I seemed a little edgy, but I'm not used to getting roused out of bed that way."

"You were just concerned about getting the concrete poured."

He looked at Michael's unruly hair, then leaned forward to kiss him. "Good morning, handsome. I believe those cinnamon rolls would hit the spot."

A ranch hand driving a pickup truck had delivered the portable cement mixer while Justin was brushing his teeth. After looking it over, they moved their chairs near the new foundation, where they sat in the quiet of a desert morning, staring at their handiwork while eating warm cinnamon rolls. They heard a hawk and looked up in time to see it swoop down for some hapless critter two hundred yards north of the house. The day began as they always do with the early sun warming their face.

Michael looked over at Justin, curious. "What are you thinking about?"

"I'm wondering how the new walls are going to look. I hope they'll blend with the house without looking too much like an add-on. Don't you think the stones we brought up from the river are a good match?"

Michael glanced at the piles of stone. "Yeah, I do."

"Me too. But the mortar in the house has aged. There'll be a difference between the mortar in the new walls and the old."

Michael looked at him, amused. "My lover is a perfectionist. Really, I don't think the mortar will stand out that much."

A truck appeared in the distance, coming toward the house. Justin recognized what it was. "That's a utility truck from the electric company. I forgot to tell you that Bernard did us a favor. He has a friend over there, and he got the guy to agree to upgrade our electrical service at no charge."

Moments later they watched the truck pull off the road in front of the house. A lanky six foot kid got out and slammed the door, then ambled toward them, his utility belt already strapped on. The boy looked to be in his early twenties, a week old stubble on his jaw and chin, his cheeks festering with what looked like chronic acne.

Justin nodded.

"You the owner?"

"We are," said Justin.

He took a piece of paper from his shirt pocket and looked at it. "The order says to upgrade your service, so I'll be up on that pole out front changing the transformer. They sent along a hundred amp panel box with fuses. You'll have to show me where you want that mounted."

The panel box surprised Justin. He wasn't expecting it. "I guess we'll just replace the old box on the south side of the house."

"Okay." The boy looked around at the stacks of material about the property. "What all are you doing here?" he asked.

"A little construction project. We're adding two rooms to the house."

"Looks like you could use a service plug out here."

"No doubt about that," said Justin.

"I'll run one for you before I leave."

Justin looked at Michael with a grin. "Don't you just love living out here in west Texas?"

Michael had been studying the boy's face. He stood and approached the young man, taking his jaw in hand and turning the face toward the sun. Stunned, the boy's eyes found their way back to Justin.

"He's a doctor, son. Let him have a look at that condition you've got there."

"Have you been putting any medication on this?" Michael asked.

The boy nodded, his jaw now free of Michael's grip. "I've been trying some stuff I picked up at the drugstore."

"I don't think you have to live with this. Wait here and I'll be right back." Michael went into the house and opened his medical bag. He took out a small bottle of tetracycline and a prescription pad. Back out side, he handed the boy the pills and wrote out a prescription. "Follow the directions on that container and pick up this ointment. Wash your face with anti-bacterial soap every morning and before you go to bed at night. There's no guarantee, but it ought to clear that up in no time at all."

The boy looked at him with an expression of bewildered gratitude. He nodded, then turned without another word and walked back around the house to his truck.

Justin reached over and took Michael's hand when he sat back down. "Well Doctor, looks like you might have made his day, and on top of that, you bake one damn good cinnamon roll."

"What's next?" asked Michael, changing the subject.

Justin looked at the new slab. "Looks like we bought way too much cement now that Mr. Gordon sent over enough to finish the foundation. But that's okay. Instead of a wooden deck, our veranda will have a concrete and satillo tile floor."

Anxious to begin erecting the stone walls, they would have to wait a couple of days for the concrete foundation to cure. They spent the rest of the day installing forms for the veranda's foundation. By five o'clock they had installed the forms around the parameter of the veranda. A grid of rebar lay on the ground within them. Justin sat down on the cross section he had just nailed in, propping his elbows on his knees.

"I just realized I don't feel like working until sundown."

Michael sat down beside him. "I'm ready for something to eat myself."

"Not chili I hope. That stuff we had last night was pretty close to awful."

"You noticed that too?"

Michael took off the deer skin work gloves he had been wearing to saw the rebar. The blisters were still red and angry but at least they weren't worse. Justin reached for his hand to have a look for himself. He lifted the palm to his lips to give it a sympathetic kiss.

"I hate this," he said.

"The gloves worked fine. I'd rather worry about dinner."

"Got any ideas what we should eat?"

"I've been fantasizing about a steak."

"That's a perfect idea!" Justin leaned toward him a drew a breath near his shoulder. "Umm, you've worked up a little west Texas manhood today. Are you planning to wash it off?"

"Right now, actually."

Justin reached down and adjusted the reaction inside the crotch of his jeans, not at all surprised that just one breath of Michael's skin could cause it to happen. "Then I guess I'll get the steaks ready while you shower."

A few minutes later Michael was standing under the water

jug, his hair lathered with soap. With suds in his ears he didn't hear the pickup approach, or hear its door slam. After pulling the rope to rinse his hair, he opened his eyes and saw Collin Gordon inspecting the new slab. He quickly grabbed the towel and dried off, wrapping it around his waist and strapping on his sandals. He walked over toward the old rancher.

Mr. Gordon turned as he approached, his eyes sweeping over Michael's near naked form, his tongue pressed firmly against his cheek. "I guess you boys are going to enjoy the modern convenience of running water when you finish this project."

Michael nodded. "Yes, sir. The more I think about it, the better I like the idea."

The old man looked back at the newly poured foundation. "Mighty fine work here. That stone looks like a good match, too. Where'd you get it?"

"Off the bottom of the river."

The old man's eyes widened and he glanced back over the several piles. "You're kiddin'!"

"No, sir."

"Bet that took some doin'."

Justin came out of the house and joined them.

"Good to see you, Mr. Gordon. Did you stop by to make sure weren't building something that might have a negative impact on the neighborhood?"

The old man laughed. "No. I wasn't too much worried about that."

"We sure appreciate you sending over the concrete. It saved a lot of time and a backache."

"Well, we're neighbors, son. I'm proud to help."

"We're grilling steaks for dinner. How about joining us?"

The old rancher considered the invitation for a moment. "I believe I will. Best call Juanita and let her know she won't have to fix the old grouch anything for dinner." He took a cell phone out of his pocket and looked at it as if he'd have to figure out all over again which buttons to press. "Never thought I'd see the day I'd be talking into a little gadget like this," he said, punching buttons in frustration, then handing Justin the phone. "Can you dial my number on that thing?"

Justin punched in his number and handed the phone back to him when he heard it ringing. When Mr. Gordon put the phone back into his pocket, they all when into the kitchen to sit down and have a beer.

Lifting the can for a swallow, the old rancher ignored the glass Justin had placed on the table before him. "I've got some hands who finished a new fence yesterday. I could send them over to help you boys finish up that project out there."

As anxious a Justin was to see the house finished, he couldn't imagine anyone but Michael and himself pounding every nail and setting every stone. He looked at Mr. Gordon diplomatically and said, "Thanks for the offer, but you know how it is. It's something we want to do with our own hands."

The old man nodded with a gleam in his eyes, perhaps reminded of some of his own projects from the past. He glanced between the two of them, his lips pursed as if he wasn't quite sure of how to approach whatever had crossed his mind. He finally spoke.

"I got a good friend up in Midland, an oilman. Known him for years. I asked him one day why he never got married, and I guess he decided to take me into his confidence. He admitted he was homosexual." Collin said the word as if uncertain of its exact pronunciation. "I wasn't really all that surprised. After all, he had certain mannerisms that more or less implied he might not be partial to the ladies." He paused glancing between them again. "But you two. There's not a damn thing about either one of you that gives you away. Now that's a hard thing to figure."

There was a glimmer of amusement in Justin's eyes. "Well sir, it wasn't something I figured out overnight myself."

"Is that something you figure out, or do we have a shortage of women here in Big Bend?"

"No shortage of women, Mr. Gordon," said Justin. "We have them in every size and shape."

"Did you bother to try out any of 'em before you got tangled up with this California doctor here?"

"Well, I suppose you could say tried one out back home in Jasper. It didn't work out well."

Mr. Gordon nodded. "I see. Well, I never understood it myself, but I admit it ain't the only thing I don't understand. It's remarkable, two strapping young bucks like you. Seems you're both happy with it though." He paused, then added, "You know my wife passed on early last year, but we had a mighty fine half century together. What we had was worth more to me than all the oilwells in west Texas, and I can't help but wonder if you two aren't going to miss out on having something similar."

"I wouldn't worry about that, Mr. Gordon," said Justin. "Of course it's different in obvious ways. Look at it this way: if you compare a man's psyche to his perception of good music, you'll find that some men enjoy Willie Nelson, while others prefer

Bach. Men are born with different sexual preferences as well."

"Good way to put it, I suppose."

A knock came on the door.

"It's open," Justin called out.

The boy from the electric company opened the door and looked in. "It took longer than I expected since that first transformer was defective, but I'm done now. The circuits you have in the house are hooked up to the new box. That box gives you the capacity to pretty much add anything you want."

Justin came to his feet and approached the young man, handing him a twenty dollar bill. "Michael and I want to buy you a couple of rounds for your good service."

He pushed the money into his pocket. "I appreciate that."

"We're going to grill steaks here in a few minutes," Justin said. "Want to join us?"

"Can't. My aunt will be waiting with dinner by the time I get home." The boy then looked at Michael. "Thanks Doc. I'm going to pick up that prescription first thing in the morning."

Michael nodded and the boy turned and walked back to his truck.

Collin Gordon was looking at Michael, who, under the weight of the old man's gaze, folded his hands before him on the table.

"That boy called you *Doctor*," he said. It was a statement that sounded more like a question.

It was also a subject Michael dearly wanted to avoid. He answered as simply as he could. "He's living with a pretty bad case of acne. I just gave him a prescription that might help clear up his face."

Squinting, Mr. Gordon's eyes seemed piercing. "He might not have ever known about that prescription if you weren't here to give it to him."

Michael shrugged. "Any good doctor will stay abreast of recent drug releases."

The old rancher scooted his chair closer to the table, leaning in on his elbows. He had thought long and hard on the purpose that had prompted this visit, well aware of the sensitivities evoked by bringing it up. He had lived a long life of simply tackling his challenges, so as always, he plowed right in. "Well, that brings me to the reason I came out here this afternoon."

Michael braced himself to listen respectfully to whatever Mr. Gordon might say. He anticipated another arm-twisting.

The old man rubbed his mouth, then said, "There's a few things I'd still like to accomplish before I'm gone, and I hope one of them will include you. I've done a lot of thinking about this since you operated on the Gutierrez boy here awhile back. And I did a little checking up on you, Dr. Anderson. I had a feeling you might be one of those *good doctors* you just mentioned, but I had no idea you're a renowned heart surgeon. Your amazing career is almost breathtaking."

He paused, glancing at Justin. Michael looked at him closely, puzzled by the definite emotion he had detected in the old man's voice. Mr. Gordon then looked back at Michael. "With all you have accomplished, I understand now why you came out here. It has to do with that little girl who died on the operating table."

Michael cringed.

"I thought so. I wish I could say I understand why you quit, but I don't. Not after all those remarkable years of success. You're blessed with the ability to save lives and it's as simple as that. I'm just surprised they didn't tell you in medical school that you'd face making a mistake one day. Lord knows I've made plenty of mistakes myself."

"Ever make one that cost an innocent child her life?" Michael asked bitterly.

The old man sighed. "Can't say that I have, son. But I have made big enough mistakes to get myself sued a time or two."

Michael looked at him, aware of his obvious implication.

"Yes, I also know about the lawsuit, that you refused to contest it or even testify in your own defense. I know all about that. I also know you've amassed a small fortune in mutual funds and stand to lose it all if you practice without a good malpractice insurance policy. Is that why you don't want to open an office out here?"

"No," Michael said bluntly, his tone defiant.

"I didn't think so." He paused again before going further, for what he was prepared to talk about next threatened even more emotional pain for Michael. "There's something else that came to my attention. I took an uncommon interest in learning all I could about it because I've never had the good fortune to have my own son. I know about your father."

Michael closed his eyes. It seemed that everything he'd like to avoid thinking about was being thrown at him at once.

"Your father is a hard-nose Navy man, the kind of a man who has helped make this nation's military might second to none in the world, but he's also the kind of man who doesn't deserve the love and respect of his own children. I'll tell you, if I had a son and found out he wanted to be with other men, I might get mad and kick a garbage can or something, but I'd keep on loving him."

Michael bowed his head when a tear ran down his cheek.

Justin listened tensely, biting down on his lower lip. He ached, for the man he loved so dearly was agonizing under the weight of the old rancher's blunt words. The strongest urge came over him, an urge to go over and protectively fold his arms around his pained lover. But he also had great respect for his wise old neighbor, sensing something positive would somehow come out of all of this. He sat stiffly, wrenching his fingers against his palms, and listened quietly as Collin Gordon continued.

"Michael, I know the man well, though I've never met him. Done business with those kinds of bastards all my life. God blessed him with a son, and in spite of the fact that his son went on to become one of the finest surgeons in California, he still wasn't satisfied. He's lived a life handicapped with a mentality so narrow it allowed him to be estranged from his own son. How utterly sad for him. I may be a hard-headed old west Texas rancher, but I recognize one dimensional thinking when I see it. He couldn't accept your homosexuality." The old man shook his head. "How I pity that poor man. How I envy him for having a son."

A brief silence fell over the room. Mr. Gordon reached over and gently placed his hand on Michael's. "You're an intelligent man, Michael. You must know why I came over here to bring these things up."

Michael looked at him. "Yes. It's because I'm not facing all of this on my own."

"Maybe, then maybe you are in your own way. I'm just a

neighbor, but I'm also an old man who cares about what happens here in Big Bend country, and I couldn't be more proud to have you here. It's good you bought this land with Justin. It means you plan to stay, and I hope to get to know you a whole lot better." He hesitated a moment before adding, "I know Justin's father deserted him when he was a child, and … well I guess I've become a sentimental old fool, but with the circumstance we have here, I'd like to think of both of you boys as the sons I never had."

Justin hardly knew what to say. The old man's sentiment had struck a cord in his own heart.

Michael looked up, tears now streaming down his face. His emotion was a maze of anger, frustration and confusion. "If that's the case," he blurted in desperate need of some rational thought, "you have a daughter, too. Her name is Jody and she's planning to marry a guy we don't even know."

Collin Gordon smiled calmly. "There, you see, all of that is going on and I'm not even aware of it. We should spend more time together so important things like that don't escape me. Now I'm curious to know more about your sister. For example, I like to know if you approve of this boy she's going to marry?"

Justin spoke: "We don't know him, but they'll both be here for awhile in a week. We plan to get to know him better then."

"That's good. If you like, I can have my office check him out, too." Mr. Gordon took a swallow of beer, looking at Michael over the can. "I can't define exactly what it is, but Michael, there's something about you that touched my heart. Justin here, I've always admired him. He came to my wife's funeral. Out of the hundreds of people who were there, he was the only one who came up and said something that made me feel better, and forgive me because I always tear up when I think about it. He simply took my hand and said, 'Mrs. Gordon was a fine Texas lady.'" He paused to rub his eyes, then continued. "But you, Michael … there's something special about you. I have a sense that your real motivation is to help people, not the financial rewards. In spite of the glory you've enjoyed in San Diego with all of your success, I believe you've basically always wanted to help those who need your special skill. Now here you are in the Big Bend, where there are many who are desperate for the kind of help you can provide.

"I'm talking about people who eat cold beans out of a can because they have no way to cook them, people who pound corn into tortillas. We used to call them wet-backs, but now I believe we call them illegal aliens, and whether our government likes it or not, they're here. And Michael, they're good people, some of the best I've ever had to pleasure to know; but the sorry truth is, when they get sick or badly injured, some of them just simply die. They're afraid of deportation if they seek help.

"So I'll put my cards on the table. I'm thinking about, shall we say, an undergound clinic, someplace our Spanish speaking neighbors will know is safe when they need medical help. Of course I'm not excluding the locals. You'll find from time to time one of them will get drunk and fall out of his own truck or shoot himself in the foot. But I'm mainly talking about the Mexicans. It's their backs that make these ranches around here work. They're the ones who've made the thankless contributions to agriculture and the glittering skylines of Texas cities. Simply put, they do the work no one else wants to do, and we owe them for it.

"And the thoughtful men and women who live in the Big

Bend all know we have to give something back, just for the privilege of living in country like this. We can't come here and suck in the air and walk across this wonderful land without making some sort of a contribution. So here's my offer: I don't have your talent to help people with my own hands, but I have money, and use it for this purpose I gladly will. I'll set up a trust with unlimited funds. It will provide for any conceivable expense our underground clinic might have, such as malpractice insurance, medicine and supplies. You'll call the shots. There'll be money for anything you need, now and long after I'm gone. I intend to give back every penny I have before I depart this world, and this is the best way I know to get started." He looked at Justin.

"And Justin, this isn't just about Michael. I plan to leave my ranch to the State of Texas, to be turned into a state park, with the proviso that you are named the administrator. If you accept this position, my plan is to fund your salary and pension because in you, I know my land will be in good hands."

Justin looked at him in disbelief. Thinking that Michael had been the only focus of their conversation, he was shocked that he too had been included in Collin's future plans.

"Mr. Gordon," said Justin, faltering, "I don't know what to say."

"You don't have to say anything. Just think it over. In the meantime, I'd like to come over here from time to time and have a beer with you boys. There's no harm in treating you two as my adopted sons, and through you both I'll give back what I've taken; and in helping me with this, you'll also be making your own contributions.

"That's the deal," he concluded.

"You know you're welcome here anytime," Justin said, getting to his feet to get another round of beer. He still didn't know what to say. "I'm a little overwhelmed. I think I'll go out and put those steaks on the grill and let all this soak in," he said, setting the beer on the table.

Michael watched him carry a tray of steaks out of the house then looked over at the old man. "I wish I could simply agree to what you want me to do, but I have to think about it. I came out here convinced I'm a curse on the medical profession. It's not easy to get past that. I wouldn't defend myself at a trial because what I did was indefensible. So I want time to think about it. I'll give you an answer by the time we finish the work on our house."

Mr. Gordon nodded. "I can't ask no more than that, son. Enough said."

"Then I'm going to fry some potatoes while he cooks the steaks."

Justin stood staring at the sizzling beef in a daze. Beyond his concern for Michael, he himself now faced a decision that would change his own life, a position with far more responsibility than he shouldered now. And there was something else bothering him. He had known Collin Gordon since his first few weeks in the Big Bend, but he had never seen this side of him, these sentiments of an old man. Why had he sounded fatalistic when he outlined his plans? As Justin thought about it, it occurred to him that there might have been something left unsaid.

The three men were cutting into their steaks a few minutes later. Justin watched the old man, wary of his changed demeanor.

"Mr. Gordon …"

"I'd like you boys to call me Collin," he interrupted.

Justin glanced at Michael. A first name basis with this so highly respected gentleman would take some getting used to. "Uh, Collin, you know I'm honored by your confidence in me, and by your offer, but … I don't mean to pry, but you seem tired. Is something wrong?"

There was a hint of weariness in the rancher's eyes. "You mean besides getting old?"

"Yes, sir. While you were telling us about your plans, I detected a sense of urgency in your voice."

"I didn't realize it was obvious already."

Justin and Michael were now both looking at him.

The old rancher laid his fork aside. His heavy eyelids lifted toward Michael. "I would have been talking to you about this before long anyway, so you might as well know now. I was in Midland a couple of weeks ago. Saw my doctor up there. I was diagnosed with lung cancer."

Michael closed his eyes and released a long breath.

"Damn!" Justin blurted, angrily banging his fist down on the table.

Mr. Gordon looked at him. "I'm eighty-two years old, son. It's not in the cards that any of us live forever."

"What kind of treatment are you undertaking?" asked Michael.

The old man picked up his fork and resumed cutting his steak. "Treatment?" he said. "If you're talking about chemicals or radiation, I won't be wasting what time I have left with that sort of thing. I plan to get my affairs in order, then see you for some painkillers when the time comes. I'll die on my ranch, in my own bed. But this is why we have limited time to accomplish what we've discussed here tonight."

The room fell silent again. Mr. Gordon seemed to relish the grilled ribeye, obviously resigned to an impending certain death. It was disheartening news, and for Michael, it was an added dimension of pressure to make a commitment, for the old man had upped the ante by including him in his legacy. It took his mind from the harmony of a desert night, back to the relentless demands of his life in San Diego. He felt tense. Collin Gordon sensed his apprehension, he seemed to be reading his thoughts.

"It's different out here, Doctor Anderson. It's not at all like what you've left behind. You can practice medicine here without the burden of a bureaucracy or an insane litany of rules. These are humble people here. They mend fences and pound nails and toil to give their children a better life. Instead of expectations, they have dreams and prayers. They are grandmothers who need help with the pain in their fingers, and mothers who need help bringing their babies into the world, and men who need their injuries tended to."

He looked at Justin. "You don't have to look so distraught. We're talking about positive things here."

"I don't want to lose a good neighbor."

"Well, you can't be too surprised by the fact an old man is going to die. And besides, you're going to be too busy to be concerned about it."

"I was thinking about that, too. The idea of turning your ranch into a state park is overwhelming."

"Yes. It's not a small undertaking. My lawyer has been going back and forth to Austin for the last couple of weeks. Looks like, since I'm funding the project, we'll have the opportunity to operate it with a high degree of independence. The bureaucrats are insisting we follow a few basic regulations, but that aside, I believe we can establish a park with some real west Texas flavor. You'd want to convert the house into your adminsitive offices, but the compound is also large enough to establish a museum." He paused as his dream seemed to take form in his mind. "Think about that, Justin. We could commemorate the Comanches who were among the first to inhabit this land, and then all the great early settlers who came before us. I've been piling up artifacts in that big barn over there for years."

They continued their dinner at a casual pace, mingling the conversation with local gossip and history. The old rancher seemed calm and at peace when he stood up to leave at eleven o'clock. Perk trotted in front of them as they walked with him out to his pickup truck. They watched tail lights grow small in the dust as the sound of tires crunching over the gravel road faded into the night.

"Not an easy man to resist, is he?" said Justin.

"No."

"How do you feel about his offer?"

"I don't know," Michael said, looking at him. "How do you feel about running a new state park?"

"Like I told him, it's overwhelming, but I'm intrigued. Fact is, I never imagined anything like that coming my way. Guess I'll talk to Bernard about it."

But for the sound of Collin Gordon's truck crossing the gravel road now almost lost in the distance, another lonely silence again lay over the desert. Standing in soft light cast by the moon, they turned to survey silhouettes of the new foundation and the piles of materials and stone, the night air of early Spring like silk upon their arms. The mysterious song of this ancient land lay foremost in their minds, for now the vague melody had new meaning. It all seemed so strangely different. By virtue of a dying old rancher and his grand designs, were they to be further drawn into pages of its history? Justin placed his hand on Michael's shoulder, and they walked together back into the house to clean up the kitchen and turn in for the night.

Justin was the first to get in bed. Centered atop the sheet, his back resting upon a pillow propped against the iron headboard, he watched Michael enter the room and slip out of his jeans. It had been a long day of labor in the sun, they were exhausted, and the revelations of Collin Gordon's visit had made them emotionally weary. Justin spread his legs as Michael sat between them, and then leaned back against Justin's chest. He rested his head on Justin's shoulder, aware once again of one of his favorite times of the day.

Justin wrapped his arms around him, resting his hands on Michael's belly, leaning the side of his face against sandy brown hair. He sighed. Nothing equaled having Michael in his arms, the feel of his warm weight against his chest, the clean smell of his hair. He closed his eyes, aware of Michael's breath with the rise and fall of his chest. What did it matter that somewhere, a million miles from the sweet solitude of their desert haven, pulsing with the frustration of relentless ambition, so much of the world labored to achieve unattainable happiness through their material goals and their allusive dreams of peace?

Perk jumped up on the bed and curled up next to Justin's leg, the dog's fluffy hair tickling his skin, and Michael's weight grew languid as he began to drift off to sleep. It was another easy desert night. Soft moonlight from the window filled the room. His dog lay sleeping and content. As the heat of his lover's body spread warmth through his arms and chest, he wondered if the turmoil in Michael's mind would permit him to be involved in Collin Gordon's clinic.

CHAPTER 19

Jody and Brian arrived a week later. By then, the concrete foundation for the veranda had been laid, and the new walls were about one foot high. The masonry was a much slower process than either of them had anticipated, as each stone had to conform to an irregular space in its place on the wall. Just under one foot thick, it was a labor equal to the creation of art, each stone put in place its own small success. They doggedly sorted through odd-shaped stones to find each exact fit, using a level all the while to be certain the wall was going up perfectly straight.

Jody had found two couples who were not only willing to assume the leases on her and Michael's apartments, but who also bought most of their furnishings. Beyond that, what her acquaintances didn't buy, she gave to the Salvation Army. Their residential tie to San Diego had been severed. She flew into El Paso with Brian and from there they rented a SUV to drive to the Big Bend. Michael and Justin were working on the wall when they arrived. When they pulled off the gravel road in front of the house, Michael was shocked. Shannon Mason was in the car with them.

"Who's the girl?" Justin asked, standing next to Michael near the wall.

Almost speechless, Michael collected his wits to answer. "Her name is Shannon Mason. She's a nurse I worked with at the hospital."

"Were you expecting her to come with them?"

"I didn't have a clue."

Caught off guard, Michael wasn't unhappy with Shannon's arrival, just surprised and a bit anxious, and agitated that Jody had not told him in advance.

"You know," Justin said, watching the threesome getting out of the car, "I've lived in this house for three years now. Day in and day out nothing ever happened. But since you've moved in with me, it seems this is the most popular place in west Texas. Between visitors and people showing up for medical emergencies or psychological counseling, it's gotten down right risky to walk outside naked."

The new visitors approached, all smiles. Jody threw her arms around Michael's neck, then stepped back to introduce Shannon to Justin. He smiled and nodded and took her hand to welcome her. She glanced between him and Michael as if to size up what she knew to be their relationship. Then she stepped forward to give Michael a hug.

She had been apprehensive about the visit. Now she was determined to keep it from becoming awkward. Though she always knew that Michael was a sensitive man, he was also very masculine—it had shocked her to learn he was gay. It had also dashed a fantasy she had nurtured for a long time. He had been the only man that she had ever allowed into her life, who, in just looking at him provoked sexual thought. Like others who knew him, she found him attractively rebellious, confident and thoughtful, a man not just extremely sexy, but slightly enigmatic, now confirmed by the fact he had coupled with a handsome black man in the desert. She had labored through adjusting to his sexual orientation, and had accepted the reality that he could never be the man in her life, but she wanted for all the world to be his friend.

"The staff misses you, Michael," she said disarmingly. "It hasn't been the same since you left. But I know you've moved here to stay. Jody told me all about how happy you are here."

He felt a bit awkward, aware of what her feelings for him had been before she learned he was gay. He was at a complete loss as to why she might have wanted to come to Texas to see him. "It's good to see you, Shannon. I still feel guilty for leaving you as abruptly as I did that day. I hope you understand."

"Please, Michael, don't feel guilty. I just wanted to see you again. We parted friends, remember. I'm so happy you've found peace of mind out here."

Brian had shaken hands with Justin. Now he stepped toward Michael, his hand extended. "Hello, Michael. I appreciate you guys letting us stay with you for awhile. I never knew the country was this beautiful out here until I came out with Mr. Kirkland." He looked at the stone work of the new walls. "Looks like things are moving right along."

Michael looked at the budding walls, dazed, dealing with the emotions that had surfaced by seeing Shannon again, and standing face to face with the man who wanted to take his sister away. "Uh, yeah, it's going well." He looked back at Brian. "We didn't have much time to get to know each other that night."

"No, no we didn't. I know Jody has told you all about what we've been doing and what we've been talking about."

"Yeah, she has … congratulations. I was beginning to think she's too picky to ever find a man she'd like to live with."

Brian turned and looked at her with a dopey grin. "I'm the

lucky one."

Michael looked at her, too. "Sis, I'd like to hear about how you settled our affairs in California. Would you walk with me for a moment?"

Justin began explaining to Brian and Shannon what they were doing to the house as Michael and Jody strolled a few yards out into the desert. Out of earshot from the others, he turned to look at her. "Why didn't you tell me over the phone Shannon was coming? I was completely unprepared."

"I didn't know myself. She joined Brian and I for dinner one night and we talked for hours. Of course we told her about you and Justin. Then she just showed up at the airport, just before we had to board the plane. She was lucky to get a ticket on the same flight. There wasn't time to call you."

"You could have called when you landed!"

"Michael, we were talking about all kinds of things. I didn't think about it. What's the big deal?"

"Why did she want to come? I hope it wasn't to ask me to go back to California."

"You don't have to be so uptight about this, Michael. Shannon knows you're happy out here. It's like she said, she's a friend. She wanted to see for herself how you're doing. Just visit." Jody paused in thought, then added, "But I'm pretty sure she's at odds with her career at the hospital. She said just enough to make that picture pretty clear. She wanted to see you, but I also believe she wanted to come out with us to get away from there for awhile."

Perk had trotted out behind them. Jody knelt and gave his ribs a frisky rub. "This little pooch gets into your heart. He's the only dog I've known that I miss when I'm away from him."

"At odds with her career? How do you mean?"

"She made comments about how impersonal everything is there, how most of the staff is more concerned about covering their asses above everything else. At the airport she made a comment about how San Diego makes her feel homesick."

They looked in her direction. She and Brian were listening to Justin describe how the new rooms were to be built.

"I know she doesn't care much for living in the city," Jody said. "She's a midwestern girl you know. She's lonely. I asked her if there were any romantic prospects in her life. There's none. Even though she's gorgeous, she's not the kind of girl the average dumb fuck would recognize as someone they should get to know." Jody looked back at her brother. "She talked a lot about how much she enjoyed spending time with you. When she was helping me pack your books, she broke into tears."

"Sis, there's no chance she came out here hoping there might be a chance for me and her is there?"

"No chance, Michael. Even though she didn't fully understand what it means to be gay, she does now. We talked about it at length. There's nothing complicated here. She's lonely. She needed a vacation and she values her friendship with you."

Michael studied the ground.

"Are you excited about getting to know Brian better?"

"Now that's exciting."

"Don't be sarcastic."

"Is he a little bit preppie, or is that just my imagination?"

"Preppie! I certainly haven't thought of him that way. He might be a little conservative about some things, he's a

Republican you know, but he's liberal where it matters. He has no problem with you and Justin being gay."

"That'll help, now that he'll be staying with us for a couple of weeks."

"Well, this visit was his idea so we're both looking forward to it. Just a short walk out behind your house is an adventure. And he was getting a little burned out. It was obvious he needed some time away from his office."

"Sis, aren't you two moving a little fast with this relationship? I mean, Jesus, you're moving to Houston. What do you know about humidity and mosquitos and big hair?"

"Relax, my charming brother. Let's just enjoy some time together. Brian was really looking forward to coming out here. He's hoping you and Justin will let him help on the house. Just get to know him and I think you'll like him."

Michael took a long, thoughtful look at the light in her eyes. He had never seen her glow with such contentment. It softened the lines of her face. He smiled. "I already do, Sis. If he makes you happy, I like him." He looked back at the small group. "Now all we have to do is figure out what the sleeping arrangements are going to be."

"Let the adventure begin."

They walked back through the creosote brush and dagger plants and rejoined the group. Justin suggested a quick tour of the property and its accommodations. The contraption rigged for showers intrigued both Shannon and Brian. Their thoughts were obvious as they stood looking at it, trying to envision what it would be like to actually use it to bathe. Jody explained to Shannon the procedures in using the outhouse, to never venture out to it barefooted and approach slowly at night. She also cautioned her to not be alarmed when she looked out and saw men peeing on the ground behind the house.

Inside, Justin showed them how to pump water at the sink, and after briefing them on where everything was at, he went into the bedroom and came back out with a regional map.

They gathered at the kitchen table, where Justin spread out the map. Jody joined them with Tecate and sliced lime from the refrigerator, just as Justin began running his finger along the parameters of their property.

He pointed at a certain spot on the river. "Our land includes this river frontage along here. The property line is in the middle of the river, beyond which is Mexico. It's very scenic along here and I bet Michael will take you all to see it when I go back to work in a couple of days."

"Pretty impressive piece of property, Justin," said Brian. "I know Mr. Kirkland enjoyed selling it to you and Michael. What are you going to do with it?"

"Walk on it," said Justin.

Brian smiled and glanced at Jody. She shrugged.

"And when we get the barn built, we're going to ride our horses on it," Justin added.

Shannon was looking around the room. She seemed to be absorbing every detail of the old house.

"Do you like our house, Shannon?" Michael asked.

There was a gleam in her eyes. "I've never seen anything like it. I love it. I loved driving through the desert. It's not hard to understand why you chose to live here."

Michael was anxious to talk to her in private. He still felt guilty that he had inadvertently misled her in their relationship in California. Now he wanted her and Justin to become friends, and he also wanted to find a way to brighten her morale with her career in San Diego.

Justin looked at his watch. "We have a half load of mortar left in the mixer," he said, getting to his feet. "There's just enough time before dinner to use it up."

"Dinner!" Jody blurted, "I forgot we have groceries in the car!" She stood. "We stopped for some ground beef so I could make hamburgers tonight."

Shannon went with her to the car for the groceries.

Justin looked at Brian. "We'll help you bring in the luggage before we get started on the masonry."

"No," said Brian. "Go ahead and get started. I'll take care of the luggage."

"It would sure be nice if the guest room was finished," Michael said, looking at the window they planned to knock out.

"Don't concern yourself on our account," said Brian. "I brought along an inflatable mattress. Jody and I can sleep on the floor over there," he said, nodding toward the living room. Shannon has already said she'd be perfectly happy on the couch."

Michael looked at him, wondering why he couldn't just settle into the fact that his sister was suddenly sleeping with a man who meant a great deal to her. Beyond simple concern, it made him feel selfish. It was like a burr he couldn't get out of his jeans.

Justin was quite happy with the situation, especially since he now knew it didn't mean giving up his bed and the intimacy of his nights with Michael. He found himself intrigued by Michael's awkward adjustment to Brian, and Shannon's surprise visit was another interesting element that promised to spice the next few days. He wondered how their visitors would adjust to the primitive accomodations, if either of them would be able to screw up the courage to take an open-air shower.

Brian joined Justin and Michael after he had taken all the luggage inside. He removed his shirt and now stood bare-chested like the other two men, his body lean, like that of a runner. Though his skin was a beautiful olive color, his hairless chest was rather pale.

"You might want to wear sun screen out here, Brian," Justin suggested.

He looked down at his chest. "Jody said she'd be out in a few minutes. I'll ask her if she has any." He looked around at what they were doing, then asked, "Is there anything I can do to help?"

Justin reached for the shovel. "I'll show you how we get mortar out of the mixer. If you'll keep that mortar board full, we'll get through the rest of this batch a lot faster."

Justin scooped a shovel full of mortar from the mouth of the mixer and slopped it onto the two foot square plywood board next to Michael, who was fitting the wall with another stone. Brian took the shovel, then stood by, watching the care they took in packing the mortar around each new stone, all the while keeping an eye on the mortar board.

After awhile, Michael looked over his shoulder and said, "Do you sue many people, Brian?"

"Actually, I've never sued anyone. I'm not involved in that kind of law. I basically advise clients on their contractual needs when they're negotiating real estate deals. I probably have the same view a doctor has concerning lawsuits. I'm exposed to malpractice litigation too, based on bad advice I might give, or a flawed contract I might draw up." He shoveled a scoop of mortar onto the board.

Michael looked at Justin. "I like him better already."

Brian laughed. "I generally expect to take it on the chin about being a lawyer. I've long since gotten use to lawyer jokes."

"Jody told me you're a religious man. Should we watch what we say around you?"

"I suppose I am religious. I'm Presbyterian and I go to church on Sundays. Jody went with me last Sunday. But I hope you don't feel uncomfortable because of it, and you certainly don't have to watch what you say around me. I'm not *that* religious."

"And you two have talked about getting married?" Michael asked, failing to hide the concern in his voice.

Justin looked at Michael. "You going to ask all twenty questions at one time?"

"Oh, it's okay," Brian said before Michael could answer. "I want him to feel comfortable with us as soon as possible. Besides, I have the advantage. Jody has told me all about both of you, and you know very little about me."

"So you've talked about it?" Michael repeated.

"We're trying to be at least a little practical in how we feel about each other, so that's why we're going to live together for awhile. In truth, I would marry her tonight, and that I *can't* explain. I've heard about this sort of thing, you know, love at first sight."

"Yeah," said Justin, moving a couple of inches down the wall on his knees. "I believe that's something Michael and I know a little something about."

"I thought it was something you'd see in a movie," Brian went on to say, eyeing the mortar board. "I never gave it much thought until it happened to me. It's a powerful emotion. I'll confess that it sometimes makes me feel like a silly teenager, but something hit me the moment I walked into your house that night and saw her. It was like my eyes had settled on the woman I wanted to spend the rest of my life with. I was not only drawn to her beauty, I felt like I knew her, intuitively, just by the look in her eyes."

Michael looked up from the stones he was sorting through. "I think that was obvious to everyone there that night."

Brian produced a doubtful smile. Judging by the tone of Michael's voice, he couldn't tell if he was winning over Jody's brother or not. He ventured on. "Well, when I actually began to get to know her, she was just as I had imagined. When she allowed me to kiss her that night, I was immediately compelled to have her in my life. I'm still awed by it. I had to resist telling her what was going through my mind. Nothing would do other than to get her to go to Houston with me. I was desperate to come up with the right words that might inspire her to go."

Michael had turned back toward the wall, testing the fit of another stone. "What would you have done if she hadn't gone with you?" he asked.

"I wouldn't have gone back with Mr. Kirkland. I would have stayed here in Big Bend, consumed with getting to know her. I can't explain it any better. Nothing like that has ever happened to me before."

"Looks like things went well for you two in Houston," Justin said over his shoulder.

"I'll say," said Brian, lifting his foot and resting it on the shovel blade. "On that first morning we awoke together, I knew I never wanted to wake up again without her beside me. I knew that moment I had to find a way to get her to move to Houston, to live with me, to forsake all that awaited her return in San Diego. I have never wanted or needed anything so deeply. There has never been anything in my life so important that nothing else mattered. It happened just that way, and all I can do is hope you can understand it."

Michael had stopped his work. He now sat on the ground, his arms wrapped around his knees, his back resting against the new stone wall. He was staring at Brian, seemingly speechless.

Justin looked at him and then turned to look at Brian. "Trust me," he said casually. "He understands it." Justin looked at him again. "You've read *Romeo and Juliet*, Michael. It happens to heterosexuals, too."

"You didn't think she's a little too headstrong?" Michael said dumbly.

"That's precisely one of the reasons I love her. She's not intimidated by anyone. Her tolerance for crap is zero. I've known so many women who've tried to mold themselves into what they thought I wanted, it makes me sick. I've known women who simply can't hide the fact they're more impressed by my career and social circles than they are with me—the guy who sniffs his armpit to see if his deodorant is holding up, and who lets go a loud belch after a cold beer. I've been discouraged time and again by self-possessed women whose agendas are born from some misguided psychological gene. I've spent more time than I care to think about with women who are hopelessly superficial and material in nature.

"Not Jody. She wants to live. She could care less about the latest fashion trends that might impress the right people, yet she impresses everyone she meets. She could care less what people might think about her, yet they are drawn to the dynamic of her personality. She simply doesn't care if she forgot to shave her legs or if her hair isn't perfect. There is nothing about her personality I don't admire. She doesn't try to stroke my ego, which makes me want her approval all the more."

Michael looked down at the ground. Anything that he could have possibly wanted to hear from the man who wanted his sister, had just been said by Brian. He felt joy in his heart, and an instant kinship with the man who seemed destined to be his brother-in-law. He looked up at the eager young man. "You're not bothered by the prospect of having a gay relative?"

"Bothered? That's not the right word. I've known a few gay men, usually those who are more outwardly gay than you and Justin are. Effeminate I mean to say. Curious would be a better word. You can place me among those who agree it must be within the natural order of things. But I am curious. I'd like to better understand how one man can be attracted to another; when for me, a woman such as your sister can possess every thought my mind can produce."

"It's no more complicated than the power of the genes, my friend," said Justin, fitting in place another stone. "Everything you just said about Jody reflects the same feelings a gay man can have for another man."

Michael looked at his lover, his outstretched arms as he patted wet mortar around the stone. He thought of how wonderful it felt being in them. He thought of their day's labor, the sun bearing down upon their skin, the bouquet of sweat it would bring to their bodies. *Yes*, he thought, *the power of the genes.*

"I'll also confess," said Brian, "I'm intrigued by the fact you guys are racially different."

Michael looked at him and smiled, certain he was going to enjoy getting to know his future brother-in-law.

"Think we'll be able to explain it to him?" Justin said, watching him shovel another scoop of mortar.

Michael had resumed his work on the wall. It was work in slow inches as the mortar ran out, as the wall continued to gain the height of another layer of stone.

"We have much more in common with you than you might think," Michael said, looking at Brian. "It's no more than one person loving another with the added element of a sexual attraction. You're the born with genes that determine the nature of that attraction. Our racial difference?" Michael looked at Justin and smiled. "I rather like the variety of color."

Brian eyes shifted between them. "Jody and I talked about sharing childbirth and about how we will raise our children. You don't regret missing out on that?"

"I think we'll leave that chore to you and Jody," Michael stated flatly.

Brian looked at Michael with a hint of bewilderment in his eyes. "So when you look at a beautiful woman, you never wonder what it would be like to go to bed with her? You never have a fantasy of holding her in your arms?"

"I never have," said Michael.

Justin thought of the confusion that had haunted him before

he met Michael. "It was different for me," he said, going on to relate the story of his failed engagement, concluding with: "And she was beautiful, Brian. So it doesn't matter, does it? Even though she was beautiful, and even though I didn't realize I was gay, it still interferred with my relationship with a girl I cared a great deal for."

Michael looked at his watch. "We're getting close to dinner time," he said, and then began to look for the next stone to mortar onto the wall

Brian watched the two men go about their meticulous work of fitting stones and packing mortar, captivated by the ambiance of their proximity. Had he not known what was between them, their subtle affection would have eventually made it abundantly clear. He marveled at the symmetry of their new wall, the loving care used in its formation, and its conformity to the ancient wall they were connecting it to. A calm came over him, with the warm sun upon his back, with the woman he loved not more than a few heartbeats away. He realized that he liked Michael and Justin, and felt he had been accepted by them. He sensed the potential for interesting new friendships to develop, the kind of friendship that came with no ulterior motive. He looked west, scanning the far horizon, struck again by the vastness of the desert. Here he could unwind, learn things his harried life in Houstion would never permit, and for the first time that he could remember, he actually tasted a sweet fragrance in the air.

By the time the hamburgers were ready, thay had placed a new layer of stone over the entire length of the wall. They gathered at the table and piled their hamburgers with onion and lettuce and pickle, and while they ate, they listened to stories Justin had accumulated during his years as a park ranger. Then he told them about Collin Gordon's magnanimous offer.

"That's wonderful, Justin," Jody said. "I think you'd be a perfect choice to run a state park." She looked at Michael and decided not to comment on Mr. Gordon's idea for him. He was fidgeting with his napkin, obviously at odds with his thoughts on the subject.

But, unaware of Michael's emotions, Brian asked, "Michael, do you plan to take him up on his offer to establish a clinic?"

Michael looked at him, stunned. "I haven't decided yet."

Brian glanced at Jody, wondering if he had said something out of line.

"My brother hasn't decided if he wants to return to the medical profession or not," she said, regretting she had not told him about Michael's sensitivities on the subject.

"Sis, let's not talk about that tonight," Michael said to insure that everyone understood it wasn't a subject to bring up. He handed Perk the leftover beef patty that still lay on the platter.

Shannon watched him with interest. She remembered well his emotions just before he left San Diego, and it was obvious now that those emotions were still raw. It made her heartsick. Not only did she care for him as a personal friend, she felt regret that his talent might go to waste. And she was intrigued by Collin Gordon's plans to establish a clinic, certain that Michael would be perfect for it. The concept inspired her imagination as she sat listening to the others. Though she wasn't quite sure how, it occurred to her that she might be the catalyst in getting Michael past his emotional dilemma.

Justin went on to describe his challenge in working for

Bernard. Brian talked about the dynamics of Houston, and his long family history in law. No one could interpret what might be on Shannon's mind. She simply seemed to enjoy listening to the others.

She offered to help Jody clean up the kitchen after dinner. Brian went into the living room to organize their luggage and arrange the inflatable bed. Justin went outside with Michael.

"I'm going to take a shower," Michael said, looking to see if the jug was full. It was. Justin had filled it that morning to let the day's sun warm the water.

"I think I'll work on that septic tank line then. I'll take one after you."

Standing with his back to the house a few minutes later, Michael was blotting off his chest when he heard someone come out the back door. He turned. It was Shannon. She looked startled, her eyes wide as he stood naked near the poles. He wrapped the towel around his waist as she quickly turned to go back into the house.

"Wait!" he called out.

She turned again as he approached with a disarming smile.

"I hope I didn't embarrass you," she said with a weak smile.

"It seems to me you're the one who is embarrassed."

"I *am* embarrassed!"

"Why? You're a nurse. You've seen hundreds of naked men."

"It's different with you."

"Is my navel in the wrong place or something?"

"You know why."

"I suppose I do, and I still feel guilty about that. I hope you have forgiven me?"

"I have," she assured him, though she had come to believe that she would never meet another man she admired as much as she did Michael.

After an awkward silence, he said: "If you came out to take a shower, I can go inside and make sure no one comes out."

Her face reddened. She looked in horror at the jug and two poles. "I couldn't possibly take a shower out here! Not out in the open like this."

"Then that'll be another new experience for you on this vacation—two weeks without a shower."

She looked again at the makeshift rigging. The weight of her extreme moral upbringing sat on her shoulders like an ever present troll. Just looking at it made her feel vulnerable.

"We're doctors and nurses, remember?"

She looked back at him, still blushing.

He nodded toward the new chairs. "Let's sit down for a minute."

They sat down and he took her hand and kissed it to help her relax.

"I'm glad you have forgiven me, but I still feel like a bastard for not telling you about myself when we were spending time together. I don't know why I just assumed that you knew."

She drew a deep breath. "You shouldn't feel guilty, Michael. You never misled me in any way. Frankly, I never understood why you were still single. Of course I know now." She looked at him. "And I *am* happy for you."

"But you're not happy for yourself though. Now I'm worried about that."

"Why would you think that?"

"Jody said something about it."

"I never told Jody anything like that."

"It must have been obvious in what you *did* tell her."

Shannon looked out across the desert and sighed, thinking about some of the things she had said to Jody. It dawned on her that anyone could have gotten the impression that she was unhappy. "When I was in school I dreamed about going to California to become a nurse. I suppose I had an impression of what it would be like, but it's not at all like I thought it would be."

"In what way?"

"For one thing, it's not the same with you not there. It's … colder. No one seems to really care about anyone else. It's a monotonous routine where everyone seems bent on self-preservation." Her eyes followed the western horizon, the colors of the setting sun now coming alive in the low clouds. "It's easy enough to understand why you have chosen to live here."

The towel slipped off his leg when he crossed it over the other. Noting her reaction, he avoided the obvious gesture of adjusting it.

"I'm lonely, Michael. I didn't notice how much so when you were there. You wouldn't think I'd feel lonely at the hospital, surrounded by other people all day long, but it's even worse there."

A tear had formed in the corner of her eye. Michael thought back on his assessment of the hospital and likened it to a hellhole, though he refrained from telling her this. He wanted nothing more than to find words that might comfort her, but he found himself at a total loss.

"Have you considered doing anything else?" he asked gently.

"I thought about going back home, but I can't. There's really nothing for me there, and I would feel defeated. That would be even worse."

The sun was dipping below the horizon, a fiery ball casting red hues across the land. Justin had quit digging out more lateral lines for the septic system, and had approached the shower. No more than a silhouette in the twilight, he stripped off his jeans and reached for the rope to tilt the jug. Shannon slumped slightly in the chair, trying to pretend no more than a casual awareness. Michael was amused by her reaction.

He watched Justin for a moment, water cascading down over a firm black body aglow with the final hues of a setting sun, his arm uplifted as he began to lather himself with soap.

"He's beautiful, isn't he," Michael said casually.

"Uh, Michael, this is awkward."

He glanced at her. "Don't women enjoy looking at naked men?"

"Well, they do, but ..."

"He won't mind if you look at him. He'd look at you if it were you over there. So would I. Actually, I had thought about asking you to go to Black's Beach with me one Sunday, before everything flew apart back there. It's a natural thing, isn't it, to admire the human body. It has a certain innocuous effect, like adding a disarming and sensual dimension to a friendship. Nudity feels natural, but you have to let it. I've always thought it a shame that people deny themselves this simple pleasure."

He noticed her gaze had drifted to Justin's shadowy form, and he believed this vacation was going to be good for her. He leaned back in the chair, his eyes fixed on the last remants of yet another magnificent sunset. That, and the fresh dry air, and the quiet of a vast land had had its healing effect on him, and he believed it would for her, too. He could see it in her eyes, her desire to leave old baggage behind, to grow and reach out for her own slice of life.

"I've been worried about him," Michael said, watching Justin reach for a towel.

"Justin?" she asked.

"Yes. We have an escaped killer on the loose somewhere around here. He killed a little boy in the park, and Justin is taking it personally."

"Oh my God!"

"I wouldn't worry about it too much," Michael said with assurance. "It looks like the guy has gone somewhere else."

"They didn't catch him?"

"No. But I think Justin is the only one who thinks the creep is still in the park."

With Michael's assurance, Shannon discounted her concern that a killer might be in the area. Her thoughts drifted back to the conversation at dinner.

"Why didn't you want to talk about that clinic at dinner?" she asked, aware she most likely already knew the answer.

Michael stiffened. "You know why."

"I don't agree with that, Michael."

"Join the crowd. No one else does either."

"Do they need doctors out here?" she asked.

"I wouldn't know."

"Evidently your neighbor, Mr. Gordon, thinks they do."

"Then I suppose they do."

"I would take that offer in a minute," she said wistfully.

His head snapped toward her. It was like she had thrown on a light switch, but what the light illuminated was not immediately clear.

She looked at him. "I would. There's no doubt in my mind. I can't imagine anything I'd rather do."

"You'd pack up and move out here? You'd be interested in getting involved with a charitable clinic?"

"The majority of my education was in general practice. I only went into specialized training because I thought it would be more rewarding, but it's not. You have no idea of how much I'd love to be involved in a clinic like that."

This revelation took him by surprise. He wasn't quite sure what to make of it. He looked at her, trying to make something coherent from a swirl of thoughts, and then Brian stepped through the door.

He stood squinting into the shadowy light for a moment at Justin, who was now drying himself off. He looked down at Shannon and Michael, who were observing his beffuddled expression.

"Not overly modest, is he?" Michael said simply. "Just consider it an addional feature of an outdoor shower, the possibility of an audience when you bathe."

"Uh … so it seems," he said, adjusting his sensibilities as Justin approached, the towel wrapped around his waist.

Stepping past them to enter the house, as he reached for the door knob Justin turned and said, "Looks like I forgot to go in for a clean pair of jeans before I rinsed off."

Jody was mopping the old, uneven tiles of the kitchen floor

when Justin paraded through. She looked up and watched him disappear into the bedroom. She looked over at the back door, wondering how the eccentric bare reality of a community shower had affected Justin's other rather conservative guests.

The evening passed with the old Zenith parting with some static and a few country tunes, and with Tecate and the camaraderie of light conversation. They turned in at eleven o'clock. After turning off the light, Justin got into bed and rested his arm over Michael's chest. They lay for a moment listening to the quiet of the desert, then Justin moved his head closer to kiss Michael's neck.

"Have you formed an opinion of Brian yet?" he asked.

"I think he's grand." He looked at Justin. "I'm a little worried about it, but mostly relieved. She's so damned picky, I didn't know if she'd ever find a man to settle down with."

"That's the thing—she isn't predisposed to hasty decisions. Even though it seemed quick, obviously she thought it through."

Michael looked at him. "You're right. Plus they'll be here for a while. We'll have a chance to get to know him a lot better."

Justin stroked the side of Michael's face. "I regret telling them about Collin's plans for a clinic. I just didn't stop and think that it would have an effect on you. It seems you can't get a break, Michael. Everytime you turn around someone is trying to get you back into the medical profession."

"I'm glad you brought it up. Shannon said something interesting about it while we were outside."

"She did?"

"She said she'd take Collin's offer in a minute."

Justin got up on his elbow. "You're kidding!"

"She was serious. There seemed to be no doubt in her mind."

"That *is* interesting."

"She'd be good at it. I'm thinking it might be a good idea to introduce them."

Justin thought for a moment, then said, "He might be interested in that. But I think he already knows he could find a doctor for the job if it came down to it. I got the impression he wants you. He seemed comfortable planning it with you involved. And I can understand that. You have a natural ability to put people at ease. The Mexicans he talks about would trust you. I'm sure he considers that important in what he wants to accomplish with the clinic."

"Shannon would be a better choice."

"A good choice, maybe yes; a better choice, no."

Michael let out a weary sigh and closed his eyes. Justin looked at him and smiled, then laid his head back down. With a whisper of cool fresh air from the window, he pulled him in tighter and they fell asleep in a soft glow of starlight.

At daybreak Michael went into the kitchen to find Jody mixing batter for pancakes. Brian was sitting at the table, yawning, his coal black hair askew.

"Sis, we're not used to someone cooking all the meals around here," he said, kissing her forehead. He looked out the window. Shannon was making her way back from the outhouse, stepping gingerly in her housecoat and slippers over the rocky desert crust.

"I love cooking in this kitchen," Jody said. "Sit down and I'll bring you some coffee."

A few minutes later all five were melting butter on their pancakes.

Michael glanced at Justin with a wink, then said, "Well, Brian, you got a little sweaty in the sun yesterday. We're all hoping you plan to begin your day with a shower."

Brian looked around at the faces smiling back at him, perplexed. He lifted his elbow to sniff his armpit.

"I think you missed the point, honey," said Jody. "I bet they just want to see if you have the guts to get naked."

"Oh! Well, even if I did, seeing me naked could be a disappointment," he said, stuffing his mouth with a forkful of pancakes.

"I certainly didn't think so," Jody shot back.

Justin joined in. "Well, Brian, I'd be happy to refill that jug for you."

He looked at Shannon, the only one besides himself who harbored reservations concerning outdoor showers.

"Don't look at *her*," said Michael. "You might be able to screw up the courage to give it a try, but you're not going to see Shannon out there taking a shower. She plans to wait until she gets back to civilization, some two weeks from now."

"I didn't say that exactly, Michael. I said I didn't think I could take a shower out in the open like that."

"It's the only shower we have," said Michael.

"What a shame," said Justin. "And such a lovely creature you are, to deny this barren land such a delightful image."

"I don't know why any of you would want to see me nude," said Shannon. "You two are gay, Jody is a woman, and Brian is obsessed with *her* body. I know that because he can't seem to take his eyes off of it."

"Are you kidding?" said Justin. "I'm certain Brian would like to see you naked and I bet Jody would too."

"Don't be ridiculous, Justin," Jody retorted.

He looked at her, grinning. "You wouldn't admit it if you did."

"I would too!" she protested.

"Well then, do you secretly like to look at other women when they're naked or not? Yes or no."

She hesitated with her answer, then said, "Okay, I admit it, yes. I think all women secretly compare themselves to other women."

"What about you, Shannon? Do you like looking at naked women?" Justin asked.

"Good Lord!"

Justin didn't let up. "Come on, girl. You do … go ahead and admit it."

"Fine! I admit it. From time to time I am curious about what other women might look like naked."

"There you are," said Justin. "It's not so hard to just be open with it after all, is it?" He looked back at Jody. "Would you like to see Shannon naked?"

She scowled at him. "Just how far do you plan to take this?"

"Answer that one question and we'll change the subject."

She looked over at Shannon, and her eyes fell to her chest. "Okay, I'll admit that too. I've wondered if your breasts are that perky when you're not wearing a bra."

"I wish!" Shannon blurted with little thought, realizing only then the issue had embarrassed her.

Michael pored more syrup on his pancakes, delighted with the conversation.

Brian was looking at Justin inquisitively. "Why would a gay man want to look at a naked woman?" he asked. "Yesterday you said … "

"Good question," Justin interrupted.

"Yes, that is a good question," said Michael. He looked at Brian. "For the same reason we walk out into the desert to look at a cactus in bloom, or watch a hummingbird draw from that feeder out there. To give our eyes the pleasure of natural beauty in yet another form."

"And to make her chill out," added Justin. "No one should spend two weeks out here and go back as tightly wound as they were when they arrived."

"Have you showered out there, Jody?" Shannon asked.

"I have. And rest assured, these guys have no qualms about staring at you, gay or otherwise. But I have to admit, it is fun. I'll miss taking a shower in the sun when the new bathroom is finished. There's something invigorating about it."

"I'm willing to do it!" Brian announced.

They all looked at him.

"When?" asked Justin.

He pursed his lips in thought. "Right after breakfast," he said brazenly. "And anyone who cares to is welcome to observe."

Then they turned their gaze on Shannon.

"Why is everyone looking at me?" she protested. She glanced across their smiling faces. "Okay, okay, let me think about it. God, I never realized taking a shower could be such a challenging ordeal."

"I think we might have her," said Justin, blotting a spot of sticky syrup from his lip with a napkin.

Justin went outside to refill the water jug when they finished eating. Shannon went with him. Brian went into the bedroom. Michael stayed behind to help Jody clear the table.

"Justin sure is animated this morning, isn't he?" Jody said, scraping plates over the garbage can.

"Yeah," said Michael, "and I'm glad. It's taken his mind off that mess over in the park. He refuses to believe the killer left the area."

"Why?"

"I don't know."

By the time Michael and Jody went outside, Justin had arranged a semi-circle of chairs not ten feet from the towering poles. The morning shower had indeed become an event. Coffee mugs in hand, they took their places in the chairs and awaited Brian to come out of the house.

"I bet he's hung like a horse," Justin said in anticipation.

Michael looked at Jody. "Sis, is he?"

Sipping her coffee, Jody looked over the rim of the mug. "I'm not going to spoil the suspense."

Brian finally emerged, still clad in his flannel pajamas. He stepped toward the shower much like a condemned man might trudge toward the gallows.

"You wear those pajamas when you sleep?" Justin called out.

Jody was tempted to answer for him, but decided to let him hold his own.

"I did last night," he replied in his approach. "I am a guest in your house after all, and we are in mixed company."

"Looks like he wasn't aware of the rules," said Michael.

"What rules?" said Shannon.

"Pajamas are against the rules," Justin stated flatly.

"For women too!"

"There's no discrimination of any kind on this property."

"I'm glad I'm not Catholic," Brian mumbled. "I'd have to confess all of this when I got back home." He stepped toward the two poles and tested the rope. The jug tilted slightly. He let go the rope and reached for the top button of his pajama top.

"The pillars of conservative prudism now come tumbling down," said Michael with his finest early morning humor.

It took what seemed like a protracted length of time for Brian to remove the top. His bare chest heaved with a deep breath, his olive skin now tinged with pink from the few hours of afternoon sun the day before. When he pushed his thumbs under the waist band of the pants, he glanced across their faces again, then turned his lean frame in the other direction.

"Now wait a minute!" protested Justin. "I thought you were going to be a good sport."

Brian looked back over his shoulder, then, with no small reluctance, he turned to face them. He hesitated a moment longer before he found the courage to deal with the bottoms, finally leaning forward to push them down his long thin legs.

His audience cheered and applauded as his face turned red, his knees seemed bound together. He stood before them naked, a dopey grin fixed on his face, fumbling for what he should do with his hands.

"Goddamn! Are all you Spaniards hung like that?" Justin blurted. "I knew it! I knew he would make me look like an idget!"

"An *idget*?" said Jody, amused.

"Just look at him! You don't know what I'd give to be hung

like that. It ain't fair!"

Jody feigned indignation. "I'm shocked, Justin. I've always assumed gay men were more sophisticated in their thinking than that," she said.

"Bullshit. He's hung like a horse, just like I thought."

As the subject of their intimate focus, Brian felt lightheaded. He had never imagined finding himself in these circumstances, though the tingles across his skin were not so very unpleasant. In fact, as his pounding heart began to settle, he felt a rush of exhilaration.

Shannon lowered her head and rubbed her brow, but then found her eyes drawn back toward the self-imposed exhibition of a lean and quite handsome nude man.

Now resigned, Brian stood under the jug and pulled on the rope. He shuddered when cold water came pouring over his head. "Shit! I didn't realize the water was going to be this damn cold," he said, shivering.

"Okay, Jody," said Michael. "Get over there and wash him before he freezes to death."

"Michael, you're kidding!"

"This is not a passive event, little sister."

She got to her feet and approached her hapless future groom. He was now braced for almost anything. First, she lathered his rich black hair, then moved quickly to his chest and arms. Except for his shivering, he stood as rigid as the poles he was between as she hastily washed his lower body, stiffening further when her hands came up between his legs.

She looked up at Brian's red face. "I'm doing this as fast as I can," she said, not sure if he was embarrassed or just plain cold.

"You're turning me on!" he hissed through his teeth.

"Sorry," she said, standing back up. "There, we're done. Go ahead and rinse off. We'll find a way to get even with those two later."

Shannon gaped in stunned amazement, nervously aware she would be coerced to go next, yet she wanted to do it desperately. Her whole life equaled no more than a series of cautious steps, and she yearned for a little adventure, such as that before her now. Her heart began beating faster with her inner struggle to expand the limits of her courage. She thought of Justin the afternoon before, how he had so casually showered publicly. But he was a man, and so was Brian, and men have more inclination to do such things. If only Jody would volunteer to go first, but that was not on this morning's agenda. Her new friends were captivated in finding out if she had the guts to get naked. And if only she did, instead of quietly fretting over what her mother might say.

Jody blotted Brian's back and then handed him the towel. After he dried his chest and wrapped the towel around his waist, he combed his fingers back through his wet wavy black hair, looking at Shannon.

"Guess whose turn it is now," he said wryly.

Jody saw the alarm in Shannon's expression. "You don't have to do it if you don't want to … does she, Michael?"

Michael leaned forward and looked down at the ground. He had come to know Shannon well during the course of their friendship in San Diego, aware of how badly she wanted to break out of her shell. He hoped this dare might be a way to do it; yet it pained him to see her struggle.

"Of course not," he said, and then he looked at her. "Brian did, but you don't."

"You're wrong!" Shannon shot back, defiantly, albeit nervously. "I *do* have to. I've never dared to do anything silly in my life, and it's about time I do. I'm a sport too."

"Right on, girl," said Justin in light encouragement.

"Just give me a minute," she said, finding the courage to bring herself to her feet.

"It's not as difficult as you're thinking it will be," said Jody. "It really is kinda fun."

Timidly, she stood. She stepped toward the poles, her hands at the tie of her housecoat. She averted her eyes from the others, holding her breath as she pulled open the housecoat and then let it fall from her shoulders. Standing in the morning sun, in silk panties and lace bra, she felt compelled to draw her arms across her chest. She looked up at the jug as she twisted her arms behind her back to unfasten the bra, her nervous fingers finding the clasps all but impossible.

The camaraderie of the morning had turned to reverence as they watched Shannon set out to prove to herself that she could go forth with a bold pursuit. Frustrated with the clasp, she fumbled with it, determined to know the sensation of their eyes upon her nude body. She had imagined it before, that fairly common fantasy of undressing before others, for it had dawned on her how utterly exciting that might be. But so unlike a fantasy, this was unnervingly real. So now she would test her mettle. It came with chills and hot flashes of electricity running down her arms and legs. It caused a fast beating heart and short breaths so quick and shallow. But still, it was a dare that made her feel alive in a way she had never felt befoe, a challenge so sensual it almost made her dizzy.

Justin stood and stepped forward and placed his hands on her shoulders, hoping to calm her. He realized that for Shannon this was more than getting past her modesty, that she had made it important to follow through, and had resolved to challenge her inhibitions despite the anguish it may cause.

"Relax, lovely lady," he whispered. "We teased you in good fun. I hope that didn't make you feel obligated to do this."

"No. I'm just nervous."

"You could give it some thought, maybe jump in another time."

"That's my problem, Justin. I'm always giving everything so much thought. I'm thinking my whole life away."

He smiled and nodded. "Then let me help you." Her shoulders still in his hands, he guiding her beneath the awaiting jug.

She let her arms fall to her side and took a deep breath. Standing behind her, he gently unfastened her bra, lifting the straps from her shoulders. Her breasts fell slightly with their full weight. He paused, looking at her shoulders and arms, at the thousands of tiny bumps of gooseflesh spreading across her skin. He knelt, placing his hands aside her hips, then he slowly slid her panties down her silky white legs, and he heard from her a small gasp. She stepped out of the panties and turned to look at him as he stood, and she melted in his disarming smile. She watched his eyes follow the soft curves of her form, and his lingering gaze brought a sensual calm deep inside her belly.

"You are a brave and exquisite creature, lovely lady," he said, smiling at her again. He then looked up at the half full jug. "That water is quite cold this time of day. Are you ready?"

She nodded and he took hold of the rope. A rush of cold water cascaded down over her short blonde hair and she gasped, at once folding her arms over her chest. The water splashed over her small shoulders, and ran down over her breasts, dripping from the hardened peaks of her nipples, down over her belly and through the thin tuft of blonde pubic hair, and on down her quivering legs to the sand. He saw again the gooseflesh and felt a protective instinct to take her into his arms to warm her. Instead, he reached for the soap. What this lovely good sport had decided to endure need not be prolonged.

"You can wash your hair later, in the kitchen sink," he said softly as he began to lather her shoulders.

She stood shivering, enchanting as a siren as Justin's hands glided over her pale flesh, the sun at last warming her skin, and from his hands came a different but so pleasant form of warmth. He washed her gingerly, her breasts and arms and back, and again he reached for the soap.

"Oh, God!" she sighed as his hands then came down over her belly.

"Are you okay with this?" he asked tentatively.

"Yes. It's just I've never been bathed by a man before," she said, closing her eyes, the chills coursing through her no longer caused by cold water. Though it may have been the most sensual experience of her life, it was also much like a young girl being bathed by her father. But that could never deliver the sensation of all those eyes upon her, of Justin's hands so caring and gentle.

His hand came fleetingly between her legs, brushing past her nether lips nary hidden by their slight scattering of fine blonde hairs. His other hand came down her back, down over the feminine curve of her shapely hips.

"I'm amazed you haven't already attracted a special man, someone who would be lucky enough to be here in my place," he said, swirling the soap over her soft, silky skin.

"Me too," she said, her eyes still closed, allowing herself to enjoy the luxury of his hands.

Justin felt that if any lady deserved the loving attention of a special man, his hands were upon her now. He considered her idea of moving to the Big Bend country, to help establish that clinic, and he wondered if such a man existed for her here.

Now sharing the sentiment of Shannon's bold endeavor, Michael watched how carefully his lover handled this most courageous lady, how easily Justin had called upon the dynamic of his compassion, and his heart swelled with the good fortune to be loved by a most extraordinary man.

Justin knelt and his hands left a wake of soapy lather down the length of both of her legs. He then stood and took ahold of the rope again. Her eyes still closed, he said, "Here it comes again. Are you ready?"

"Yes," she whispered, gritting her teeth, and the water poured over her again, taking the soap in fast rivulets to the sand.

He quickly blotted her head to toe with the towel, and she stood in the warmth of the sun and opened her eyes, now calm and effervescent with early sunlight glistening on her skin. She looked up at Justin, and then turned to look at the others, and a smile of wonderment came to her lips. She held her hands before her, looking at them. Then she looked down at her own nude body.

"Look around you, lovely lady," said Justin. "Now is your time to breathe, to take in all that is around you, while all of your senses are so keen." He looked up into the sky. "You have those few feathery clouds drifting by, and the morning sun warming the earth. They are for you." He stretched out his arm toward the horizon. "You have some of nature's most incredible work for as far as the eye can see. A desert awaiting to embrace you and inspire new dreams. Mountains with the power of songs you've never heard." He held his hand before her. "You have the fine sculpture of this beautiful body, nature's most exquisite creation yet, and you have now shared it with your friends. These are the things that give our lives real joy, God's gifts with true meaning. They are life's simple pleasures that are universally lost on the vast majority of mankind. I've always found that so incredibly sad."

Her shoulders drew in. "Wow," she said, looking back up him. "I've never experienced anything like this before. I can't describe it. It's like waking up and breathing fresh air for the first time. I'm not sure I even want to put my clothes back on right away."

"That's okay by me," Brian said happily.

Jody gasped and slapped his knee. "You don't have to be so enthusiastic about that!" She looked back at Shannon. "But girl, I don't blame him. You really do have a beautiful body."

Justin stepped over and picked up his chair, prepared to take it back inside and then start the day's work on the new wall. He looked back at Shannon, who stood in awe, gazing out across the desert.

"You don't have to hurry to put your clothes back on. Strap on your sandals and take a walk out there just as you are. Let your body have the whole morning in the sun. You'll find that the desert will become a part of you."

He picked up the chair, as did the others, and Shannon turned toward the desert as they walked back toward the house.

CHAPTER 20

A week passed. The new wall and the community of their friendship had grown with its passing. Justin had returned to his duties in the park, but since rumors of the serial killer still lingered, Big Bend was still almost deserted, so Bernard had suggested he check out at noon, to allow him more daylight to work on the house. Brian had taken to the art of mortaring in stone, and with his help, the wall had reached shoulder height. Perk had adjusted to the camaraderie and found quite tolerable all of his guests, and the little dog reveled in the never ending attention, as at least one of them was always ready with a good belly or neck rub. All inhibitions that had been smuggled in from the city about the open-air shower had faded away, as had the confinement of sleeping in pajamas. They found little time to read, for their conversations often went on past midnight. With the flavor of a variety of opinions, they discussed politics, religion, sexuality, and life in the city as compared to laid back harmony of the desert. They were easy friends, and family, and in this few day's time the haunting mystery of the desert had found its way into their souls.

Shannon thought often about the new clinic. It had taken a place in her mind in the form of a dream, a fantasy in which she would be a part, and she ached to find a way to discuss it with Michael. Finally, for want of a better tact, she decided to simply bring it up.

She waited for the end of the day, when Michael usually took his shower, to approach Justin with her thoughts. He was inspecting their day's work on the wall when she walked up. He stood listening while she explained what she would like to talk to Michael about. Justin glanced over and noticed Michael was already drying his hair when she finished. He let out a long sigh.

"I know why you're reluctant to talk to him. It's like you're peeling a scab off a sore that never heals by just bringing it up. But Shannon, I believe with all my heart that down deep inside he'd love to set up that clinic. No one understands it really, but he simply can't find a way to convince himself he should do it. I've agonized over it, and I can't find a way to help him. But you've worked with him. You know that part of him better than anyone. Maybe you can find a way to help him."

"I wish I knew how to help him, Justin. It seems like he's fighting his own mindset and can't find a way to prevail. But I think the clinic would be as good for him as it would for me. If I could be part of something like that, it would finally give my life some real meaning. And I love it out here so. You don't know how I dread going back to San Diego."

Justin recalled a previous conversation he had had with Michael. "Michael did suggest we talk to Mr. Gordon about you. He said you'd be better at it than he would."

"That's ridiculous. He would have to be involved," came her instant reply.

"Maybe not. Maybe this is the reason you were compelled to catch that plane out of San Diego."

"I'd rather talk to Michael," she said without further thought.

"Well then, maybe you'll find a way to bring him around."

She turned and watched Michael start toward the house. She hurried and caught him before he reached the door. Distracted for a moment by the dimensions of his body, her eyes swept over him before resting in his gaze. Little did he know the effect he had had on her in San Diego, how he had inadvertantly disabled for her the prospect of any other man. The likelihood of finding another man his equal, to Shannon, seemed all but impossible. She had not been able to go to work for two days after he left the hospital, for she had stayed in bed and sobbed.

Now she knew they would never be lovers, nor hold each other through the night, nor explore the nuances of each other's intimate secrets. But she had come to the desert to see him, confirming that they would forever be friends. And their friendship being so much more than naught, this had mended her heart; and if there was another man for her somewhere, she would have to rely on fate to bring them together.

He turned and looked at her, aware at once she had something on her mind. "Do you have a few minutes to listen to something I've been thinking about?"

He looked over her shoulder at Justin, who was watching them. He sensed what was coming. "Uh, of course I do." He reknotted the towel around his waist and they sat next to each other in the new chairs.

"I don't want to go back to San Diego," she began. "I'd rather move out here and help you start that new clinic." She held her finger to her lips to hush him when he began to speak. "Just listen for a minute. I think I understand as well as anyone why you're reluctant to practice medicine. I was in the operating room with you that day, remember? But Michael, I'm not doing anyone any good with what I'm doing now, especially myself. I don't like the people at the hospital, and I don't like San Diego, not that I want to be critical with any of that. It's me. I guess I'm not cut out to be a city girl, or to be part of a hospital bureaucracy. I want to do something real with my hands. I want to look into a patient's eyes and feel trust. I can help people out here, people who otherwise have no hope. I want to go home at night knowing I have a reason to exist." She looked at him, taking a hopeful breath before she continued.

"I know you aren't ready, and maybe you never will be, but you could set it up. I could help. I can run it from there, with your advice when I need it. I can wait, and hope that one day you'll be ready to join me."

"Can I say something now?" he asked.

She nodded enthusiastically.

"I've already given this matter a great deal of thought, and I agree with you. I'll ask Justin to call Mr. Gordon."

She gulped a swallow of air, hardly able to believe her own ears. She was elated. She had expected resistance, even an argument, but he had simply agreed with no reservation. It was a fantasy on the urge of coming true. Her enthusiasm began to bubble like shaken champagne.

"When?" she asked excitedly.

"Now." He waved Justin over, and as he approached, Michael said, "I know you know what we were talking about. Do you want to call him?"

"It'll only take a minute," Justin said, heading then into the house.

Collin Gordon arrived by the time dinner was ready. He

walked into the house, went straight to the stove and lifted the lid on a big simmering pot to look inside.

"Goddamn, that smells good!" he said, looking at Jody. "What is it?"

"We're having spaghetti and meat sauce, Mr. Gordon."

"Call me Collin," he said. "When will it be ready?"

"It's ready now," she replied.

He turned toward her. His eyes drifted down her front and back up, his brows lifted. "You must be Michael's sister, Jody."

"That would be me," Jody said, the smile in her eyes reflecting her enchantment with the crusty old man

"You two look alike. Same nose. 'Course you're much prettier."

"Why, thank you, Collin."

He looked into the living room. "I don't know some of you people, but get on over here. Dinner is ready!"

Justine introduced Brian and Shannon as they walked into the kitchen. The old rancher nodded, then took his chair at the head of the table.

"You boys need to buy a bigger table," he said, watching everyone squeeze in.

"We make our own furniture around here, Collin," said Justin.

"Of course you do," he said, forking spaghetti onto his plate. "How about passing some of that sauce down this way?" he said, breathing in the delicious aroma as he took hold of the bowl.

The food made a quick round and everyone began to eat, watching with delight the old man savor his food.

"Is that garlic bread over there?" he asked, nodding at a plate piled with bread.

Jody smiled and handed him a piece.

"So you're an ambulance chaser," he said looking at Brian, his mouth full.

"I haven't chased many ambulances lately, sir," Brian answered.

"He a commercial real estate attorney," Jody said defensively.

"Ah," he said, nodding. "Noble profession." He looked at Shannon. "And young lady, you're a nurse?"

"Yes, sir. A registered nurse. I worked with Michael when he was in San Diego."

"So that's how you two know each other. Well, if he left someone like you to come out here and live with Justin, I guess there really is no hope for him."

Michael spoke: "Collin, she's the best nurse I've ever known. She's why we called you tonight."

"I'm way too old for her, Michael." He looked back at her. "But then …"

"We're thinking you're interest might be in her professional skills."

"In what way?"

"The clinic. She wants to move out here and be a part of it. She wants to run it, and she's qualified to do so."

His attention seemed to shift from his enjoyment of the food. He looked at her again, this time a long, thoughtful gaze, then he turned to Michael again. "I was hoping you had decided to run our clinic."

"Well, sir, I haven't decided to do that, but I'm willing to help her where I can."

The old rancher's face reddened and his brow furrowed over squinting eyes. "Damn! What is it with you temperamental doctors?"

"Why me?" Michael argued. His nostrils flared with a frustrated, angry breath. "Why does it have to be me? How are you so certain I'm the right one?"

Justin looked at Michael, distraught. He wasn't surprised Michael had reacted angrily, aware that his emotions festered just under the surface.

Collin studied him for a moment. "Son, fifty years ago I was walking across some land up in the Permian Basin. I accidently stepped on a little cactus. Damn needle from it went through the sole of my shoe and right into my big toe. I sat down and took off my shoe and suddenly had the strongest sense I was sitting right on top of a big pool of oil. I left my shoe there so I wouldn't lose that spot, then hobbled back to my pickup truck. Against the advice of everyone I knew, I bought that piece of ground and sank a well. To this day that well produces more oil than any other project I've been involved in. That's how I know you are the right one."

Michael looked down at his food, then looked back at the old rancher. "If you have that much faith in me, then have faith in what I'm telling you. It's a good idea. She'll make it work just like you want it to, maybe better. All you have to do is give her a chance."

"I don't have to make a lot of money, Mr. Gordon," Shannon said anxiously.

He laughed. "Angel, you could write your own check if you could do this for me. No, not for me, you'd be doing it for the people who live here."

"She could do it, sir," Michael assured him. "And I would always be around if she needed me."

He looked at her long and hard, then startled everyone by slamming his hand down on the table. "Give me two weeks to get it organized."

He took another large forkful of spaghetti.

"Now that's what I love about west Texas," said Justin, grinning. "No need for feasiblity studies or long-winded strategic meetings."

Shannon was all but breathless. She got up, went over and threw her arms around the old rancher's neck. He smiled at the others. "Sure hope my wife is not up there reading my mind right now."

The old man, his mouth full again, looked at Brian. "So you know a little something about real estate?"

"Yes, sir, I do."

"Then tomorrow, I want you to go over to Lajitas. Find a piece of ground that would be an appropriate location for our clinic. Negotiate the price and set up the contracts and a closing date. Don't tell anyone I'm involved or they'll try to get more money for it." The old man's eyes narrowed. "And young man, don't make any plans to bill me for this. Consider it your contribution to a good cause."

Brian smiled. "Be happy to do it, sir."

"Michael, I want you to sketch out a floorplan for the clinic. You know the layout we'll need. Make it as complete as you can so my architect can take it from there."

Michael nodded.

Mr. Gordon looked at Shannon. "Young lady, what do you plan to do to help?"

She was still almost too excited to talk, but she managed, since she had already put some thought into starting the clinic. "We'll need a list of medical supplies and equipment. I can do that. I'll call the suppliers I know in San Diego and find out who we need to contact out here."

The old rancher looked at the piece of garlic toast in his hand. He took a bite, nodding. "Well, kids, it looks like we're on our way."

CHAPTER 21

Two days later, Shannon and Jody drove to the El Paso airport. They had made reservations to fly back to San Diego, to pack Shannon's belongings and shut down her ties to California. Near the final security check point, Brian stood with his arms around Jody's waist while the others waited patiently nearby. He wanted to go with her, but he was obligated to follow through on that real estate deal for Mr. Gordon. Now he didn't want to turn her loose.

Michael feared they might miss their plane.

"Okay, okay, she's only going to be gone a few days," Michael finally said.

That night after dinner the three men sat in the living room, reading. Michael and Justin glanced at Brian from time to time. The young man seemed lost, his gaze often drifting from the pages of the *Wall Street Journal* to rest in hapless thought on the opposite stone wall.

"Collin seemed to be happy with that lot you have under contract, Brian," Justin said.

Brian's gaze shifted to Justin, who was stretched out on the sofa.

"Uh, yeah, I heard him say that," Brian said hazily, his mind still distant.

Justin and Michael exchanged glances, smiling. Justin spoke again: "Plenty big enough for the clinic, easy to see from the road, and I thought it was a pretty good price."

"Yeah, I thought so, too," he said, glancing sullenly from the newspaper that had dropped to his lap.

"What are you thinking about, Brian?" Michael asked.

Brian looked at him. "Didn't Jody say it would take three or four days?" he said.

"That's what they said."

"I would have gone with her if Mr. Gordon hadn't needed help to buy that property. We got a pretty good contract," Brian said wistfully.

"Yeah, we were just talking about that, weren't we?" said Michael.

"Brian, you look like a lost puppy," Justin said.

He sighed. "I was just thinking about Jody. I'm already used to having her around. I didn't realize how long four days could seem."

"He really is a goner," Michael said.

Justin was looking at Michael sprawled out in the over-stuffed chair. "Yeah, I believe he is, and I'm pretty sure I know how he feels."

Two days later the three men were topping out the new stone wall. It blended almost perfectly with the old walls. An inside stone wall, waist high, divided the new bathroom from the guest room. They would use drywall and plaster to take it to the ceiling. Justin was completing the final stages of the bathroom plumbing when the cell phone rang.

He handed the phone to Michael. It was Jody. Brian stood nearby, eager to talk to her.

"I wanted to talk to you first," she said. "Brian is going to be upset. This is going to take longer than we hoped."

He glanced at Brian. "You're right. He is definitely going to be upset."

"I'm not too happy about it myself. Anyway, the hospital accepted her resignation without prejudice when they learned her service was immediately required to open a charity clinic."

"That's good."

"But there's some criticism flying around about the way you left town."

"I don't give a damn about that. Why is it going to take longer to get back?"

"Crating and shipping Shannon's stuff is more involved than we realized. We decided it would be quicker to just rent a truck and drive it back. Did Brian find her a rent house?"

"Yeah, he did, over in Lajitas, but I'll let him tell you about it."

Michael handed Brian the phone, then watched the disappointment spread across his face as he listened to the explanation of why their return would be delayed. They talked for a few minutes and when he finally turned off the phone, he leaned on a saw horse, staring at the ground, dejected.

Michael walked over and placed his hand on Brian's shoulder. "You know, I really am going to enjoy having you for a brother-in-law."

A few days later Shannon was arranging her possessions in her tiny rent house. It was situated among other small houses on a hillside overlooking Lajitas. Walking distance from the general store and the new site for the clinic, the house was more than Shannon had hoped for. With its small back porch providing a good view of the eastern horizon, she could watch the sunrise with her morning coffee. Now free from a life that made her miserable, she was in heaven.

The masonry of the new rooms was complete, including the meticulous tile work on the oversized bathtub. The tub was large enough for them to sit and stretch out their legs and lean back against an inclined tile surface, facing a window that overlooked the mountains along the western horizon. They had framed in the windows, and Justin started the plans for a pattern of rafters.

"This is really nice," Brian said as he stood looking down into the new bathtub, his hands planted on his hips. His morale and easy going demeanor had returned to normal with Jody's return.

Michael nodded. "I'm looking forward to giving it a try."

"I'm amazed at how all of this is coming together without a blueprint. It's like it's all just coming out of Justin's head."

"I know. We do what he tells us to do, and the next thing you know, the house is bigger."

"Are you still planning to ride with him in the morning?" Brian asked.

"Yes." Michael had never accompanied Justin on a patrol of the River Road. He was looking forward to it. "Do you and Jody have any plans while we're gone?"

"We're going to do a little hiking in the dessert, down on the south end of the property."

Michael glanced over his torso, now golden brown from his hours in the west Texas sun. "Don't forget the sun screen," he said. "When you took a shower yesterday afternoon I noticed your legs and ass are still lilly white."

"Why do you think I'll need sun screen?"

"Because you're going with my sister, and she'll notice how private it is down there, that's why."

Brian thought about the casual accord between his new friends. It had never occurred to him that he would find himself taking an open-air shower in mixed company. Even Shannon had abandoned her midwestern modesty, sun bathing nude with Jody and disrobing without reservation to take her showers. He somehow felt different from the man he was when he left Houston, like the knots had vacated his neck and shoulders.

"The time sure goes by fast out here," he said. "But I've always been a city boy. I'll be ready to get back to Houston."

"Well, you'll need another break from it before long," said Michael, "and you two will have your own room next time you come out here."

The cell phone rang. Michael followed the direction of its sound and answered it. It was Bernard asking for Justin.

Justin walked over from the stack of lumber he had been sorting through, and Michael handed him the phone.

"I'm glad I caught you," said Bernard.

"What's up, Bernard?"

"It's happened again. Another kidnapping. This time a little boy by the name of Benito Garcia. He lives over in Lajitas with his mother and brothers and sisters."

Stunned, Justin stood staring into thin air for a moment. "I knew that sonofabitch was still around here someplace."

"The state police believe it's the same fugitive, too. No reports of the guy turning up anywhere else. The FBI are on their way back in."

Justin looked at his watch. "It's four o'clock. Do you want me to come in?"

"No. Sit tight. I'm leaving here shortly. It'll be a long day tomorrow. In the morning just go about your routine, but stay near your radio. No point in you driving all the way back over here tonight. I'll let you know what's going on by radio."

Justin turned off the phone and slumped against the stone wall, shaking his head in disbelief. He looked at Brian and Michael, who were watching him with concern. "Let's go in the house," he said, suddenly emotionally exhausted.

Shannon was sitting at the table, looking through medical supply catalogues she had brought back from San Diego. Jody had started dinner. She turned and watched three somber men take a seat at the table. They all listened as Justin related the sad news.

Michael was up at six o'clock the next morning awaiting Justin at the kitchen table. Coming out of the bedroom a few minutes later, dressed in his uniform, Justin joined him for a quick bowl of oatmeal. He had gone to bed preoccupied with little Benito's misfortune, and still was.

"I won't be in the way by going with you today, will I?"

Justin looked up at him from his daze. "No. I'm a little

depressed. I'm glad you're going to be with me."

"You never did believe that fugitive left Big Bend, did you?"

"No."

"Do you have any ideas?"

"I still think he's found a place to hide out in the park. I thought I'd take another look around the old Marsical Mines."

Perk rode atop Michael's lap went they left the house. The days warmed quicker now that Spring had settled in. Driving east toward the park, the glare of morning sun was in their eyes and dry wind splashed over their faces. Another day of wispy white clouds and rich blue sky lay ahead of them as they pondered the intrusion of a deranged killer in their area, and now the fear that yet another child might be found dead.

Justin turned off onto the River Road, and the Jeep bounced along at a steady pace over the rutted primitive surface. The park was still all but deserted, as most campsite reservations had been canceled for the next several weeks. The vast wilderness of Big Bend had lost its appeal in the face of a killer still on the loose.

It took an hour and a half to reach the old abandoned quicksilver mine, its production having ended in the nineteen twenties. They drove up a long sweeping slope to reach the mine, through the skeletal remains of a few dozen small stone houses in which the miners from days gone by had dwelled. The mines, bored in several places some distance up the mountain side, yawned like haunted mouths in the rock. Sprawling before them a steep apron of ground lay strewn with ghostly structures from the distant past. Though often explored by adventuresome tourists, it was eerie nevertheless, with signs posted that warned of toxic poisoning from the lingering presence of mercury.

Michael scanned the craggly mountainside, the wounds in the rock left behind by men long since gone, and he imagined this landsacape harbored a good many places in which a fugitive could hide. Justin turned off the ignition and looked over at Michael.

"I'm going to walk around that area up there a bit. If the kidnapper has been up there, he might have left behind a few signs. It shouldn't take longer than thirty or forty minutes."

"You don't want me to walk up there with you?" said Michael.

"It would be best if you stay here close to the radio, in case Bernard tries to get in touch with us."

Justin stepped out of the Jeep and Michael watched Perk trot along ahead of him up the hillside. He looked small in the distance a few minutes later, disappearing then reappearing as he got up into irregular terrain. Staying within earshot of the radio, Michael got out of the Jeep and strolled about. With vultures circling in the eastern sky, he studied the flowering desert plants and walked up on a roadrunner that dashed quickly from view. As always, the land lay calm and quiet, the warm sun upon his skin, and when he unbuttoned his jeans to urinate, the wet splash on the hard crust seemed like the only sound being made on the whole face of the Earth.

An hour later, sitting atop the Jeep's hood, he watched for Justin's return. It was taking longer than anticipated, and he began to worry that these old mines might harbor dangerous falls.

He heard sudden footsteps behind him. He whipped around, shocked by the unexpected appearance of a solitary man. Instantly alarmed, he saw long scraggly hair, large arms and tattoos, and a grin much like evil. Michael's eyes widened as he began to realize what this might be, his chest filled with dread.

CHAPTER 22

"You don't look like no park ranger, mister," said the man, his crude appearance an appropriate match to the uneducated tone of his voice.

"I'm not," said Michael, trying to conceal his nervousness.

"That's a ranger's Jeep you're sitting on there."

Michael slid off the hood of the Jeep, planting his feet on the ground and taking a deep breath. "Yes it is. I'm with a park ranger. He'll be back down here any minute."

The man grinned broadly. "No he won't."

Michael's forced smile slowly melted. "What did you say?"

"That ranger ain't coming back down here."

Michael's hands knotted into fists. He could hardly believe his ears. His mind simply rejected the possibility that something had happened to Justin. Whatever this awful man meant to say couldn't be what it sounded like. "Yes. Yes he will. He just took a short walk up that hill. He'll be back down any minute."

A hint of anger flared in the man's eyes. "I said no he won't! I got him tied up. He's up there all right, but he's tied up like a pig. He ain't never coming back down here."

Michael stood, terrified. His heart pounded with incredulous disbelief. He stared at the man, struggling to stay calm and collect his wits.

"I ain't seen no one 'round here for days, mister. What you doing here anyway?"

"Uh, we're just driving through," Michael said, his mind swirling with confused thought. Now fully aware of the severity of the situation, he struggled for a way to deal with it. "Why would you want to tie him up? He's a park ranger. You can get into a lot of trouble by doing something like that."

The man laughed. "I figure you two are looking for me, ain't ya?" The man's demeanor turned threatening. "You walked into a world of shit, mister."

Michael's eyes widened on a revolver the man took from his dirty overalls. The barrel looked large aimed at his chest.

"Know what happens inside ya if ya get shot with a gun like this? It's a 357 Magnum. Your guts turn to soup."

Michael did not have to be told. He had operated on more than his fair share of gunshot wounds in the ER. He was staring at a madman, wishing for all the world that he and Justin had not ventured up this way, his heart racing with utter helplessness. The man scowled, his scraggly auburn hair flithy, a strand of it dropping over one of his eyes. His grimey face was leathery, from too much sun rather than age, and a deep scar distorted the symmetry of his left eye.

"If you want to live to see the sun go down, you're gonna tell me what you're doing up here. You're a cop of some kind, ain't ya? This has got something to do with that Mexican kid I snatched. You FBI?"

It was Michael's worst fear. This maniac was indeed the kidnapper. His mind spun in a whirr of confusion. Profoundly intimidated in the glare of this man's cruel bearing, the gun aimed at his chest, these were circumstances he could not have been less prepared for. No rational thought came to his mind. He stood staring, disbelieving. It had overwhelmed them so quickly, like a sudden storm of infected air. He realized, despite his enormous desire to believe otherwise, that they had been sucked into a nightmare that promised to disrupt their world; and as knots drew tight in his chest, he struggled for a way to cope.

"Okay, mister, get behind the wheel of this Jeep here. We're going to move it under them trees yonder."

Michael glanced over at a stand of trees a few hundred yards from where they stood. He looked back at the man, who waved his gun impatiently toward the driver's seat.

"Go on, get in there."

The man got into the passenger seat beside him, now pointing the gun at his head.

"I'll blow your head off if you make any sudden moves, mister. Now crank this thing up and drive it into that ravine. We're gonna hide it in them trees."

The Jeep labored over the rugged terrain. Hoping to leave an obvious trail, Michael drove over a number of creosote bushes. Moments later, he pulled it to a stop in the shade under the stand of cottonwood trees, next to a battered Ford Explorer, the vehicle Michael assumed the man had stolen. He turned off the ignition and closed his eyes, again struggling to collect his thoughts. His instinct to survive had kicked in. Right now it was important to stay calm, to focus on what the man might say, to respond accordingly. *Stay calm, Michael. Don't lose your head. Just do what he says, and try to find a way out of this.*

"The park ranger is my friend. Is he all right?" Michael asked, turning toward the man.

"Yeah, sure," the man said, making sure the radio was turned off. "He's all right. I had to whack him up side the head when he came charging after me, but he's all right."

Not surprised that Justin had tried to attack the man, he felt relief that he at least was still alive. Justin was up there some-where, tied up, and Michael knew now that this man had hit him, probably with the gun. He wanted to see him, to care for him, to help him in any way he could. *Keep yourself alive, Michael. Don't make this man angry. Listen to him. Do what he says. Stay alive. Use your wit to survive.*

"Go on and get out of the Jeep. Start walking up that way." The man waved the gun toward the hillside. "Remember, no sud-den moves."

Wheezing from the effects of smoking, the man ranted as they climbed up the rocky terrain. Michael listened carefully, hoping to get a better picture of his mentality, a better under-standing of how they might be able to deal with him.

"Things been calm and peaceful around here lately. I knew it! I just knew taking that kid was gonna set the law off again. I was-n't planning on doing it, not with things lookin' so good around here. Just ran out of cigarettes. Just wanted to find someplace to get some. Wasn't planning to pick up no kid. Little shithead was playing out by the damn road. Not another soul in sight. Just playing by the road all by himself. Shit! Next thing I know, I got that kid in the car with me and forgot the damn cigarettes. Hey, mister, you got any cigarettes on you?"

"I don't smoke," said Michael.

"Guess I don't either. Ain't had one in three days. Hey, mis-ter, you ever see a kid get so scared he pissed on himself?"

Michael cringed, trying to conceal his reaction.

"I tell ya, it's something. That little Mexican kid just pissed on himself. Made those little britches smell real sweet. You ever smell anything like that, mister?"

They trudged on. Michael's emotions ran with anger, revulsion, and fear, swirling in his mind like the wind on a stormy sea. *Humor this bastard. You can do it, Michael. Humor him and stay alive.*

The sordid comment had reminded Michael of the missing boy. "That boy's parents are awfully worried about him. Did you let him go somewhere?"

"Ha! That's a laugh."

"Then where is he?"

"You're full of questions, ain't ya?"

Michael glanced back at him. The man's face had reddened from exertion. "Just one. I don't know what to call you."

"So you want to know my name, huh? Think you're gonna slip away from me. Get back down here to that radio in the Jeep. Call in and tattle on me. Is that it, pretty boy. You want to tattle on me? Get me in trouble?"

"I just wanted to know what to call you, that's all."

"Sure. Okay. Well, let's see … I kinda like Wayne. Why don't you call me Wayne?"

"Okay, Wayne. My name is Michael."

"What's that nigger's name?"

Michael's jaw tightened. The word had an even more negative impact coming from such a vile mouth.

"Uh, who are you talking about, Wayne?"

"You know who. That park park ranger I got tied up. What's his name?"

"Listen to me, Wayne, it's not going to help us work anything out if you use words like that."

"Fuck you!" He pushed Michael from behind. "Do I whack you up side the head too, or do you tell me his name?"

"His name is Justin."

On they went, stumbling up terrain increasingly steeper. The cresote and scrub had thinned, the slope now more barren. Looking back, the desert sprawled for miles. Michael could no longer see the road. A place so remote, just the isolation instilled new fear. They topped the hill and followed a path that narrowed and rounded an embankment. It eventually opened into a small clearing. At the back of the clearing it looked like the mountain had been gouged out. Not a cave, but more like a deep overhang of rock, its shadowy recess slightly higher than a man's head.

"In there," said Wayne, pointing his gun toward the shadows.

It took Michael's eyes a moment to adjust to the dim light. He made out a figure sitting against the wall of rock. It was Justin, his hands bound behind his back, his legs stretched before him with bound feet. Perk lay beside him, his chin resting on Justin's leg. The dog had lifted his head when they appeared.

Justin had just a few moments before regained consciousness. He had had scarcely enough time to realize the full scope of his predicament, having broken into a sweat struggling against the ropes before he saw it was useless. He had hoped that Michael had somehow detected trouble and gotten away, that he had gone for help, and was safe. His heart sank with Michael's appearance. Now they were both caught in the same snare. Far less concerned for his own safety, he dreaded more than anything the possibility that something could happen to Michael. He believed he could endure anything this heathen might dish out, except that.

Pushed from behind, Michael stumbled in and Perk stood up growling, the hair at the back of his neck raised in warning. Michael had never seen the little dog react this way. He ran forward viciously, growling at the kidnapper.

"Perk! Come here, boy," Justin called out with quick panic, but the dog pursued his brave advance.

"Goddamned mutt," snarled the kidnapper, aiming his gun at Perk.

They jumped, then went rigid when the gun sounded, an echoing, almost deafening explosion inside the enclosed walls of rock. Perk rolled violently some two or three feet, a motionless, unnatural heap of fur. Michael stood in horror, staring in disbelief. He knew at once the little dog was dead.

Justin struggled in a blind rage against the bindings of his arms and legs, his eyes blood furious at the sight of his lifeless dog. "You bastard!" he raged, rendered helpless by the tight, knotted rope. "You worthless, dirty bastard!"

Michael stepped forward and dropped to his knees beside Perk. He reached out, stopping short of lifting the dog, unable to comprehend what he should do. He turned his head to look at the killer, his eyes filled with hate, and in the blink of an eye he attacked.

"Michael! No!" Justin yelled frantically, but it was too late.

The butt of the gun came crashing down atop Michael's head. He collapsed, folding unconscious to the hard earthen floor.

It was more than Justin could bear. He ceased his struggle against the ropes, his body tight with both anger and fear. He stared at his unconscious lover, flooded with relief when he detected the rise and fall of his chest. His eyes then slowly lifted up to rest on the killer. Hatred shot from them like daggers. Now more than ever he wanted to live, to survive if for no other reason than for the one chance to get his hands around the killer's throat. It was the only thought that calmed him, this grim ambition that now evolved into a single-minded purpose.

He watched the killer drag Michael to the opposite side of the den, then bind him in the same manner he himself was bound, and he dread what they were sure to suffer, this nightmare of captivity with a threat of a bitter end. The killer left Michael laying unconscious on his side, his arms and legs bound tight. Justin watched painfully as the killer lifted Perk by his tail and flung him aside the rock wall near the opening of the den. He turned to look into the shadows at the back of the den, where lay the lifeless body of Benito Garcia, nude. The boy had not yet shown any sign of life.

"I hope everyone has calmed down now," said Wayne, looking over at Justin with a taunting grin. "Like to get your hands on this gun I bet," he said mockingly.

Justin had steeled himself with hate. He sat staring at the killer, a prisoner bound helplessly by sound rope and knots, unable to conceal his contempt. He would wait. Nourished by vengence and hate, he would survive. And he prayed no further harm would befall Michael. The killer would eventually make a mistake, or perhaps the state police would stumble on this hideout just as he had done. But he vehemently prefered a lucky break to rescue, for he wanted more than anything to kill the man who killed his dog with his own bare hands.

"Is the boy still alive?" Justin asked bitterly.

"Sure he is." Wayne turned his head to look at the boy. "Look at him back there, sleepin' like a little angel. The kid has a lot of spunk in him. Should have seen the fuss he kicked up when I split that little brown ass of his. I like it when they bleed. Makes it good and slippery."

Justin turned his head, unable to bear the sight of this brute.

"Looks like that friend of yours has a little spunk too. I didn't think he had it in him to come after me like that."

Justin looked again at Michael, wishing he would come to. He ached to know that he was all right. It came on him with a whole new kind of weight, this moment of anguish in seeing someone you love more than life get hurt. The full force of his love had gripped his heart, and seeing Michael in the shadows, knocked unconscious, bound unmercifully, seared through his chest like hot lead.

And his shoulders were burning, already. Sitting with his back to the vertical rock wall behind him, his legs stretched out toward the center of the den, Justin squirmed his arms in an attempt to keep the circulation going. The pain in his wrists, bound tight near the small of his back, had dulled. He noticed that his hands had begun to feel numb, so he leaned forward a bit, opening and closing his fingers the best he could, which brought back some of the feeling

The killer was pacing in an antsy, nervous state of mind over his own set of concerns.

"So now I have to figure out what to do with you two. I figure the FBI is gonna get back in the picture. Them state boys too. They won't give up so easy this time. Damned if those urges I get don't cause me a lot of grief." He stared at Justin in thought for a few moments. "They got those road-blocks back up yet?"

"I wouldn't know."

Wayne shook his head as if he didn't believe Justin's answer. "I noticed something a little odd about you awhile ago, when I whupped that one over there. It got to you pretty bad, didn't it? I figure that's the key to gettin' the truth out of you. Suppose I whack off one of his fingers. That worth telling me another lie?"

"Look, asshole, I've got nothing to gain by lying to you, but if you hurt him again, I swear, you won't get a dime's worth of cooperation out of me. It's like I said before, I wouldn't know if the road-blocks have been set back up. I just found out you took the boy last night."

"What were you doing up here?"

"You already know why I was up here. Trying to find your worthless ass."

The killer smiled. "Kinda surprised when you found me, weren't ya'?"

"You can grin all you want to, but you were right when you said they won't give up so easily this time. You only got a minute's peace because they thought you eluded the roadblocks the last time. They're going to smoke you out this time."

The killer nodded. "That's why you're still alive, nigger. Oops, sorry, you're friend said I shouldn't call you that."

Justin paused with a smug smile, then said, "Don't be concerned about me, mister. I don't fret over words, especially when they're uttered by morons."

"You're gonna pop-off one time too many if you're not careful."

"Sure thing, brave man. You've got me tied up and you've got the gun. I know you don't have the guts to turn me loose for a little one to one, so go ahead and tell me why you're planning to keep us alive?"

"Insurance. I figure you'll make a pretty good bargaining chip with the law, unless they give up again. And that'd be just fine with me. Then I can blow your head off."

"Sounds like you understand your situation pretty good," said Justin. "But don't count on them giving up. They know you're holed-up around here somewhere."

"Maybe." The killer rubbed his bearded jaw in thought. "You know, I like you better than that one over there. That dumb ass tried to act friendly with me on the way up here. He thought I'd fall for something that stupid. You know better."

"He may be a dumb ass, but remember what I told you. You hurt him again and you'll get nothing from me."

Michael remained unconscious another two hours. When he came to, the killer had left the den for some reason. It was a struggle, but he finally managed to sit up. An enormous pain throbbed on top of his head that ran all the way down his spine. He glanced around, groggy, and saw Justin watching him with concern.

Justin closed his eyes with relief.

"Where is he?" Michael asked.

"I don't know where he went."

"That bastard killed Perk!" Michael said, suddenly feeling sick in remembering the sight of it.

"Michael, listen to me. I could kill him for that alone, but right now we have to focus on staying alive ourselves. This maniac is ruthless. He has no conscious whatsoever. I want you to keep your mouth shut. Don't try to talk to him. If he asks you a question, give him a guick unvarnished answer, but don't try to reason with him, or befriend him. Do you understand me?"

Michael nodded. "Justin … how are we going to get out of this?"

"I don't know yet. Just keep believing we *will* get out of it. We have the Garcia boy to worry about, too."

"The Garcia boy?"

Justin nodded toward the back of the den.

"Oh my God!" Michael gasped.

"He's still alive, but I don't know what kind of shape he's in. The bastard raped him."

Michael started scooting toward the boy.

"What are you doing?" Justin said hotly.

"I'm going to get back there and have a look at him."

"You can't do anything to help him with your hands tied! Goddammit, Michael!"

"If he's alive, at least I'll be close to him when he wakes up."

It took exhaustive effort to get close to the boy. He lay motionless, but Michael could see him breathing. In the shadowy light he could see dried blood on the boy's buttocks and the back of his legs.

"I think his rectum is ruptured," Michael said grimly.

"Get back over there where he left you, Michael!"

"No."

"Damn it!" he said, looking at Michael with exasperation. "God, I don't know what I'd do if I lost you. If you make this guy mad, he'll kill you as easily as he killed Perk."

"I can't let this boy wake up on the cold ground alone."

"Okay," Justin said anxiously. "Stay there, but let me handle the killer. Promise me, Michael."

"I promise." He scooted as close to the boy as he could, hoping to help keep him warm, and though he was never a religious man, he prayed.

CHAPTER 23

Jody had made sandwiches for her and Brian at one o'clock that afternoon. They had taken advantage of having the house to themselves that morning, as their appetite for each other still showed no signs of abating. After lunch she had gone outside with her novel to read another chapter or two. Brian had decided to do a little digging on one of the septic tank lateral lines. It was was three o'clock when he stepped out of the two foot deep trench and joined her for a break.

He saw right away a look of concern that tightened her face. "What are you thinking about?" he asked.

"Hasn't Justin been getting home quite a bit earlier than this?" she asked.

Brian looked at his watch. "Yeah. He's been getting home around one or two o'clock. He told me his boss is giving him the afternoons off to work on the house since the park has been so empty. It's a little after three already."

She looked down at the ground in thought.

"Are you worried about them?" Brian asked.

"I just wish Justin had said something if he thought they were going to be gone all day. I don't know what time to expect them since that kidnapper turned up again. Maybe he's involved in that manhunt somehow."

"Is that why you're worried?"

"I know it's silly, but that guy is still out there somewhere. I'd call them, but both of their cell phones are in there on the counter." She lifted her hand and looked at the back of it, her skin still a little red from the dishwater. "I guess I've worried about Michael all my life," she said, her sisterly love expressed by distant thought.

"Just think about how big that park is," Brian said assuringly. "What are the chances of Justin and Michael running across the killer?"

She looked at him. "Do you think Justin would have taken Michael along if he intended to look for the fugitive today?"

"I doubt it. I asked him about it last night. He told me the state police excluded the park rangers from the manhunt."

"Maybe so," said Jody, "but I know he's been following tire tracks on his own. Michael thinks he gets hunches and won't let go of them without checking them out."

"Well, they'll be getting back any minute," Brian said, wiping his face on the shirt he had left on the arm of the chair he was sitting in.

She stared out across the desert for a few moments, and then returned her attention to Brian. "I made fresh coffee a few minutes ago," she said. "Ready for some?"

"I'm ready for some more of you," he said, attempting to shift her mind to more pleasurable thoughts. Glancing down at how the t-shirt fell over the contours of her chect, his eyes lit with the memory of their morning together still lingering in his mind.

Her smile didn't quite mask her concern for Michael and Justin. She reached out and ran two fingers across Brian's sweaty, gritty chest. "You would get on top of me like that?"

"I'd get on top of you if I was covered with tar and feathers."

"You know they'd show up for sure if we got involved in that."

"I guess I'll do a little more digging then."

He took up her hand and kissed it, and then got up to return to the trench. Jody lifted her novel and started the next chapter. At five o'clock, she picked up her cell phone and punched in Bernard's phone number, waiting for what seemed like an eternity before Bernard came to the phone.

"Hello, Jody. Sorry, but it's a madhouse around here."

"I was wondering, Bernard, is Justin gone on a stake-out or something?"

"Stake-out?" he laughed. "I'm afraid that sort of thing isn't in our job description."

"Michael went with him today. They haven't come home yet."

She heard a prolonged silence on the phone.

"Bernard? Are you there?"

"You haven't heard from them all day?" he asked.

"No," said Jody, detecting something odd in Bernard's voice. "Why? Should I have? Do you think something is wrong?"

Another silence, then, "Uh, I tried to get him on the radio all afternoon, but his radio has been turned off. Never got an answer. I was so damn mad at him for leaving his radio off, I was planning to call him there. I would have already if it wasn't so crazy around here."

"What's going on, Bernard?"

He looked at the men perched around his conference table across the room, FBI agents and state detectives. They were arguing about procedure and strategy. "God only knows," he said, at once troubled by this news.

"What should we do?" she asked, her concern now elevated.

Bernard tilted his head to look at the wall clock. There were maybe three hours of daylight left. He put the phone back to his ear. "Jody, I don't think you have anything to worry about, but it is a little strange that Justin's radio has been off all afternoon. I'm thinking there might be something wrong with it. Could be they're late because they're having trouble with the battery or the alternator on the Jeep. I believe I'll drive over there and cover as much of the River Road as I can before dark."

"Call me as soon as you find out anything," said Jody. "Will you do that, Bernard?"

She heard another silence and then a click.

Bernard stared at his desk for a moment. He had mentioned battery trouble to Jody, and that could be exactly why Justin's radio wasn't working and why they had not gotten home, but his mind had drifted to more ominous possibilities. Bernard knew Justin had been out there looking for the killer. Did Justin coincidentally have battery trouble, or had he found the killer?

Bernard thought about the River Road, a sixty mile long stretch of primitive road not much more than a goat path, and some of it nearly impassable. He walked over to the radio and called the ranger who patrolled the area nearest the east end of the River Road, and explained to him what was going on, and told him to enter the road on that end, that he himself would go in on the west side and they would meet in the middle. If Justin's Jeep had broke down, they were almost certain to spot it.

Watching the confusion at the conference table, Bernard set the microphone back on the desk. His anger burst into flame over the bickering across the room. He walked slowly toward the table, seething, and pushed in between two men.

"SHUTUP!" he yelled at the top of his lungs, Slamming his fist on the table.

There was instant silence.

"I just found out I've got a man missing. No one has heard from him all day. I couldn't get him on the radio all afternoon. I'm worried something has happened to him, and that it might be connected to this case. He's the best man on my staff. Now why don't we get those goddamned helicopters in the air and make a few passes over the southern section of this park?" They stared at him as he paused a moment to calm down. "If you look at the map on the wall behind you, you'll see an unimproved road that follows the Rio Grande for about sixty miles. His name is Justin Brooks and that's the road he was patrolling today."

At five o'clock, Brian stabbed the shovel into the ground when he saw Jody go inside the house. He approached her in the kitchen.

"I'm going to start dinner," she said, taking some ground beef out of the refrigerator. "Collin will be here by six o'clock."

"Who did you call when I went back to the trench earlier?" Brian asked.

"Bernard."

He heard the disappointment in her voice. "Evidently Bernard didn't know why Michael and Justin would be this late," he said.

"He thinks they might have battery problems."

Brian nodded in thought. "Well, that makes sense, doesn't it?"

She looked at him. "I can't help but worry about them. You know why."

"You're going to miss Michael when you're in Houston, aren't you?"

"Yes. But it doesn't matter, Brian. I won't miss him any more in Houston than I would have if I had gone back to San Diego."

He stepped forward and placed his hands on her shoulders and leaned a bit to kiss her on the forehead. He was beginning to worry, himself.

"Meatloaf sound good for dinner?" she asked.

He tilted his head back and smiled. "Sounds perfect."

And hour later, a knock came on the back door. Brian got up from the table and opened it. Collin Gordon stepped in and glanced around. He had noticed that Justin's Jeep was not parked outside.

"Good work on that contract, young man," Collin said with a light slap on Brian's shoulder. "Good price too. I figured you to be as sharp as you look."

The old rancher had already detected the somber mood in the house.

"What's wrong here?" he asked, looking from Jody, back to Brian.

"Justin and Michael haven't come home from the park yet," said Brian. "We expected them back shortly after lunch. Bernard couldn't get them on the radio all afternoon. We're a little worried, Collin."

Collin looked again at Jody, who confirmed their concern with the expression on her face. He shifted his eyes to the floor in thought, and then looked at Brian a moment later. "Hasn't

Justin been over there poking around for that fugitive here lately?"

"Yes," said Brian.

Collin lifted his large, broad-rimmed hat and ran his hand back over his head. "Is your phone handy, young lady?"

"Go ahead and have a seat, Collin. The phone is right there on the table."

The old man sat down and picked up the phone, handing it then to Brian. "Every time I look at one of those gadgets, it looks smaller than the last one I looked at." He stated his ranch foreman's number and watched Brian punch it in, reaching for it when it started ring.

"Hola," came his foreman's voice from the small phone.

"Miguel, it's Collin. Listen, the missing boy, Benito, isn't Ernesto Garcia his uncle?"

"Si, Señor."

"I want you to call Ernesto up. Ask him to come over. I want to talk to him. I'm on my way there now."

Collin Gordon laid down the phone and looked at Jody.

"Bernard thought they might be having trouble with the Jeep," she said, hoping to hear Collin endorse that possibility.

"Probably just what it is, young lady. Nevertheless, I think I'll skip dinner tonight. I've got an idea, just in case."

"Just in case?" she said, realizing that worse possibilities had also occurred to Collin. A tear streaked down her cheek. With a fugitive killer in the area, her imagination refused to rest.

"I was just thinking that this might be something we don't want to leave to chance. Since the kidnapper snatched another child, Big Bend is crawling with law enforcement officials, but it seems that could be a problem in itself. There might be too many. I've heard there's discord in how to conduct a seach in an area the size of Big Bend. if we don't hear from Justin and your brother by tomorrow morning, it looks to me like it'll be time we take this matter into our own hands. I don't know what happened to those boys, but it could be they're in trouble. Could be it's related to that kidnapper. Either way, we have a fugitive loose down here, an animal, and I think it's time he finds out he came to the wrong part of the world to snatch children."

Jody was desperate to believe her brother's absence was not connected to the fugitive. She had thought of a dozen other rational explanations, none very satisfying. Now standing next to him, she looked helplessly at the old rancher. "Oh, Collin … I'm praying they just ran out of gas in some remote place. I can't bear to think they might have run into that kidnapper."

"Well, we'll have a better idea of whether they have or not if they don't turn up by tomorrow morning. Whatever happened, we'll find them, and the Garcia boy." He reached over and squeezed her hand before he stood up. "I'm leaving now, but I'll keep you posted on how things are going. If they show up tonight, have Justin call me, no matter what time it is." He glanced at Brian and then back at Jody. "If we do have to go over there to look for them. don't fret if it takes a while. It's big country over that way."

Brian closed the door when the old man walked out, then returned to the table.

"Did you get the impression he seemed certain he could find out what's going on?"

She looked over at the back door. "Yes, I did get that impression."

"You know, if I was that kidnapper, I don't think I'd want Collin Gordon out after me."

Collin had sold his house in Midland and his penthouse in Dallas when his wife died. He loved the Big Bend country and had for years, it was now his only home. He couldn't abide a criminal coming along and infecting it; and like everything significant that had happened in his long life, it had happened because he had caused it. Now it was time to stop a reign of terror.

Ernesto Garcia, a stocky Mexican national, was waiting on the front porch of Collin's sprawling ranch house with Miguel when the old rancher drove up.

"Let's go inside," he said, walking past them on his way to the front door.

They went into the den, where Collin walked over and stood before his massive fireplace, his chin between fingers and thumb in thought. He turned and looked at the pair. He had talked with a neighbor earlier in the day about the discord in the Mexican community over Benito Garcia's kidnapping. "I reckon there' been a lot of talk about what happened to little Benito," he said in Spanish.

Both men nodded.

"I just found out Justin Brooks and Michael Anderson are missing."

They knew Justin, and they recognized Michael's name as the

doctor who saved little Julian Gutierrez's life.

Collin continued. "I think they might have stumbled across the kidnapper when they were over in the park looking for him today. I've had a feeling all along that maniac was holed up over there someplace." He studied their faces for a moment, their expressions set in anger over an innocent boy falling prey to an intruder. "I hear the men around here are up in arms over this."

Both men nodded again.

"Well, I've got an idea," Collin said. "I want you two to be prepared to round up as many men as you can when you get up in the morning, and get back over here by noon. Tell them to bring plenty of water and blankets. Anyone who can get a hold of binoculars should bring those too. And tell them to be ready to stick with this as long as it takes. We're going to fan out over the southern section of the park and find the boy, and those two men if they haven't turned up by morning."

"What are you doing back there with that boy?" the kidnapper growled when he returned to the den.

Justin sat up, quickly alert. "Calm down, Wayne. He's just trying to keep the boy warm."

"Ha … I was keepin' him plenty warm before you two showed up."

"Has he had anything to eat?"

The kidnapper held up a dead jackrabbit. "Had one of these just yesterday. Dang rabbits ain't hard at all to catch with a good snare. I'm gonna cook this one right after sundown."

Michael's heart quickened as the crude man approached and stood towering over him and the boy. He knelt and rolled the boy onto his back, then took a hold of his jaw and turned his head from side to side, inspecting his face. "Little punk sleeps like a rock." Then, lifting Michael's feet, he took a close look at the knotted ropes. "You musta looked like a worm crawling over here."

Wayne then turned his head and stared at Justin for a long while.

"You can turn that boy loose you know," said Justin. "You have us for hostages now. Looks to me you're through with him and he'll just be getting in the way. Let him go. It could make a difference at your trial. Showing a little mercy could keep you off death row."

"You still thinkin' I'm gonna get caught?"

"Always a chance of that, Wayne. You might as well buy yourself a little more insurance just in case."

The kidnapper looked again at the boy, in thought.

It seemed to Justin that Wayne was considering his suggestion. Gratified that he might be able to influence the crude man's thinking, Justin continued to study his mannerisms and reactions. He watched the kidnapper pick up the rabbit and walk back to the mouth of the den, standing in the glare of late afternoon sun, looking around at the immediate terrain. He looked up into the sky, as if any minute he expected to see the helicopters again. Then he sat down and leaned back against the rock. Ten minutes later, he was snoring.

Justin's eyes shifted to Perk's lifeless body, and he stared at the little dog for a long while. For Michael, the sadness settling on his face was nearly unbearable.

"Justin … why don't we see if we can get him to bury Perk?" came Michael's compassionate voice from the shadows at the back of the den "It's hurting you too much to see him lay there like that."

"No. I don't want him buried up here, by him."

"We'll take him home then, when we get away. We'll bury him out back."

"Be careful what you talk about, Michael. That asshole could be listening to every word we say."

Justin's eyes were still resting painfully on the twisted mangle of fur, his thoughts alive with memories. "He came to west Texas with me when I first came out here," he said reflectively. "Perk was just a puppy then. Got him from a neighbor in Jasper, just before they were going to take the whole litter to the pound. I could tell he loved the desert. He jumped out of that van the first time I stopped in the park and romped around with such excitement. We took a long walk into the desert. It was cute how his little head shot this way and that every time he kicked up a lizard. We both seemed to know right away that Big Bend was going to be our home. And since then, whenever I've been lonely, I could always count on him to be my buddy, no matter what."

Michael thought about the joy Perk had brought into their lives. It was impossible to believe the little dog was gone. The weight of Justin's broken heart was more than he could bear. One thing was certain—their dog's brutal murder made an already grim situation all the more real.

The pain atop his head had turned into a dull ache that radiated down into his shoulders. Michael knew the gash must be bad, he could feel stiffness in the hair at the back of his head, obviously dried blood. Now his arms ached, twisted as they were behind his back, and he had to keep adjusting his weight to keep his hands from feeling numb. The only thing that distracted him from the soreness in his body was the mental anguish of this miserable luck, and that was worse than the physical pain.

"Of all the times for you to be with me," Justin said wearily, "why did it have to be this one?" It was seeing Michael bound and curled on the earthen floor that took Justin's mind from his own agony: his lover, the beautiful man he held in his arms while they slept at night, the magnificent surgeon who had spent his life helping others, being treated like a sub human. Worse than the pain in his hands—the numbness and burning—was a relentless ache to kill, to get his hands free and get them about Wayne's throat.

"Don't feel guilty about that," said Michael. "Thank God I'm here. I would have lost my mind had you disappeared and I not know where you were. I can't stand to even think about it."

"They'll never spot this guy from a helicopter. Not here. He can hear their approach and hide long before they're overhead."

"Then how do you think they'll find us?" Michael asked.

Justin thought about the strategy meeting he had observed during the last manhunt, the complexity in organizing a search in such a vast land. It seemed hopeless. He knew helicopters would be ineffective. Even his own search of this area around the Marsical Mines revealed no evidence of this hideout—in fact he might never have realized anyone was here, had the kidnapper not approached from behind with a gun. It was maddening, this recurring, sinking, helpless feeling, churning in his stomach like poisonous bile. But he couldn't allow Michael to suffer the same despair, not if he could help it, though he found it increasingly difficult to assure him with confidence.

"They'll find us, Michael. They'll ratchet up their effort this time. They'll know the kidnapper doesn't intend to leave Big Bend. Everyone involved will be determined to catch him before another child falls victim."

Justin's eyes moved with loathing to the unconscious criminal, sleeping so peacefully without guilt on the sandy floor, the filty overalls and matted hair, lost on how any human could perceive the world the way this man did. Though he had known racists and greed and ruthless ambition, he had never hated anyone. Now it was beyond hate, for he ached to kill a man, and it served well his will to live, if for no other reason than to kill him with relish.

CHAPTER 24

The kidnapper built a small fire near the mouth of the den at sundown, just inside the ceiling of rock so the flames couldn't be seen from the air. The smoke drifted up and moved across the rock toward the open air, unseen in the black of night.

They watched him skin the rabbit, placing then the small carcass on a makeshift spit. The smell of roasting meat soon wafted into their nostrils.

The boy stirred and Michael leaned over him to see his eyes, longing to sweep him into his arms to comfort him. He awoke with a start, looking up at Michael in utter fear.

"Shh," Michael whispered, displaying his most disarming smile, and the boy seemed to calm just a bit. "Do you speak English?" Michael whispered.

Though he didn't, the boy understood this question and shook his head. His innocent brown eyes moved over Michael's bound body, reflecting his quick understanding that he had been joined by new captives. Michael nodded toward Justin, who was watching them. The boy stared at Justin for a moment, then he looked back at Michael, shivering. The air temperature had fallen sharply when the sun went down.

Michael, almost forgetting his own misery for a moment, resented the boy's inhumane circumstances, especially since he also needed medical attention. He had no idea how much damage the boy had suffered.

Michael looked through the shadowy light cast by the small fire and called out defiantly, "Wayne, where are the boy's clothes?"

The kidnapper looked up and squinted through the dim light. "We lost 'um out in the desert someplace." He sounded testy.

Justin tightened at the sound of Michael's voice, scared to death he might say something to anger this maniac and get himself killed.

"This boy is shivering. It's too chilly to be in here with no clothes on. Is there a blanket around here or something?"

"Yeah, sure, I've got an electric blanket. It's just there's no place to plug it in."

Michael was growing angry. "Then untie my hands for a minute so I can get my shirt off and put it on him."

"You're an annoying fucker, ain't ya?"

"Drop it, Michael," Justin seethed.

"He's freezing. I won't drop it."

"Goddammit! If I let you give him your shirt, will you shut up?"

"Yes."

Wayne walked to the back of the den and turned Michael around. He yanked up Michael's bound hands and labored over the knot until the rope came loose. Michael rolled his sore shoulders and rubbed his raw wrists, and then pulled the shirt over his head. It fit the boy like a sack, giving him room to draw his knees up under it, close to his chest.

"Get your hands back behind your back," huffed the rude man, his fowl odor tainting the air.

He tied the coarse rope angrily as Michael focused his thoughts. He imagined a calm desert morning, awaking in the sensual warmth of Justin's arms, and it helped just a bit to take his mind from the pain.

When satisfied the rabbit had finished cooking, Wayne sat down near the fire with it. His elbow on his knee, he held it by the end of the spit, pulling off pieces of meat and stuffing them into his mouth.

In Spanish, Justin asked Benito if he was hungry, and the boy nodded.

"You can talk that boy's language?" asked Wayne.

"Yeah. He said he's hungry."

Wayne motioned with his hand for the boy to approach. Benito looked at Justin, who nodded. The boy got to his feet and walked apprehensively across the den, Michael's pullover shirt dropping down below his knees. He stood frozen in fear near the kidnapper, his small stature trembling in the soft flicker of fire light. Wayne handed him the spit, having already eaten half of the roasted carcass.

"Go ahead, kid, eat some of that. Give some of it to your new friends too."

Justin repeated in Spanish what the kidnapper had said.

He ate hungrily, for he had been captive long enough now to eat anything given to him. After a few bites, he stepped toward Justin, pulled off a piece of meat and held it before the bound man's mouth. Justin leaned forward and took it between his teeth, aware he would have to eat anything available to keep up his strength. After he swallowed a few pieces, he nodded toward Michael. The boy took the carcass to Michael and extended a piece of meat. Michael smiled and shook his head. He had never had less appetite for food, especially something like the greasy meat between the boy's fingers.

Justin spoke up again. "Wayne, we need some water now. And you're going to have to untie us so we can go out and take a leak."

Resting with his back against the rock, the kidnapper shook his head. "Looks to me like you two are going to be more trouble than you're worth."

"Sorry, Wayne," Justin said sarcastically. "I'll try to interrupt your busy schedule as little as possible."

"Wise ass."

He stood and picked up a plastic jug half full of water and took it over to Michael, setting it on the ground near Michael's bound feet. "I'll try this one time. Any trouble out of you and you'll shit in your pants before I untie you again."

"Do exactly as he says, Michael," Justin said sternly.

Wayne untied his feet first. "Stand up," he then demanded.

Michael struggled to his feet. Wayne turned him around and untied his hands, backing up then a few feet and pulling the pistol from his filthy overalls. Michael picked up the jug for a drink.

"Where'd you get that water?" Justin asked.

"Out of the river," said Wayne.

"It's contaminated. It needs to be boiled before we drink it," Justin said.

Michael quit drinking and looked at the jug.

"Sure thing," said Wayne. "I'll just go into the kitchen and do that right now." He looked at Michael. "You want some of that water or not, pretty boy? Either way, I don't give a damn."

"Just a couple of sips, Michael," said Justin. "Then give Benito a swallow or two."

After Benito took a drink, Michael sat the jug back on the floor. Wayne, standing a few feet away, held the gun aimed at Michael's chest.

"Now here's how we're gonna do this. You and me are going outside so you can take a piss. Then you're gonna untie your friend over there. Any sudden moves, you're dead. You're gonna tie him up again after he takes a piss, good and tight, just like he is now. Got that?"

Rubbing his wrists, Michael nodded. Bound unnaturally for so long, his legs felt shaky as he stepped toward the mouth of the den. Wayne followed him, ever vilgilent as Michael walked a few paces into the open void of the night. He unbuttoned his fly and urinated on the ground as the kidnapper observed his every move.

Back inside, he untied Justin, then watched him struggle to his feet. Justin arched his back, staring intently at Wayne.

"Go on," Wayne snapped, waving the gun. "Just outside over there. One mistake and this pretty boy gets it first."

When Justin returned, he took his same posistion on the floor. Following Wayne's instructions to the letter, Michael reluctantly knelt to retie his lover's arms behind his back.

"Do it right, Michael," said Justin with a wink. "He'll inspect the knots when you're through."

Michael saw the wink. His heart quickened. He went through the motions of tying the rope, leaving the knots loose, certain that is what the wink had meant. He looked at Justin with a tight swallow, fearing the man he loved so dearly was planning a dangerous risk. With the task completed, Michael started to get to his feet.

"Now get back over there where you were," Wayne ordered. His tone was impatient and harsh.

Michael took his position next to Benito, looking up at the kidnapper who towered over him.

"Now I have to tuck this gun away to tie you up. You tried me once when I shot that dog. Try me again and it'll be the last thing you ever do."

Michael sat complacently as the brute tied his legs. He then rolled onto his side so that his hands could be bound, his emotions charged with turmoil and violent hate, and now he feared Justin might do something to get himself hurt, or worse. He closed his eyes with dread. *Please, God, whatever he does, let it work. Please, let us out of this and don't let anything happen to him.*

Wayne stepped toward Justin and leaned over him to test the ropes. Justin exploded violently, thrusting his feet hard at Wayne's face. Wayne reeled backward and fell, looking back at Justin with disbelief. Justin peeled the ropes from his wrists and ankles and was upon the stunned man in the blink of an eye, his hands going for the bearded throat. They rolled in a whirl of sudden vilence, one man clawing, grasping at the other.

Alarmed and helplessly bound, Michael's heart stopped. Benito cowered beside him, hugging Michael's shoulders as closely as he could get.

The fight continued, both men now on their feet. Justin charged as Wayne's fist came flying with full force, catching Justin aside the head. Justin fell to his knees, staring, blinking at the floor as if he had been knocked senseless. Wayne's booted foot came next, catching Justin in the stomach, knocking the wind from him. Justin collapsed, gasping, his head spinning.

Wayne leaned forward, bracing himself on his knees, gasping for breath, his eyes fixed on Justin. Michael tensed, nearly out of his mind with fear that Wayne's anger would prompt him to execute Justin. Wayne's head twisted around and his eyes rested on Michael, who felt a sudden overwhelming, debilitating sense they weren't going to get out of this alive.

"Think you're pretty smart, don't ya?"

"Wayne, I don't know how to tie ropes," Michael pleaded.

"I ought to just fuckin' blow the both of you away." He looked back at Justin, rubbing his nose, which had taken good blow and was bloody. "But I think maybe your friend here has learned his lesson."

Wayne wiped the blood from his nose on the back of his hand, and then drug Justin back to his place near the rock wall, where he retied him.

An hour later, propped uncomfortably against solid rock, Justin watched the small fire slowly die out. Why Wayne had not killed him earlier, he didn't know. But the fact he didn't had been enough to hang onto a small glimmer of hope. The kidnapper had reclined on the ground just beyond its dimming light. Justin's heart had still not returned to its normal rhythm, he worried so that Michael might make a mistake or say something to anger the killer. Desperate and with nothing to looe, Wayne could easily demonstrate his rage by shooting Michael, or simply decide he didn't need all three hostages.

The minutes grew long into the night as the fire died and turned cold. The den had turned into acold, pitch black void. A aura of utter vulnerability lay over the remote space, like the unending and silent moan of a war orphan. It was cold, yet Justin could feel a light sweat across his forehead as he stared out at the soft cast of moonlight on the desert fawna just beyond the mouth of the den. How desperate his struggle to hang on to some small hope, the forbidding odds seemed so great. How he ached to reach up and rub his eyes, to stand and stretch the relentless pain from his limbs. He began to shiver as the chill found its way into his bones, and the long torture of night lay before him like eternity.

To sustain his sanity, Justin drifted mentally from the den, reliving in his mind those moments with Michael, those wonderful bits and pieces of life they shared everyday. He cherished the memory of that first time he came upon him staring at the river, that instant spark he had felt for a distraught and lonely man. How quickly they had found themselves carried by the compelling power of a mutual attraction. He closed his eyes, the pain that radiated through his shoulders abating as the warmth of Michael's body took form in his mind. Like an escape into a conscious dream, they made love in his mind's eye, and he was warmed by images of passion. He relived one of their typical mornings together, awakening in each other's arms, allowing those blissful moments to linger before starting a new day. He saw them sharing the easy chores of breakfast, and he thought of their long days on the river gathering stone, their careful mortaring of each one in its place on the new wall. But still, on the fringe of this conscious dream, lingered a relentless horror like a waiting ghost in the night.

If he had taken a single moment of it for granted, he would

never, never, do so again—if only they might find a way to survive this ordeal. But hope collided with throbbing pain as the agony in his swollen wrist crept up his bound arms. It settled in his shoulders with its unyielding grip. It burned, and death seemed to lurk in the dark. Each minute grew long, increasing the torment throughout his body, and that awful fear. Though he tried, he could not find a position that would allow him to sleep, and the night continued to grow more and more unbearable. Each minute loomed like an endless increment of time, one followed by the weight of yet another, and Justin found himself praying. *Please, God, let me live. Let me get Michael out of harm's way. Let me get Benito back to his family. Let me have the wisdom to get us out of this. I promise, as I've always tried to do, I will be guided by the conscience You have given me—always.*

Michael also lay shivering on the ground, drifting fitfully in and out of the reality of this horrid dream. Benito lay sleeping, snuggled as close as he could to Michael's chest. It seemed the night's chill had displaced his soul, as his lungs filled and relaxed with labored drafts of air, for now his guilt came with fowl breath. Yes, he was to be blamed for this misfortune. It was he who had lived an insane lifestyle that resulted in a young girl's death. So everything he had found in the Big Bend was no more than what could have been, if he had been the man who deserved it. But he was not. And aside from Benito's and Justin's suffering, this was surely his just reward. But then, their suffering also served to enhance his, for what else could be worse than having to witness his lover suffer such an ordeal, or bear that endured by this small boy? It was justification born in guilt, the only rational explaination his mind could produce, and it weighed on him with its ugliness as he shivered on the fringes of a fitful sleep, his jaw so tightly clamped the pain inside his head rivaled that searing through his twisted arms.

Though he may have deserved this end, why Justin and a small boy? Why must they endure a punishment that belonged solely to him? The boy moaned and Michael opened his eyes. Little Benito awoke in pain. He winced and his small hands reached down to his bottom, drawing his legs toward his chest. What could cause someone to brutalize a child, to impose such a misguided ordeal? Michael yearned to have his arms free, to take the boy up tight. Then Benito began to quietly sob. It added the horror of an unending nightmare, making it even worse for Michael. What torture could surpass not being able to comfort a tormented child?

By mid-morning the next day, Michael and Justin both were fighting a growing state of despair. It was around high noon when Wayne stepped out into the clearing and took a long draw on the water jug. He held it up to look at it, as if checking its contents, and then without explanation he carried it dangling at his side from view.

Justin waited awhile, watching the direction he had gone. "I bet he's going to hike over to the river to refill the jug. He'll be gone awhile." He looked at Michael. "I've got an idea. I'm going to tell Benito to try to untie your hands. You'll need to lean forward a little."

This sent another wave of panic through Michael. "If he gets the better of you again, he might kill you, Justin."

"I don't intend to give him that chance," said Justin. "Sit up so Benito can get to your hands."

"Shouldn't he untie yours first?" Michael said.

"No. If that asshole comes back, I don't want the boy over here by me. He'd know we're up to something."

"What are you going to do if we get our hands untied?"

"Did he do anything with the Jeep?"

"He had me move it under some cottonwood trees in a shallow ravine and made sure the radio was off. You could see them from where we parked."

"Did he look in the glove box?"

"No," Michael said.

"Good. I have a thirty-eight revolver in there. I saw the trees you're talking about. I'll try to get down there."

"How? We don't know where he hid our shoes. How can you cover that much of this terrain barefoot?"

"I'll just do it. So are you ready?"

Michael leaned forward as Justin spoke to Benito in Spanish. The boy looked at the knots and went about trying to untie them immediately. Michael could feel the fumbling work of his small hands. The fruitless attempt went on for at least ten minutes before the boy began to cry. Michael couldn't stand it. The boy's small hands were no match for the tight knots. Justin told Benito to give up, assuring him that it was okay, and in the helpless silence that followed, all three of them sat with blank stares, and all three sank deeper in despair.

CHAPTER 25

Some fifty men had gathered in Collin Gordon's den the next day by noon. He had pinned a large map of Big Bend National Park to the wall. He stood before it prepared to outline his plan. They listened solemnly as he spoke.

"Odds are the fugitive we're after is hiding out somewhere in the southern section of the park, in the general vicinity of where he kidnapped that first boy. If so, I don't think the law enforcement agencies that have shown up are going to find him with their walking boots and helicopters, and they don't have enough dogs to sniff him out. Too many places over there to hide. Even if this guy is out walking around, he'll hear a helicopter miles before it gets to him. He'd just duck into a ravine. So it seems to me the best way to find Benito and our two friends is to stake out this section of the park." He moved his finger along the River Road on the map. "We'll find positions in the higher elevations through here and sit and wait for the guy to make a move."

Collin Gordon looked across the somber faces. They were a ragtag bunch of dirt-poor ranch hands, wearing their well-worn jeans and sweat stained shirts, a few with straw hats. Most of them had managed to get their families out of Mexico, while a few of them slept on any available floor in order to send their meager earnings back home to loved ones. All of them appeared ready to do whatever necessary to find Benito and rid the land of a menace.

"I want you men to divide into groups of six. Each group is going to take one of these sections I've drawn on this map. Each group will disperse into its section, discreetly, and each man will find a vantage point that will give him the best view of a large area of land. When you find a good look-out, lay low and watch what goes on as far as you can see around you. Eventually, one of you will spot someone suspicious. That's when you'll come get me. I'm going to be right here at this little store," he pointed at the map. "That's where I'll be waiting. When we find him, I want to deal with this guy myself."

Collin's eyes shifted to his foreman. "Miguel, we went over all of this earlier this morning. I want you to coordinate the groups and be the liaison between them. Make sure the men are well placed within each section."

Miguel nodded, and within thirty minutes, he had them organized in groups of six or seven men. A caravan of just under a dozen pickup trucks sped down Collin's long gravel drive, kicking up a good cloud of dust all the way to the main road. In their surveillance of the entire route along the River Road, with each man watching from a discreet vantage point, Collin Gordon believed they would eventually spot the fugitive and discover his hide-out. All the bastard had to do was set out for food or water.

Jody moved nervously around the house, beside herself for something to do. What little sleep she had gotten during the night had been fitful. Sitting at the table in the kitchen, her third cup of coffee before her, she decided she should call Shannon.

433

When she heard Shannon's voice, she relayed the disturbing news.

"Oh my God!" came Shannon's gasping reply.

"Shannon, Brian and I are waiting to hear from Collin Gordon here at the house. Why don't you join us?"

"I'll be there in thirty minutes."

Brian joined her, taking her hand. He found it difficult to believe the harmony of the desert had been disrupted by something like this, exactly the kind of thing he was more used to reading about in the headlines of city newspapers. "I have an urge to do something. I thought about going over to the park to search for them myself."

"I thought of that too, but you know it's not realistic. We don't know anything about that park, except that it's huge. We wouldn't know where to start. We're just going to have to depend on Collin or the police to find them."

The phone rang. Jody was glad to hear Collin Gordon's voice. He described to her the logic of his plan, and though it might take time, he assured her that he was confident it would work.

It made sense to her. She felt relief in relating the plan to Brian, and he nodded in thoughtful agreement.

"He sounded certain they would find them," she said optimistically.

Brian looked down at the table top in thought, rubbing his forehead with his fingertips. "You know, Jody, I don't know what it is about that old man, but I believe I'd bet on him."

Collin Gordon sat on an old wooden chair on the covered porch in front of the general store. The weathered boards beneath his boots creaked everytime he adjusted his weight, worn by decades of footfall: someone stopping for a jug of water, or a fresh plug of chewing tobacco, or a cold bottle of beer. He sat staring out across the desert, a mug of coffee in his right hand.

Occasionally, a local or a passing tourists pulled off the road onto the gravel in front of the store. When they stepped up on the rickety wooden porch, Collin nodded, though no smile came to his stoic lips. They would nod in passing and enter the store, the old screen door banging closed behind them. A white owl had taken a perch in the cottonwood beside the building, awaiting dusk; and Collin looked up at it from time to time, wondering which of the two of them had the most patience.

And long silent minutes turned into hours.

Collin sat quietly with his unwavering resolve, staring out across the land that he loved, confident one of the Mexican look-outs would sooner or later spot the kidnapper. They would find this man who had made his final mistake by coming here, for a small army of angry men had dispersed across the park, all of them determined to end his short reign of terror. And the army had grown in number, for one by one they came, the friends and relatives of those already stationed on the cliffs and ledges, relatives from Mexico's interior and friends from as far away as Ojinaga and Marathon. The kidnapper had made the mistake of taking one of their own, something that could not go without recourse, the outcome for his latest young victim still in question. Collin was also now convinced that Justin and his young doctor friend had fallen prey, and that too could not stand.

Every hour or so Ellie, the lady who ran the store, would come out with a pot of coffee to refill his cup. She liked to wear late nineteenth century style dresses and a bonnet, telling folks it seemed to enchant the tourists who stopped by the rustic store. When the day approached late afternoon, she brought him out a ham sandwich.

"Think you'll get that kidnapper, Mr. Gordon?'

"That I do, Ellie. It's just a matter of time."

"I'll swear I'll never understand the likes of a man like that," she said with a look of incredulity.

"I guess a man is born every now and then with his wires crossed, Ellie. Nothing else makes sense, does it?"

"No sense at all," she said in summary.

His eyes fixed on the desert, she set the sandwich on the chair beside him. And then, after scanning the horizon, she looked down at the old rancher, believing with all her heart that if anyone could find that awful fugitive, it would be the man now waiting patiently on her front porch.

When she went back inside, Collin reached for the sandwich. After eating it, he got up and stretched his legs. Just after the sun went down, Ellie came back out. She was ready to close the store and go upstairs to her apartment for the night.

"When do you plan to go home, Mr. Gordon?"

"I don't plan to go home, Ellie, not until we get this job done."

"You intend to sleep out here?" She felt concern for an old man sitting in the cool night air.

"I might doze a bit, yes."

Her hands took a firm position on her hips. "If you're going to sit up all night, least you can do is come upstairs and take yourself a nap on my couch after being out here all day. Then you can bring a blanket back down with you."

"Now, Ellie, I won't be disrupting your evening with my snoring, but I will take you up on that blanket. If I get sleepy, I'll just tilt this chair against the wall and take a little snooze."

She stared at him a moment, shaking her head. "If you're going to be hardheaded about it, I'll go get you that blanket."

The night passed with no word from the park. The sun warming his face awoke Collin at daybreak. It would be another hour before Ellie came downstairs to make coffee. He walked stiffly behind the building and peed on the ground, hidden behind the scraggly limbs of a mesquite tree. Whatever his old body had endured spending the night in that hardback chair, he figured it wasn't near what his young friends might have suffered. He was worried, yet he forced himself to believe those two boys and the child were still alive. In his mind, they were simply too good of men to befall such a cruel fate.

On the morning of the second day, Michael could feel his sanity slipping. At some point during the night, he had lost his ability to restore his faith that they would be rescued. His thoughts were coming in a straight line of despair, his will threatened to succumb to the horrors of captivity. All he could do was try to keep his mind blank, for any thoughts at all led him back to his feelings of guilt, which he could not come to understand were irrational.

He had spent much of the night thinking about his life in San Diego, those hectic years at the hospital, managing to recall a few specific cases that brought him at least a small reprieve. They were those cases where he had saved a life, or had performed an operation that freed his patient from a wheelchair, cases which implied he had not lived his life entirely in vain. But stampeding over the dim glow of this small reward, came the swirling memories of his empty nightlife, his endless search for something that could never be found in the carnal haunts of men's clubs and parlors and bathhouses. How he loathed himself for so abusing this wonderful gift of life. It was as if he had spit in the eye of freedom, and scoffed, and only now recognized life's great value, only now that his freedom had been so rudely taken away.

But no, he argued in his mind, trying desperately to control the demons that were stabbing at his brain—he had recognized life's value before now. That had happened the moment he set eyes on Justin, and it grew by degrees as their lives merged from one day to the next. And in thinking about it over and over again, what Michael actually recognized now was how much he had to lose, and as such, the pain of his loss even more enormous; it threatened to include his sanity. Indeed, this was the pain so hard to bear, more so than that which numbed his arms and hands, this seeing his chance at happiness cut short—*Oh God*—after so many empty years. This, coupled with the guilt that he had not yet had time to compensate for his many sins, that he had not had time to simply enjoy being alive, that he had not had enough time to love and be loved by the man who had stolen his heart.

For three days, Justin had used every opportunity to regain a spark of cooperation from Wayne. It was almost as if he had found in this a way to cope with the long, endless hours, for it had been no small challenge. It seemed Justin found it imperitive that they be allowed to relieve themselves in some cilvilized manner, for he wheedled and cajoled until he finally got a small compromise. It was humiliating, but Wayne agreed to let Benito come around with a can, unzip their jeans and aim for them so they could pee in the can; humiliating, but not so much so as sitting in jeans soaked with their own urine.

And from Justin came finally another plea, as if it had become his life's endeavor: to let them attend to their bowel movements outside of the den. Wayne eventually relented, aware his two captives had been worn down and now posed very little threat. One at a time, he untied them and allowed them to go outside, all the while holding his cocked gun aimed at the other's head. Justin complied with no hint of resistance, thoroughly convinced another attempt to break free would result in Michael's immediate death.

Justin had taken to daydreams to wile away the waiting, and to lessen his body's pain, dreaming of what it might have been like to grow old with Michael, and then realizing that such dreams revealed his subconscious fear that they could never come out of this alive. Yet he envisioned two old men glancing at each other from time to time, smiling with the memories of a lifetime, glad in their old age they had walked the long miles together. It brought him comfort, this dream;

and with it, he also realized that he would give everything he owned for one final wish: to be at the back of this den, bound as he was, to just be close to Michael, to be near him when they drew their last breath.

Collin Gordon's eyes narrowed on the battered truck as it reeled off the road, onto the gravel in front of the store. He had just spent his third night on Ellie's porch, listening to the distant howls of the coyotes and watching the white owl swoop from its perch in the cottonwood into the starlit night. He adjusted his weight in the chair awaiting the two Mexicans to get out of the truck. Off and on throughout the night he had dozed, but he had not left the porch other than to relieve himself near the Mesquite tree behind the building.

Now weary from the three uneventful days of their waiting pursuit, Ernesto and Miguel stepped up onto the porch. The old rancher greeted them in Spanish.

"You men bring any news?"

Miguel, his ranch foreman spoke: "Pedro Escobar got here yesterday. We put him on a lookout over by the old quicksilver mines. He spotted a man out there this morning. A gringo. Looked like he was out there alone. He had long stingy hair and a beard. He wore dirty clothes."

Collin Gordon nodded. "Could Pedro tell what that man might be doing out that way?"

"He came out of high ground carrying a water jug. He walked out into the desert and checked two or three rabbit snares, then headed off toward the river with the jug. This is all Pedro reported when Ernesto stopped by his station to check on him."

Collin looked down at the floor boards in thought. "It adds up, don't it? Out there by himself. Snaring rabbits for food. Drinking water out of the river. Boys, we just might have our man." He looked at Ernesto. "Me and Miguel will take my truck over to Pedro's lookout. We'll try to pinpoint where this man is holing up. While we're doing that, you get word to the other men to get on over there. Tell them to approach quietly so that guy won't spot them. I want to try to corner him by surprise so this don't turn into something ugly. That shouldn't be too hard to do if he's hiding somewhere on that hill behind the mines." He looked at his watch. "We should have plenty of time finish this job by sundown."

They stepped off the porch and walked to their trucks. Before getting behind the wheel, the old rancher reached behind the seat and took out a holstered, western style .44 Magnum. He strapped it on, then got in and started the truck. With haste, they were less than an hour away from the Marsical Mines.

The three days had taken their toll. Michael, Justin and Benito were haggard and filthy. They were hungry, but they had lost the will to eat what little Wayne passed their way. They were resigned to the inevitable, though within both of them that one tiny spark of hope would not die. But then, really, Michael wondered with his increasingly incoherent thoughts, what was the significance of a man's life in the elements of this vast wilderness—surely not more than that of any insect. A man could come and go on the wisp of a breeze in time in an unforgiving wilderness like Big Bend, even if it came at the mercy of a man called Wayne who had been brought into this world with no soul.

How, he wondered, might that final moment unfold. Would he and Justin simply close their eyes and go to sleep, having said goodbye to each other with one last vague glint in their eyes; or would Wayne wake up in a foul mood and take a notion to rid his miserable life of another nuisance? These were the thoughts that came with the dulling pain, during a lifetime of three days of despair, each passing with fading anger and dimming hope. What did it matter they had heard the helicopters a couple of times, when the noisy machines might as well have been flying over Mars, their fly over confirming nothing more than no evidence of the fugitive in this area? Why allow themselves to be tortured with more false hope?

Michael was all but oblivious to the pain in his arms when Wayne stepped forward and yanked on them to make another of his obsessive inspections of the bindings. It was then Michael saw the sudden shadow. His eyes widened. The shadow loomed on the sun-lit rocky surface just inside the mouth of the den, a clear silhouette of a solitary man. His breath stopped the moment he saw it. As Wayne kneeled before him, Michael stared at the looming shadow, blinking his eyes, thinking it might be an illusion; but no, it clearly belonged to a man in a broad rim hat, obviously standing just outside the den. The shadow moved, growing larger, and then Collin Gordon appeared.

The tall rancher stood centered in the entrance, his determined stature sure and straight, his eyes sorting from the shadows what had unfolded before them. Wayne looked up at Michael's face. He knew at once that Michael's eyes had found something that threatened him behind his back. His head jerked violently around. Alarmed by the sudden appearance of this lone figure, he came quickly to his feet, stopping short of a spontaneous attack. His hand ached for the weight of the gun hidden just inside the upper flap of his overalls, his impulse to grab for it acute. A growl of anger roiled up from his throat.

"Who are you?"

Collin's eyes had adjusted to the gloom. A faint, satisfied smile curled the corners of his thin lips. "I'm the last man on Earth you wanted to see show up here."

"Yeah," hissed Wayne. "You look like just an old man to me."

"That I am, an old man holding a 44 Magnum."

Wayne shuddered visibly. He tensed as his hand moved ever so slightly toward the overalls.

"Those fingers of yours get much closer to your overalls, mister," said Collin, "and all your choices will disappear."

"What choices?"

"Whether you die where you stand, or take your chances with our slow grinding justice system."

Michael, revived by a rush of adrenalin, watched the criminal with near disbelief. It was as if his vile body could not abide what he himself could not control. It seemed to well from within him, some unexplained intolerance, and his body trembled all of a sudden as might the ground before a massive earthquake. Wayne's hand began to shake and from him came an ungodly roar. He charged forth, his hand groping for the gun, his impulsive anger a violent display of madness.

Collin Gordon raised the long barrell of his Colt and squeezed the trigger. A deafening explosion resonated like a clap of thunder off the solid rock walls. Lifted completely off his feet, the kidnapper lurched back through mid air and fell to the ground like a sack of wet cement. The round had struck the center of his chest, shattering bone and vital flesh. The death had been mercifully quick. In his final moment, the beast who called himself Wayne had not had time to bleed or draw a last breath.

Collin Gordon stepped near the corpse, nudging the ribs with the toe of his boot. "My God! We share this world with some truly awful creatures." He shook his head. The kidnapper had died with that last snarl fixed on his face. "One thirty-nine cent bullet," he said looking at the twisted corpse. "Looks like it might have been the best money I ever spent."

Miguel walked in behind him and stood looking around in disbelief.

"Untie these boys, Miguel," said the calm rancher.

The Mexican took a large pocket knife from his pocket and made short work of the ropes binding Justin and Michael.

Michael sat up. Ignoring the pain in his arms, he picked up Benito and held him tight, staring hypnotically over the small shoulders at the ghastly corpse. It took, it seemed, a significant effort to actually believe the man was dead, that such omnipotent wickedness could so easily be destroyed by the simple firing of a gun.

Justin had crossed the den to sit down by his little dog. He recoiled when he reached out and found the body cold and stiff.

"Looks like you boys got a taste of hell up here," said Collin, walking over to rub Benito's head. "Miguel, go on down to my truck and bring back that bottle of water."

Michael helped Benito get to his feet. He then got to his knees and from there he stood slowly, rubbing his wrist, his knees weak and wobbly. He placed his hand aside Benito's face and drew the boy close to his side. "Collin, I've never been so glad to see anyone in my life." Staring at the old rancher, flooded with the emotion of an unexplained miracle, he added, "I can't understand how you could have found us."

Collin smiled and placed his hand on Michael's shoulder. "You're fixing to see for yourself how you were found, son."

Collin Gordon turned to look over at Justin. "Right now, I'm just glad we found you three still alive." He shook his head. "Dang hard to figure why anyone would want to kill a little dog."

Michael's eyes melded on Justin. They both were safe. His heart sailed with relief in their unexpected rescue, but it also beat with aching grief. Though they had been found, and their days together could now go on, he was painfully aware it would take a long time to adjust to life without Perk.

One by one, and in pairs, and in groups of three or four, the Mexicans began to collect just outside of the den. When Ernesto walked in, Benito took off toward him, and found himself swept up and smothered in his uncle's embrace.

Michael's emotions swirled in a dozen directions. He had been subconsciously prepared to die. He had feared even more than that seeing something happen to Justin. Those fears that had churned in his stomach, that were so utterly real now melted away like a bad dream, and he found himself in the grip of a new round of emotions. Tears ran down his face as he looked with bewilderment at the gathering of men outside the den, as he came to the vague realization they must have had something to do with their rescue.

"Who are all those men, Collin?"

Collin Gordon wrapped his arm around Michael's shoulders and passed his hand before the group.

"They're your neighbors, son." He pointed at a man near the back. "I believe you know Juan Gutierrez. You saved his son's life, Dr. Anderson. You asked how I found you. These men are the answer. Not me. They found you. They all know who you are and that's one of the reasons they're here. They all know you saved Julian Gutierrez that night when you operated on him. You have become a hero to them, and in turn they have saved your life. You're a fortunate man, Dr. Anderson. You have their friendship and trust, and for you they would do anything. These men and their families are the people I spoke of that night at your house when I talked about the clinic, the people who would benefit from your services. This would be a good time to decide whether or not you'll be there for them."

Michael stood trembling. On the verge of sobbing, he stared across the unsmiling, somber faces of some fifty men, his eyes wet and blurry. They stood shoulder to shoulder, their objective accomplished, waiting to learn if Collin Gordon needed them for anything else.

Almost too emotional to speak, Michael fumbled for his words. "Forgive me, Collin. I'll never forget this. Forgive me for being so stupid and selfish. Please tell them they can count on me. Tell them they'll have their own clinic as soon as we can get it open. And I'll be there all right. I'll be there to help them anyway I can. There's no doubt in my mind or no power on earth that could keep me from being their doctor."

Collin Gordon slapped him on the back. "You're a good man, Dr. Anderson. That was the right decision."

"Benito ..." Michael gasped with the sudden recollection of the boy's ordeal. "We need to get him to a hospital. He has internal injuries."

"I understand," said Collin. "I've got my cell phone right here, and I can even dial the numbers on this one myself. I'll call Bernard for help."

Anxious for this day to end, Bernard sat down at his desk to take the call.

"What can I do for you, Collin? …What did you say? …What do you mean Benito Garcia needs a hospital? You found him? …You found the kidnapper! … What?" Bernard's jaw fell open. "You shot the kidnapper? …He's dead! I can't hardly believe this, Collin. These law enforcement agencies have just this afternoon revised their strategy to get started… Justin and Michael were there too! …Were they both all right? …Thank God! …Yeah… Yeah, I can get a helicopter down there… No more than thirty minutes… Yes, I'll call Michael's sister. Shit! I can't fucking believe this! …Sure, I'll tell the FBI, but they might not be too happy you shot the bastard." Bernard laughed. "No. You can tell them something like that if you want to, not me. I still want to retire in a couple of years, peacefully… Okay… Sure… We'll talk again soon."

Bernard hung up the phone, shaking his head. He looked down the hall at the two agents still standing in the front room, pondering their reaction to this news. Then he exploded with laughter.

Justin had gotten to his feet. Michael approached and stood beside him. "Justin, I wish there was something I could say."

Justin wrapped his arm behind Michael's neck and pulled him close. "Oh Michael!" he said softly, his lover warm in his tight embrace. "All that matters now is we're both alive and together. I was so worried you were going to be killed. I've never been so scared of anything." He looked back down at his dog. "Don't worry about this. I can get over it in time. We'll bury him out behind the house, just like you said that first day."

Rubbing Justin's back, Michael looked down at the dog. "I'm so sorry we've lost him. Everyone loved Perk. He was part of us."

"I'll be all right. I just thought he'd be around a lot longer, that's all." His heart still heaving with emotion, he looked for a long moment at Michael. "I was so worried. God I was worried. Oh, Michael … if I lost you …"

Michael smiled and placed his hand at the back of Justin's head. "You know, I believe I'm hungry. It's funny. Right now I'm thinking about a big steak."

Collin Gordon had made the call for assistance. He was talking to the Mexicans, telling them to go home to their families. They began to disperse. Ernesto was sitting on the ground in the afternoon sun, holding Benito in his arms.

Collin walked over and stood next to Michael. "Bernard said he could get a helicopter up here in thirty minutes. They'll fly the boy into Alpine. I'm guessing the state police or the FBI will be here any minute to turn this into a crime scene." He glanced around at the frightful conditions of their captivity. "And by the way, Bernard sounded damn glad you boys are okay."

"Thanks to you, Collin," said Justin.

"Not me, Justin. Don't give me credit for something your neighbors did."

"Did you have neighbors like that in San Diego?" Justin asked Michael.

Michael turned and watched the last few men pass out of the clearing. "Hardly. I didn't know my neighbors in San Diego, and they lived just twenty feet from my front door."

Collin spoke: "Well gentlemen, I think things have turned out as they should. Miguel went down the hill for your Jeep. He'll bring it up as close as he can, and we'll get you two home. I'd say a couple of day's rest and a few beers are in order."

Michael didn't bother to rest during the next two days. After Jody nursed the gash on his head, he found himself immersed in planning the clinic with Shannon. Justin didn't rest either. After they buried Perk, he got involved in building the new rafters for the roof of the house. On the second day that Michael and Justin were back home, Brian and Jody drove their rented SUV into El Paso, presumably to run some errands and pick up a few supplies. They returned that late afternoon with a frisky, brown and white

Cocker Spaniel puppy.

Elated, Michael and Justin broke from their projects to sit down facing each other on the ground behind the house. Their legs crossed before them, the puppy vied for attention with its prancing back and forth between their legs. They took immediate joy in playing with the dog as it licked their hands and its little tail wagged with excitement.

"I prayed quite a bit when we were up there," Justin said soberly.

Michael looked at him. "Me too."

"I promised God I'd never take anything for granted again."

"Sounds pretty close to some of the promises I made."

"I won't, Michael. I will never again take anything I love for granted."

"Me either."

The puppy climbed atop Justin's leg and lifted his paws up on his chest. The little dog stretched its neck to lick his chin. The sun had inched toward the horizon, the western sky now fired with red and orange. Michael and Justin both turned, their eyes drawn by the wonder of another west Texas sunset.

ABOUT THE AUTHOR

A resident of Dallas, **Martin Brant** has spent most of his life as an entrepreneur, which has given him the opportunity to meet and know people from all walks of life. His love of writing began in high school and is now his primary career. He enjoys the work of authors like Norman Mailer, Anne Rice, Ken Follett and Fyodor Dostoevsky. Celebrating human diversity, Martin's tales are written to intrigue and entertain those who enjoy reading something a little different. He would love to hear from you at martinbrant@msn.com .

Dear Reader,

Many thanks for choosing my debut novel. I hope you enjoyed reading it as much as I enjoyed writing it. As you know, the character's sexuality is entwined in the storyline. I believe this aspect of being human is as fascinating as the challenges the characters in a novel face, including the way they express their intimate feelings. I also believe the majority of gay and bisexual men lead everyday lives and are low profile with their sexuality, though they may suffer conflicts with their predilections. When they find themselves facing uncommon challenges, they are the men and the stories I write about. Excerpts from future novels can be read at www.martinbrant.com.

I would love to hear what you think. Your opinion can be a wonderful inspiration or can enhance my learning curve. Either way, I would love to hear from you at martinbrant@msn.com.

I would also like to thank Niani Colom at Genesis Press, Inc. for giving me the opportunity to share these tales with you.

MB

A SONG IN THE PARK

2005 Publication Schedule

January

A Heart's Awakening
Veronica Parker
$9.95
1-58571-143-8

Falling
Natalie Dunbar
$9.95
1-58571-121-7

February

Echoes of Yesterday
Beverly Clark
$9.95
1-58571-131-4

A Love of Her Own
Cheris F. Hodges
$9.95
1-58571-136-5

Higher Ground
Leah Latimer
$19.95
1-58571-157-8

March

Misconceptions
Pamela Leigh Starr
$9.95
1-58571-117-9

I'll Paint a Sun
A.J. Garrotto
$9.95
1-58571-165-9

Peace Be Still
Colette Haywood
$12.95
1-58571-129-2

April

Intentional Mistakes
Michele Sudler
$9.95
1-58571-152-7

Conquering Dr. Wexler's Heart
Kimberley White
$9.95
1-58571-126-8

Song in the Park
Martin Brant
$15.95
1-58571-125-X

May

The Color Line
Lizette Carter
$9.95
1-58571-163-2

Unconditional
A.C. Arthur
$9.95
1-58571-142-X

Last Train to Memphis
Elsa Cook
$12.95
1-58571-146-2

June

Angel's Paradise
Janice Angelique
$9.95
1-58571-107-1

Suddenly You
Crystal Hubbard
$9.95
1-58571-158-6

Matters of Life and
Death
Lesego Malepe, Ph.D.
$15.95
1-58571-124-1

2005 Publication Schedule (continued)

July

Pleasures All Mine
Belinda O. Steward
$9.95
1-58571-112-8

Wild Ravens
Altonya Washington
$9.95
1-58571-164-0

Class Reunion
Irma Jenkins/John
Brown
$12.95
1-58571-123-3

August

Path of Thorns
Annetta P. Lee
$9.95
1-58571-145-4

Timeless Devotion
Bella McFarland
$9.95
1-58571-148-9

Life Is Never As It Seems
June Michael
$12.95
1-58571-153-5

September

Beyond the Rapture
Beverly Clark
$9.95
1-58571-131-4

Blood Lust
J. M. Jeffries
$9.95
1-58571-138-1

Rough on Rats and
Tough on Cats
Chris Parker
$12.95
1-58571-154-3

October

A Will to Love
Angie Daniels
$9.95
1-58571-141-1

Taken by You
Dorothy Elizabeth Love
$9.95
1-58571-162-4

Soul Eyes
Wayne L. Wilson
$12.95
1-58571-147-0

November

A Drummer's Beat to
Mend
Kay Swanson
$9.95

Sweet Reprecussions
Kimberley White
$9.95
1-58571-159-4

Red Polka Dot in a
Worldof Plaid
Varian Johnson
$12.95
1-58571-140-3

December

Hand in Glove
Andrea Jackson
$9.95
1-58571-166-7

Blaze
Barbara Keaton
$9.95

Across
Carol Payne
$12.95
1-58571-149-7

Other Genesis Press, Inc. Titles

Acquisitions	Kimberley White	$8.95
A Dangerous Deception	J.M. Jeffries	$8.95
A Dangerous Love	J.M. Jeffries	$8.95
A Dangerous Obsession	J.M. Jeffries	$8.95
After the Vows	Leslie Esdaile	$10.95
(Summer Anthology)	T.T. Henderson	
	Jacqueline Thomas	
Again My Love	Kayla Perrin	$10.95
Against the Wind	Gwynne Forster	$8.95
A Lark on the Wing	Phyliss Hamilton	$8.95
A Lighter Shade of Brown	Vicki Andrews	$8.95
All I Ask	Barbara Keaton	$8.95
A Love to Cherish	Beverly Clark	$8.95
Ambrosia	T.T. Henderson	$8.95
And Then Came You	Dorothy Elizabeth Love	$8.95
Angel's Paradise	Janice Angelique	$8.95
A Risk of Rain	Dar Tomlinson	$8.95
At Last	Lisa G. Riley	$8.95
Best of Friends	Natalie Dunbar	$8.95
Bound by Love	Beverly Clark	$8.95
Breeze	Robin Hampton Allen	$10.95
Brown Sugar Diaries &	Delores Bundy &	$10.95
Other Sexy Tales	Cole Riley	
By Design	Barbara Keaton	$8.95
Cajun Heat	Charlene Berry	$8.95
Careless Whispers	Rochelle Alers	$8.95
Caught in a Trap	Andre Michelle	$8.95
Chances	Pamela Leigh Starr	$8.95
Dark Embrace	Crystal Wilson Harris	$8.95
Dark Storm Rising	Chinelu Moore	$10.95
Designer Passion	Dar Tomlinson	$8.95
Ebony Butterfly II	Delilah Dawson	$14.95

Erotic Anthology	Assorted	$8.95
Eve's Prescription	Edwina Martin Arnold	$8.95
Everlastin' Love	Gay G. Gunn	$8.95
Fate	Pamela Leigh Starr	$8.95
Forbidden Quest	Dar Tomlinson	$10.95
Fragment in the Sand	Annetta P. Lee	$8.95
From the Ashes	Kathleen Suzanne	$8.95
	Jeanne Sumerix	
Gentle Yearning	Rochelle Alers	$10.95
Glory of Love	Sinclair LeBeau	$10.95
Hart & Soul	Angie Daniels	$8.95
Heartbeat	Stephanie Bedwell-Grime	$8.95
I'll Be Your Shelter	Giselle Carmichael	$8.95
Illusions	Pamela Leigh Starr	$8.95
Indiscretions	Donna Hill	$8.95
Interlude	Donna Hill	$8.95
Intimate Intentions	Angie Daniels	$8.95
Just an Affair	Eugenia O'Neal	$8.95
Kiss or Keep	Debra Phillips	$8.95
Love Always	Mildred E. Riley	$10.95
Love Unveiled	Gloria Greene	$10.95
Love's Deception	Charlene Berry	$10.95
Mae's Promise	Melody Walcott	$8.95
Meant to Be	Jeanne Sumerix	$8.95
Midnight Clear	Leslie Esdaile	$10.95
(Anthology)	Gwynne Forster	
	Carmen Green	
	Monica Jackson	
Midnight Magic	Gwynne Forster	$8.95
Midnight Peril	Vicki Andrews	$10.95
My Buffalo Soldier	Barbara B. K. Reeves	$8.95
Naked Soul	Gwynne Forster	$8.95
No Regrets	Mildred E. Riley	$8.95
Nowhere to Run	Gay G. Gunn	$10.95

Object of His Desire	A. C. Arthur	$8.95
One Day at a Time	Bella McFarland	$8.95
Passion	T.T. Henderson	$10.95
Past Promises	Jahmel West	$8.95
Path of Fire	T.T. Henderson	$8.95
Picture Perfect	Reon Carter	$8.95
Pride & Joi	Gay G. Gunn	$8.95
Quiet Storm	Donna Hill	$8.95
Reckless Surrender	Rochelle Alers	$8.95
Rendezvous with Fate	Jeanne Sumerix	$8.95
Revelations	Cheris F. Hodges	$8.95
Rivers of the Soul	Leslie Esdaile	$8.95
Rooms of the Heart	Donna Hill	$8.95
Shades of Brown	Denise Becker	$8.95
Shades of Desire	Monica White	$8.95
Sin	Crystal Rhodes	$8.95
So Amazing	Sinclair LeBeau	$8.95
Somebody's Someone	Sinclair LeBeau	$8.95
Someone to Love	Alicia Wiggins	$8.95
Soul to Soul	Donna Hill	$8.95
Still Waters Run Deep	Leslie Esdaile	$8.95
Subtle Secrets	Wanda Y. Thomas	$8.95
Sweet Tomorrows	Kimberly White	$8.95
The Color of Trouble	Dyanne Davis	$8.95
The Price of Love	Sinclair LeBeau	$8.95
The Reluctant Captive	Joyce Jackson	$8.95
The Missing Link	Charlyne Dickerson	$8.95
Three Wishes	Seressia Glass	$8.95
Tomorrow's Promise	Leslie Esdaile	$8.95
Truly Inseperable	Wanda Y. Thomas	$8.95
Twist of Fate	Beverly Clark	$8.95
Unbreak My Heart	Dar Tomlinson	$8.95
Unconditional Love	Alicia Wiggins	$8.95
When Dreams A Float	Dorothy Elizabeth Love	$8.95

Whispers in the Night	Dorothy Elizabeth Love	$8.95
Whispers in the Sand	LaFlorya Gauthier	$10.95
Yesterday is Gone	Beverly Clark	$8.95
Yesterday's Dreams, Tomorrow's Promises	Reon Laudat	$8.95
Your Precious Love	Sinclair LeBeau	$8.95

Order Form

Mail to: Genesis Press, Inc.

P.O. Box 101
Columbus, MS 39703

Name _____
Address _____
City/State _____ Zip _____
Telephone _____

Ship to (if different from above)
Name _____
Address _____
City/State _____ Zip _____
Telephone _____

Credit Card Information

Credit Card # _____ ☐ Visa   ☐ Mastercard

Expiration Date (mm/yy) _____ ☐ AmEx   ☐ Discover

Qty.	Author	Title	Price	Total

Use this order form, or call 1-888-INDIGO-1	**Total for books** _____
	 Shipping and handling:
	   $5 first two books,
	   $1 each additional book _____
	 Total S & H
	 Total amount enclosed _____
	 Mississippi residents add 7% sales tax

Order Form

Mail to: Genesis Press, Inc.

P.O. Box 101
Columbus, MS 39703

Name _____
Address _____
City/State _____ Zip _____
Telephone _____

Ship to (if different from above)
Name _____
Address _____
City/State _____ Zip _____
Telephone _____

Credit Card Information

Credit Card # _____ ☐ Visa ☐ Mastercard

Expiration Date (mm/yy) _____ ☐ AmEx ☐ Discover

Qty.	Author	Title	Price	Total

Use this order form, or call
1-888-INDIGO-1

Total for books _____
Shipping and handling:
  $5 first two books,
  $1 each additional book _____
Total S & H _____
Total amount enclosed _____
Mississippi residents add 7% sales tax

Visit www.genesis-press.com for latest releases and excerpts.